COPPERHEAD

Book One: Son of the Silver Fox

COPPERHEAD

Author's forward

I have on my desk an early 1800's daguerreotype of a handsome young man. He is dressed simply but elegantly, in a modest homespun coat with a high white collar and black cravat. He looks out of the gilded frame defiantly, as if daring anyone to challenge his right to be where he is, to be *who* he is. The young man is dressed as a white man, but he is native. He is my talisman. He is my promise that this tale is important. Even though the sitter in the portrait is from a later time, in my mind's eye – and I am an artist – he *is* Copperhead. This book belongs to him, and to all of those who believed in my telling his tale. Special thanks to Becky, Janie & Karen who read the novel, and to Karen again and Paula who proofread. Also to the members of Gallimaufry for their support, and my family. And last, and most importantly, to God.

This book is a work of fiction. All characters in this book are either the work of the writers' imagination or used in a fictitious manner.

COPPERHEAD Book One: Son of the Silver Fox
© Copyright 2008 by Marla F. Fair

All rights are reserved. No portion of this book may be reproduced or transmitted in any form or by any electronic or mechanical means, including photocopying, recording or by any information storage and retrieval system, without the written permission of the author except where permitted by law.

ISBN 978-1-4357-2938-4

Cover Art & Design by Marla F. Fair

Lady Faye's Press books available online at
www.marlafair.com & www.a-writersgroup.com
email: dfair@woh.rr.com

First edition: 2008

COPPERHEAD

Prologue
North Carolina 1774

Wudigeas opened his eyes.

Above him the forested world was an ocean of green – swirling, swaying, spiraling down. Down. Down.

The native boy attempted to lift his head but found it would not obey. A bare leg twitched instead. One golden-brown hand slid down his side to land in the thick clotted grass.

Grass. Clotted with his blood.

Even though the field of battle was far away, Wudigeas still smelled smoke. It clung to him as did his shame. He was alive. The others. His brothers....were not.

Weak. Weary. Beyond hope, he turned his face into the grass and cried. Mother earth cradled him, her welcome scent filled his nostrils, her voice, a caress of the wind.

A wind speaking wisdom words he did not want to hear.

Why do you weep like an old woman wearing ash?

"Mother," Wudigeas answered, "I am weary. Let me come to you."

You are young. You have not yet built your lodge.

"I do not want to live. I have shamed my family and myself. I...."

Because you ran.

A sob escaped him. Trembling fingers clawed the matted grass. "Yes...."

You ran toward life. There is no shame in this.

"But my friends...." he protested.

You shame them now, Wudigeas. If you die, who will tell their story? Who will make them live?

The green world closed about him. He did not know if night had fallen or if, as he wished, he was about to die. He could not remember the time of day, or the day itself. He only knew that as he ran from the battlefield a white man had shot him in the back and left him for dead.

"Mother? Are you still with me? Mother...."

In reply, a warm wind arose. It lifted the ends of his copper-brown hair, rattling the beads and stirring the finger-thin feathers that decorated it. A band of clouds, brooding above, broke to reveal a bloated moon. Close by the underbrush rustled.

A featherlight footfall brought the creature to his side. Its silver face was narrow – tipped with a pair of pointed ears and split by eyes golden as the grain in the white man's fields. The fox tilted its head and gazed at him. Then it stepped forward and pressed a wet muzzle against his fevered skin.

Wudigeas' fingers found a purchase in the animal's thick coat.

Then he knew no more.

George Foxwell was an uneasy man. Seldom did he take his nightly constitutional so late. And even less often did it lead him into the woods beyond his son's estate. This night, though, something drew him there. It was not the heady scent of young myrtle and yellow jasmine on the breeze, nor the argent light of the waning moon. It was a sense of something waiting. Something wanting – no, *needing* him – that called him forth into the trees and the soft susurrations of their shadows below.

His son would have laughed at him. William was a practical man.

That was why he had avoided him when leaving the manor. George ran a hand through his grizzled hair, commanding the graying waves to come to order, and then turned and looked back at Foxwell Manor. Even at this distance the candlelight blazed, lighting the fine and fancy world behind the expensive glass windows – a counterfeit daylight as false as the laughter of the party-goers who danced and drank and died a thousand little deaths beneath it.

Turning back to the trees and their rugged honesty, George Foxwell shook his head and sighed. "Where did we go wrong, Maggie?" he asked aloud, hoping for just a moment that his question might conjure up the shade of his dead wife. Though mystical, the night held no such comfort. Margaret was long dead. She had died before the last war and he had not been with her. He had been in His Majesty King George's service then, commanding savages in the battle against the French invaders known as the Seven Year's War.

Commanding *and* killing them.

George adjusted his black tricorn hat with its white cockade and straightened the collar of the regulation scarlet coat he still wore. He had grown weary with killing after the war and had resigned his commission and retired to North Carolina to his son's home. William was considered a fine officer and highly regarded by the Crown. He had just received a promotion to colonel and was the man of the hour.

Would that his *father* could have found something admirable in the only surviving child of his loins.

George Foxwell began to pick his way through the dense underbrush, drawn to a road familiar from the day. The dirt path beat into the earth by the passage of hundreds of hooves and padded feet, led to a hollow filled with ripe berry bushes and tall sweet grasses. The hollow was surrounded by moss-covered boulders and backed by a stream that tumbled down in a little waterfall to end in a clear pool which lay cupped in the hand of the land, its still surface shining like a dark mirror. He often came here to think. It was far enough away from the house to afford him some privacy, but not so far that he could not hear one of the grandchildren if they called.

George swept aside a low-hanging branch and began the descent into the hollow. A late rain had left the grass slick and heavy with dew. A tenacious mist clung to the surface of the pool. Wisps of the gray stuff rose above its placid surface like sacred spirits in a dance. He had just reached the pool's side when a sense of movement halted him. George hesitated, uncertain. Above one of the boulders the mist parted to reveal a large four legged shape. The beast's keen eyes pinned him as it bared its sharp sallow teeth and began to whine. George's hand went for his pistol.

Then he remembered he had left it at the house.

He *was* getting old.

George waited a moment. Then he spoke to the silver fox as he would to his English hounds – showing respect for both its power and intellect. "Well, boy, what is it you want? I am afraid the meat on the bones of this old man would prove gristle in your hungry mouth."

The fox stared at him. Then it pawed the rock and looked behind.

"What is it, boy?" George asked, puzzled.

The animal cocked its head. It barked once – sharply – and then disappeared down the back of the boulder.

George Foxwell frowned. He had spent enough time among the savages to know an omen when he saw one. A shiver ran the length of him and he grew chill in the warm spring air. What was it he had thought before?

That something was waiting? Wanting. *Needing* him.

His son, William, would have called it 'utter nonsense' to believe in such things. George Foxwell shrugged. It probably was. Still, his life had been saved, he couldn't say *how* many times, by those same savages and their superstitious beliefs. And more often than not the things they spoke of came true.

Things that went beyond the world William could see.

George searched for a good size branch and found one thick as a man's fist. Quickly honing it to a cane, he used it for balance as he worked his way up and over the boulder, heading for a place just beyond the waterfall. He spotted the fox as it entered a stand of thick grasses near the pond's edge.

"Hold up, boy! This is an *old* man you are leading on," George Foxwell huffed as he parted the grasses and followed the animal into the underbrush. "I can't – "

George's boot struck something solid. In spite of his makeshift cane, he lost his balance and tumbled to the marshy ground. His ancient joints screamed as his hands and knees struck the earth and bore the brunt of his weight. He paused for a moment, breathing hard.

Then he smelled it.

Blood.

"God's wounds!" George exclaimed as he reached out and touched the still form lying face down in the grass. Whoever it was his skin was still warm, but from the look of him, he was not long for this earth. The light of the silvered moon above revealed a lean form, well-muscled, clothed in leather leggings and swamp boots. Silver and brass rings decorated his unusually long dark hair, as well as beads and pale thin feathers. George placed his hand on the savage's chest. His skin was fevered. His breathing shallow. His sinewy form bathed in paint, sweat, and blood. Taking hold of his chin George lifted the Indian's head and turned his face into the light.

He was just a boy.

As George rocked back on his heels, considering what to do, the silver fox reappeared in the tall grasses beside him. Baring its teeth, it growled to attract his attention. The older man did not move. The fox was extraordinarily large and well within striking distance. He did not want to startle it. As he had in the past on the field of battle, George Foxwell turned and held its gaze, proving he was not afraid.

The fox returned his stare. Then it bowed its head and placed its chin on its paws and whined. A moment later it crossed to the Indian boy and nudged his side.

Was this – this *savage* – what the fox meant to lead him to?

What was one half-dead Indian to him?

George looked at the boy's face. It was strong-boned. A handsome face, once proud, now clouded with pain. He was young – twelve, maybe thirteen at most – but still a warrior to his people. It would be best to leave him here. Let him die. His son, William, would never accept an Indian at the house – even as a servant.

In fact, William would probably shoot him on sight.

George continued to stare at the boy. Then again, he thought as he scratched his bare chin, the party at the house *was* a farewell gathering held in his son's honor. William was returning to England on the morrow before undertaking a new tour of duty that might well last a year....

Or an eternity.

The old man rose and, with the silver fox still watching him from a tramped down nest of matted grasses, removed his scarlet coat. He knelt and gently lifted the boy up. Sickened by the blood that poured over and through his hands, George placed him on it, pulling the lapels with their thick brass braid close over the boy's chest. Even if he managed to get him to a place of safety where he could heal. Even if the boy had not lost so much blood that he died before he got him there. Even if –

George had no idea what the future held for either of them.

The boy moaned and stirred as George picked him up. His deep brown eyes flickered open and his cracked lips formed a question. George did not know the boy's language, but he knew what he asked.

"Why?" he echoed softly as he began to bear the Indian boy toward the house. "Why?"

"God alone knows."

COPPERHEAD

Chapter One

"Miriam. Psst! Miriam. Come here!"

With a sigh young Miriam Foxwell halted in her gardening and turned her head with its torrents of golden ringlets toward her elder sister Kate who was charging across the well-manicured back lawn of the manor house. In Miriam's hands the green plants were responding, gifting her with both seeds and happiness. Above her head one of their mother's caged canaries was singing the song God had granted her. The spring sun was brushing the hedgerows and topiary animals with gold dust, making a heaven of her small plot of earth and turning it into a peaceful haven – a sanctuary far away from choices and chores, and the expectations of her rigid Mama Charlotte and Papa William.

Miriam shook her head. "No, Kate. I am happy here."

Kate anchored her hands on her hips and huffed. Then she approached and knelt by Miriam's side. Her sister's luscious copper locks were piled high beneath a molded straw hat edged with fine silk ribbon, their spiraling ends resting on her highly fashionable, partially exposed breasts. Over a delicate cambric chemise Kate wore a day coat of expensive yellow brocade and a bright blue petticoat. Kate was sixteen and four years her senior. Already a woman. Miriam loved and hated her all at once. Kate was so bright. So beautiful. Boys fell at her feet, and she used them to wipe the dust off of her elegantly embroidered and beaded slippers. Miriam wanted to be just like her. And nothing like her.

Miriam didn't know what she wanted to be.

"Go away, Kate," she murmured as she returned her trowel to the rich brown earth and began to dig.

"But I have a secret," Kate whispered in her ear. "Don't you want to know it?"

Miriam shoved a ringlet away from her eye, smudging her nose with dirt. She daubed the sweat from her forehead with the back of a white muslin hand and then returned to digging. "I don't."

"Oh, I think you *do*...." Kate sat down beside her. She cocked her head, displaying the stuffed white dove perched perfectly on the crown of the straw hat their soldier father had brought her from London. "After all, you're the only one of us who is close to the *old* man."

Miriam was watching an earthworm, waiting for it to crawl past before continuing. She scowled at Kate's words and turned to look at her sister. "You mean Grandpapa George?"

"I mean *crazy* old Grandpa George."

"You've been listening to Papa," Miriam scolded.

"Yes, I have. Papa is a great man, meant for great things," Kate remarked as she straightened her skirt. As she did she noticed one of the stable boys not far off, walking a horse their father feared had gone lame and – with a little quirk of her lips – deliberately lifted the cloth so her embroidered stockings and ankles showed before continuing. "Papa is right about the old man. Grandpa George *is* crazy. Papa said the war with the French left him that way."

"He is *not* crazy!" Miriam shouted, driving her trowel into the earth, almost skewering the lethargic earthworm. "He's kind and gentle and loving! And he – "

"And he has a *terrible* secret in his studio."

Miriam fell silent. It looked like this secret just *might* be something that would get Grandpapa George in a lot of trouble. At least that was what the wicked gleam in Kate's green eyes said.

Kate rose to her feet. She eyed the stable boy who had stopped nearby and, with a smart little bump, plumped her rumpled gown and ordered the basket panniers beneath it before marching away. "But then, I don't suppose *you* want to know. If you did, you might have to admit the old man *is* crazy as a loon and ought to be locked up – just like Papa says."

"Where are you going?" Miriam called after her, a little afraid of the answer.

"To get James and John, you ninny. Where did you think?" Kate threw back over her shoulder.

James and John were their brothers. James was three years older than Kate, and John a few years younger. Both were older than Miriam. Only her sister Anna was littler than she.

"Are you going to take them to the studio?"

Kate turned back. "Of course, I am. So if you want to see the *animal* Grandpa has caged in his rooms, you had better hurry. They'll kill it quick and throw the carcass to the wolves."

As she watched her sister walk away, Miriam's perfect lips pursed and a frown marred her heart-shaped face.

Animal?

With a sigh Miriam laid her trowel down and rose to her feet, brushing dirt and dead leaves off her apron. She shook the skirts of her deep orchid gown free, making certain to press the pleats into their proper places as her Mama had shown her, and then she left the garden with its brilliant blossoms and fragrant foliage behind and headed for her grandpa's sanctuary.

Grandpapa George's studio was within a stone's throw of the manor house and nestled in a grove of trees, hidden away from casual view. Though Foxwell Manor was given over to rice and other lucrative crops, Miriam's father's passion was fine horses. The building had been a holding place for sick ones once upon a time, before the proud beautiful animals had grown so numerous that another larger and more accessible facility was erected. The structure stood abandoned until their grandfather had come to live with them a year and a half before. Grandpa George liked to paint, and he had asked their father to give him the small brick and wood building for a workshop.

Miriam picked her way across the shadowed lawn, her petticoat lifted high in her gloved hands. She knew the way well. Whenever she could, she would come to visit her grandfather and sit for hours watching him bring the blank canvas he had lovingly stretched and prepared to life with all manner of people, birds and beasts. Perhaps if Grandpapa George had an animal in the studio it was for study. Maybe it was the fox she had seen at the edge of the garden the night before. The large powerful beast had both frightened and fascinated her, its coat shining silver in the waxing light of the moon.

Miriam glanced back at the house. Her papa's negroes would be lighting the torches. The day was waning. Mama would be unhappy if she was not in soon. Still, she *had* to know what it was Kate had seen. The pallid light of the late spring sky lit her way, casting weird shadows on the path as it filtered through a bank of low-lying clouds. Miriam checked over her shoulder several times, expecting to find her brothers and her tattle-tale sister hard on her heels.

But there was no one there.

At the door of the studio Miriam hesitated, her hand on the latch. Kate had said her brothers would kill the animal within. Did that mean it was feral? Maybe even sick or rabid? Fear suddenly gripped her. Backing off, she moved to the base of one of the windows that opened onto the interior and stared up at it. At twelve Miriam was the size of a ten year old. Her father called her his 'Lilliputian Princess' after the race in Mr. Swift's novel about Gulliver. Most of the time opening a door or sitting in a chair was a challenge. Climbing to the window of her grandfather's studio and peeking in seemed as great a feat as scaling Hadrian's Wall. Glancing about, Miriam located a supply crate propped against the studio wall. She righted the crate and placed it beneath the window and then stood on it, raising up on tiptoe.

The moon's argent light fell in an eight-pane panel, touching the top of a low table before casting itself in a quilt of light on the wooden daybed her grandfather used to take his afternoon naps. Miriam gripped the edge of the windowsill and pulled herself up for a better look.

The bed was occupied.

Rubbing dirt from the window glass with one of her white gloves she leaned forward, squinting, trying to make out who was in it. One thing she knew for certain, it was *not* her grandfather. The figure was too small and it had a mop of dark hair that lay half-exposed above the hand-stitched edge of the blanket. Miriam's pale brow furrowed as she searched the interior of the studio for a sign of the animal her sister had mentioned, but saw nothing.

Nothing but the sleeping figure on the bed.

Emboldened by her discovery and overcome with curiosity, Miriam slipped off the box and approached the door again and placed her hand on the latch. She lifted the latch and pulled on the door with both hands only to discover that, contrary to his habit, her grandfather had locked it! Miriam scrunched up her nose, anchored her hands on her hips in unconscious imitation of Kate, and huffed. She thought a moment and then a wicked smile lit her elfin face.

Her brother James had shown her another way in.

Miriam glanced at her silk gown. It would mean taking a dressing down from her Mama and probably bed with no supper – maybe for a week She glanced at the window and thought about the mysterious figure on the bed.

It would be worth it!

Moving to the back of the studio Miriam crouched down and pulled at the loose vent set in the foundation. One time James had removed it and had her wiggle through since he was too big. Their grandfather had locked the door that day too. He had had her brother's birthday present – a fine hand-tooled leather saddle – hidden there.

Wriggling through the vent was not so easy as she thought. Apparently in spite of her own fears, she *had* grown. By the time Miriam made her way in, her flaxen curls were askew and hanging in her eyes, her apron was gone, and she had torn the shoulder of her purple gown. Next summer, she would no longer fit.

Then it would be Anna's turn to wiggle in.

Miriam emerged into the side room once used to prepare the sick horses' feed. Moving quietly, for fear of waking the sleeper, she entered the main room and walked toward the bed, passing her grandfather's soldier straight lines of paints and brushes on the way. The figure on the cot had the blanket up to its ears. A lock of hair crossed the blanket's binding and it was long as a girl's. Miriam twisted her skirts nervously between her fingers. Did her grandfather have a girl in here? A servant, maybe one who was in trouble with her Papa? It would be like Kate to make a big thing out of that, even if Grandpapa meant only to give the girl shelter.

As Miriam drew closer she realized the cast of the stranger's shoulders was too broad for a girl. The angle of the partially exposed cheek, strong and high-boned. Interwoven with the long coppery brown lock was the remnant of leather strip decorated with brightly colored beads, and a pair of hawk's feathers. Miriam made a strangled sound in her throat. Terrified, she shifted back, upsetting the low table and knocking the metal plate and fork on it to the floor.

Waking the Indian up.

The sleeper jerked. He turned and looked at her, his dark eyes startled. Then he threw the covers aside and sat up, revealing a bronzed chest already covered with battle scars – though he could have been little older than her brother John – and long muscled legs sheathed in leather. The Indian's eyes never left her as he slipped to the side of the bed and crouched there as if ready to spring.

She couldn't help it. Miriam screamed. She backed away toward the door, her gloved hands raised defensively before her. Halfway there she turned and started to run. Her soft kid slippers caught in her voluminous skirts as she did and she tripped and fell, bloodying her lip.

And continued to scream.

The Indian watched her from his purchase near the bed, unmoving. He waited until she drew a breath and then held out a hand as if to say, 'I mean you no harm." When she remained silent, he rose slowly and took several steps toward her, saying something in a language she could not understand. Then he grew pale and began to shake. Sweat rolled down his bare chest and his breathing became labored. He muttered something, swayed, and fell to the floor.

Miriam sobbed as she fought for control. Looking at the Indian, lying there helpless, he *did* remind her of an animal –

A wounded one in need of help.

Her father, one of His Majesty's soldiers, had taught her not to show fear in the face of the enemy. Shamed by her own weakness, Miriam pulled herself together and approached the Indian, more than half-expecting his sudden weakness to be a ruse to lure her in. When he failed to take advantage of her close proximity – when he did not move at *all* – she knelt beside him and hesitantly placed one hand on his naked shoulder. For a moment, he didn't stir. Then he slowly lifted his head and met her gaze.

His eyes were the deep brown of the silt in her garden. Wide and full of pain. She saw in them neither hatred nor any intent to harm her.

Only fear.

"Please," she said softly as tears wet her cheeks. "Please, let me help you back to the bed. I am sorry I screamed. I thought…." Miriam frowned as he shook his head, not understanding. "No," she finished softly, reaching for him, "I *didn't* think."

A crashing noise turned her head toward the door. Her brother James' lean figure stood framed within it, silhouetted against the dying light outside. James' riding crop was in his hand. He had struck the door with his booted foot, breaking the boards and splintering part of the wood. James cursed and struck his palm with the whip as he advanced into the room. Her brother John trailed close behind him, looking frightened and unsure. In the yard outside Kate stood shrieking as if she had just sighted a party of painted savages fifty strong with bloodied tomahawks and clubs coming over the rise.

"James, no!" Miriam placed herself between the fallen Indian and her brother. "You don't understand! I'm fine. He's done nothing – "

James wouldn't have it. He gripped her by the shoulders and threw her out of his way. She fell, striking her cheek on the cabinet that held her grandpa's brushes, scattering them all over the floor. "Get out of here, Miriam!" he ordered. "John take her away! I will take care of the *vermin* infesting Grandfather's studio."

James' voice was cold and thick with a lust for violence. Miriam moved toward him, intent to grab the crop from his hand. John caught her before she could and pulled her kicking and flailing through the door. James spoke again just as her feet cleared the threshold.

"This is a man's work, Miriam. Take Kate and go back to the house. Now!"

Kate was white as a winding sheet. She grew even more so when she saw Miriam's bruised cheek and split lip. Kate reached for her hand, seeking comfort. When she pulled away, her elder sister began to wail again and, lifting her petticoat, turned tail and ran blubbering like a baby toward the manor house. John followed close behind, too frightened to remain. She watched the pair until they entered the great brick building, knowing that they would rouse their Mama and soon she and the servants and staff would come spilling out of the house to see what was the matter. Miriam turned her tear and dirt-streaked face back toward the studio. Even this far away she could hear the sound of James' crop striking the Indian's flesh. She held very still. So still she became aware of her own fast beating heart, of the birds winging high over her head – so still in fact she could hear the frogs trilling on the banks of the pond half a mile away.

But from the Indian she heard nothing. No cry of pain. No words begging for mercy.

COPPERHEAD

Nothing.

Compelled, Miriam moved toward the studio. A shout from close behind stopped her. She turned to find her beloved grandpapa George moving faster than she had ever seen him. He was shouting and waving his hands. Miriam tried to make out what he was saying, but fatigue and relief and fear washed over her all at once.

And she knew no more.

When Miriam woke up she was in her bed. Doctor Wallington was there and he bled her, leaving her weak. Now, several hours later, she was alone except for her aged nurse, Martha, who sat close by snoring. Miriam watched the old woman through half-lidded eyes for some time to make certain she was not pretending, and then cast her sheet and blanket aside and slipped off of the bed into her soiled shoes. She tiptoed to the door and listened, and then opened it. Outside the corridor was empty.

The house was asleep.

Returning to her wardrobe Miriam pulled a robe over her white nightgown, bound it under her small breasts and then slipped down the stairs, careful to keep alert for the night watchman and her father's dogs. She passed the two black hounds on the stair. They were snoring, satiated with their supper and too lazy to care.

The brisk night air struck her making her light-headed as she stepped outside, but she pressed on in spite of weariness and fatigue, driven by a need to find out what toll had been exacted for her curiosity. Just outside the studio she hesitated. The broken door hung on its hinges and opened onto the interior. The light of a single lamp shown inside. Her grandfather sat beside it, his head down, one hand on the Indian's bare shoulder. Miriam watched for a moment and then decided perhaps she was not wanted and started to turn away.

"Miriam" Her grandfather's voice was tired. Thick with worry and grief as it had been when her Grandmama Margaret had been sick. "Come here, child."

For a moment she wanted to break and run to the house. It was as if she somehow sensed that this moment marked the ending of one thing, and the beginning of another. Her grandfather called again and Miriam left the moonlit night behind to enter the shadowed interior of the studio. A tin lamp cast a wheel-spoke circle of light about the cot on which the Indian lay.

Her grandfather reached out and took her hand and drew her near. He met her wide-eyed gaze and then, with his other hand, touched her battered cheek. "Miri, are you all right?"

She nodded.

"He did nothing to harm you?"

She could see in her Grandpapa's light blue eyes the fear that the Indian had caused her wounds. She shook her head. "No. It wasn't him. I fell."

Grandpapa George squeezed her fingers and released them. He shifted in the chair and sighed, and then seemed to relax for the first time. As he ran a hand across his grizzled chin, he breathed, "I thought not. I don't believe it is in him."

Miriam waited. When he said nothing more, she asked, "Will he live?"

The older man placed his hand on the Indian's chest. The scarred skin beneath it rose and fell rapidly as if he was running a race, or fighting some unseen foe. His golden-brown skin was broken in several places where her brother's crop had drawn blood, and there were multiple bruises and a contusion on his face. Miriam could see now that his back and chest were bandaged as well, though her grandfather assured her that was due to an old wound and not something her brother had done.

"He clings to life, this one, though there is no reason for him to. He is a stranger in a strange land, torn from his kin, and left to the care of an old man who does not know his language. One who cannot even keep him safe from a pair of adolescent thugs."

"He's a savage!" Miriam proclaimed as if that explained everything from Kate's shallow behavior to James' irrational fury. Then she felt foolish.

"And so that gives your brother the right to beat him within an inch of his life?" Grandpapa George turned a disappointed eye on her. His words were harsh. "Miriam, I expected more of you than that."

"Grandpapa...."

"Look at him, girl! He breathes. He *bleeds*. He has a mother and father who are missing him. Sisters, brothers, who love him. A tribe. A family. He wants to love and be loved. He is *human*. Like you and me." Her grandfather cast a despairing look toward the open door and the manor house beyond. "More human than those brothers of yours – and their narrow-minded self-righteous father."

Miriam wasn't listening. The Indian had turned his face into the moon's light. Beneath the dried blood and traces of worn paint, the bruised cheek and swollen eye....

He was beautiful.

"What are you going to do with him?" she asked, breathless.

"Do?" Grandpapa George ran a hand through his graying hair as he rose from the chair. "After tonight? God only knows, Miri. If I can convince your mother he will make a fit servant, there might be a chance for him to remain. Still, your brothers will be merciless. His path will be hard no matter what I decide. I had hoped to clean him up before anyone saw him. Cut his hair. Make him presentable. Perhaps try to convince them that he was not an Indian – "

"But he is, Grandpapa."

The older man stopped and looked at her as though struck to the heart. His hand came down on her head and he ruffled her tousled curls. "Yes. He is. And we must never let him forget that. No matter what happens."

"May I...may I sit with him, Grandpapa?"

"You will be missed in the house."

Miriam smiled shyly. Before leaving her room, she had stuffed her pillows under the coverlet. And her nurse was asleep. "Not for a while. Please."

He frowned but did not refuse. "Very well. I will see what I can do about getting him some clothes fit for your mother to see him in and then return. But when I do, you must to bed, child. You have had a hard day. We all have."

With one last look at the sleeping figure, Grandpapa George departed.

Miriam turned back to the pitiful creature on her grandfather's cot. Some dream fluttered beneath the Indian's eyelids and he murmured, speaking words she could not understand, though she sensed by their tone that he was crying for someone or something he had lost. Miriam sat beside the bed and watched him for some time. Then she dared to reach out and touch his golden skin just above the wrist. It was feverish, but other than that felt just like hers.

She had not expected that.

Chapter Two

"Dear God in Heaven! George, what *were* you thinking?" Charlotte Foxwell looked up from her embroidery. Her deep brown eyes flicked to the expensive Persian carpet that graced the heart of pine floor in the drawing room, wondering if her father-in-law's endless pacing had worn a hole through the hand-tied pile yet. "George! For Providence's sake, hold still!"

"Charlotte, I.... I don't...." George Foxwell stopped and turned toward her, his face wrinkled with chagrin. The older man threw his hands up in defeat and fell heavily into the great tambour-work wing chair that rested before the fire – the one her absent husband, William, usually occupied. Once seated William's father rested his head in his hands and murmured, "I don't *know* what I was thinking."

Charlotte stifled an exasperated sigh and, ignoring for the moment the slipped stitch on her otherwise perfect needlework, placed the embroidery hoop on the mahogany table beside her that held a wine glass and the remnants of a mid-morning snack. Then she laced her pale perfect fingers together in the lap of her Dutch chintz gown.

"Certainly not of the children," she scolded. "Exposing them to a *savage* – "

Her father-in-law looked up. His words were hasty and unacceptable. "Charlotte, he is not a 'savage'. He's a human being."

"He's an *animal*, George, and deserves to be treated as such." Her jaw grew tight. The tip of her upper lip quirked and her right eye twitched – the first warning signs of an impending headache. Charlotte pressed two fingers against her temple to impede its progress. She was furious! Savages with their paint and beads had burnt their home when she was a child and murdered her eldest brother. They had nearly killed her husband more times than she cared to think about. She was sick to death of her father-in-law's misplaced kindness and generosity. "He must be put down before he grows up to do more harm."

"Charlotte! He's a child. Like *your* children. He's – "

Her fingers gripped the wooden arms of her toile sewing chair. If possible, her patrician knuckles grew even whiter. "He is *not* like my children! That animal is not fit to polish my children's boots, or to empty the pots they piss in!" Charlotte paused and then asked in an even, more controlled voice. "Did you not tell me, George, that the savages train their male offspring, almost from the time they can walk, to hunt and kill?"

"To hunt *animals*. Yes."

Charlotte kept the triumphant smile she felt from lifting the corners of her perfectly blushed lips. "And did you not *also* tell me that by the age of twelve they are considered adults? The boys, warriors?"

He nodded. "Well, yes. In certain tribes, but – "

"How old is this savage?"

Her father-in-law hesitated. "I can't be sure," he said at last.

One elegant eyebrow arched. "Guess."

"I would place him at about twelve. Perhaps older," George admitted quietly.

"Old enough, then, to be a *threat*." Charlotte rose in queenly fashion from her seat and approached the old man where he sat before the fire. Theirs had never been an easy relationship. In spite of the fact that his son was the quintessence of propriety, George Foxwell was an avowed eccentric who had no sense of the proper social order and whose actions were often embarrassing. Her husband, William, despaired of him. And yet, in spite of his faults, Charlotte had to admit that the old man was legend – a seasoned campaigner and a decorated veteran of several of His Majesty's wars.

Whatever he might be, George Foxwell was no fool.

Softening, Charlotte leaned forward and touched his hand. "George. Father. What is it you see in this Indian? Can you make me understand?"

He placed his hand over hers. Meeting her perplexed stare, he answered with a snort. "Charlotte, my dear. How can I possibly hope to make *you* understand what I do not understand myself?"

"Try," she insisted, disengaging her hand and straightening up. "Give me a reason not to have the groundsmen drag the savage from the studio and snuff out his life before he grows up to murder all of us in our sleep!"

Her father-in-law fell silent for a moment. George rose from his seat and began to pace again. She frowned at the path his regulation British boots cut in her carpet as much as at his words.

"Charlotte, you are an intelligent woman," he said as he turned toward her. "One who is able to think things through for herself. It saddens me that you have bought into William's deranged animosity toward the native people of this land." Her father-in-law held a hand up to cut off her comment and continued. "Yes, there are 'savages' among them, but then, are there not among our kind as well? What would *you* do if a foreign invader broke down your door, threatened your children lives, and then drove you off your land? Would you not fight back? Is that not what *we* are about – protecting what it ours by rights? What did we fight the last war with the French for? For our right to be *here*, in this province, on this rich and bountiful land." George took a step toward her and opened his arms wide, encompassing the drawing room with its elegantly appointed furnishings, the broad French windows and the sun-kissed land beyond. "But to own *this*, another had to be displaced."

Charlotte drew a deep breath, keeping her anger in check and reminding herself that she was attempting to give him a chance to make some sense out of all of this. "You *cannot* compare us to the savages."

"And why not? Are we not all God's creatures?"

"As are the beasts of the field and the fish that swim in the sea," she replied calmly. "Really, George, you are not going to say the savages have rights! This bountiful land is wasted on the Indian. He is *not* industrious. He does not plow or plant. Their women are made to work as drudges while their men smoke pipes, fight among themselves, and engage in drunken orgies! God has given us dominion over the red man so that we may educate him in His ways."

The moment the words were out of her mouth Charlotte knew she had been had. Like the brilliant commander he was, George Foxwell had maneuvered her into a position of his choosing – one with little or no defense.

Her father-in-law smiled as he approached her. "Then, Charlotte, is it not *God's* will that we educate this boy? Make an example of him? *Show* his people what they can become?"

Charlotte remained silent for a moment. "William would never allow it. Even if I conceded."

"William does not need to know."

She shook her head. "I will not hide a thing like that from my husband."

George took her hand again. He pressed it between his own, and then spoke softly, "If – by the time William returns – he can tell the boy is a savage and he disapproves, then I will send him away from here. But I do not think he will be able to tell. The boy is bright! I have seen it in him. He will learn, and he *will* adapt. He can change."

Charlotte noted the fire that lit the old man's eyes. It had been some time since she had seen him so passionate. In the last few years, since the death of his wife, George had seemed lost – almost distracted.

"What about the children?" she asked at last. "They know what he is."

"Children are children. Today they are enemies. Tomorrow they may be the best of friends. Besides the boys will soon be at school – "

She pulled her hand away. "No. I will not have an *Indian* in my children's lives."

George nodded without hesitation. "Very well. Whatever you say. If I keep him as my boy, is that acceptable? He can live in the studio."

Charlotte nodded, but then added quickly, "If he *ever* so much as raises a hand to one of the children – "

"He won't. I will see to it."

Charlotte studied the old man, wondering which one of them was crazier. Then she pressed her fingers to her temples again. The threat of a headache had developed into a reality – just as it usually did when she dared to cross swords with General Foxwell.

"You had better," Charlotte warned as she moved past him and pulled the cord that would summon her serving maid. "I am holding you personally accountable. Remember that."

Sister Kate had taken a fright the night before and was in bed with a chill. James and John were away with the neighbor boys hunting. The nursemaid was watching little Anna who was asleep, and Mama had retired to her rooms with a headache.

She was free!

Miriam was in the larder. She gathered a few things together and placed them in a basket, covering them with a linen napkin, and then headed down the long corridor that led to the entry. Her hand was on the latch when she heard someone call her name. Starting guiltily, she turned and found her grandfather emerging from the drawing room.

He looked tired.

"Grandpapa? Is something wrong?"

As he came to her side, the older man placed one hand on her shoulder and fingered the light cloth that covered the contents of the basket with the other. "And where might you be gadding, my girl?"

She shrugged. "Nowhere. Everyone else is gone or asleep. I thought I would –"

"Go visit the Indian?"

Miriam's gaze dropped to the pine floor beneath her freshly-laundered slippers. She spoke without meeting his eyes. "I feel bad for screaming and getting him hurt." She shifted the linen cloth and exposed the neatly ordered biscuits and jam within as well as a few other little items – a book, an apple, and one precious piece of chocolate. "I was going to take these to him."

Grandpapa George knelt so his eyes would be on a level with hers. Then he forced her to meet his stern gaze. "Miriam, you must not come to the studio again," he said.

"But Grandpapa! Why not? You said – "

"I know what I said." She watched as he cast a glance back toward the drawing room. "I made a promise to your mother that I would keep you safe."

Miriam shook her ringletted head and insisted, "He won't hurt me."

Grandpapa George rose to his feet. He walked to the door and looked out one of the tall thin windows that framed it, toward the line of trees that masked the studio "You can't know that, Miri. Neither can I. The boy is a savage creature from a savage race, born to the wood and forced to do what is necessary to survive." He turned and met her puzzled stare, his look grave. "He may have already killed, Miriam. He is old enough."

"Killed? You mean – "

"Yes. Killed a man. If he has been in battle...."

"But, he is no older than John," she declared, scarcely believing it possible.

"If John did not have this fine house, if he did not have a father who has property and provisions aplenty – if John were *forced* to forage and live off the land, and to defend whatever small portion of it is his own, then he might have killed by now as well. This boy is an Indian, Miriam. *You* told me that." Her grandfather placed his hand on the latch. "Never forget it."

Miriam watched him walk out the door and then, driven by a need she could not explain even to herself, she bolted after him, calling, "Grandpapa!"

He turned to look at her. "Yes, child?"

She held the basket out. "Then, will you take this to him? And tell him I am sorry?"

Her grandfather regarded her for a moment, a curious expression on his face, and then he returned to her side and took the basket. "I will give it to him. But I cannot tell him anything. I do not know his language. He will have to learn ours."

"Can't you send him home?" she asked suddenly, thinking how she would feel if she had to leave behind everything she had ever known – her Mama and Papa, James and John. Even her silly old nursemaid Martha.

Grandpapa George took her hand and led her to the foot of the stone stair and then sat with her. He kept hold of her hand and patted it as he talked.

"I can't take him home because I don't know where his home is. I have no idea where he came from, what tribe he belongs to, nothing. And he cannot tell me. And I fear, by the time he can, he will no longer remember the way home. He is all alone, Miriam. All he has is me."

She placed her hand on his and squeezed. "Us. He has 'us', Grandpapa."

"No, child. Your mother will not hear of it." Her grandfather released her hand and stood up. Bending down he planted a kiss on her forehead. "I will take your basket to him and tell him of your kind and generous heart. He may not understand my words, but the biscuits were very good this morning and *those* he will understand." He looked at her a moment and then, with a smile, added softly, "You are a blessing to me, child. Do you know that?"

Miriam jumped up and caught him in an embrace. "I love you, Grandpapa."

Miriam loved him.

But she wasn't going to listen to him.

Later that morning she watched as her grandfather mounted his fine black horse, Molly, and headed down the pebbled lane. While her father, William, was in England, Grandpapa George was in charge of the family business since John and James were too young. Not only did he have to oversee the plantation's one hundred and twenty slaves and the hired laborers who bossed them, but he had to handle the export business as well as manage the care of the manor's several dozen horses that were her father's pride and joy. Today, Grandpapa George had to go to the town to arrange for the sale of a few of those horses to a local magistrate. And since the Indian was too weak to go with him, that meant he was still in the studio.

Alone.

Miriam wasn't certain what it was that compelled her to seek him out. She told herself it was because she felt guilty. She didn't want to admit that it might be just plain curiosity. Whichever it was, it made little difference. The moment her grandfather was gone, she slipped out of the house and headed straight as a bee to its tree for the small wood and brick studio nestled in the shadowy grove.

The door had been patched together and was shut with a makeshift padlock. Fortunately, her grandpapa knew nothing of her secret entrance. Miriam loosened the vent cover again and wriggled through. Once inside she paused to straighten her hair and skirts so she would be presentable. She was wearing a fine white pinner apron over a pale blue closed gown of Irish linen today and had her hair pulled back in a tail. But as she plucked the pleats and ran her fingers along the apron's hem, she hesitated. Would a savage know if she was presentable?

Did he even know what *presentable* meant?

The door out of the annexed room that led into the main studio had been pushed to, but was not locked. She placed her hand on the painted wood and slowly shoved it inward. Then she peered around the edge. The savage was there, sitting on the bed. He was dressed like her brothers now in a linen work shirt and a pair of tan fall front breeches. But there any similarity ended. His lower legs and feet were immodestly bare, and his coppery hair hung in a wave that washed halfway down his back. The midday sun was streaming in through one of the studio windows and it cast his face into shadow since his head was bent. Miriam could tell he was looking at something, but she could not see what.

Hesitantly she pushed the door open and stepped into the room. She waited a moment and when he did not stir, cleared her throat. When he failed to respond to that, she tried calling out 'hello.' When he still did not move, she frowned, at a loss. Maybe he was deaf.

Was there such a thing as a deaf Indian?

Miriam moved farther into the room. She stopped when she noticed the basket with its half-eaten biscuits and jar of jam on the low table beside the bed. Her grandfather had brought it to him as he promised.

And now she knew what was in his hands.

"It's an ABC book," Miriam told him softly as she approached. "My Grandmama Margaret made it for me when I was little. She painted the pictures herself."

Through the wave of gleaming copper hair she could just make out his face. The golden-brown skin of his cheek was split; the edges of the wound painted a deep purple by her brother's cruelty.

And her foolishness.

"I am *so* sorry," she said, her voice trembling with rage and shame. "I didn't know that they would beat you. I didn't want them to. I didn't mean for it to happen. I was just...." Miriam reached out toward him, "I was afraid."

The Indian's head shifted slightly as though he might look at her and then, faster than thought, he captured her wrist with his hand. Two seconds later she found herself lying on the daybed with his strong muscled form suspended over her.

Miriam trembled down to her toes, but she refused to scream. *Never* would scream again. "Well," she snapped, mimicking her sister's arrogant tone, "what do you intend to do? Scalp me?"

The Indian's fingers went to her pale ringlets as if he understood her words. He scowled as he undid the blue ribbon that held her hair in its tail, and then grinned wickedly as the pale curls fell loose about her face and shoulders. He pointed at her apron and then pulled at the pin that fastened it to her gown.

Miriam froze, unsure of what to do. Kate had told her once about a boy who had done the same thing. He had taken the pins from her apron and then tried to unpin the bodice beneath. Kate had also told her what to do if a boy ever tried the same thing with her. So Miriam did it. She slapped him.

Hard.

The sound of her palm striking the savage's skin startled them both. So did the blood that ran down his cheek. The blow reopened the wound her brother James had inflicted. Miriam started to apologize but before she could, he started for the pin again.

Shoving his hand away, she scooted back until she was at the end of the bed. "You are *not* a gentleman!" she declared.

The Indian stared at her, seemingly puzzled by her behavior. He shook his head and then sifted through the bed linens as though in search of something. Abruptly he swooped toward the floor and returned –

With her grandmother's ABC book in his hand.

The Indian turned a number of pages before he found what he was looking for. "U-s-qua-i!" he declared indignantly, one light brown finger jabbing the vellum sheet.

Miriam dared to move forward so she could glance at the water-colored image gracing it. It showed a paper of pins.

She relaxed and nodded, though she kept a hand on her apron. "Pin," she said. "That is a 'pin'."

The Indian's split lip twisted and, for a moment, he looked as if he had taken a bite of something distasteful. Then he spit it out. "Pin?"

"Yes," Miriam laughed, pointing toward her apron and then back to the book. "This is called a 'pin'. It is a piece of metal fashioned to keep your clothing together."

"Clo-th-ing?" he repeated.

"Yes." Miriam reached for his arm, but halted when he stiffened and grew wary. "May I show you?" she asked, pointing toward his shirtsleeve.

He looked skeptical, but nodded.

She touched the linen of his sleeve. "You are wearing 'clothing'. This is a 'shirt', and these," she added, pointing toward the tan cloth that covered his legs, "are breeches. You are wearing a shirt and breeches. Like a proper boy would."

The Indian stared at her a moment and then indicated her grandmother's book with a nod, as if to say, 'Show me.'

COPPERHEAD

"Oh, not everything is in there," she replied, knowing he couldn't understand. "I can't remember what Grandmama Margaret painted for 'C', but it wasn't 'clothing'. Can I look?" She asked for the book. The Indian reluctantly surrendered it, and only after she promised to give it back.

That he somehow seemed to understand.

Miriam began to page through the ABC book. She had given it to her little sister Anna when she got too big for it, but when she first thought about coming to visit the savage, had located it and tossed it in the basket thinking that maybe she could use it to teach him their language.

And here she was!

Miriam opened it to the letter 'C'. "Do you know what this is?" she asked, showing him the drawing of a small feline curled in a great wingback chair.

He nodded and said proudly, "We-sa'."

"Wesa?" she repeated. "Well, maybe it is called that where you come from, but here we call it a 'cat', and you shall have to learn to call it that too. Can you say 'cat'?"

Again the frown. The pursed lips and the awkwardness of forming words one had never known. "Ca-h-t?" he managed.

Miriam laughed. "That will do. Now what else shall we...."

She had been thumbing through the book. The Indian, who was sitting quite close by her now, stopped her with a finger on one of the latter pages. He smelled like soap. Her grandfather must have scrubbed him. The paint was gone from his face and he was really quite handsome in spite of the fact that he was far too thin and had the look of a convalescent. His dark eyes were intense and fastened on the spot where finger met paper. "Hv-?" he asked, indicating the drawing.

Miriam tore her eyes away from him and looked at the page. A brilliantly colored snake was coiled on it, one with a copper head and distinctive chestnut colored bands on its back and sides. "That is a snake," she said.

"S-nake?"

She smiled. It would not take him long to learn. He seemed eager to know. "Yes. A copperhead. We have them in the yard sometimes, though they prefer to stay in the lowlands where there are lots of vines and grasses. Grandpapa said a copperhead will only attack when it is threatened. And then, only in defense." Miriam paused. She was talking too much. He couldn't have any idea what she was saying.

"Wudigeas," he said, pointing at the picture of the snake and then at his golden-brown chest where it showed beneath the linen shirt. His voice was strangely insistent, as if it was vitally important she understand. "Da-qua-dov, Wudigeas!"

Miriam shook her head. "I don't – "

Unexpectedly, he grabbed the book from her and threw it on the floor in a fit of anger and frustration. It landed in a heap, the precious hand-painted pages bent and broken by their contact with the stone tile. The Indian stared at it a moment and then moved to pick it up. He flipped the pages until he found what he wanted and then, cradling it against his body as if it were something precious, approached her and held it out, pointing once again at the brilliantly colored snake as if asking her to confirm what it was.

"It's a copperhead," she repeated.

He nodded. His finger touched the picture of the snake and then returned to his chest. "A-ya! Cop-per-head."

She frowned and then, suddenly, understood. "Oh! Your name! That's your name. Copperhead?"

He smiled. White teeth breaking in a face of gold. His deep brown eyes lit with delight as he pointed at her and asked, "Ga-do-de-tsa-do?"

Miriam's frown deepened. "Gado what?"

He nodded, pointing to himself. "Cop-per-head." Then he pointed to her. "Ga-do-de-tsa-do?"

"Who am I, you mean? Miriam," she answered, extending her hand out of habit, just as her Mama had taught her. "Miriam Elizabeth Foxwell."

"Mir-ee-am," Copperhead repeated slowly, as if committing it to memory. And then to her surprise he took her hand as if he were a gentleman come to court.

She pulled it away, a little too quickly, and settled on the edge of the cot. Copperhead came to sit beside her, bringing the book. Once there, he handed it to her with a nod.

Miriam opened it. She pointed toward the first page with its bright splash of red and green.

"Apple," she said. " 'A' is for apple."

Chapter Three

George Foxwell ran a hand across his stubbled chin and stared at the destruction left in the wake of the Indian boy's violent outburst. He had thought they were making progress, but something had changed.

He only wished his remarkable houseguest could tell him what.

Upon returning from town, he had been called away for a fortnight on business for the Crown having to do with the new commander of his old regiment. It was a 'request' he could in no way refuse. It had troubled George to leave the boy alone, but he had little choice. Now he knew he needn't have worried. Obvious little signs – a square of parchment with a child's scrawled letters next to a finer hand, a piece of chocolate, a beribboned basket containing a few berries – visible amidst the broken furniture and shattered glass, told him someone had been in the studio during his absence. George suspected it was Miriam, though he couldn't understand how the girl had gained entry when he – and the servant set to feed the boy – were the only ones with a key. It worried him to think of the two of them alone. He had no idea what morals the boy had. Though George had fought side by side with Indians for nearly a decade, his civilian contact with the red man had been limited.

For all he knew the boy could be mature enough to be not only a warrior, but a father.

Careful to keep his gaze averted from the place where the boy had chosen to hide, George up-righted one of the few chairs left intact and took a seat. He adjusted the fit of his regulation scarlet coat and then leaned back, extending his long legs and crossing his spit-polish black boots. The last few years – in the absence of Margaret's gentle but firm reminders – had added a few unwanted inches to his midriff. George's buff-colored waistcoat now had more than the *bottom* button left fashionably undone.

A small contingent of His Majesty's soldiers had returned to the estate with him. Several of the men he had been sent to deal with had turned out to be the sons of his old regiment mates. The dozen or so who accompanied him were headed farther south, deep into Cherokee lands, and he had offered them the hospitality of his son's home on their way.

With Charlotte's permission, of course.

They had arrived amidst a shower of budding trees, just as the late spring sun was setting. George introduced the young men to Charlotte and the children and then left them to her graces, making a rather pathetic excuse about checking on the horses that his daughter-in-law saw through immediately. Promising to return in time for dinner, he had begged their pardon and then hastened to the studio to check on the captive guest he had so uneasily left behind.

He had found the boy sitting on the cot with his strong-boned face turned into the dying light, a book balanced on his knee. Even though the Indian could not read, the pictures seemed to fascinate him and he wanted to know what they were. Over the course of several weeks George had begun to use this fascination to exchange words and had come to realize that the boy was Cherokee or Tsalagi. 'So-qui-li' was the word for 'horse. 'Gas-gi-lo' for 'table'. He had thought they were developing a rapport, and might even become friends. While in Salem he had purchased a picture book of the heroes of the Bible, thinking the martial images would appeal to the boy. He held it out and spoke to attract his attention. The boy had turned, a smile of welcome on his face.

And everything changed.

The Indian boy's lean form had gone rigid. His eyes – usually intelligent, keen, and eager to learn – became the eyes of a wild thing at risk. He began to breath heavily and backed away, shouting something in his own tongue. Hoping to calm him George had approached, his hands out-stretched in what he thought was a universal symbol of truce. The boy denied the gesture and retreated further, first into a dark niche at the rear of the studio and then – using a tabletop as a springboard – into the exposed rafters of the ceiling.

At that moment one of Charlotte's maids had appeared, declaring it was time for dinner. Not being desirous of offending his daughter-in-law any further, George had laid the picture book on the cot and – with one final word of encouragement – gone to take his place at the table.

The dinner wore on and it was not until close to midnight that he was able to return to the studio. George opened the door to find a tempest had taken place in his absence. The picture book was on the floor. Its colorful pages ripped out and strewn about like autumn leaves. The cot had been up-ended, the linen bedding shredded and tossed aside in a tangled heap. His paint pots had been opened and their contents hurled about, creating a violent rainbow of rage on the interior walls. Chairs had been smashed, and one in particular had been used in an abortive attempt to break out the window. Shards of glass littered the tile floor. After wreaking this destruction the Indian boy had retreated to his perch near the ceiling where now, from a sanctuary of shadows, he watched him. On the tile beneath the savage's perch was a growing pool of blood. George did not know if it was from the old wound to his back, or if the Indian had cut himself in his desperate attempt to escape.

While bidding goodnight to the children, George had noticed Miriam avoiding him. Drawing her aside he had spoken to her sternly, asking if she had been in the studio during his absence. She had, of course, lied and said she had come nowhere near it. She had also slipped and made him certain that she had. In reply to his assertion that the Indian could and most likely *would* prove dangerous and she dare not trust herself alone with him, Miriam had replied matter-of-factly. 'Copperhead would never hurt me, Grandpapa.'

Copperhead.

George shifted back in the chair and looked up. The light of the lantern he had carried with him caught the boy's eyes, making them appear feral. Had he indeed brought a viper into the bosom of the family? Was the Indian only waiting for an opportunity to strike?

Would Copperhead, if given the chance, murder them all in their beds just as Charlotte had predicted?

George licked his lips and then said calmly, "I am not leaving until you come down. I need to know what is wrong. If I have done anything to offend you, I apologize."

As he waited George wondered how much – if anything – of what he said the boy understood. Could he tell by the tone of his voice that he meant him no harm? If Miriam had been schooling him, the Indian might understand more than he thought.

"Copperhead. I expect a reply."

After a moment of silence, there was a grunt in answer to his having employed the Indian's name. George had thought perhaps that would work. The fact that he knew it would connect him immediately to Miriam and give him some power over the boy.

"My granddaughter – Miriam – tells me we have nothing to fear from you, Copperhead. Is that the truth?" he added to reinforce the connection. The scowl returned to George's face as his gaze went from the up-turned cot to the broken window. "From what I see here of your handiwork, it begs the lie."

The shadowy form above him shifted. "Mir-i-am?" the Indian asked.

George nodded. "Yes, Mir-i-am. I know she has been here."

"Mir-i-am Copperhead's friend."

Dear God! Whatever the deepest hellhole was on this untamed continent, that was where he was going to find himself if Charlotte ever discovered the truth about this pair. Stifling a sigh, George replied gently, "I am – George is Copperhead's friend too."

"*No*! George *not* friend. *Never friend!*"

The vehemence of the boy's shout surprised him. "Why not?"

There was a pause. Then six words. "Coat. Apple coat. Enemy. *Not* friend."

Apple coat? Now what in the world did *that* mean?

Apple coat. Coat. Apple. George glanced down at his coat. As he did his gaze fell on a torn page from the ABC book Margaret had painted. The one Miriam had brought to the boy. 'A is for apple' his dear wife had written, and illustrated the words with a bright *red* apple. George looked at the furtive figure clinging to the rafters. Copperhead had never seen him in uniform before. The boy had been unconscious when he found him and carried him to safety. He had not worn it since.

It was his British red coat the boy feared.

"Is that it?" he asked, rising and removing the coat. "Is this what you are afraid of?"

The Indian said nothing and his silence said all.

George crossed to a tall clothes press he used for his aprons and supplies and laid the coat in one of its drawers. He closed the drawer tightly and then returned to the chair and sat down. "I have put it away. Now, please come down."

"No!" the boy shouted.

George leaned back and placed his hands over his face. It seemed what trust he had built with the boy about *who* he was, had been destroyed by the reality of *what* he was when wearing his uniform. He was no longer the man who had rescued him and saved him from a certain death, but a British officer and Redcoat.

George Foxwell rose wearily to his feet and crossed to the cot. He righted it and, after locating the torn and paint streaked feather ticking and placing it on the ropes, lay down on his back.

"When you are ready," he said without looking at the Cherokee boy, "I will be here." And then he rolled over and pretended to sleep.

Copperhead might be held captive in the white man's lodge, but in his mind he was home.

The wood floor beneath him was the grassy plain on which his family's lodge stood. The beam he crouched on, the sturdy branch of the ancient tree he and his elder brother had proclaimed their hiding place. The faces lining the room, gazing at him from the depths of brown and gold frames, were the faces of his people watching from the land of the dead. And the blood that clothed his all but naked frame, running as a red river from his wounds, was a path to the broken and burnt bodies of his father, his mother, his brother, and all the others.

Red as the coats of the men who murdered them.

Copperhead did not know how old he had been when it happened, for the People did not count the years as the white man did, marking the day of one's birth with noise and celebration as though that one day were more special than another. The People lived from sunrise to sunset, from plentiful harvest to the lean time, from birth to death all in one journey. His elder brother had been a man when the British came, and so Copperhead knew he had still been a child. The sister closest to him in age could not walk yet, and his little brother was still suckling. He was old enough to carry a bow, but not yet able to string it. His father spoke kind words to him that final day, promising him it would not be long before he could wear the paint and run with the older boys, but it did little to soothe him. This day was not the day, his father said.

This day he must remain behind, in shame, with his mother and the little ones.

Copperhead did not understand. Anger like a swollen river broke in him, overflowing in disobedience and rage. He remained behind, as he had been told, but as soon as the sun set he sneaked out of his mother's lodge and followed his father and the other men. He should have known his choice was not an honored one, for as soon as he set out the night turned its back on him. Clouds overtook the moon and the stars fled. Soon he was lost. He wandered for hours, cold and alone, until at last he tripped and fell into a ravine and knew nothing more.

Until he awoke to the sound of gunfire and the cries of men.

Frightened as a toothless old woman Copperhead crawled on his belly into a stand of tall grasses and clung to the hillside, burying himself deep in its cloaking shadows. The flash of steel striking flint lit the night. Smoke and the acrid smell of gunpowder choked him and brought tears to his eyes. Loud commanding voices, not of the People, followed by the thunder of the stranger's guns assaulted his ears as he burrowed his way into the mud and trembled.

He had no idea how long he laid there – cold, quaking, growing sick in mind and body. The People do not count the hours nor live by hands of gold that march in an endless circle running their lives. The People are born anew each day, and know in their hearts that each night holds the promise of rest and replenishment.

But not this night.

Copperhead did not remember rising, but he remembered parting the stiff grass and peering through. He remembered the face of the moon reflected on the still black water. The moon – whose earlier absence had denied the path to his father – now revealed a path he did not want to take. The men of his village lay before him, dead and dying. His father, Bear Paw, was within arms' reach. He lay on his back, his eyes wide open and focused without seeing on the mottled sky. Copperhead watched his father's chest rise and fall with labored breath. He shifted forward, ready to forsake the safety of his grassy nest to touch him, but then there was another flash – not of a gun this time, but of the light of the bloated moon. It struck golden braid on a sleeve of scarlet and glinted off the tip of the bayonet –

As it pierced his father's heart.

Copperhead did not move. He couldn't. Though he could see, he could no longer feel. He watched as the British soldier who held the bayonet turned to speak briefly to another man. Then, pressing a shining black boot against his father's throat, he jerked the weapon out. Blood poured from Bear Paw's lips, red as his killer's coat.

His father cried out once and then, was silent forever.

The moon fell from the sky before the men in red coats departed. When he found the courage to move, Copperhead searched the banks of the ravine and found his elder brother and his uncle, and many, many others.

All cold and dead.

He would have wept for them and sung the ancient songs, but he had no time. Not before he smelled the smoke on the wind.

The hours it had taken him to run away, it took also to return. Copperhead arrived at his mother's lodge just as the sun rose to reveal this new shame. The grassy plain was char. The ancient tree where he had perched with his brother, embers. His mother's house was no more. A body lay before it, burnt beyond recognition, a baby swaddled in ashes fused for eternity to its skeletal arms.

His sister was gone.

And it was all his fault.

Copperhead had no idea how long he sat unmoving in the midst of the ruins of his life. The sun and moon came and went without notice. The men in the red coats did not return as he prayed, and so he waited for the angry spirits of those he had betrayed to rise and take him. For the carrion birds that circled overhead to pick his bones. For one of the wild beasts watching from beneath the canopy of rustling leaves to strike and tear out his heart.

He did not have the courage to kill himself.

At last, he thought his prayer had been answered. From the living womb of the forest a pack of rawboned wolves emerged. They circled him, their jaws slavering, their empty bellies howling with hunger. He watched them with only mild interest, lacking the energy to stand and embrace what he desired.

As the circle tightened and death grew close a silver-gray shadow appeared, not from the wolves but from the emptiness surrounding them. It growled and leapt between him and the rapacious pack. Copperhead could not see it clearly, for his eyes were all but closed, but he did not think it was a wolf. Snarling and snapping, it drove the others away, turning them from him to feast on the charred flesh of those he loved.

Diseased with grief, sick, fevered, Copperhead remembered only snatches of what happened next. A pair of dark eyes. A warm muzzle pressed against his skin. The unwanted comfort of a blanket wrapped around his aching body and being lifted up. A wrinkled hand touching his forehead. A voice, like his father's.

And then sleep.

Blessed sleep.

Copperhead awoke to the reality of his loss, only to find that his maternal grandfather had survived the massacre. The wise old man had been among the party of warriors who, a few days before, had accompanied a contingent of British soldiers on an abortive raid against their mutual enemy, the Shawanoese. The raid failed when the provisions were lost along the way. Without food or powder the men – including Copperhead's father – had refused to fight and instead returned to their home. His grandfather, Walker, had argued with his daughter's husband along the way. Bear Paw believed the British commander when he said there would be no hard feelings. Walker did not and so, along with another of the elders named One Feather, Copperhead's grandfather turned back to spy on the men in the red coats.

Walker returned too late with the knowledge he gained to save his family.

His father, his brothers and his mother died, and his little sister was taken to be sold into slavery because, on their way home the warriors had found and captured a few free-roaming horses that had once belonged to the British army. The soldiers used this 'horse thievery' as an excuse to punish the People – mutilating and scalping the dead before burning more than half of the village to the ground.

Copperhead mended slowly. Many, many days passed before he uttered a word. And when he spoke it was only to tell his grandfather of his desire to die. Walker nodded, understanding, but assured him the Great Spirit would be saddened by his death. When he asked why, his grandfather spoke of a vision that had come to him the night before they found him. A vision of a silver fox. The powerful animal had come to Walker and told him that his daughter's son had need of him, and that Copperhead must live, for one day the fox would have need of *him*. The fox told Walker it slept by the boy's side to keep him warm so he would not die, and would keep close watch until the old man came to care for him.

And so Copperhead returned to what was left of the People and was reared by the old men of the village. It was under Walker's guidance that he became a man. He studied hard and mastered the ways of the warrior, running faster and jumping higher, shooting straighter and killing quicker than any of the others – earning the name the Beloved Woman of the village had given him.

In time the British soldiers returned with new offers of friendship, saying the enlisted men who had burnt their village had been renegades out for themselves. Their actions had not been sanctioned by the King, and they had been taken and punished for their crimes. Though his grandfather doubted the soldiers spoke the truth, the fathers and many of the young men of the village accepted their words, for they had need of the goods the white men carried in their wagons. Copperhead *knew* they lied. He watched them swagger through the village, arrogant and boastful, flashing false smiles, courting the young girls with their bright beads and fancy cloth, and promising weapons and liquor to their brothers if they would look the other way. He watched them and he waited.

Waited for the day when he could avenge those who had died.

Copperhead was his elder brother's age when that day came. Many years had passed since the slaughter of his family. One day an old woman recognized a soldier who walked among them as one of the officers who had been in the village the day his family had died. He told his grandfather, but Walker cautioned him to do nothing, reminding him of the vision of the fox. He was meant for greater things than vengeance, the old man said.

Copperhead did not care. Fire and fury burned within him. He tried to raise the men of the village against the British. They would not listen. They did not want to lose the favor of the men in the red coats. And so, against his chief and his grandfather's wishes, he enlisted his friends – those who had also known loss in that raid so long ago. In secret they met and in secret they plotted their revenge. The journey would be a long one. The man lived far to the north. But that would make the victory greater and paint their names upon the face of history.

But there was no victory. No spoils. The British officer did not die.

Only Copperhead's friends.

And again, *he* was alive. Saved, this time, not by a silver fox but by a man wearing a red coat.

It shamed Copperhead that he had mistaken the red coat's actions for kindness. When he woke to a world of pain, the old man's face looking down at him had reminded him of his grandfather, Walker, and that had put him off his guard. Now he knew George Foxwell for what he was – his enemy. He did not know why the red coat held him captive – to study him or to take pleasure in his pain – but he knew he could not let the old man live and use what he had learned against the People.

Copperhead's muscles were aching. Blood-loss left him dizzy and barely able to keep his purchase on the beam. He ran a quaking finger over the surface of the broken shard of glass he had collected from the floor. It would only take a second. He could be on the red coat and cut his throat before he had time to call out. He *should* do it, for the People, for his mother and father, for his brother. His sister. He should….

One thing stopped him.

Miriam.

Copperhead had watched her and the old man from his sick bed when they did not know he was awake. She loved him. If he killed the red coat, she would grieve. And would his action be justified? Miriam's grandfather was not the man who murdered his family, even if he did wear the same uniform. And if he killed George Foxwell out of vengeance, where would it end? Miriam's brothers, or Miriam herself, would call out for his blood. And if he died, then one of the People would come and kill them. The scarlet river of vengeance would be ever flowing and know no end.

Copperhead let the glass shard fall. It struck the stone floor and shattered. When the old man did not jump, he knew he was not pretending. The red coat had actually fallen asleep, trusting that he would not kill him.

Leaving his perch in the rafters, Copperhead dropped silently to the top of a table and then slipped to the studio floor. He limped slowly to the side of the bed and stood there for some time, watching the old man breathe.

Then he lay on the floor beside him and curled up into a ball and fell into a heavy sleep.

George Foxwell opened his eyes to find that the day had dawned and he was still alive. Mildly surprised, he yawned and shifted only to realize that Copperhead was seated on the cot near his feet, watching him. The boy's chest and legs were painted in his own dried blood, but apparently the cuts – though bleeding profusely – had been mostly superficial. At least he had not bled to death.

George made certain Copperhead was aware that he was awake and then shifted into a seated position. For a moment they simply stared at one another. He cleared his throat and said softly, "I am sorry for whatever happened to you. For whatever the men in the red coats did. But I assure you, we are not all the same." He knew the boy had no idea of what he was saying, but hoped the tone he employed would convey something of his regret.

Copperhead continued to stare at him but said nothing.

George studied the Cherokee boy. The bruises from James' bashing were healing. But there were other scars, marks of honor, won no doubt through trial and cherished in victory. He would put his age closer to thirteen now, maybe fourteen. Definitely a man in the eyes of his tribe. Copperhead's face was strong-boned, the cheeks high, the nose straight, and his mouth tolerably large – all well within the sensibilities of what one might call 'handsome'. His eyes were the deep brown of tilled earth and his skin, a rich gold in tone. But it was his hair that struck the older man the most. In spite of the blood matted near his face and the fact that dirt and debris had become entangled in it during his rampage, the boy's hair was not black or even deep brown, but the rich color of a chestnut roan. Copper as the head of his namesake. He wore it very long for a warrior. From what George understood the Cherokee often shaved their heads when going into battle, fearful of offering their enemy an easy handhold. Was it a mark of defiance that Copperhead had not?

Or the sign of an independent spirit?

George shifted again and supported his aching back as he swung his feet onto the floor. It had been some time since he had spent a full night on the daybed. The ropes definitely needed tightening and the ticking was far too thin. The family goose had better look out for him, for the fat gray bird would soon be lacking a few tail feathers! He grunted as he rose to his feet.

The boy watched him closely, but *still* said nothing.

With a slight frown, George turned toward the door. "Well, Master Copperhead, as it seems we will accomplish very little sitting here staring at one another in stony silence, I think I will go to the manor house and see about getting us something to break our fast. Charlotte's cook, Malindy, makes some damn fine Johnny cakes when her mind is on her busi – "

George stopped. In front of him lay the Bible book of heroes. The pages from the book had been gathered together and replaced in a haphazard fashion within the calfskin binding. The volume was a mess. But it was also a sign. Apparently a truce had been declared.

At least for the moment.

George turned back to find the boy's dark eyes had taken on a wary cast, as though he feared some sort of punishment. The older man stifled the satisfied smile that tickled the edge of his lips. He placed his fists on his hips and with a scowl, looked about the room. The morning light revealed even more damage than before. It would take hours just to clean the paint from the walls.

"Well, Copperhead," George began, careful to keep any sound of condemnation or annoyance out of his voice, "I could use some help cleaning up."

Chapter Four

Miriam had not seen Copperhead in nearly five months. She had gone with her mother and her sister Kate to visit their grandmother Augusta Colbert who lived in Charlotte's Burg. During their lengthy absence her grandpapa had apparently discovered the loose vent cover and nailed it tight. When she knocked on the door late on the afternoon of their return, Grandpapa George had come out to tell her how disappointed he was that she had lied to him, and then turned her away. Mortified, Miriam had run back to the manor house and burst into her room, flinging herself on the bed, and cried and cried until her nurse decided she must have taken a chill on the journey and announced to the staff that the young mistress was surely going to perish of the ague. Martha called Miriam's mother and her mother called the doctor, and the doctor called for a fleam and a bleeding bowl.

After the bleeding, somewhat subdued, Miriam inquired meekly if she might not sit in her chair by the window. Her mother had frowned but agreed to ask the doctor. Doctor Wallington had nodded, adding that the diversion would be good for her. Martha had clucked like an old hen and muttered under her breath that it was too soon, but had done as she was told and helped Miriam to rise and walk to the chair. Once seated, she was smothered in quilts and coverlets in order to prevent a reoccurrence of the chill.

From the sanctuary of the soft stuffed wingback Miriam watched the autumn leaves fade from a fiery red, gold, and orange to pale pink, saffron, and peach. She fell asleep several times without meaning to and awoke to find the world outside her window dark as Copperhead's eyes.

Martha was nowhere to be seen. The old woman had probably crept off to her own bed that was attached to Anna's room. Miriam let the coverlets slip to the floor and rose unsteadily to her feet. Her head was muddied from the loss of blood. Wearing only her white dimity nightgown she opened the window and stepped out onto the balcony, embracing the brisk air and the clarity of the lapis lazuli sky with its diamond-dust stars.

The night was still. The breeze almost absent. There was a definite promise of winter in the air. A gentle mist was falling, but she would not have been surprised to see a snowflake float down from Heaven. Though it was only mid-November it smelled like snow. Leaning on the ledge of her balcony, Miriam closed her eyes and tried to imagine what it would be like to be torn from everything she knew. To be thrust among strangers who did not speak her language. To be hated and rejected for what she *was* and not for anything she had done.

She couldn't imagine it.

Though she was often discontent and did not want the things her parents wanted for her – a rich husband, a fat dowry, and high standing in society – still it was all she knew. And she was accepted *because* of what she knew. She would never have to fight for anything. *Prove* anything. Well, that was not quite true….

She would have to fight to be Miriam.

With a sigh she started to turn back into her room. A glimpse of motion on the south lawn stopped her and made her turn back. Something was moving across the green, alternately highlighted by the moon and hidden by the shadows of the soldier-straight row of trees that fenced the manor house. Miriam narrowed her eyes as she leaned on the ledge, trying to discern what it was. It might have been an animal. Or a man. She couldn't tell. But whatever it was, it was moving fast and sure, as if accustomed to stealth and the lack of light.

Quickly crossing to the clothes press that dominated the southern wall of her room, she pulled a light robe from it and tossed it around her shoulders. It would be foolish and unwise to venture outside, but she felt she should find her mother or the night watchman, Michaels, and alert them that someone was on the grounds.

The manor house was hushed. As Miriam descended the stair the tall case clock on the landing struck half past two. She had not realized it was so late. The hall was unexpectedly cold. A chill breeze lifted the trailing ends of her golden hair. With a start, she realized the front door was standing wide open. Shivering, she pulled the collar of her robe close about her throat. Perhaps it *would* be better if she returned to her room and waited until morning. Michaels had undoubtedly seen whatever she had seen and that was why he was not at his post.

Turning on her heel, Miriam began her retreat up the stair. The unexpected sound of metal striking wood and rolling away stopped her. She froze, and it was only then that she discerned voices coming from the direction of the drawing room. She listened for a moment and then, intrigued, completed her descent and stepped into the entry hall. Her silk slippers were silent on the patterned pine floor. No one would have known she was there – *if* the men who were robbing her house had not chosen that moment to grab their sacks overflowing with sterling and coins and make a break for the front door.

One of them nearly ran her over in his haste to escape.

"Blood and hounds!" the man cursed and then called out in a fierce whisper to the other lagging behind. "Someone's seen us!"

"Who?" a rough voice answered.

By this time Miriam had started to back away. The first man, who was dressed in a ragged military uniform, caught her by the arm and dragged her into the square of light cast by one of the sidelights flanking the door. She didn't know him, but he seemed to know her. "It's the young one. What's her name? Mary?"

"Miriam," the second man answered as he moved into the light. His brown frock coat was old and mud-stained. His face unshaven. A thick scar ran from beneath his left eye to the tip of his lip, lending him a perpetual and evil sneer. "Miriam Foxwell," the man snarled as he dropped the sack he held and stepped toward her. "Captain Will's dainty little prize!"

It was then she recognized him. The villain's name was Jack Caruthers. He had been in her father's employ some time back and had been dismissed under suspicious circumstances. Her brother James had told her that Caruthers had been caught red-handed altering the manor's books. For some reason their father had not preferred charges, but had dismissed the man outright, sending him away with only the shirt covering his flailed back.

Caruthers took her chin in his callused hand and pinched it. "I don't suppose we can trust you to keep quiet. *Can* we, my girl?"

"Don't hurt her!" The light from the open door was eclipsed as a third man appeared. To her surprise Miriam turned to find Michaels, the night watchman, nervously eyeing the two of them and the stair beyond. "It's not worth it, Jack. William Foxwell will hound you to the very edge of Hell if something happens to her."

"He will, will he?" Caruthers' grip tightened on her chin. "I bet this one is worth quite a lot then. He's a *topping* man, ain't he? Foxwell? Got more cash than he could ever use himself. Maybe we'll just relieve him of a little more of it." He pulled her closer and it was then she smelled the rum on his breath. "What do you suppose old Captain Will would pay to get *this* heavy baggage back?"

Miriam began to tremble uncontrollably. Her terrified gaze went to her father's man, her deep blue eyes pleading with him. Michaels had always been kind to her. She couldn't understand how he could be a party to this.

Michaels lowered his head. His voice was thick with shame and regret. "I'm sorry, Miss Miriam. I had no choice."

"Stop your whining! Grab the bag while I get the baggage." Caruthers indicated the spilled sack of silver at his feet with a brusque nod and then, in one swift movement, spun Miriam about and picked her up, tucking her under his arm. A filthy hand clamped over her mouth.

"Jack! No!" Michaels cried out, loud enough to alert the house. "You're drunk as Davy's sow! This will only get you hung!"

"They'll be rope enough for three in the end, Michaels," Caruthers promised with a growl. "Now grab the swag and let's get out of here."

Copperhead had escaped.

He had not gone very far, but even as far as he had gone would have angered the old man. While he did not yet understand all of the white man, George Foxwell's, words, he knew their meaning. His grandfather, Walker, said many of the same things. *You are reckless. You do not listen. You will only get hurt.*

Death awaits you if you do not learn to control your anger.

Copperhead sat perched on the pinnacle of the studio roof, cloaked by a mantle of trailing leaves and moss. On one of the many days he spent alone, he had found a hidden door in the ceiling. This night he had used it to escape the warm comfort of the studio. A warrior should not be too comfortable. It made him soft.

And weak

He had shed the confining work shirt the old man made him wear and was clothed only in a pair of soft leather breeches. More than five moons had passed since he had come to live among his enemies. His wounds were healed. And even though a weakness remained in his back where the white man's ball had entered his flesh, he was well enough to leave.

What troubled him was the fact that he had not.

Copperhead shifted and stood. The angle of the slanted roof with its red oak shingles did not make it easy, but he had perched on rocks thrust from the face of the mountain before and he did not fear that he would fall. His thoughts were many this night – of the white man, George Foxwell, and of Walker, his mother's father. Of the family he had loved and lost. And of the spirit-fox who had saved him and challenged him to seek his destiny.

Copperhead's fingers coiled into fists as he thought of the shame he bore. A storm rose within him – a tempest of rage and confusion that threatened to wash him away. Forcing his fingers open, he closed his eyes and lifted his hands toward the sky and pleaded with the One Who Dwells Above for a sign. As he waited, reveling in the wind that lifted his long hair and the spray of icy rain that stung as it painted his muscled chest a glistening bronze, he sought to clear his mind so that when the answer came it would not be drowned out by his own voice –

Or by thoughts of the white girl, Miriam.

Guarded words spoken from directly below him opened his eyes. He crouched on the steep roof, uncertain of who it was. The moon had drawn a mask across its pale face and the yard below was a sea of impenetrable shadows. With the grace and agility of his namesake, Copperhead slipped from the roof and landed silently on the wet grass. He followed the hushed voices for several minutes and then....

He saw his sign.

From the trees a powerful form emerged, moving with four-footed sureness. The silver fox waited until he met its yellow eyes, and then turned and ran along the path leading to the deserted garden behind the manor house.

And Copperhead's destiny.

The moon had retreated behind a bank of clouds and the night was nearly black. Miriam squirmed in Caruthers' arms, desperate to break free, but his grip on her was sure as death. The villain paid scarce attention to her futile efforts, though he struck her once across the face when she bit his hand and threatened he would drag her by her hair the rest of the way if she tried it again.

The man in uniform whom she did not know had gone ahead. Her father's man, Michaels, walked by their side. Shame had settled on the night watchman's shoulders forcing them down. Michaels never lifted his head. Never looked at her.

They had passed her grandfather's studio on their way to the Pleasure Garden, but his rooms were dark. He and Copperhead were probably asleep. Miriam wanted to scream, to call out, to let them know she was in danger, but she didn't. It was not only Caruthers' hand clamped over her mouth that stopped her, but the sight of the aged flintlock pistol, primed and loaded, hanging off his hip.

Behind the studio was a stand of live oak trees and just beyond them, within the Pleasure Garden, an abandoned maze and zoo. The former owner of the estate had kept exotic animals on the grounds. Now the cages and the convoluted hedges that surrounded them were untended and untenantable. As they approached the derelict area Michaels halted, startled, and turned to face Caruthers.

"What was that?" Michaels asked, his breath a white cloud in the cold night air. "Did you hear it? That howling? I thought Harter tied up the dogs."

"I warrant I did," the third man insisted as he drew his pistol and reached for the regulation cartridge box hanging at his hip. "I don't hear anything – "

Then Miriam heard it. An eerie keening. It wasn't a hound – she knew the sound of the dogs from long acquaintance – but she was not quite certain it was human either.

"Sounds like it's coming from inside the maze," Caruthers growled. "Harter!"

Harter was looking up into the tall trees that framed the entrance to the garden. His eyes went wide with fear as he turned back. "Aye, Jack?"

Caruthers nodded toward the maze. "Get in there and check it out."

"Me?"

"Who else? The bleeding King of England?" Caruthers shoved Harter with his free hand and then reached for his own weapon. "Now get going!"

"What about him?" Harter indicated Michaels. The night watchman had moved into the shadow of the trees as if seeking the source of the uncanny sound.

"I need to keep my eye on him. Now go!"

As Harter reluctantly disappeared into the Pleasure Garden, Jack Caruthers pulled Miriam close. The man stank of rum-soaked fear and sweat. "Don't think me a paper-skull, Miss Blue Stocking. If this is a trick, you'll pay for it in blood! Was someone else with you in the foyer?" He lowered his hand, allowing her space for an answer. "*Speak!*"

Miriam gasped, sucking in the crisp night air. "No! No one."

"You'd best be telling me the truth." Caruthers placed his hand over her mouth again and moved with her toward the opening in the walled garden. Once there he shouted, "Harter! Harter, what have you found?"

Silence was his answer.

With a scowl Caruthers turned back, searching for Michaels. "Get over here, you milksop! Go see what the matter is!"

The night watchman appeared at Caruthers' elbow. When he spoke his voice was hushed, his words haunted by his own weakness. "This is wrong, Jack. I said I would help you steal the silver, but I will *not* put a child's life in jeopardy. Let Miriam go. Let her go, or I swear I will return to the manor house and tell them all I know!"

"You do and I will tell your master just *what* you need the money for," Caruthers threatened, his gruff voice laced with joyless mirth. "Old Captain Will knows no mercy. That pretty little wife of yours will bide in the pillory, her shame exposed for all to see." He caught Michaels' arm with his free hand and shoved him forward. "Now get in there!"

Michaels did as he was told, his shoulders slumped in defeat as he moved slowly toward the opening in the garden wall. Then, without warning, he spun, ran back, and struck out, knocking Miriam free and carrying the thickset Jack Caruthers to the ground. The two men struggled, rolling amidst bracken and dead leaves, and for a moment it seemed Michaels had the upper hand as his fingers found the villain's throat. But Caruthers was several stone heavier and powered by spite and an all-consuming greed, and it was not long before Michaels lay pinned to the ground beneath him.

Then Jack Caruthers drew his pistol and began to use its butt to beat Michaels about the head.

Miriam backed away, horrified, as the night watchman's blood spattered her white gown and skin. She ran, but the dark night blinded her to danger and she tripped and fell heavily to the cold earth. Within seconds Caruthers was on her. His fingers gripped her hair and he used it to pull her to her feet, laughing as she squealed in pain.

"I told you'd I'd drag you from here to Hades if you tried anything!" he shouted. Lowering his voice Caruthers added, his hand sinking toward her breast. "Maybe, my girl, if you're *nice* to me, you'll live long enough for your rich father to ransom you. Though there's no guaranteeing what shape the baggage will be in by then – "

There was a crack just above them – such as a foot made when snapping a branch. And then a high-pitched whine. Miriam gasped as blood spattered her nightdress a second time and a pool of red spread across the pockmarked forehead of Jack Caruthers. His gunmetal eyes went wide. His scurrilous face grew slack.

And then with a groan the brute tumbled to the ground.

Numb in spirit and body, Miriam stumbled backward and fell just as a dark form dropped from the closest tree and landed near Jack Caruthers' unconscious form. The villain's body shook, as if whoever it was wanted to make certain he would not rise again, and then the anonymous figure moved on, creeping menacingly toward Michaels who was rising, his head a bruised and bloodied pulp.

The moon chose that moment to make a reappearance, its argent light streaming down to light the derelict zoo and the path before it. With relief and horror Miriam recognized her savior, just as the slender bronze form lifted a wrist-thick branch to wield it like a club.

"Copperhead! *No!*" she screamed, running toward him. "No! You mustn't!"

The Indian whirled toward her. His mouth was a razor-line. His eyes, savage and fierce. His muscled chest, oiled by the chill night mist, glistened and heaved.

Copperhead was a creature of the forest, totally foreign to her, and the bloodlust was on him.

"No! Copperhead, you mustn't hurt him! Please, *listen* to me!" Miriam pleaded. She did not want him to hurt Michaels, but even more she feared what would happen to him if he *did*. "Put down the branch. Please! Michaels tried to help me."

Copperhead's eyes went from her to the broken man and back again. He either did not understand or did not trust her. But he also did not move.

"You *must* believe me. It's all right." Miriam quivered from the cold as she said it. With the moon, as she predicted, had come the first fall of snow. It crusted her eyelashes and lay as a white cloak upon the land. Her slippered feet left dark prints as she moved toward him and reached for his hand. "Please…. You have saved me."

Copperhead met her gaze. He dropped the makeshift club as he nodded his head. Then he took her hand.

And the gates of Hell broke open.

A ring of torchlight surrounded them. There were shouts and the cacophonous noise of dogs straining at the leash. A shot was fired. Voices – familiar and unfamiliar – cried, "There he is! There's the savage!" And "The girl? Is the girl unmolested?' Miriam saw her grandfather's troubled face, but lost him quickly in the crowd of wrathful, fuming humanity that surrounded her. A woman screamed – she thought it might be Martha. Someone took her hand but lost it. And then someone else swaddled her in a warm woolen blanket and told her not to be afraid, hushing her as she tried to speak.

Miriam was lifted up and quickly borne away even as a vengeful tide of righteous but wrongfully placed outrage swallowed Copperhead and hid him from her sight.

COPPERHEAD

Chapter Five

It took two days to get anyone to tell her what had happened. And two more to get any of them to listen to the truth.

The fright and the cold night had left her unable to rise from her bed. Attended and shielded by Martha, Miriam heard nothing until her brother James came to see her and crowed that he had been there and witnessed it all. The savage had been thoroughly thrashed for daring to touch her, James proclaimed proudly, and then shackled like the animal he was and thrown into one of the empty cages in the abandoned zoo to await judgment. Only Crazy George's intervention had kept Copperhead from being lynched outright. The night watchman, Michaels, had barely escaped with his life and had fallen unconscious. He'd been hailed as a hero for his attempt to protect her, and borne away solemnly to his home. Jack Caruthers had given a statement, claiming he caught Copperhead in the act of abducting her. Of his companion, Harter, her brother had no word. The silver and jewels now – along with Caruthers – were apparently missing.

James was certain that Copperhead must have had an accomplice who had absconded with them in the chaos following the savage's arrest.

Miriam sat stunned through James' narration. Then she began to cry, and refused to stop crying. James went to fetch their mother. When the lady Charlotte appeared it was with the doctor. Miriam was labeled 'excitable' and only by promising to remain quiet and to meditate on her many transgressions, did she escape being bled again.

The following day she lay languid and forlorn, refusing to eat or to take visitors. Visions of Copperhead beaten and brutalized, his neck stretched to breaking by a rope, haunted her infrequent sleep. She had seen men hung before. Robbers and brigands strung up alongside the road, their bloated black bodies left as a warning.

'Just as they deserve' her father had declared.

As the clock on the landing struck quarter 'til midnight, there was a knock at her door. She supposed it was Martha with a last tray of food to try and tempt her. "Go away!" Miriam shouted as she pulled the coverlet up over her head. "I don't want anything!"

"Miri, it's me," a weary voice declared. "Grandpapa."

Miriam lowered the coverlet as the door opened and her grandfather came in. He looked to have aged twenty years over night. As he came to the side of her bed he began to apologize, but she stopped him and clasped his hands between her own.

"Grandpapa, it wasn't him! Copperhead didn't try to hurt me. He saved me! You have to get him out of that awful place. You *have* to!"

"Saved you?" He sat on the bed beside her and pressed a hand to her forehead. "Are you feverish, child?"

She struck it away. "No! Why won't anyone listen to me!" Tears streamed down her cheeks. "You're all wrong! That horrid man, Caruthers, he robbed the house. Him and a man named Harter. I caught them at it. Michaels was in it with them. He must have let them in. They were kidnapping me, but Copperhead came out of the trees and stopped them!" Miriam grew sober very suddenly, her deep blue eyes wide with the memory of that moment and all that followed. "Copperhead was *terrifying*, Grandpapa," she finished, her voice hushed. "But he saved me."

Her grandfather rose and paced at the side of her bed. He seemed almost afraid to believe her. "Is this true, Miriam?" he asked at last, stopping to look at her. "You are not lying just to save him?"

She sat up on her knees and held out her right hand. "I will swear an oath on the Good Book, Grandpapa. I will swear it on my life!"

"Dear God!" He fell heavily into the chair beside her bed. "Dear Lord in Heaven…."

When he said nothing more, Miriam grew bold. "Have you seen him?" she asked.

Grandpapa George shook his head. "I could not. I was so…." His voice broke on the word. "So *ashamed* for having brought this evil to my son's family. My worst fears were suddenly realized. Your mother, Charlotte, said – "

"Mother hates Copperhead. Just because he is an Indian."

He held a hand up to quiet her. "Your mother has cause to hate the Indians. Do not judge her too harshly, Miriam."

She had heard the stories. When her mother had been Kate's age the Catawba had looted their home and killed her brother. Mama cried when she talked about it, and so she did not do so very often. Miriam slipped off the bed and approached him. "What will you do, Grandpapa? About Copperhead?"

He thought a moment. Then he rose to his feet. "I will go to see Michaels. With God's mercy, I will be able to get him to speak before they hang the boy."

She could not believe it! "Grandpapa, no!"

"Yes, child. The Crown's representative was here. Judgment has been made. He has been sentenced to die two days from now."

"But no one was killed!"

Her grandfather laid a hand on her shoulder. "Miriam, Copperhead did not need to kill. He touched a white girl. That is all that it takes, I fear."

Miriam paled. "Because of me, then. Because of *me*."

He caught her about the shoulders and hugged her close. "We will save him, Miriam. *That* I promise! Now, I must go to Michaels and bring him back – even if it is in a cart – to speak on the boy's behalf." Her grandfather kissed her on the top of her head. "You rest, dear child. You have been through enough."

Miriam begged to go with him but he would not listen, and so she watched from her balcony as her grandfather mounted his black horse and flew off in a fury into the cold wet night. She returned to her room then and shoved a small wooden stair up against her clothes press. Mounting it, she removed her quilted petticoat and thick woolen socks from one of the top drawers and then donned them along with last year's winter dress; a cream-colored woolen gown embroidered with rich burgundy roses. Tossing a thick cloak about her shoulders and tying it, she returned to the balcony. The main stair, she was certain, was being watched. Miriam stared at the tall Sycamore tree butted up against the balcony. It had been a long time, but if she was cautious she could stand on the window's ledge and just reach its lowest hanging branches. Careful lest she fall, she moved into the tree and then shimmied down its trunk as she had when she was little, landing with a small thud on the frosty grass. The clock on the landing had just struck quarter past twelve in the morning. Several hours should pass before anyone missed her. It was risky, but she had to chance it.

She had to see him.

Miriam resolutely crossed the lawn, seeking out the abandoned garden with its maze and zoo in spite of the horrific memory of the events that had unfolded there only days before. As she hurried along, gathering the thick folds of her woolen cloak close about her throat, a light snow fell, landing on her eyelashes and tickling the tip of her nose. Her breath painted the night air white and her winter shoes, made of leather, crushed the frozen grass beneath her feet. She stopped several yards short of the Pleasure Garden entrance. One of her father's men had been posted as a sentry there and another prowled the green wall's dark perimeter. Miriam had played among the dead vines and broken archways of the maze many times with her brothers, and knew of a back way in. The tall hedge that surrounded it was missing in some places – just wide enough to wiggle through.

COPPERHEAD

Waiting for the sentry to turn his back, Miriam slipped unseen across the lawn. Once she was in the garden, she went to the zoo and moved from one abandoned cage to the next, searching for some sign of life. As she neared one of the larger ones, used once upon a time for a cheetah or a bear, the cold crisp air carried to her nostrils the foul scent of human filth and old blood. Drawing a deep breath and steeling herself, Miriam slipped around its side to peer in.

Copperhead was chained to the wall and sat with his head lowered, shivering. His once bright copper hair was dull and without luster, and littered with mud and debris from the cage floor. The leather breeches her grandfather had given him were torn, revealing welts on his calves and thighs. All about him lay the refuse of a caged human being – remnants of half-eaten food, a stagnant bowl of water, his own filth.

Miriam choked back tears as she crept close to the bars and called his name. "Copperhead? Copperhead, it is Miriam."

His eyes opened and he sighed. But he did not look at her.

"I am *so* sorry. All you did was try to help. Why can't they see that?"

With a soft groan Copperhead straightened up and leaned his head back against the wall. The deep brown eyes he turned on her were set in cradles of bruised flesh. "Not see," he licked his lips and replied in broken English, his breath creating a pale blue cloud. "Never see *me*. Only Indian."

Terrified that the sentry might have seen her, Miriam slipped forward and glanced at the path before the cage. The man was leaning against the broken arch just inside the garden wall. Someone had brought him a steaming mug. He was drinking it to warm himself and paying them no mind. She returned to Copperhead's side and reached through the bars. His ice-cold fingers were just within reach.

"I will make them see what I see," Miriam insisted as she squeezed his hand. "I will make them see *you*."

Copperhead pulled his hand away. "No."

'Yes! Grandpapa is going to get Michaels. He will tell the truth. I will make him! Mama and the others will *have* to admit that they are wrong." Miriam pressed her face between the bars. "You have to believe me. There are good people among us. They will know the truth when they hear it, and they will set you free!"

Copperhead glanced forward and then stiffened. Turning toward her, he whispered, "Go, Miriam!"

She shook her head. "Why? I don't understand."

As he rose shakily to his feet, he nodded toward the cage door.

The sentry was approaching, carrying a plate.

"Go!" he repeated.

"Only if you believe me. Otherwise I will stay here no matter what. Do you?" she demanded. "Tell me you do!"

Copperhead turned and met her desperate stare. A hint of a smile lifted the edge of one split lip. He nodded.

"I believe *you*."

George Foxwell hesitated, his hand poised above the rough wooden door. The house that Michaels lived in was of moderate size – homely, but mean. It was half a day's walk from the manor house and perilously close to the river used by the locals for disposing of waste and refuse. The miasmic vapors were powerful here. On his way George had seen several children sitting by the roadside, nearly incapacitated with coughing. One had left blood on the filthy sleeve it employed as a handkerchief.

Such foul air would bring many to an early grave.

It disgusted him. Obviously his son did not pay the man enough to escape this dung-hole. It probably took all the family had just to keep Michaels in clothes fine enough to suit William, and to allow him to work at the manor house. George growled and again cursed his son's avaricious nature. All William cared about was gain – in prestige, in power – *and* in capital.

Bringing his hand down on the door, George rapped loudly three times. Then he waited. When there was no reply he rapped again, sharply, three more times. Finally, the cracked and peeling door creaked open to reveal a haggard face – one belonging to a child. When the girl saw him – in his fine frock coat of forest green and cocked hat, leaning on a mahogany cane tipped with silver – her watery brown eyes grew wide within their framework of pallid yellow hair and she stuttered a greeting.

"S-Sir?"

He removed his hat and locked it under one arm. "Miss Michaels, I presume? Is your father home?"

"He's abed," the girl answered with a short glance behind.

George nodded. "I understand. I know he was injured. Your mother then? I would like to speak with her."

"What do you want with Ma?" a gruff male voice demanded even as a callused hand took hold of the door above the girl's head and pulled it open.

If the sickly girl was about eleven, this young man must be thirteen or fourteen. He was dressed as a common worker. His knuckles and nails were black, which indicated employment as an apprentice to a smithy, or perhaps a puddler who worked with iron.

"Ma don't want to see no one," the boy insisted.

"What is your name, young man?" George asked, employing the command tone he used with raw recruits.

The boy's jaw set but he answered, already all too keenly aware of the powerlessness of the poor. "Albert," he answered. "Albert Michaels."

"Well, Albert, tell your mother that George Foxwell would like to speak with her. I promise I will not keep her long."

"Foxwell? From the manor?" the boy asked. "Master William...."

"No. His father. Now, please hurry. Time *is* of the essence."

"Have you come to take Pa away?" the girl whined, tears entering her eyes. "He ain't done nothing wrong. Please, mister, please...."

"Child," George touched her dull blond head as he turned to her brother. "Albert, you must believe me, I wish your family no harm. Your father is in the position to save the life of someone who is...dear to me. I need to talk to him – or your mother. Now."

"Albert. Jenny. Move away. Let the gentleman come in."

It was a light voice, one that should have belonged to a young woman. The vision that greeted him as the door slowly swung inward was instead one of a woman well past her prime. Mistress Michaels had been lovely once, and the remnants of that former beauty clung to her as faded petals to the stem. Her hair had been copper. Now it was brass, and had gone gray at the edges. Her deep brown eyes were wide and well set, but ringed with sallow circles born of too little sleep and too much worry. And she was thin. *Very* thin. George had seen her before, but never up close. Until shortly after his return from the city, she had been employed as a washwoman at the house. He had never heard what cause had brought about her dismissal.

George crossed the room quickly and greeted her. "Mistress Michaels. It is of the utmost importance that I speak to your husband. And that he accompany me back to the manor."

She looked startled. "Richard is sleeping," she answered. "And may not leave his bed."

"Has the doctor seen him?" Even before he spoke to Miriam, George had sent the family physician, Dr. Wallington, to check on the night watchman. After all, Michaels had saved his granddaughter's life.

Or so he had thought.

"Aye, the man was here. He said wasn't nothing he could do." Michaels' wife gathered her shawl about her shoulders and moved to sit beside the meager fire that burned low in a stone fireplace. Picking up a stocking she had been darning, she began to turn it over and over as if seeking the spot where she had stopped. Her weary eyes flicked up, searching his face, and then returned to the task as she added ruefully, "There never is."

Mistress Michaels knew something of the truth. He was certain of it. And probably thought he had come to arrest or confront her husband. It was hard to imagine what she was thinking. A woman, fearing a life alone. A husband imprisoned. And there were at least two or three more children. George could hear them above, barking. The cough sounded serious.

The Michaels household was one with too little cheer and *far* too much pain.

"Mistress, I would like to assure you that I am not here to bring harm to your husband, or to you." George turned and looked at the boy and girl who were watching them warily from the shadows near the stair. "May I speak freely?"

Her eyes went to her son. "Albert, take Jenny and go check on your sister and brothers."

"Ma. I don't want to go...."

"Please, Ma," Jenny echoed.

"Do as I say! Both of you."

The surly young man stared at his mother hard and then, with a nod, took his sister's hand and headed for the stair. Mistress Michaels waited until they disappeared into the darkness at its head and then offered him a seat. George accepted her offer and sat, alighting with care on a rickety old wooden bench near the fire.

When she said nothing, he spoke. "I was not there that night, until near the end. I saw your husband being taken away. I am sorry."

"Richard was sorely beaten," she answered softly, crossing her hands over the darner lying in her lap. "Albert swears he will get the men what done it. But he don't know...." Mistress Michaels paused. She met his inquisitive stare squarely, her head held high. "Wasn't no more than he deserved for what he done."

George was startled by her words. "Mistress! Your husband was instrumental in saving my granddaughter – "

"After putting her in danger in the first place. 'Twas the hand of God what saved the young miss, and caught Richard and made him face what he become." She drew a deep breath and turned to stare at the fire. "He's a good man, my Richard. A good man, Master Foxwell. But times are hard...." Her voice fell away to nothing and a single tear ran down her cheek.

George waited a moment and then asked gently, "Do you have any idea why your husband would have let those men into the house?"

She nervously fingered the tattered stocking. She nodded and then, unexpectedly, a sob escaped her. " 'Twas for me!" she declared. "For me...."

"Mistress? For *you*?"

Her gaze went to the stair up which her children had departed. "Can you hear the young ones?"

"Coughing? Yes."

Her large brown eyes reflected a world far off and decades away. "Day and night, night and day I heard that. My brother died horribly of the Chin cough, sir. I remember it well. I couldn't bear to have the same happen to our little ones." She looked at him. "What with the rent and all my husband has to have for his work, there's no money left – not for broth, not for the medicine they need. Richard asked Master William for more work. He said there was none to be had. I was desperate...." She turned away, shamed. "One morning, I took what I needed from the manor house larder – eggs and bacon. Honey to sweeten their tea...." Her face mirrored the anger she felt and her voice took on the crimson tone of hated. "He was there, that *villain*! He saw what I done."

"Villain?" George shifted forward, anxious to know more. "What villain?"

"The one what beat my Richard. Jack Caruthers."

So Miriam *had* spoken the truth. "Caruthers threatened to tell William what he had seen, didn't he?" George asked. "To expose you and see you sent to the pillory?"

"If Richard did aught other than what he asked. Aye." She placed the darner on the table and knit her hands together in her lap. Tears filled her eyes now. "He didn't want to do it. But it was only money. And, Master William, he has *so* much...."

George could tell all *too* well by her tone what she thought of Master William.

"Mistress Michaels..." he began.

"Maggie," she said softly, sniffing.

George hesitated. Margaret. His wife's name. Fighting back his own memories, he asked her, "*Is* your husband well enough to speak to me?"

Maggie rose to her feet. She lit a candle with a taper from the fire and then headed for a room at the back of the small house.

"No," she answered, "but he will anyway. Come with me."

The light that filtered from the narrow street outside into the Michaels' bedroom was meager, but it was enough to reveal the hellish aftermath of the brutal beating the man had taken. The night watchman lay in his bed, his head swathed in bandages. What little flesh was left exposed had turned a sickly purple green and was swollen so it almost eclipsed his eyes.

Almost.

When he asked Michaels what had happened, George could see enough of those eyes – and the horrific truth written in them – to know that what Miriam had told him had been gospel.

Copperhead *was* innocent.

George moved into the room and took a seat by the injured man's side. Michaels reached out a quaking hand and laid it on his sleeve. "Have they harmed the boy?" he asked, his once strong voice reduced to a throaty whisper.

"They hang him tomorrow." George did not mean the words to be harsh or to carry judgment.

But they did.

Michaels coughed and shifted. He forced his battered body into a half-seated position and leaned against the headboard. "You must stop them, Master Foxwell!" he declared. "If not for that young man, Master William's child would be dead – or worse." He drew a deep breath and coughed again. "Jack Caruthers is a vile man. If not for Maggie, I would never have...." Michaels lowered his eyes as his voice trailed off.

George nodded, acknowledging his confession. "I do not condone your actions, Michaels, but I understand what a man can be driven to. War peels away the layers until the true man is revealed. I have seen soldiers I would have thought incorruptible, corrupted. Some reduced to thievery. Others driven to betrayal. I know the likes of Jack Caruthers. He *would* have followed up on his threat. Your wife would have been exposed and sent to the pillory for nothing more than trying to feed her children." George smiled ruefully. "I had my own 'Maggie'. I know what I would have done to protect her."

"It was wrong." Michaels drew a great shuddering breath. It was obviously hard for him to breathe. "And I *knew* it was wrong. This is my payment for choosing the easy path – this beating."

George spoke as he rose to his feet. "And your penance is to come back with me and save Copperhead. God has left you a chance at redemption. You have it in your power to save an innocent life."

"He's a good boy. I've talked to him before. Seen him in the stable," Michaels acknowledged. "He deserves better."

George nodded. "Yes, he does. So you will come with me?"

"God only grant the journey doesn't kill me," he answered.

George took the hand Michaels offered and pressed it between his own. Hard times could drive good men to desperation and desperate acts. He sensed no malice in Richard Michaels, only hopelessness and despair. Turning back toward the door that led to the common room of the house, George offered gently, "Now, let's see what we can do about getting those children some medicine."

His jailer had returned.

Copperhead could not help but grow tense as the key slid into the iron lock and clicked, and the cage door swung in. His bruised lip and swollen eye were testimony to the last time the man had entered his cage and beaten him for spilling a bowl of putrid gruel.

But this was not his jailer.

"Dear Lord! Are you animals?" a familiar voice demanded, shaking with fury.

"*He's* the animal, Guv'ner," a mocking voice replied. "Them filthy savages are *all* animals. You'd best keep back. He tore the skin of my arm with his nails."

"You will release him now!" George Foxwell declared.

"Not me. Take the keys if you like. I ain't going near him – unless it's with a stick!"

A few more words were exchanged. There was a sound – like metal striking stone – and then a tall dignified figure entered the cage. Miriam's grandfather quickly crossed the short distance to him and knelt at his side, heedless of the filth and debris that stained his expensive green breeches.

"My boy," he whispered as he inserted the keys into the shackles that held him. "What have they done to you? Copperhead, can you speak?"

Copperhead made no answer, but rubbed his wrists where the cuffs had cut into them.

The white man rocked back on his heels, staring at the irons in his hand. "I am sorry. I should have come sooner. I thought....I *feared*...." His voice broke. "I was afraid I was wrong and that William was right – that no savage could be trusted. That you had only waited until you had my trust to try to...." George Foxwell's eyes met his. They were tortured. "Can you ever forgive me?"

Forgiveness. It was something in the black book from which this man liked to read. Something spoken of by the one the white men called, 'Lord'. Copperhead made no reply, uncertain what it was the older man wanted.

"I see," he said, nodding. "I will have to win your trust again. That is only fair since my actions of late have betrayed it." He paused and then added, almost reluctantly, "It was Miriam who saved you."

"Mir-i-am?" he asked.

"She would not let it rest. She made me listen – listen to the *truth*. I am sorry I ever doubted you."

"Where is Miri-am?" Copperhead asked.

"Resting. Recovering. As you should be. Will you give me your hand, lad?" The older man held his out. "Let me take you from this vile place."

"Where?" he asked. "Where…will you take me?"

As George Foxwell caught him by the shoulders and helped him to stand, the white man's eyes found his. "Home, boy. Home," George said. "With me. And I promise you *on my life* that I will never let them take you from it again."

Weak from lack of food, exhausted, Copperhead leaned into the old man's strength and allowed him to help him out of the cage. Squinting in the light, he limped at George Foxwell's side, past the jailer who had beaten him, through the arched opening in the hedge, and toward the studio he had called home for nearly half a year now. Copperhead knew the white man meant what he said, but he knew as well that Foxwell's words were meaningless. To the other white men who inhabited this world he had been thrust into, he would never be anything but an animal. If they did not cage him again, they would find another way to destroy him. Just as they destroyed anything that was not like themselves.

"Copperhead?" George Foxwell asked. "What is it?"

He shook his head. The old man would not understand. How could he? He was not of the People. He did not know what it was to have a warrior's heart. This day, amidst the filth and beatings, the warrior in him had reawakened. He knew now what he must do. *Why* he was here. He would use what time he remained among the white men to learn from them – to learn their language and their ways.

In order to destroy them.

From this day forward all who were white were his enemies.

Miriam was thrilled. Copperhead was a hero.

It was, however, not what her mother Charlotte wanted to hear. Even after Grandpapa George told her the truth, she had worked to delay Copperhead's release. Kate told her she had overheard their mother praying that the savage would die before the amnesty papers could be signed.

Thanks to her grandpapa and Michaels' testimony, her mother's prayers had gone unanswered.

As had her own.

She had not been there to see Copperhead set free. For three days she had been confined to the house for her sins and forbidden to go anywhere *near* the studio or garden. But even worse than that was the unwelcome news her brother James had brought when he visited her.

She was to be sent away.

Miriam halted outside the studio door and brought her fist down on the mended wood knocking one, two, three times. She smiled weakly as her grandfather opened it.

"So your sentence has been lifted," he said as he ushered her into the candle lit room. "And I am no longer a pariah?"

"Mama is away, and James could not keep me from coming. But it is only to say 'goodbye'."

"Scotland it is then," her grandfather remarked. "But you must not look so down-hearted. This is a fine opportunity for an educated young lady on the verge of womanhood."

"I do not want to go," she murmured as she took off her heavy gloves and flung them on the cot. Then she plopped down beside them.

Grandpapa George came to sit by her. "Miri, it is for the best. This... *affection* that has developed between you and Copperhead, there is nowhere it can go. Even if he manages to learn to fit into our world, Copperhead will never be more than a servant or tradesman – and always an outcast. That is no life for you."

"He is my friend," she replied stubbornly.

Her grandfather's words were hard. "Miriam, you are grown enough to know that cannot be." When she said nothing he stood and walked to the door, pausing with his hand on the brass latch. "Copperhead is outside chopping wood. I will send him in and give you a moment alone to tell him goodbye."

Miriam waited as the studio door opened and then closed. Several minutes later it opened again. A soft fall of steps brought him to her side. She did not look up for fear of what she would find. She expected Copperhead must hate her now. He had been ill used – and all because of her. As he sat beside her, she felt the cold bleed off of his wool coat. The scent of the outdoors – of winter and of pine – was heavy in his hair and on his clothes.

"I am leaving," she declared without preamble. "Mama has decided I must go away. To school." Miriam sighed as a single tear escaped her eye and trailed down her cheek. "To Scotland."

"Scotland...is far...away?" he asked.

"Very," she replied, sniffing. "I could be gone for *years*. Who knows if they will ever let me come back to visit." Miriam turned toward him. She winced when she saw the bruises on his face and neck, the broken skin and angry welts. "Will you be here when I get back?" she asked quietly.

It was what she had to know. What she must make him promise – what she *needed* him to promise to be able to say goodbye.

"Well?"

Copperhead was silent for a long time. Then he reached out and took one of her hands and placed it between his own which were cold and already callused from menial work.

He nodded.

"I will wait."

Chapter Six
Three Years Later

The trip to the estate had been a trying one. When she stepped from the carriage, Miriam was exhausted and wanted nothing more than to retire to her room. They had arrived at the manor by the southern road, and so had passed the studio on their way in. Bittersweet memories of three years before flooded through her at the site of the small wood and brick building. Memories that brought her no joy. Only pain. She had hidden her tears in fashionable laughter so her companions would not suspect, and then excused herself saying she felt a headache coming on. Now, in the darkness of her room, she wept for what might have been.

And for the Indian boy who had died.

Later that night Miriam joined the others in the dining room for a light supper and then retired with them to the drawing room. Her brothers James and John were horrid! It was Christmas break, and they had returned from their time at Oxford older and more arrogant than ever. Her sister, Kate, of course, hung on their every word and worked her charms as she listened to them, all the while seeking to draw the attentions of the classmate who had accompanied them home. Master Charles Matthew Spencer was the son of minor English nobility – his wealthy father owned nearly two hundred thousand acres in South Carolina, or so Charles claimed, with nearly nine hundred under cultivation. Kate thought he was perfection itself. To Miriam he was a popinjay, over-dressed in a fine raw-silk suit of deepest umber edged with silver thread. Charles' collar was starched and stretched so far towards his chin that it made the fact that he looked down his long nose at everyone seem almost a necessity.

The problem was Master Charles Matthew Spencer did not share her sensibilities. Or care for her sister Kate. He seemed interested only in her. Nearly three years at a fine girl's school in Edinburgh and reaching the advanced age of fifteen had taught Miriam many things.

How to suffer bores was not one of them.

Miriam stifled yet another yawn. She primped her pale saffron skirts and shook her golden hair free of her shoulders. Then she leaned on her elbow. It and she were propped on the arm of a fine dimity sofa. Charles was regaling the family, yet again, with tales of his wondrous exploits and conquests on the hunting field. At this moment the fool was pretending to ride a horse, striking his thigh with his dinner knife as though it were a whip. As she slid toward the sofa's seat, losing her battle with boredom, her sister Kate jabbed her sharply in the ribs. Miriam yelped and sat up.

Charles mistakenly thought she was screaming with delight and intensified his efforts to impress her.

Across the room her grandfather sat, his chin cradled in his fingers, watching her. They had not yet had time to speak. Grandpa George occupied their father's broad wingback. Charles' father had served under him in the Seven Years War and so his presence – on this rare occasion – had been required. The wedge that Copperhead's brief presence at the manor had driven between him and her mother had never been removed. Charlotte Foxwell tolerated her father-in-law but, according to Anna, they had no more contact than was necessary.

Miriam sighed and looked at her fingers knit together in her lap. She would never forget the day during her first year at school when the letter had arrived telling her Copperhead was dead. It was a casual aside in one of Anna's lengthy notes. 'Oh, by the way,' her little sister wrote, 'Grandpapa's Indian died. Mama said it is for the best'.' When she read that, something in her died as well. In reply to her query, Anna wrote back explaining that their grandfather said Copperhead had died of a sickness – something picked up on a trip to Charles Town. It had been near Christmas. Miriam had not even bothered to ask about going home that year. There had been nothing for her at the manor then.

As there was nothing now.

She did not know to this day what, if anything, her grandfather had admitted to her mother about her visits to the studio, or if her mother had figured it out on her own. She had been away a little more than three years, and in that time had only been permitted to come home twice. And even those visits had been well supervised. Her mother explained to Anna that her sister was 'foolish'. She was not about to take the chance that Miriam would run off and find some other poor orphan or lost soul to take a fancy to. In Scotland she had been carefully schooled and taught her proper place in the order of things – which was to marry and bed someone like Master Charles Matthew Spencer and produce a brood of shallow, self-absorbed brats for him and for posterity.

As Charles finished his latest tale to a hearty round of applause, Miriam saw her mother lean over and whisper a word in Kate's ear. Her sister rose with a demure little curtsy and made her way quickly to the ormolu-encrusted harpsichord nestled in the corner of the vast room. To the pretended delight of everyone – including their guest – her mother announced that Kate would give an impromptu concert. After a servant rearranged the chairs, creating a space for the captive audience, Miriam rose and headed like a lamb toward slaughter for the seat her brother

James had saved her. As she did, another servant entered and moved to refresh the fire. She noticed him because he was not negro, and she didn't recognize him. The young man was tall and well dressed. His bearing was proud – he moved more like a foreign prince than a menial. His waistcoat was cut of an elegant brocade, a rich golden silk worked with whorls and geometric patterns of bronze and gold. His shirt was of the finest linen, costly and brand new. His breeches were the same bronze as the design on the brocaded vest and were fastened at the knees with golden buckles that matched those on his leather shoes. The young man's hair was fashionably cut and bound at the back with a golden ribbon, but was not pomaded. It was the color of autumn leaves.

Distracted, Miriam missed the fact that Charles had offered her his arm. Snubbing him without meaning to, she skirted the chairs and James and stopped at her grandfather's side to kiss him on the top of the head. He smiled up at her and patted her hand. Miriam frowned. Her grandfather seemed even more distracted than usual. Following his gaze, she realized he was watching the servant go about his business at the fire.

"Grandpa?" she asked.

He had aged since she had been gone. His hair was white as snow now and his skin had a thin, frail look – like waxed parchment. Her father's tour of duty in the East Indies had been extended and Grandpa George had been left to run the estate and manage the family business. Something he had often remarked he had no desire or talent for. As a military man everything had been clear-cut. High society was a place of shadows, and walking among them had drained him.

Her grandfather's pale blue eyes met hers and he placed a finger against his lips. Shaking his head, he cast a quick concerned glance at her mother.

Miriam followed his gaze. He needn't have worried. Her mother was occupied impressing Charles with Kate's less than modest talent.

"Grandpa, what is it?"

Her grandfather's hand gripped hers and squeezed it. He rose from the chair and embraced her while whispering in her ear. "You must forgive me, Miri. It was necessary. Come to the studio when you can." With that cryptic word he left her and crossed the room to speak to the young man tending the fire. As she watched, her grandfather touched the back of the servant's neck affectionately and then, with a quick whispered word, exited the room.

The servant continued in his work, carefully separating the embers and employing the bellows to breathe new life into the coals before adding fresh logs. He ran the back of his hand over his forehead, wiping away the sweat, and then rose and turned toward her.

Miriam gasped. Loud enough that her mother turned to stare at her. She quickly tore her eyes away from the young man whom she had recognized as her Grandpa's 'dead' Indian, and hastily covered up her surprise by executing one of the most unexpected and dramatic swoons in feminine history.

Charles must have been hovering nearby for he caught her before she hit the Persian carpet. Kate remained seated at the harpsichord, her eyes even more green than was their natural wont. As her mother came to her side and Charles helped her to sit in her father's chair and began to fan her, her brother James did the one thing Miriam had hoped to prevent – he turned his attention to Copperhead who remained, somewhat perplexed, standing by the fire.

"You, boy! Go get Martha," her elder brother ordered, his tone well practiced with disdain. "Tell the comb-brush we need the smelling salts and vinaigrettes. *Boy*, do you hear me?" James snapped his fingers and then without waiting to be obeyed, turned back to take command of the scene.

Miriam couldn't breathe. And it wasn't that her stays were too tight. James had looked *directly* at Copperhead and yet not seen him. How could that be? How could he not know him?

And *how* could Copperhead be alive?

Why had her grandfather lied and let her think him dead? What possible reason could he have? Miriam drew a deep, cleansing breath and curbed the anger rising within her. There *had* to be a reason. Her grandfather would not have caused her such pain if there had been another way.

As Charles continued to fan, Miriam glanced at Copperhead again. His skin had paled. Grandpa George had probably planned it that way. Placing him in the manor house would have kept him out of the sun and caused his deep golden-brown color to fade. His beautiful long hair had been cut and styled in the current fashion so that the queue hung only a few inches past the shoulders. And he had put on weight. But there was no mistaking his compelling brown eyes or the way he held himself – as if he were the equal of any within the room.

Or their better.

But then that was also a part of her grandfather's plan. In James' eyes – and in her mother's – a savage could never have pulled off such a charade. Perhaps Grandpa George was passing Copperhead off as someone from the East Indies where he had once been stationed. Or he might have told her mother that he had purchased him from one of the many soldiers who passed through Charles Town.

Miriam cleared her throat and sweetly asked Charles to fetch her a cup of punch. He responded with alacrity and took off for the opposite end of the room. Explaining to her mother that she was cold, she rose quickly and crossed to the fire just as Copperhead retrieved the coal bucket and turned to leave.

Their eyes made brief contact. In his she saw no spark of recognition, but then that was how it would have to be played. Miriam held her head high and addressed him in a superior tone.

"I will no longer have any need of the salts. You may go now."

Copperhead's dark eyes flicked to her mother and to Charles who was working his way toward her, a glass of golden punch in his hand.

"Yes, my Lady," he said softly as he bowed, and then he exited the room.

Toward midnight George Foxwell heard a knock at the studio door. He was in the annexed room that had in the last year been converted back to a haven for sick horses. His own passion might be painting, but it was not Copperhead's. The boy had needed something to do with his hands – and with his anger. Taking care of the horses proved therapeutic for him. George placed the blanket he had just folded on a low worktable and went to unlock the door, shifting the extra bolt before opening it.

He knew even before he did who it was awaited without.

"Miriam," he sighed as she stepped past him and entered the room. "What can I say?"

His granddaughter lowered her hood and shook her golden ringlets free. She avoided his eyes and instead moved into the room, turning this way and that as if searching for something.

Or *someone*.

"No one knows I have come, Grandpa George," she said at last. "They think I am resting in my room. I must talk to him before I am sent away again."

"Are you to return to Scotland so soon?" he asked softly.

Miriam shook her head as she removed her cloak and draped it across her arm. "No. But Mother has my social schedule filled. And what little time she has permitted me, Charles will try to monopolize."

He studied her. Then he said, "I sent Copperhead out. He may not return before dawn."

A slight tremble shook her diminutive frame. Even though Miriam's pale saffron gown was ill suited for the weather, he did not think it was from the cold.

"Out? Out where?" she asked.

"To carry a message to a man about a horse."

"Oh," was all she said. Miriam fell silent for a moment as she studied the transformed studio. "I hear Kate's horse is here," she remarked, sounding only mildly interested.

He nodded. "Kate is not the most...expert of horsewomen. She was impatient and the horse twisted its leg and threw her. It is mending. As to Kate...."

"Who takes care of them? The horses?" she asked, ignoring his attempt at levity.

"Jackson," he answered. "And Copperhead. Though he is most often called Woody now, short for Woodward – his supposed surname."

"Woody?"

"It was as close to his Cherokee name as English could come."

"I see." Miriam paused as if uncertain of what to say next, or even what to do. Then, with a little twitch of her lips, asked sweetly, "May I sit with you a while? I have not spent any time with you in three years. Where *were* you each time I visited?"

"Three years," George repeated, brushing off the question. "It seems much longer."

"Yes, it does," she answered, her voice reflecting some of the pain of separation she must have felt. Once Charlotte had made the decision, Miriam had been gone in less than a week.

It had been hard on Copperhead as well.

"Scotland is lovely," she continued, moving toward one of the two chairs before the fire, "but it is not home. I wish I did not have to go away again." When he said nothing, she turned and looked at him, a wistful smile lifting the corner of one perfect lip. "You do not need to fear, Grandpa George. It is not only for Copperhead. I am *not* that child who wiggled through the vent and sat up all night with an Indian boy studying letters."

As she took a seat, George held his hand out for her cape and then crossed to hang it by the fire. "No, of course not. You are a lady now. Why, in France young women are engaged and married by your age."

"And in the Indian villages?" she asked softly as she turned her face to the fire.

"Miriam," he cautioned.

Her laugh was a painful echo of the child's he had known and loved. "Grandpa, how could one who has feasted with princelings think of falling in love with a child of nature? Do you really think I would want to spend my life living in a lodge stringing beads and pounding corn meal with a rock to make cakes for my naked brown children?" Miriam's fingers were knit together in her lap, her knuckles white as the bone beneath. She drew a deep breath and turned to look him in the eye. "Well?"

He leaned on the mantle beside her. "You play the part well, my girl. But it is not you."

Her small shoulders first squared, and then slumped. Miriam leaned wearily back in the chair. After a moment, a more genuine smile quirked at the edges of her lips. "I bribed one of the boys in the local theater troupe to instruct me. I *had* hoped to be able to convince Mama that I am become what she expects of me."

George laughed heartily and then leaned forward to take her hand and patted it. "Your mother does not know you as *I* do. She will *never* suspect that you are still a spirit untamed."

Miriam fell silent again. Tears welled in her eyes and spilled down her cheeks. When she looked up at last, it was to ask the question he had dreaded.

"Grandpa, how...how *could* you let me think he was dead?"

He knew his answer would not please her. He released her hand and sat in the chair opposite her. "It was for the best. For everyone. Copperhead. Your mother. You...."

"For the best! How can you – "

"Miriam. You are my granddaughter. I love you. How could I *not?*"

"We were just friends. You make it sound like something more," she snapped, growing heated.

"I know. And that is why I feared it would become in time – something *more*. Miri, Copperhead must remain dead to you. There can be no future there. You know that." He paused and then added with regret, "I am sorry I brought this on you."

Miriam remained silent. At war with herself. She sat for some time unmoving, her tears watering her folded hands. At last she asked, in a voice so low he could barely discern the question, "How is he, Grandpapa? Is he happy?"

"Happy? Copperhead is.... Well, he is alive." When she fixed him with a puzzled stare, he continued, "I cannot tell if something of the spirit in him is broken, or if it merely waits to burst forth, like rushing water frozen in ice. There are times when he seems content, and times when the rage in him boils over." George reached out and squeezed her fingers and then rose. He walked to the wall and placed a hand on the stones beneath the window. "These walls have seen *many* coats of paint," he added with a wry smile.

"Could you not have sent him home?"

"You asked me that once before. No, I could not. I do not know where his home is, and neither does he. The path back is lost in memory.

Copperhead knows only that he came from the south. That is all."

She stood and joined him beneath the window. It was the same one she had peered in when twelve years old to look for the 'wild' animal her sister Kate had told her was hidden there. "Then he is all alone," Miriam said softly. "And truly a stranger in a strange land."

"Yes. It is likely he stays only because he has no where else to go."

She touched his arm briefly. "I imagine it is more than that," Miriam remarked as she moved toward the table and fingered a book laying on it. "What do you do with your time? The two of you? Have you taught him how to paint?"

"Other than walls?" George shook his head. "No. He tends to the horses, and each evening we read and work on his speech. It is quite good now. I can't imagine anyone could guess his origins. And I have taken to reading to him out of the Bible. He listens, but I fear he does not understand. His eyes light not at God's goodness or His promised salvation, but with the tales of revenge and death." He joined her at the table, feeling very old and feeble. "I pray.... I pray I have done the right thing, child. Perhaps...

"Perhaps I should have let him die."

Miriam said nothing, but circled his waist with her arm and leaned her head on his breast. "How have you kept it from Mama? Is she not suspicious?"

He shook his head. "That was where the charade began. A few months after you left, I took him away from here, to the lodge your father keeps in the hills. When I returned, I told Charlotte we had been to the city and he had died. In reality I left Copperhead at the lodge with a man of mine and – after setting others to attend to business here at the manor, and telling your mother my country had called me – I went back." He squeezed her hand where it rested on his waist. "Your leaving hit Copperhead hard, as did his unfair treatment. I think he blamed me for both in a way. For a time he was uncontrollable. We struggled long and hard. He tore the clothes I put on him. He threw the books I had brought along. And when I read, he would scream so loud he could not hear. But slowly, I think he came to understand I cared. That I was not going anywhere. And that I was not going to give up." George shifted free and went to sit in the chair again, weary almost beyond words. "Within the first half year he was able to read primers. Now he reads from the Bible to *me*."

Miriam followed him. "And no one has recognized him since your return?"

He shook his head. "Do you think James knew him tonight?"

Miriam laughed. Genuinely this time. "How could he? He would be looking for a 'savage'."

The sound of the door opening made them both start. Snow and wind blew in along with a tall sinewy figure draped in a long black woolen cloak. Just past the threshold the man stopped and tossed back his hood, and shook free his coppery mane so it framed his high-boned cheeks.

It was Copperhead.

Miriam turned to look at him, astonished. "Grandpa George? I thought you said you had sent him away...."

He touched her cheek and gently kissed her forehead before moving away.

"I lied."

Against his better judgment her grandfather left the two of them alone.

Copperhead hadn't said a word since his return to the studio. He crossed to the hearth and hung his cloak by it to dry, and then turned and walked into the annexed room that held her sister Kate's gray filly. Her grandfather had it half-right. Kate *was* a poor horsewoman. But Miriam knew she had been riding the animal too hard, trying to impress Charles, and had nearly caused it to break a leg. As she followed Copperhead into the infirmary, the mare limped forward to greet the taciturn young man.

"My grandfather tells me you no longer go by Copperhead," she remarked casually after watching him retrieve a set of brushes from a drawer and set to work combing the horse's pale coat. "What is it people call you?"

His dark eyes flicked to her face. They crackled with an inner rage. "'Foxwell's bastard'," he growled. "Among other things."

Miriam scowled. She had hoped to find him in a better mood. "Grandpa says you had been learning. And that you speak English well."

"When it is permitted," he replied as he knelt and began to stroke the animal's long legs with one of the brushes. "Most often it is not."

He was deliberately avoiding looking at her. Miriam knelt so she was on a level with him. "Copperhead, are you angry with me?"

He had reached the horse's injured leg. Copperhead laid the brush down and began to undo the bandage. "No," he replied.

She watched him for a moment and then remarked softly, "I thought Grandpa said he had been reading to you from the Bible."

He glanced at her as he rose and turned back to the chest of drawers. "So what if he has?"

"Has he never read the part about not telling a lie?"

Copperhead stopped, the brushes still in his hands. Then he turned and looked at her. "What do you want of me?" he asked.

She rose as well. Tears formed in her eyes. "I want my friend back."

Copperhead laid the brushes on the chest. His eyes locked with hers. Within their fathomless brown depths there was an ineffable sadness that seemed an immutable part of him now. "Miriam, you know that is not possible. *Now* more than before."

"But why?"

His lightly tanned fingers stroked the mare's white mane. "You are a woman now."

A single tear fell and ran the length of her cheek. She struck it away in anger. "But I don't *want* to be. I don't want to be married off to some oaf like Charles Matthew Spencer, to be bred for stock! Or to spend my life giving teas and entertaining supercilious women who exist for no other purpose than to gossip about the ones who could not – or would not – come." Miriam stamped her foot so hard the horse shied and whinnied. "I don't and I *won't!*"

Copperhead laughed at her as he patted the mare's neck.

"You!" She looked around for something and finding an empty feed bucket, grasped it by the handle and threw it at him. He ducked and it missed his head, instead hitting the wall. "It's *not* funny!" she cried, breaking into tears.

Copperhead looked stricken. He sobered quickly. "The women in my village would not be treated so," he said quietly.

Miriam sniffed and wiped her nose on the sleeve of her expensive saffron gown. "You remember then, what it was like? Living as an Indian?" she asked.

He nodded.

"Then why have you not tried to go back?"

Copperhead met her eyes briefly before kneeling to retrieve the feed bucket. He rose and moved silently to replace it.

"Copperhead? Talk to *me!*"

She saw him go rigid. Then he faced her. The scent of the cool December night still clung to him, to his pale golden skin and shining copper hair. His linen shirt was partially undone, revealing a tight muscular chest beneath, traversed with scars. Approaching him, Miriam reached out to touch the remnant of another wound – one set high on his cheekbone. Left there years before by her brother's riding crop.

He caught her hand. "I did not go because I promised you I would wait. Now that I have seen you, it *is* time to go."

"Go?" She had only just found out he was alive. And now he was leaving? "Go where?"

"Back to my people," he said, releasing her and pushing past. "I do not belong here."

"But Grandpa George said you do not know where your people are."

He turned to look at her. "I will find them."

"But the horses!" she pleaded, desperate to get him to stay – if even for an hour. "Grandpa says you take care of them now. What will they do without you?" Miriam hesitated, and then she continued, unashamedly honest. "What will *I* do without you? Would you leave me here? With James and John, and Kate?" Miriam shuddered, suddenly chilled, and hugged herself tight. "With *Charles*?"

He shrugged. "Soon you will be gone again. Once you have left, there will be nothing here for me."

"What about Grandpa?"

Copperhead nodded. "He has been kind to me. I do not wish to hurt him, but – "

Desperation made her bold. She went to him and caught his hand and pressed it between her own. "Please, Copperhead, please, don't go! Stay with me – "

"Miriam," someone called from behind her.

The pair started guiltily even though they had done nothing wrong. Miriam dropped Copperhead's hand and turned toward the sound of the familiar voice. She found her grandfather as she had expected.

What she had *not* expected was the look on his face.

"What is wrong?" she asked as she moved into the main room where he stood.

Her grandfather spoke to her, but his eyes remained on Copperhead who had followed her and stood in the door of the annex. "Neither your mother nor Kate are feeling well. She is worried about you. It may be something they ate. She has sent James for the doctor."

Miriam heard Copperhead shift uncomfortably, anxious to escape and return to his work. In spite of her grandfather's disapproving stare, she turned back to him. "You must promise me that you will be here when I return," she insisted. "Or I will not go."

"I will see that he does not leave," her grandfather assured her, coming to her and placing his arm about her shoulders. "Now is not the time for him to go. The winter has been unseasonably cold this year. A storm is on the horizon. We shall be cut off tomorrow night at the latest – by ice or snow." He glanced back at Copperhead. "And we will need every hand to survive."

Copperhead nodded. And then, without a word, returned to his work.

Grandpa George led her to the door and opened it, ushering in a cold withering blast of wintry air. With one last glance at the tall figure in the annex, Miriam tossed her dry cloak about her shoulders and ran to the manor house.

Three days later both Kate and her mother were dead.

COPPERHEAD

Chapter Seven

Miriam put the quill down and shoved the amber inkstand aside. She leaned back in the upholstered chair that fronted her late mother's plum pudding mahogany desk and placed trembling hands over her face. She had tried to write to her father at least half a dozen times, but the words would not come. What could she say? That fate was a cruel and harsh mistress? That God seemed not to care?

That, for the fact that she had had no appetite that night, she would – most likely – be dead?

It had been two months. Only two. The doctors could not explain what had happened to her mother and sister other than to say that it was a bilious fever resulting in corruption, brought on by the consumption of a plate of contaminated oysters. Though at least one physician, just returned from a convention in Philadelphia, thought the deaths most likely were the result of a miasma – an unseen vapour in the air – coupled with overexcitement and the general nervous dispositions of the deceased. Kate and her mother had shared a plate that last night and had offered her some, but she had no appetite and had refused. After the church service their Grandmother Augusta took little Anna to live with her in Charlotte's Burg, deeming it improper for a girl her age to grow up without a firm adult hand. James and John returned to Oxford. Though her grandmother protested, Miriam was deemed old enough at fifteen to go to housekeeping, and so she had been handed the keys and the responsibility for maintaining the day-to-day functions of the manor. Her grandfather was to run the estate until her father's return later in the year.

In one brief horrific moment her family was gone.

With a wistful smile Miriam glanced down and fingered the cloisonné watch with the consular case that hung from her belt chatelaine. The chatelaine, decorated with pearls and jewels, had been her mother's. The gold watch was a recent gift from her grandfather to show his confidence in her and her ability to perform her new duties. So, she was not *quite* alone. There was Grandpa George.

And Copperhead.

Miriam sighed as she turned her face into the late afternoon light and gazed out of the palatine window in the drawing room. Her feelings for the transformed Indian were complicated. And made even more so by the sudden radical change in her life. Where before there had been only moments snatched – a book shared by candlelight, a brief touch of hands, the meeting of eyes – all a part of a child's flirtation with something wonderfully mysterious and monstrously dangerous – now they were thrust together on an almost daily basis.

And now that they were, she was afraid.

Shifting the chair back Miriam rose and obsessively straightened the folds of her emerald and rose chintz gown, forcing order into her now chaotic world. She adjusted the soft merino wool mantle she wore so it covered her shoulders. It was early February and the world outside was silent. Snow and ice remained on the ground. Her responsibilities, which seemed all but overwhelming, were actually light now compared to what was to come when the spring planting season began. Miriam's hair was upswept now as befitted a woman with important duties, the golden ringlets packed away with her scuffed shoes and the freedom to do as she pleased. She had never really appreciated all that her mother had to do: managing the household finances, keeping track of a large staff of servants and slaves, approving in detail the plans for the new year's crop and the uses for the last year's harvest, not to mention making certain nothing came up missing or was stolen. And if it was, being the one to administer discipline and perhaps dismiss one of the staff.

She missed her mother. And she missed Kate and Anna.

She missed being a child.

A shift in the shadows near the door alerted her to the fact that someone had entered the room. Miriam struck away the tear she shed for the unfair loss of her innocence and turned, knowing before she did who had come. The late afternoon sun created a golden pool on the heart of pine floor and into it stepped Copperhead. He was dressed for travel and wore a close-fitting charcoal frock coat in the English type with a turned down collar. A pair of black riding boots showed beneath it. The boots looked to be of military issue and she wondered briefly if they belonged to her grandfather. His copper hair was trimmed to the current style, with a braided queue that hung halfway down his back.

He nodded as he removed his tricorn hat. "I am going to town. Is there anything you need…my lady?"

Miriam couldn't help but smile when he addressed her that way – though it was necessary. When they were in the house they never knew who might be listening. "Are you going to Mr. Watkins' establishment?" she asked.

A slight smile lifted the corner of his lip and he nodded.

"Let me get you a list then."

Isaac Watkins was a little younger than her father and friends with her Grandpa George. He had first been a shopkeeper at Frederica on St. Simon's Island in Georgia, and then a sutler for the soldiers in New

York. For the last two and a half years Mr. Watkins had run a tavern and dry goods store in the neighboring town. He was a kind man without prejudices, as was evidenced by the fact that his store had been burnt out shortly after it opened by townspeople angry that he was willing to trade with the local Indians.

Miriam returned to the desk and shifted a few papers, searching for the list she had begun that morning. She did not know what her grandfather had told Mr. Watkins about Copperhead, and what he had surmised himself, but he had asked Grandpa George if Woody, as he called him, could work one or two evenings a week for him in the store. Copperhead seemed to enjoy the limited freedom the opportunity presented him, though on rare occasions when she accompanied him and her grandfather to the merchant's store, the stares and whispers of the local population made her uneasy. 'Foxwell's bastard' might have been the common misnomer for her friend, but 'Foxwell's *Indian*' was just as often found on the townspeople's lips. Mr. Watkins' friendship gave Copperhead a chance to interact with people and to learn social skills, and that was something her grandfather could not offer him. In the last few months his speech had improved immensely, as had his manners and deportment. If one had not known, they would have thought Copperhead was – if to its lower levels – to the manor born.

If not for a few unguarded moments *she* might even have believed him content with his new life.

After her mother and sister's deaths, Copperhead had not left as he threatened – though sometimes she wondered if he did not regret the choice bitterly. Sometimes she would find him staring out of a window, a melancholy expression on his handsome face – looking toward the south and what had been his life. There were times when he would disappear for a few days and she would find out later that he had returned from the town with his lip split and his eyes blackened from brawling. And there were days when the pain and grief and shame and loss became so overwhelming that he reverted to his feral nature, and she would look out of an upper window late at night or early in the morning to find him perched on the cedar roof of her grandfather's studio, his white ways abandoned, clothed in nothing but a pair of leather breeches, the moonlight painting his naked chest blue; his hands raised in supplication to his native god.

"Ah! Here it is," Miriam declared with feigned enthusiasm as she shifted yet another stack of papers and found her list stuffed in-between the pages of a small prayer book. Turning back with a forced smile she read the items off to him. "Honey and maple sugar. And we are very low on sugar cones. Also I promised Anna I would send her those chocolate cookies with a cherry on top that she loves so well. So we need the chocolate and – "

She stopped. Copperhead was laughing. "What! What is it?" she demanded feeling foolish, but not knowing why.

He sobered immediately at her look and then pretended to jot the items down on an imaginary pad. "Chocolate. Sugar cones. Honey *and* maple sugar." His dark eyes flicked to her face. The hint of a smile had not vanished but only deepened. "Are you sure, my lady, you have not forgotten anything? Taffy? Butterscotch? A side dish of icing?"

Her sweet tooth *was* legendary.

Miriam scrunched the piece of parchment into a ball and threw it at him. It bounced off the shoulder of his coat and landed in the puddle of waning daylight on the floor. He bent and picked it up, straightened it out, and then tucked it in his leather pocketbook. With a gallant sweep of his hat, Copperhead bowed. He approached her, taking her hand. "Sweets to the sweet," he said, his dark eyes sparkling. "Farewell!"

Miriam couldn't help it. She giggled.

Her grandfather had told her they had moved on to Shakespeare in their reading. Still, she was amazed. Miriam glanced behind Copperhead to make certain no one was watching, and then she leaned forward and kissed him on the cheek. "Thank you for staying," she whispered as she pulled away. "And for being my friend."

Her small hand was gripped in his. It was not so callused now that he worked in the house. He squeezed her fingers and then, as footsteps echoed in the foyer and someone called her name, backed away and executed a proper bow.

"See to it that you are not late returning," Miriam ordered in her best imitation of the disdainful tone her mother had employed with servants. As Martha, her one-time nursemaid and now her personal watchdog, entered the room she added, "Charge the items to the account and bring an inventory to me upon your return, so I can be certain nothing is missing."

"As you will, my lady," Copperhead responded, his tone deeply respectful. With nary a glance at Martha, he replaced his hat and pivoted sharply on his heel and was gone.

Miriam returned to the desk and began to rummage through her papers again. She *must* learn to be organized! "I shall want my bath drawn after supper, Martha. Please lay out the pale blue gown and robe. Has there been a letter from my father yet concerning the time of his return?" She waited for a reply and when she did not get one, turned to face the old woman. "Martha?"

Her servant was not listening. Martha was staring at the door through which Copperhead had departed, a frown adding furrows to a face already fully plowed by age.

"Martha?"

The ancient creature eyed her with concern. "If I may be so bold, Miss?" she began.

"Yes?" When the old woman hesitated, Miriam snapped. "Well, come out with it. I haven't all day."

"That young man. He takes too many liberties, Miss Miriam." Martha paused and then added, "Master James says he should be dismissed."

"Master James is not here, nor is he in charge of the staff, Martha. I am." Miriam had begun to tremble. She caught the back of her mother's chair to steady herself. "Now if there is nothing more…."

Martha's weak-eyed gaze had retreated to the floor during the scolding. Now it returned to Miriam's face. The old woman curtsied and added quietly as she rose, "Nothing more, Miss Miriam, but to say that I wish the good Lord had left your mother among us. It's a terrible burden you have to bear."

Miriam's knuckles had grown white on the gilded frame of the chair. "Thank you for your concern, Martha. I will manage. Is that all?"

"Yes, Mistress."

"Then you are dismissed."

Miriam watched Martha depart and then fell into the chair quaking. What had *that* been about?

"Woody! Lend me a hand here, son! I'd need at least six to keep up with the trade tonight," Isaac Watkins, a reed-thin man with hazel eyes, a slightly hooked nose and thinning sandy hair said as he filled several tankards with a heady ale and set them down with a resounding clang on a marred pewter tray. The older man shoved the overflowing mugs and tray toward him. "Now be a good lad and take these over to the soldiers at the table by the window."

Copperhead halted at Isaac's call. He had been in the back room of the bustling establishment filling Miriam's order, carefully selecting the thickest sugar cones and the clearest amber syrup for the manor house larder, and had just reentered the tavern. He had removed his outer coat and hat upon arrival and was dressed now in a plain linen shirt with a stock collar, a pair of russet breeches with cream-colored hose, and a moss-green waistcoat with an apron over all. He parked the modest-size crate that held Miriam's order by the counter and warily eyed the frothing mugs of ale and the boisterous crowd. A regiment of Redcoats had arrived in the town and the tavern was alive with gawkers and gossips, as well as the British soldiers and those who followed them. Copperhead answered Isaac's harried request with a negative shake of his head.

"I have never waited on tables before," he said.

Isaac had already turned away to tackle the next customer. The tavern-keep pivoted sharply at Copperhead's refusal and, adopting a mock proud and haughty manner, sniffed and exclaimed, "Too good for the likes of you, eh? Won't have none of that *menial* labor?"

Copperhead knew his friend was not angry. And he knew Isaac would let him back away – even without understanding. Still, he hated to disappoint him.

Mistaking his silence for chagrin, Isaac briefly touched his shoulder and assured him, "I've watched you, lad. You're sure on your feet. There's no chance you'll embarrass yourself." The older man picked up the heavy tray and held it out to him. "Now do a body a favor and get this over to those bits of red before they start breaking the furnishings – or even worse – someone's head."

Copperhead undid the filthy apron he wore and laid it aside. Then he accepted the tray. Successfully navigating the narrow channel between tables, chairs, and men's outstretched legs, he reached the area near the window without incident. By the cut of their coats and the braid on their sleeves, as well as the silver and gold epaulets on their shoulders, he could tell all five of the British soldiers were officers. Two were seasoned veterans, forty years or more in age, with grizzled hair and the weary look of men who have seen too much war. The other three, clustered to one side as if to lend each other moral support, were not much older than he was – and therefore more likely to cause trouble. The junior officers at the table were arrogant, boastful, and more than half-pissed. Copperhead steered clear of them and placed the mugs in front of one of the older men who was sitting with his back to the maelstrom of bawling, brawling and bawdy humanity. The officer sat with his elbow propped on the chair-back, staring out the window; one hand pressed against his lips.

Copperhead turned with the tray in his hand, intent on making his escape. He nearly made it. One of the junior officers shouted something he was unable to discern in the din of the tavern and when he did not respond immediately, the soldier caught him by the tail of his waistcoat and hauled him roughly back. Copperhead fought the urge to strike the Redcoat's hand away. Though justified, any such action would only draw unwanted attention.

"Sir," he began, "release me. I have work to be about."

Already thick in the jowls at what could have been no more than twenty-five years of age, the piggish officer brought his mug down with a loud clank, adding yet another scar to the vastly abused wooden surface. "Cock and pie!" he declared, spraying the table with spittle and ale. "And just *who* do you think you are, boy? I'll let you go when I bloody well feel like it!" With that declaration the soldier increased the amount of cloth gathered in his sweaty hand, throwing Copperhead off balance so he fell against the table upsetting two of the tankards and covering himself in ale.

As the stink rose to his nostrils – and in spite of his best intentions – Copperhead lost his temper. He pivoted sharply, breaking free. Catching the soldier by the wrist, he pulled the man from his seat and brought him quickly to his knees. "If you would like to keep your bones intact, Redcoat, you will let me go *now!*" he growled.

"Well, I never!" the veteran soldier nearest the door declared as he kicked back and raised his tankard, hiding the upward turn of his lips. "Say, Billie…what shall we do with this impertinent whelp who's not worth three skips of a louse? Do we mop up the floor with him and clap him in irons for affronting a British officer – or recruit him?" He took a sip of his ale. "As senior officer, it *is* your call."

'Billie', who was still staring out the window, blinked as if emerging from a dream. He glanced from Copperhead to the junior officer and back, sizing up the situation in a second. "You! Release him!" he snapped at Copperhead. Then he pointed at the chair, ordering the junior officer to sit down. "Bring your ass to anchor, Lieutenant Jacobs!" Billie's tone brooked no disobedience.

"But, sir!" Jacobs protested as Copperhead released his grip on him. "Sir, I – "

"To the count of three, lieutenant! One. Two…."

By three Jacobs had returned to his seat – seething.

Billie wiped his mouth with a linen napkin and rose to his feet. He nodded to the quartet at the table. "I'm going out for some air. Jacobs, see that you do nothing to disgrace that uniform while I am gone."

Silence followed in his wake. At least among the officers. No one in the tavern seemed to have noticed the commotion, but then the air was riotous and most of the patrons were drunk. Copperhead caught sight of Isaac's balding head as he disappeared into a circle of soldiers and onlookers. A Redcoat private had climbed on to a tabletop and was reaching for the rope that suspended a tin light from the ceiling. As Isaac's alarmed voice rose above the whoops and the shouted wagers, Copperhead bent to retrieve the fallen tankards. While kneeling on the floor he heard one of the junior officers remark to Lieutenant Jacobs.

"That one's not worth the coin to pay the bill, Henry."

"Right you are, Nathaniel. Unless you want to give him the *monkey's* allowance."

"Ladies. Ladies….mind what you say…." The veteran officer who remained pushed his chair back and rose, tankard in hand. He nodded to Copperhead and then stepped around him, headed for the bar and a much-needed refill. As he did Copperhead heard him remark, "At least until I get out of earshot. After that what you do is your own business."

Copperhead knew what was coming but was unable to move away in time. A 'monkey's allowance' was vulgar speech for a beating.

As he rose Nathaniel caught hold of him and pinned his arms behind his back. Copperhead might have broken free if Henry Jacobs, with a wicked grin, had not shown him his regulation pistol, primed, and clutched beneath his scarlet coat. The third man in the party kept watch as the pair marched him to the back of the establishment and manhandled him into the stock room. Jacobs closed the door and then rummaged through the items on the shelves until he found some rope to bind him with. Once he had, the piggish lieutenant took hold of his collar and shoved him up against the wall.

"Keep watch, Rowlands. Alert us if Erskyn or Colonel William returns."

Rowlands laid a finger alongside his nose and nodded. Then he stepped into the tavern, pulling the heavy door to behind him.

Copperhead held very still as Henry Jacobs approached him, pistol in hand. The Redcoat looked him over, pinching the linen of his shirt between his fingers as if to check it for quality and noting with interest George Foxwell's brightly polished boots. Jacobs grunted as if satisfied and turned away, only to pivot back sharply and strike his face with the butt of the weapon. As the sugar cones and flour sacks lining the shelves began to dance about the room from the impact, Henry Jacobs caught Copperhead's throat with his fingers and squeezed.

"You need a lesson in how to talk to your betters, you half and half," Jacobs breathed with menace.

Even through the haze of stinging pain, *that* penetrated. 'Half and half' was also vulgar speech.

For a half-breed Indian.

"Well? Have you nothing to say?"

There was no point. Copperhead knew he could crawl on four legs and beg for forgiveness for his supposed sins, or insinuate what incestuous act the British lieutenant might have performed with his mother in the middle of the night – either way Henry Jacobs would *still* beat him.

Jacobs turned the pistol around and held the barrel of it to the underside of Copperhead's chin. His finger went to the trigger, but then eased off it as he said, "No." Too much noise. Too much *mess*." Henry Jacobs lowered the gun and then nodded toward his compatriot. "You see Corporal Beattie here, 'breed?" When Copperhead failed to answer, Jacobs gripped his collar again and forced his spinning head back against the wall. "*Do* you?"

Copperhead nodded.

"John Beattie is the regiment's prize pugilist. He knows how to take a man down *slowly* and make it hurt. You will pay for making me look the fool!" Jacobs released him. "Eh, John?"

"Aye?"

Henry Jacobs made a little bow as he stepped away. "The *mestizo's* all yours."

As Beattie raised his fists the door opened abruptly and Lieutenant Rowlands stuck his head in. "Henry! The tavern-keep's coming. Finish it quick!"

Jacobs acknowledged his ill luck with a curse. He nodded to John Beattie and made a motion indicating haste was of the essence. The pugilist eyed Copperhead with a grin. Beattie struck out taking him first in the stomach and then, as he fell, brought his linked hands down on his neck.

Leaving Copperhead on the floor gasping.

A pair of regulation boots blocked his line of vision and a hand gripped his braided queue. Henry Jacobs used it to lift his head to spit in his face. Then he whispered close to his ear, "This isn't over, *half-breed*. Not by a long chalk! You better watch your back from now on." A black boot struck his ribs and Jacobs let his head fall. Then the pair exited the storeroom.

Just as Isaac Watkins entered.

Isaac stumbled back as the men pushed past him, a puzzled look on his face. Then he saw Copperhead lying on the floor. Dropping to his knees, Isaac caught him under the arm and rolled him over. He winced when he saw the black bruise growing on his jaw. "Woody, lad! Can you stand?"

Copperhead nodded. He leaned heavily on Isaac as the older man helped him to his feet.

"I lost track of you for only a few minutes, lad. How did this happen?" Isaac glanced at the door through which Henry Jacobs and John Beattie had left. "Who were those men? Did they know you?"

Copperhead shot him a puzzled stare. "*Know* me?"

Isaac seemed uncomfortable. "Yes," he said at last. "From *before*."

As he allowed the older man to steer him to a large crate and help him to sit on it, Copperhead met his friend's concerned gaze. "So you know?" he asked, incredulous.

"That you are *not* my old friend George's half-breed son by some woman in Bermuda? Yes." Isaac's laugh was troubled. "I helped to start that rumor. You are light-skinned enough to pass. George knew he had to trust someone. He needed medicine, clothes...and he knew of my dealings with the natives. When George was certain it was safe, he told me how he found you." Isaac paused, as if hesitating to put it into words. "And what you are."

Copperhead's jaw grew tight. His hands balled into fists. "In the forest I would have *killed* them."

Isaac sat beside him. "Yes, and with justification. But this is not the forest, Woody." He stopped and this time the laugh was genuine. "I am not a betting man, but I venture to say I would win the prize if I *did* bet that Josiah Woodward is not your name."

Copperhead wiped blood from his lip. "No. It is Wudigeas ."

"Wuh-dih-gee...." Isaac thought a moment. "Cherokee then. Copperhead?" At his look he added, "Don't be surprised. One does not spend two decades trading with the native population without picking up a few words in his customer's tongue. Now, let's see if you can stand on your own."

Copperhead did so, though he wobbled a bit at first.

"Can you sit your horse? Do you need me to take you home?"

"I am fine."

Isaac shook his head sadly. "No, you're not."

"I have been beaten before. This is no worse than – "

"That isn't what I meant."

Copperhead looked at him. He knew Isaac Watkins well. What ever troubled the older man was of consequence. "What *do* you mean then?" he asked.

Isaac reached out and straightened his collar. "Did those soldiers get a good look at you? Well enough to see – what you are?"

He nodded. "The fat one called me a 'mestizo'."

"So he thinks you *are* from the West Indies, or Creole perhaps. That works well with George's lie. You don't think he suspected that you are a full-blood Indian?"

Copperhead shrugged, tired of it all.

Isaac Watkins walked him to the door of the stock room. Before he opened it, he asked, "Did you see the older officer? The one who left the tavern just as this all began?"

He nodded. "Yes, the men called him 'Billie'."

"Do you know who he is?"

He shook his head.

"That is William Foxwell, George's son." His hand went to Copperhead's shoulder. "Miriam's father is home now, and you are going to have to watch yourself."

Chapter Eight

Miriam awaited her father's judgment. He had returned during the night without warning and by the time she had arisen was already engaged in reviewing the estate. Now as the sun set on another day, turning the ice-covered lawn outside the drawing room window to a carpet of gold, he sat at her mother's desk in the drawing room, inspecting the receipts and business records.

William Foxwell did not like what he found.

"Miriam, my girl, besieging Fort Niagara pales in comparison to surmounting the stack of bills on this desktop!" Her father flung the papers he held onto the mahogany surface and leaned back. He braced his elbow on the gilt arm of the chair and pressed a knuckle to his lips as he pinned her with his ice blue eyes. "If you are not able to cope with your duties you must learn to delegate. There are more than enough competent members of the staff. Take Martha, for instance, she is a wise woman of formidable years, well acquainted with the business of running a manor house – "

"Mother never trusted the staff," Miriam countered quickly. "She always managed alone."

"Your mother was efficient in her duties. *Her* mother trained her well." Her father rose and walked to the window where he stood staring out at the frozen garden which had occupied so much of her mother, Charlotte's, time. "A blessing which God in His infinite wisdom has chosen to deny you."

"I can learn."

He pivoted sharply. "Not at the expense of this estate, you will not! You have no head for numbers, child. You are better suited for another life – to be the wife of someone of substance, a woman who has no other duties to attend to than the needs of her husband. A solicitor or banker perhaps. Someone in the city. I understand Charles Spencer was here when…." He paused and Miriam saw the first flicker of emotion in his face. "When your mother and sister passed."

"He was. I didn't like him," she answered stubbornly.

Her father's scowl deepened. He shook his head as he approached her. Miriam expected a dressing down such as he gave his soldiers, but when he reached her, he spoke in a softer tone and stroked her hair. "Miriam, you are no longer a child. You will reach your sixteenth birthday within the month. You must let go of these infantile fantasies. Whether or not you 'like' Charles – or anyone else – has very little to do with anything."

"But you *liked* Mother.... Didn't you?"

William Foxwell stiffened. "Your mother was an excellent woman. Competent, shrewd and wise. She gave me strong sons and three lovely daughters. I never had to bother my head about anything here at home. Charlotte handled it all. Her worth was proven by her usefulness. I do not need to put my feelings into words." He removed his hand from her head and crossed to the fire where he picked up the poker and stirred the embers, calling them back to life. "Least of all to you."

Her father still wore his colonel's uniform. The bright brass buttons on his scarlet coat glinted in the rising light. The silver epaulet on his right shoulder scintillated as it fell forward. His cocked hat had been removed and Miriam noted that his black hair had become grizzled in the more than three years he had been away.

In many ways it was a familiar stranger she faced.

"Forgive me for being so bold," she murmured.

Her father replaced the poker and turned to face her. His voice was quiet and carefully controlled – which told her he was very angry. "No. I will not forgive such impertinence. You have grown saucy in the time I have been gone. Who has been schooling you? The old man?"

"Grandpa George is seldom in the house." It was the truth. Her grandfather preferred the studio, though they did share meals several times a week. "And often away on business. I meant no disrespect, Father."

"But you serve it up, nonetheless."

"It is just...." Miriam hesitated.

"What? You can speak your mind without being forward." Her father sat in the tambour-work chair before the fire and motioned for her to take the seat opposite him. The one her mother used to occupy.

"I do not want to live in the city," she said as she obeyed him. Miriam took her seat and linked her fingers in the nest of folds created by her leaf-green dress. She too worked to control her tone. "And I do not want to marry someone like Charles Spencer. Every word he spoke while he was here was about *him*. And not only is he vainglorious, I find him boring."

Her father laughed. "You will find, my child, as you age that 'boring' has its own virtues."

"Can one not marry for love?" she asked.

Her father stretched his long legs out before the fire. The white hose and breeches of the British officer as well as his black riding boots were muddied from the day's tour of their plantation home. "Love," the word dropped into the silence like an oath, harsh and grating to the ear. "Will 'love' keep clothes on your back, or food in your children's bellies? Will 'love' till the fields and bring in the harvest? I have met many a good woman gone wrong who sold her future for the 'love' of some young wastrel." Her father shook his head. "Marriage is a business contract, Miriam, between two people. The union meant to benefit them and their progeny. Marry a man who is already established – perhaps a widower – who can take care of your needs."

"But," she hoped he did not take her words wrong, "but what if what I need *is* love?"

Her father shifted. He patted the cushion by his thigh, beckoning her to come and sit with him. When she did, he placed his arm about her shoulders and pulled her close so she leaned against his chest. "You have always been a thinker and a bit of a dreamer, my girl. But life is not made of dreams. You are old enough now to marry and have children of your own. You must put away such childish notions and assume your proper role in society. *That* is the only thing that counts."

They sat for some time in silence, watching the fire dance, until a sound close by made them both turn and look to see who had come. Miriam's breath caught when she saw it was Copperhead. Her friend was standing in the doorway, his tall lean frame silhouetted against the dying light that spilled in from the foyer behind him.

"Pardon me, Sir. Mistress," he said, making a bow. "I came to bank the fire for the night and did not know anyone was within."

"I will take care of it," her father said. "Bring me a whiskey and then you may go to your bed."

Miriam's eyes went to the bottles of liquor. They were on the sideboard on the opposite side of the fire. Copperhead would have to step into the light to pour, and then deliver the glass. "Let me get it for you, Papa," she said rising.

He caught her hand. "Let the boy do his duty, Miriam. You must learn. It is not your place to wait on me. It is his."

Miriam pulled free and returned to the seat opposite her father from which she had a clear line of sight of both men. Copperhead walked into the room, his head held high; his muscled form straight of bearing. He poured the drink and came directly toward them, his lean form illuminated by the fire's glow.

How could her father not see? He had served with Indians, fighting in the same war as her Grandpa George, but in Canada. He *must* recognize that golden-skin, the high pitch of the cheekbones, the wide and generous mouth....

"Here you are, sir," Copperhead spoke softly as he handed him the drink. He started to turn to leave, but her father called him back.

"Sir?" he asked.

Her father took a sip of the whiskey and let it lay on his tongue. He swallowed and nodded, and then his eyes returned to Copperhead. "I don't know you, do I, boy?"

"No, sir."

"Your duties are in the house?"

"Yes, sir. And in the stables."

"How long have you been here?"

"Less than a year, sir."

"And what is your name?"

Copperhead's dark eyes were fixed on the fire. "Woodward, sir. Josiah Woodward."

So far the interview had taken the accustomed form. But something about the name caught her father's attention. His ice blue eyes narrowed. "Come closer, boy."

Copperhead obeyed, moving so his face was fully revealed.

Miriam held her breath.

"You are the one who has been tending to the horses then? The sick ones?"

"Yes, sir."

"A fine job."

Her father's queries remained routine. Miriam failed to discern any indication that he found anything wrong, other than the fact that he seemed slightly distracted.

"So *you* are the young man my father, George, brought to the estate," her father continued. "From the West Indies, I hear. I have just recently returned from there. Perhaps I know of your family?"

"My family is dead, sir."

"Ah, I see." He took another sip of brandy. "And how did you come to be in my father's employ?"

"He saved my life," Copperhead answered honestly.

Miriam's father's scrutiny made *her* squirm. How could Copperhead seem so unaffected?

Her father put the whiskey glass down on the table. He leaned back in his chair and steepled his fingers before his face. "I seem to know you. How is that?"

"We met earlier, sir. Last evening at Watkins tavern. I brought your drinks."

"That's right. You're the young man Henry Jacobs took an exception to." Her father's manner eased slightly. But there was still something there – a keen interest he did not normally show in the servants. "I knew there was something. Watkins spoke of you later."

"May I go now, sir?"

"In a moment. That bruise...." Even in the flickering firelight the black mark of the pistol's butt was evident on Copperhead's chin. Her father pointed at it. "Did one of my men give you that?"

Copperhead shook his head. Keeping his voice even, he replied, "No, sir. It happened with the horses. One of them bucked and threw me against the wall."

Miriam knew that was true. But she also knew that was *not* where the bruise had come from.

"Good. I cannot abide abusive actions on the part of soldiers. It gives the Crown a bad name, and that is something we do not need right now with these difficulties over the Acts passed by parliament to finance the last war." Her father dismissed him with a wave of his hand. "You may go now."

Copperhead's eyes flicked to her face as he bowed. In them there was a quietly controlled rage. Once he had walked free in the forest, and servitude did not sit well on his shoulders.

Miriam watched him go and then turned back and waited for her father's comment. He said nothing, but leaned on his hand again and stared into the fire. As the clock in the hall struck quarter past nine, she asked him, "May I go as well, sir?"

He pursed his lips as if considering what to say. "Tomorrow or the next day we will have a 'guest'. I trust I can count on you to bring things to order, to have an appropriate room prepared, and to handle all the details," he said without looking at her.

"A guest?" Miriam sounded – and was – surprised.

"Is that not all right with you?" her father's tone was not amused. Nor was it angry. Merely tired.

"It is only.... Well, the ice is so thick. How shall they arrive?"

"By sleigh. It is excellent weather for sleighing. You will see that she is greeted and treated as family."

"Of course, sir. 'She'?"

"Judith. Judith Kingesley," her father said as he stood and crossed to the sideboard to harbor his glass. "She is soon to be my wife."

A quarter of an hour later Miriam fled the room in tears. She would have missed Copperhead lingering in the shadows had he not spoken and softly called her name. He indicated the back door and the world beyond it with a nod, and then vanished into the darkness.

They had their meeting places. Since she was older and their only ally, her grandfather, now discouraged their friendship, they had been forced to find other safe havens than the studio. One was an arbor to the west of the house. Another in the derelict zoo where Copperhead had once been incarcerated. But on cold and frigid nights they met in the stable farthest from the house in a high loft filled with soft, warm straw. There they would sit, side by side. Sometimes they would talk, but more often she would read to him. Copperhead did not say much, but then he did not need to. She knew how he felt. She felt the same.

It was like they were a part of one another.

It took her some time to leave the house. Her father did not turn in right away, but remained brooding by the fire. Martha met her on the main stair and watched her like a hawk until she entered her room, and then remained in the passageway for some time. But finally the old woman tired out and fell asleep. Miriam put on her heavy cloak and mittens and slipped past her and ran to the stable.

By the time she arrived Copperhead had fallen asleep.

He lay in the loft on a bed of straw, one hand thrust above his head; the other curled against his chest. By the light of the lantern she carried she could see the bruise on his chin her father had noted – as well as others he had not. Her grandfather had gone the next day to see Isaac Watkins, but would only say upon his return that Copperhead had gotten into a dispute with a British soldier. Miriam knew there was more. Just as she knew a simple 'dispute' would not have left purple thumbprints impressed in the flesh below his jaw.

Placing the lantern on a wooden crate they had brought there for a table, she studied him. Gone was the 'wild animal' her sister Kate had run to tell her about; the one her grandfather had brought home, wounded and dying. In his place was a handsome young man, dressed in linen and wool. Copperhead's once deep bronze skin was now a soft burnished gold and his long copper hair had been cut and captured, and bound in a tail. He was no longer an Indian.

Miriam wondered at what cost.

Before sitting beside him, she gently called his name. Sometimes when he was startled he would strike out, forgetting he was in the safety of her world. "Copperhead? It's me. I am sorry to have been so long. It is Miriam."

The sound of her voice brought a smile to his lips. His dark eyes opened and closed several times. Copperhead sat up and shook himself awake. "I fell asleep. I am sorry."

"Don't be," she said, sitting beside him. "You work hard."

He had been running a hand over his face. He stopped and his dark eyes met hers over the tips of his golden fingers. "Stoking fires and carrying pewter trays? Bringing whiskey to your father? My people would laugh and say I have grown soft." He hesitated and then added with some anger, clenching his fingers into a fist. "And they would be right."

This was the result of what she had seen earlier. The interaction with her father had humiliated him. "What would you be doing now, if you *were* still with your people?" she asked suddenly.

He looked at her, puzzled. "What do you mean?"

"What would you be doing? Fighting? Killing? *Dying*?" Miriam adjusted her heavy skirts and pulled her stockinged legs up beneath them. She circled her knees with her arms and leaned her chin on them. "My father is a warrior. And I *detest* him."

Copperhead waited. When she did not continue, he asked, "What did he say to you?"

She shook her head. "I don't want to talk about it now."

He nodded. And they fell into a silence.

Through the chill night air Miriam heard the church bell on the estate toll one and then quarter past one. She shifted and lowered her legs. Then she sighed and straightened her skirts and drew her legs up again. Copperhead did not move. He lay back in the straw with his eyes closed, though she knew he was not asleep. One thing Miriam had noted about her Indian friend was that he was not afraid of silence. Copperhead could sit for hours and say nothing. He had no need to fill the void with idle chatter.

Not being Indian it only lasted so long with her.

With a sigh she told him, "My father means to remarry. His new…wife arrives tomorrow or the next night."

"*New* wife?" he asked, sitting up. "Does he not still grieve for the old one?"

His words were a knife to her heart. Tears welled in her eyes at the pain. "Father says there is no time. The manor house must have a mistress," Miriam drew a deep breath, 'and I must have a mother." She choked and a sob escaped her. "At least Anna is coming home."

Copperhead took her hand and covered it with his own. He waited a moment and then asked her softly, "Do you know what the People believe?"

"About marriage?"

He shook his head. "About grieving. And about those who have died."

Miriam sniffed. A tear rolled down her cheek.

Copperhead looked at her, but his thoughts were far away in another place – another time. "The People believe that when our bodies die and are buried, they return to Mother Earth, from which we came. But we believe as well, as the Christians do, that the spirit lives on. When our bodies decay, they nurture the ground and become the grass that we see and the flowers that we smell and the air that we breathe." His strong fingers gripped hers. "*This* is how those we love come back to us. In the Spring, you will see your mother again. In the garden. In the plants and flowers that you love."

Miriam drew a deep breath and shuddered, and then burst into tears. Copperhead was taken aback, but caught her when she fell into his arms and held her until the tempest had subsided. When she had regained her composure she pulled back and looked up at him – so close, so caring, so....

Utterly foreign and yet, so *totally* known.

Her hand went to his chin where the bruising had caused it to swell. "Copperhead, I – "

Like an animal of the wood scenting danger he was suddenly alert. Copperhead pushed her behind him and rose to his feet. Quickly crossing the loft he crouched at the top of the long ladder and looked down into the stable. Miriam held her breath as she too sensed movement and heard voices below. Dear God! Had Martha followed them?

Or worse, her *father*?

Copperhead remained motionless for some time, listening, and then his muscled form eased. A dozen pounding heartbeats later he turned to look at her. "It is only Jackson and McNeil. Come to feed the animals. They are gone now."

Miriam rose. She pulled her woolen hood close about her face and then picked up her lantern. "I should go. Martha is likely to check in on me – though the old woman sleeps like a log, and snores like the saw cutting through it."

He rose and held out his hand. She took it and let him help her to swing out onto the ladder. When he made no move to follow, she asked him, "Aren't you coming?"

"No. Unless you need me to."

Miriam paused at the bottom of the ladder. "No, I'm fine. Are you?"

Copperhead knelt so the lantern's glow brushed his supple form. He touched his forehead. "Here, yes. But here," the hand descended to his chest. Then he shook his head.

She nodded. She had seen him this way before.

He was missing his home.

As Miriam moved across the darkened lawn she wondered again why he stayed. Copperhead was more than old enough now at eighteen or so to search out his people, though the journey would be a long and dangerous one. Still, she knew that was not what stopped him. He had spoken to her of a powerful sign that had led him to her grandfather, though he had refused to tell her what it was. And had said, as well, that he owed a debt to the older man. Miriam knew both were a part of it. But deep down inside she knew there was something more – something he wanted as much as she did.

Something they both were afraid to admit.

'Will 'love' keep clothes on your back, or food in your children's bellies? Will 'love' till the fields and bring in the harvest?' her father had asked.

Could love bridge the gap of what they both so desperately desired, and what both she and Copperhead so *desperately* feared?

Shivering with the cold Miriam entered the house and mounted the stair. Martha was still snoring.

Once in her bed Miriam drew the covers over her head and cried herself to sleep.

Judith Kingesley was not the monster she had feared, though the woman was stiff and formal and acted as if she was already the mistress of the house.

Which, in a way, she was.

Miriam lifted the pearl and jewel chatelaine from the belt of her formal lavender chintz closed gown and held it out to the tall dark-haired woman. "This should be yours."

Judith accepted it with a frown. "Didn't William say this was your mother's?"

Miriam nodded. "I have no use for it. Father says I am not capable of running a grand house like this one."

The older woman smiled knowingly and touched her arm. "Pay no attention to what William says, my dear. You will do fine." Judith placed the chatelaine in her hand and closed her fingers over it. "I am not here to take your mother's place. No one could do that. How long has it been?"

"Three months," Miriam answered.

"But a single breath in the span of a life." Judith released her hand and turned toward the fire. Her golden silk gown rustled as she moved to sit in what had been Miriam's mother's chair. Judith's eyes were large and dark and deep brown as her hair. She wore it in the old style, tightly bound at the nape of her neck in a bun, with no powder or pretense. She was not a beautiful woman as her mother had been, but handsome and intelligent. A woman chosen for her merits and not for bedding. "Come sit with me, Miriam," she said suddenly, extending her hand.

Miriam did as she was asked. Lifting her pale purple skirts she sat at Judith's feet. When she had settled in, the older woman caught her chin in her hand and studied her for a moment.

"You are lovely," Judith commented. "Very like your mother if the portraits are accurate. I can only see William in your eyes."

"Yes, Ma'am."

Judith released her and leaned back in the chair. She remained silent a moment and then asked, "Tell me, Miriam, what do you want?"

"I beg your pardon?" she asked, surprised.

"What do you want out of life? You are nearly grown. What direction have you chosen?"

"Well, I...." At a loss for words, Miriam shook her head.

"What? You can speak freely with me," Judith said.

"I wasn't aware I had a choice. Father says I must marry well, and I must marry someone who can take care of me, for I cannot take care of myself."

Judith nodded. She fell silent for a moment and then asked her, "Do you know why your father is marrying me?"

Miriam remained silent. She didn't want to be rude.

Sensing her dilemma, Judith laughed. "You need not be embarrassed. I know I am no great beauty. And though I have been educated I am no scholar either, or great wit. I will not dangle well on William's arm at social events, or shine in the midst of the ladies of London. But what I am is practical. I can run this estate and make it prosper. I can take care of William's children and maybe give him more." Growing sober she added softly, "I know who and what I am, and what it is worth, and Miriam, *that* is how I have survived."

"I don't understand," Miriam replied.

Judith rose from her seat and went to stand before the fire. "I was like you once – young, idealistic. A bit of a dreamer. I believed that one day someone would come and carry me away from the practiced and well-ordered life of monotony I was forced to endure. That he would be a dreamer too, and that our life together would be wonderful and mysterious and exciting." The older woman turned to look at her. "I thought I knew what I wanted. But I was wrong."

Miriam was growing uneasy. "Why are you telling me this – "

Judith held up a hand to silence her. "His name was Ian, and he worked for my father as a joiner. Ian's father was of the aristocracy, but his mother had been a common street wench. His father had other children, a wife, and so Ian was left to make it in the world on his own. He was young and handsome and oh, so clever. He had come from the Scottish Isles and sang like a songbird, sweet and high. My parents objected, of course. So for nearly a year we met in secret. They told me marrying him would ruin both his life, *and* mine. But I didn't listen. *I knew best.*"

A cold hand gripped Miriam's heart. She said nothing, fearing where this was leading.

"It wasn't that Ian was a wastrel or a drunkard or anything bad, but he lacked two things: ambition and position. To survive in this world, Miriam, a man *must* have ambition. He must be willing to overcome, to out-strip, and to overtake all the rest. If not, he will be trampled in the dust. And if he wants a wife, and means to keep her, he must have position. Ian loved me, but it was not enough in the end. He could not take care of me. Finally one day he left and never returned." Judith fell silent.

Miriam couldn't help it. She had to know. "What happened to him? To Ian?"

Her words were hard. "He drank himself to death." Judith knelt on the floor beside her and laid her hand on top of Miriam's own. "Your father does not know this. That is the gift I give to you, to tell you that it is true. If he knew, he most likely would not marry me."

"But why? Why tell *me*?"

"I do so in the hope that I can keep you from making the same mistake."

Miriam pulled her hand away. She rose to her feet. "I don't know what you are talking about."

Judith took hold of her arm. "Martha has spoken to me. Be glad she did not go to your father. This infatuation with the mestizo boy must end. Now."

Chapter Nine

Copperhead was working in the room attached to the studio. He paused in what he was doing when he saw a shadow eclipse the open door. It was late March. The ice and snow were all but gone. Outside the world was blanketed in dew, first frozen, and now set on fire by the rising of the sun. The early morning was his time to be alone with the horses. A time he prized. A time when he felt, just a little, like he was connected to the earth, to the heart of the land....

To his people.

He finished brushing the mane of the dappled white horse that had torn a chunk from her flesh when she had missed a jump during a hunt. She was healed now and this was the last day she would be his. He put the brush in a drawer, spoke a few soft words to her, and then walked into the studio to see who had come. The tall erect figure turned at the sound of his footsteps.

It was William Foxwell.

Miriam's father was dressed as landed gentry this day and not in his British uniform. His parrot-green frock coat was immaculate, his waistcoat ivory, and of a costly brocade fastened with pearl buttons. The riding boots he wore were of a soft-brushed leather that matched the deep umber of his breeches and hat. In his hand was a riding crop. William Foxwell moved like a man who had mastered his domain, but still lacked mastery over himself. The riding crop tapped against his thigh with irritating regularity, and he seemed unable to remain in one place for long.

"Is my father here?" William asked abruptly as he moved into the room.

Miriam's father had been home nearly four weeks, but this was the first time Copperhead had seen him since that night by the fire. Standing as a rock in the center of the other man's nervous pacing, Copperhead replied, "Master George has gone to town. He will return in the early afternoon."

"I see. Well, then, I will be about my business." William Foxwell marched to the door, but once there hesitated and turned back. "You said my father saved your life. How?"

Copperhead was not good at lying. He just wished the other man would go away. "I was shot. He found me."

Foxwell took a step back into the room. "Where?"

"In a field."

He snorted. "You dolt! I don't care if it was in a field or flat on your back in the middle of the Sahara. *Where* did he find you? This colony – or elsewhere?"

Isaac and George Foxwell told the tale of him coming from a place called the 'West Indies'. But he knew nothing of it. Not enough to *begin* to lie. "Here," he answered.

"Here?" William Foxwell spread his arms wide. "Here in this room? Here – a hundred miles away? 'Here' tells me nothing."

Copperhead fought to keep his tone even. "I was unconscious. I do not know. You will have to ask Master George."

"Don't you presume to tell me what I *have* to do, boy!" Miriam's father snarled and advanced on him. Copperhead held his ground as the older man came close, the riding crop gripped in his hand and raised with menace. "I want answers. You will stop this insolent behavior and give them to me, or I will *beat* them out of you. And there is not a court in this land that would find fault with me if I did. Do you understand?"

Copperhead nodded.

"*Do you understand*? Answer me!"

"Yes. Sir."

"That's better." William Foxwell stared at his face, as if searching for something. "Who are you, Josiah Woodward? *What* are you?"

"A man," Copperhead replied. "Like any man."

"A 'man', are you?" Miriam's father gripped his wrist without warning and brought Copperhead's arm up before his face. Then he shoved the linen sleeve back to reveal the golden-brown skin beneath. "This is not the arm of a 'man'. It is the arm of a beast." He twisted the limb and drew him closer. Foxwell's tone was venomous. "A *dark-skinned* beast."

"William!"

Both men turned. Framed by the open door and backlit by the waxing sunlight was George Foxwell. The older man entered the room, saddlebags in hand, and demanded, "What is this all about?"

William Foxwell released Copperhead and took a step back. He seemed to collect himself and then remarked snidely, "I see you know how to lie, *Master* Woodward. You said my father was gone."

"I was," George answered for him as he let the saddlebags fall to the floor. "Though, by the look of things, it seems God's will that I was thwarted on my way. Molly threw a shoe. She is tethered to a tree down the road, near the fork that leads to the town. I have spent the better part of an hour walking back." His eyes went to Copperhead. "Woody, go and fetch her for me. Won't you?"

COPPERHEAD

Copperhead nodded but did not move. His dark eyes sought William Foxwell's face. "Are you finished with me, *sir*?" he asked.

William Foxwell eyed him belligerently. "You may go. I have nothing more to say...." His ice blue eyes flicked to his father. "...to *you*."

As he passed George Foxwell, the older man touched Copperhead's shoulder briefly. "Walk her back *slowly*, Woody. We don't want her to injure her foot."

He nodded. And, with one last glance at Miriam's father who had crossed the room and was fingering one of the books on the table by the cot, exited the door.

George Foxwell peeled off his gloves and tossed them on the table. As he removed his outer coat he asked, exasperated, "William, what is wrong with you?"

"What is wrong with *you*, old man?" his son countered as he slammed the book shut and turned to face him. "You've gone soft in the head if you think you can bring this half-breed here and not suffer the consequences!"

"Who told you he is a half-breed?" George asked as he picked the saddlebags up off of the floor and placed them beside the gloves.

"It's all over the town. As are the vile rumors."

"Rumors?" A wry smile lit George's face as he pushed past his son and headed for the fire. "Since when have you paid attention to rumors, William? God knows there have been enough of them about *you* – and the fancy women of the town."

"This isn't about me, old man. Or my after dinner entertainments. Do you know what is on the lips of every old scandalmonger in the area? Word of 'Foxwell's bastard.' Foxwell's *mestizo*. Even the beggar's children bandy the word about."

George drew a deep breath and turned to look at his son. It was hard. William had his mother's dark wavy hair, and Margaret's narrow chin and crisp blue eyes. But there any similarity ended. His son's mouth was a thin cruel line set by years of adherence to his own strict code of rules, and to punishing any who infringed upon them. William's eyes were like flint, cold and inflexible. George wondered once again where he had failed him. Perhaps being gone too much. Not taking time. But then, a young man has so little time – and old men all too much.

"And does it bother you, William, what the beggars are thinking?" he asked at last.

William bristled. "*That* is not the question, old man. I will not have my honor brought into question just so the pup of some colored game pullet who caught your eye one night while you were in the isles can make a pretense at being white."

"*Your* honor?" George swallowed his anger as he reached for a copper kettle filled with water and suspended it over the fire. The morning was frigid and he needed some tea – with a heavy dose of brandy – to warm him and steady his nerves. "And here I thought you were concerned about me, son."

"I am concerned about the family, old man. They are laughing at us in the town. *Laughing*." William followed him to the hearth. "Don't you care about this family? About Miriam? And James and John? Listen here, I – "

George Foxwell met his son's indignant stare, his own temper flaring. "No! *You* listen!" he countered angrily, jabbing a finger into William's expensive ivory waistcoat. "For the last four years *I* have been here for your children. If you have seen them one day in three hundred during that time, it is a miracle on the order of the parting of the Red Sea! *I* wiped their crying eyes and put salve on their skinned knees. *I* took them hunting and taught them how to ride. Don't you *dare* imply I do not have their best interests at heart – "

"And this is how you show it? By insinuating your red-skinned bastard into their lives? By bringing him here to live among them, and making them a laughing-stock and scandal?" William drew a deep breath to calm himself. Then he asked George point-blank. "Is that *breed* my half-brother?"

George Foxwell was a man of honor. He did not make it a practice to lie. But during the war there had been times when he had had to ask God to forgive him. Times when a lie was the only way to save a man's life, his hopes....

His soul.

He met his son's withering stare and answered, "Yes. He is your brother."

Miriam saw Copperhead in the distance, walking down the lane, leading her grandfather's black mare. She went out to meet him under the pretense of finding out what had happened. Little Anna was with her. Her sister was home now. And not so 'little' anymore. Under their Grandmother Augusta's tutelage Anna had blossomed into a talkative and inquisitive young lady. At almost thirteen, she was older than Miriam had been when Copperhead arrived.

It seemed an age ago.

Miriam introduced Copperhead to her sister as 'Josiah Woodward'. Anna was unusually quiet and blushed as he took her hand and bowed over it. When he offered to allow her to lead the injured animal, she jumped at the chance. Taking Molly's reins Anna quickly outdistanced them, leaving them free to talk.

"We will have to be very careful," she began, walking alongside him. "Judith knows we are friends. That old busybody Martha told her!"

"Does your father know?" he asked.

"Why?" Miriam's breath caught. "Has he been to see you?"

He nodded.

"About me?" she squeaked. But no, Copperhead was still standing and not in shackles, so her father must not know.

He shook his head. "He did not come to see *me*, but your grandfather. But we spoke."

She waited. "And?"

"He does not like me."

"But he doesn't know you!" she protested. "In time – "

Copperhead turned toward her. "Time means nothing to such a man. His hatred runs deep. Like a hot wind it blows before him, leaving barren earth."

Miriam didn't understand. "Why would he hate you? Just because your are – "

"Not white? Yes. That is a part of it." Copperhead raised his hand and waved in response to something. He indicated her sister, walking ahead of them, with a nod. Anna had turned back and was watching them. Miriam waved as well and they quickened their pace. "But there is more to it than that."

"More?"

He hesitated, almost as if embarrassed by what he had to say. "You know of the rumor Isaac and your grandfather have spread?"

She frowned. "No. What rumor? A rumor about you?"

"There had to be some way to explain me. And my presence at the house. Your grandfather served in the West Indies as a young man, guarding prisoners of war. They have encouraged everyone to think I am…George Foxwell's son. His 'bastard' as the people in the town call me." Copperhead's jaw tightened. "And now, your father thinks so too."

Miriam thought about it. "But that would make you and Papa brothers!" she exclaimed.

He nodded. "*That* is why he hates me."

"And we cannot tell him the truth…."

Copperhead indicated the road before them. They were only a few yards from Anna. "For that, he would hate me more."

"Miriam!" Anna called, pointing ahead. "Papa's horse is at the studio. Let's go see him and grandpapa!"

"You go ahead, Anna," Miriam answered, distracted.

Anna scowled at her. Her sister's hair was blonde like her own, but underlying tones of red made it glint like gold in the sun. Anna was bigger boned like Kate had been, and already almost as tall as she was. "Are you not coming, Josiah?" Anna asked sweetly, ignoring Miriam and focusing on him. "Doesn't Molly need to go to the place where you take care of the sick horses? I was hoping we could walk together and you would tell me about yourself. Don't you have some duty to attend to Miriam?"

Copperhead's smile was gentle as he held his hand out for the reins. "Molly is not sick, Anna. I must take her to the farrier for a new shoe. We can…talk later."

The farrier was fortunately on the side of the estate away from both Anna's inquisitiveness *and* her father. Miriam nodded as Copperhead said goodbye and, linking her hand in her sister's, watched until he disappeared around a bend.

When Miriam turned back to look at the studio, her father was standing in the doorway.

Watching them.

William Foxwell leaned heavily on the Georgian mantelpiece that fronted the hearth. The hours had passed speedily enough after his disturbing interview with his father, and he had managed to lose himself *and* his outrage in the day-to-day activities of the estate. But now night had come and he was alone with his thoughts. He didn't know why, but he was still stunned. Somehow all of this seemed so out of character for the old man. Though George Foxwell was an eccentric and prone to ignore the customs and conventions of society, he took the conventions of God seriously indeed. Josiah Woodward could be no more than eighteen, perhaps nineteen years of age at most. That placed his birth date about seventeen-fifty six or seven. William's mother Margaret had still been alive then. And while a man taking his pleasure with some copper-skinned wench on a tour of duty was nothing out of the ordinary – in fact quite the opposite – the image did not fit with that of his father he held in his mind. Perhaps he was being naïve, but William didn't think so. In his heart he knew his father would not have betrayed his mother in that way.

And yet, there was the boy. If he was *not* his father's bastard, then who and what was he? And why would his father go to such lengths to protect him? All of it made very little sense.

"William. I didn't see you there."

He turned and found Judith at the entry of the darkened drawing room, flanked by her lady's maid, Caroline. "What is it, my dear?"

"I came to retrieve my embroidery," she answered. "I can stay. Or would you prefer to be alone?"

Their wedding was set for the first of June, about three months away. There was much to prepare for, and they had wanted to wait until the spring rains had passed and the roads to the manor become accessible. North Carolina as a colony was a loose collection of cities and villages surrounded by a vast wilderness teeming with wildlife and savages. Travel was never easy, but a spring thaw after such a severe winter would render it arduous indeed. William motioned for Judith to join him, and then watched as she sent Caroline to wait at a discreet distance down the hall. It would not, of course, be proper for them to be alone without some sort of a chaperone nearby. He studied his bride-to-be as she crossed the room. She was dressed in a soft open robe of butter-yellow. Judith's hair was loose for once and fell in a dark wave across the shoulders of her white shawl. The style made her appear much younger. He held his hand out. She took it and sat in the chair by the hearth.

"Are you not cold?" she asked, drawing her shawl closer. "Have you been here all evening without a fire?"

"The coals are still alive. I will get new wood and start it again."

Judith's eyes followed him to the wood-box and back as she reached for her embroidery. "I suppose the cold *is* better suited to brooding than a cheerful fire. Are you certain you are ready to banish it?" she asked softly.

As he spread the ashes and adjusted the andirons, he glanced at her. "Am I so transparent?"

She found the needle and began to pull it through the fine linen cloth. "To me."

William straightened up and reached for a log. "You are a wise woman, Judith. What do you think about this matter with my father?"

"Matter?" she asked.

He dropped the log onto the irons with a thud. "The colored boy."

"Oh. Josiah Woodward, you mean?"

"Yes." William reached for the basket of kindling beside the fireplace and, choosing a branch several fingers thick, broke it with a resounding crack over his knee. He placed the pieces under the log and then reached for another one. "Josiah Woodward."

"The young man seems very competent. The horses have never been in finer fettle, or so I am constantly told. McNeil says the boy 'has a way with them'. That he almost speaks to them, and they to him."

William huffed. "Nonsense. You make him sound like some sort of a mystic."

Judith pulled the needle up and sent it sliding through the fabric again. She did not look at him. "Something like that."

"I have spoken with Jackson. Apparently this is not the first time my father has lost all sense of sanity. There was another boy, years ago. Jackson believed him to be a savage. There was some altercation involving the children – Charlotte wrote me about it in lurid detail but actually said very little. That boy died. You would think my father would have learned."

"Your father has a generous heart."

"Generosity is best left for the parson's basket," William growled as he struck a spark with the flint and nursed it into a flame. "The boy is a risk I do not care to take. We have other servants. And many slaves. There is no need for him here. Especially now, with these rumors circulating."

Judith stopped what she was doing. "Rumors?"

Rising, William looked at her. He shook his head. "They are not for a lady's ears."

She laid her needlework in her lap and folded her hands over it. "If I am to be a part of this family, I would like there to be no secrets. I am quite grown and aware of the ways of the world."

He studied her for a moment and then nodded. "Very well. Upon my return I was informed, by no one less than our own priest, that my father had brought his bastard son to live at the house."

"Josiah Woodward, you mean?" Judith asked, growing pale.

"Yes. The child of some strumpet from the Isles." William dropped in the chair beside her. "Dear God! A *half-breed*."

She was silent a moment before she asked, "And do you truly believe this?"

"I don't know *what* to believe any more. The old man says it is so."

Judith's fingers picked at the needlework. She started to speak, but hesitated. Her brown eyes went to the growing fire and then rose to meet his puzzled stare. "Then, we have another problem."

"Another?" William reached for his pipe where it rested in the stand on the table by the chair. He struck it against the bottom of his boot and then reached for the silver jar that held his tobacco. "And *that* would be?"

"Miriam." His future wife drew a deep breath. "She is infatuated with the boy."

"What?" He sat up, pipe in hand. "How long have you known this?"

"Martha brought it to my attention when I first arrived. I talked to her – to Miriam – and told her this must *not* be."

"You should have come to me!" William declared angrily, his voice rising to a shout.

"So you could do what? Just what you are doing now? Yell? Demand! *Deny?*" Judith reached out to touch his hand. "William, that is not the way. The more you tell the child 'no', the more her heart will cry 'yes'."

"I will take the strap to her. To both of them!"

"William. Listen. Please, calm down." Judith placed her hoop on the table and moved to kneel before him. "First of all, if the boy *is* your father's, then we can just tell her. It would be *wrong*. She is a good Christian girl. She would know that." When he said nothing, she added, "But you do not think he is."

He shook his head. "No."

"If that is so, then I *beg* you, let the infatuation die a slow death. Find a reason to send him away. Put time and space between them. Perhaps Miriam could return to school." She squeezed his fingers between her own. "If you tell her she *cannot* have this, it will only make her fight the harder. Trust me on this."

He was not moved. "And you know better than *I* who am her father? You, who have only known her for a fortnight."

"William, I have known Miriam all my life. I am a woman. *You* are not." Judith smiled sadly as she released his hand and stood. She kissed him on the top of the head. "And now, in spite of the lovely fire you have built, I must to bed. But first, promise me you will not do anything rash."

He met her deep brown stare. He should have been furious with her – *would* have been with Charlotte. But there was something about Judith. Something that was *good* for him.

"If you promise you will keep no more of my children's secrets," he answered.

Judith squeezed his hand and answered with a weary smile. "No more than are necessary. Now, good night."

After she left, William Foxwell fell back to brooding. Miriam had always been headstrong and hard for him to understand. Perhaps Judith *was* right. Beating the boy or driving him away would only fire his daughter's misplaced affection and drive her farther from him.

What he needed now was information. If the boy *was* his father's bastard son, then that settled things. Miriam would be told and it would end. If he was not, then he needed to know who and what Josiah Woodward really was, and why his father was protecting him. Perhaps the information could be used to drive Woodward away.

Or to destroy him.

Tomorrow then he would begin. First he would seek out the oldest of the slaves and servants and see what they remembered about this other boy – the one who had died – and then he would speak to those who worked with Josiah Woodward on a daily basis. It should not be long before he knew the whole truth.

And then he would decide what he must do.

Chapter Ten

Miriam overheard her father and Judith making plans for her future; plans that had nothing to do with what she wanted. Plans of which she had no part. She was to be sent back to Scotland to finish school. It was not until the fall session which was nearly half a year away, but the separation from all she loved and cherished loomed before her as a chasm neither hope nor anger could surmount.

What was she to do?

She was just getting to know her sister Anna. Since Kate's death they had grown closer and were becoming friends. And she did not want to leave her grandfather. Grandpa George was nearly seventy years of age. If she went away, there was no guarantee he would be here when she came back.

And then there was Copperhead.

It was early evening and Miriam was sitting by the open window brushing her hair. The night breeze was inviting, scented with jasmine and the promise of the approaching Spring. It rustled the pale moss-green fabric of her closed robe and lifted the ends of her honey-blonde hair, tossing them about so they tickled her cheeks. Martha had told her that sitting by an open window at night was a sin. The old woman had warned her more than once to keep the shutters closed, reminding her mournfully that the night air would be the ruin of her health and send her after her sister and mother to an early grave.

Miriam thought it blather.

Besides, if she *did* get sick, Doctor Wallington was here to look after her. The older man had retired to the country shortly before her mother's death and her father had invited him to settle on land he owned. Of course, Doctor Wallington had echoed Martha's ominous pronouncement when he caught her by the window one evening.

She chose to ignore him. There was something in the night that called to her, insisting the shutters remain cased and the window open. Something that whispered of a freedom from the conventions she had been raised with – a freedom from what Miriam Foxwell was *supposed* to be. She had spent endless hours sitting in her chair gazing out at the forest that bordered the manor with its great gray tree trunks and innumerable leaves, listening to the chatter of its myriad inhabitants, and wondering about the life they shared with the dark-skinned men and women who dwelt so comfortably within its heart. Her father hated the Indians for their lack of discipline and ambition. For what he called their inability to comprehend the necessity of 'getting on in the world'

Miriam lowered her brush to her lap with a sigh. 'Getting on' meant school in Scotland and marriage to someone like Charles Matthew Spencer.

In other words – a cage.

She rose and anchored her brush on the table beside her bed and then stepped out onto the balcony. It was late April and the world was waking, returning to life after a long and weary winter. The moon was waxing gibbous, and its full light revealed tiny chartreuse leaves budding on the old sycamore outside of her window. She had even seen the heads of a few crocuses peeking through in the garden soil the day before. Feeling a sudden need to walk among the growing things, Miriam collected her light cape and tossed it about her shoulders. Then she headed downstairs. She had just reached the front door when she heard her sister Anna calling her. Not wanting to offend her, but desirous of being alone, Miriam faded into the shadows that flanked it and waited as Anna appeared at the top of the stairs. Her sister called her name again. She descended halfway and looked about, and then called a third time. Finally, with a shrug of her shoulders, Anna headed back to her room.

Most nights she would have welcomed Anna's company. But tonight she had much to think about. Laying her hand to the door latch, Miriam lifted it and stepped out into the night.

She was sixteen now and a woman. Many of her childhood friends were already married and starting families of their own, and those who were not were engaged. She had overheard Judith and her father discussing several eligible young men in the area, with the sole purpose of inviting them to the manor over the summer months so that she might 'form an attachment' to one of them. They meant to make a suitable match for her. Miriam frowned as she straightened her cloak. She very much doubted Josiah Woodward would be on their list.

Not that she was quite sure what to do about 'Master Woodward' either.

Copperhead had been in the house very little since her father's return. She had made frequent visits to the studio and stable – with Anna in tow – to see him, but over the last month had found him there less and less often. When she asked her grandfather about it, he explained that Copperhead was handling important business matters for him now. These 'matters' often took him to the town and kept him there. Miriam knew there was some truth in what he said. Even though her father had returned, Grandpa George was still in charge of the horses and involved in the other business operations of the estate. Her father was on leave from the army, but that would not last forever. And he was busy making preparations for the wedding and honeymoon. Often he was home only a few days before being gone again. He had an extended trip planned for the end of this month.

Miriam arrived at her mother's garden and paused just within its confines. The fenced-in plot of earth with its unkempt topiary animals and waterless fountain was in full view of the house. She glanced at the back face of the manor where her sister's window hung east of her own.

If Anna were looking out, she would not be alone for long.

In order to avoid that, Miriam denied the moonlight and sought the anonymity of a pool of shadows cast by the gnarled willow that overhung the manor's guardian wall. Gathering her pale skirts in her hand, she knelt and drove her fingers into the warm earth, seeking a connection. Tender shoots of new life lay buried beneath it, worming their way toward the surface. Their touch brought to mind Copperhead's words – that her mother would be reborn, here, amidst the herbs and flowers she had cherished so dearly.

Miriam wiped away a tear as it formed in the corner of her eye and threatened to spill down her cheek. Copperhead was such a dear friend at times.

And a total stranger at others.

The last time she had talked with him, he had been headed down the lane toward the town and Isaac Watkins' establishment. Copperhead had been preoccupied and had not even noticed her where she waited by the gate, looking for Judith to join her. She and the older woman were going to take a walk. When she called out to him he stopped and greeted her, but seemed anxious to be on his way. She had questioned him about his long absences, but he turned the subject and never really answered. They spoke for about a quarter of an hour, and then he had excused himself and headed for the town.

Something had changed.

She knew Judith had spoken to her father. It didn't really surprise her. If she had been married, she wouldn't have kept secrets from her husband. Still, for a few weeks she had been very angry with the older woman. And yet, whatever Judith had told him, it must have convinced her father that there was nothing between them. Copperhead had not been beaten or driven from the estate.

Though he had, in essence, been banished from the house.

Miriam rose to her feet. She checked Anna's window again and seeing no light or movement, abandoned the shadows and turned toward the studio. Earlier, while sitting at her window, she had seen Copperhead return. He had walked slowly, his chin on his chest, as if his strong shoulders bore the weight of the world. She bit her lip as her gaze returned to the manor house. So far it seemed no one had noticed her nocturnal perambulation. If she could just steal enough time to speak to him....

If Grandpa George was there and denied it, she would simply refuse to leave until he let her in.

Embracing the shadows, Miriam set off for the studio. The rising moon rode the back of a high bank of clouds, shining so brightly it turned the night to day. She kept one eye to the line of trees that flanked the wood and brick building, partially masking it, aware that if there *was* any danger it would most likely come from the river of darkness running at their feet. Just as she reached the stone path that led up to the studio door, something moved in the bushes catching her attention. She froze and waited to see if it would emerge. It did not, but shifted forward far enough that she could see its silver coat and round feral eyes. Against a backdrop of ebon darkness the yellow orbs hung, watching her.

And then were gone.

Miriam leaned against the side of the studio, her heart pounding wildly. She took several deep breaths, seeking to steady her nerves before knocking on the door. If her grandfather thought she had taken a fright, he would march her straight back to the house and that would be the end of it. As she hesitated, cloaked within the studio's cast shadow she heard the sound of the door latch being lifted. Peering around the corner Miriam saw a familiar lean figure emerge. Copperhead was dressed in his work clothes – a heavy linen shirt and breeches with a woolen waistcoat over the top – but had no coat to keep him warm or lantern to light his way. She started to hail him, but something in his manner held her back.

He moved like a man at a crossroads.

Copperhead stared at the three-quarter moon for some time, his hands lifted in supplication. Then he looked to the trees as if expecting – at any minute – someone or something to emerge from them. A moment later he began to pace back and forth. When he finally stopped, his jaw was set. He looked back toward the place he called home, and then he turned and plunged into the dense undergrowth beneath the trees.

Miriam gnawed her lower lip. She knew where she should and *shouldn't* go. But she couldn't lose him – not this way. Gathering her cloak tightly about her throat, she followed quickly, fearful Copperhead would evade her in the thickset trees.

He was moving quickly. Even in the short time she hesitated, he had gained a substantial lead. As she picked her way over the upturned roots and haphazard stones that littered the narrow footpath, Miriam called the wrath of God down upon the man who had decided that a 'proper' woman must wear soft leather shoes and skirts three feet wide.

Unencumbered by such nonsensical fashion her quarry flew fleet as the deer, while she stumbled along, snatched and held back by every stray branch and thorn. For some time she managed to track Copperhead by the flash of his white shirt through the trees and underbrush, but all too soon he outpaced her.

Leaving her forsaken in the heart of the wood.

Miriam stopped and rested her hands on the pocket hoops beneath her skirts. She drew in several great gasps of the crisp night air, hoping to quiet her fast-beating heart. It had been some time since she had run so far, so fast. She turned in a tight circle, inspecting her surroundings, suddenly aware of how vulnerable she was. The forest she had longed for from the safety of her bedroom was not so inviting from within. All about her the bare branches with their fledgling buds creaked and clattered in the wind, and the underbrush rustled and shifted as if filled with unseen threat. Miriam tried to identify some landmark – anything she recognized – but soon realized there was nothing to be seen but nameless and numberless trees.

She started to panic, but then remembered something her father had taught her. She had thought him mad at first. One warm summer's night he had awakened her and her sister Kate and brought them with him into the woods. She could have been no more than six or seven. After shuttering the single lantern he carried, leaving them clinging to him in the dark, her father had explained that the threat of Indian attacks was very real, and that flight into the trees might very well be their only hope. After that he had shown them how to use the stars and the moon to plot a course home. Kate had cried the whole time, but Miriam had listened –

And learned.

She looked up through the clashing branches and located the swollen moon. Fast-moving clouds had overtaken it, masking its lower half. That, along with a strengthening wind portended a heavy rain soon to come. If she didn't hurry, she would get thoroughly soaked and end up needing Dr. Wallington's ministrations after all.

After determining what course she must take, Miriam cast one final glance in the direction Copperhead had gone. She wondered what had drawn him to the woods this night and, if she asked him later, what he would tell her. Somehow she doubted it would be the truth.

He had shut her out. Almost as if he were pulling away.

Weary but determined, Miriam began to work her way back through the trees toward the house. Cloud-shadow now concealed the trail, making the way even more treacherous than before. She had to go very slowly so as not to trip or lose her balance and plunge into some hidden ravine. About half an hour into the journey she stopped to catch her breath, and it was then she realized –

She was not alone.

Something or *someone* was pacing her. She began walking again, listening carefully, and then halted and bent, making a pretense of shaking a stone from her shoe. Whoever it was stopped when she stopped. And not long after she began to move again, she heard the soft fall of footsteps matching her own. Even though a relative novice to the wood, Miriam was not unschooled in its lore. Recalling the feral eyes that had watched her from the underbrush beside the studio she quickened her pace, certain she was being stalked by a wild animal.

Her father had also taught her that a sure steady pace was her best protection. Screaming or flying pell-mell through the trees would only increase an animal's interest – and the scent of fear, its appetite. So for another quarter of an hour she walked as if unafraid. But when the unseen creature snarled and snapped, and she heard its heavy body break through the underbrush behind her, such lessons were soon forgotten.

Miriam panicked and began to run.

She had not gone far when the heel of her leather shoe caught on a sizeable stone and broke off. Thrown off balance by the loss, Miriam tumbled to the ground, tearing her skirts and scraping her hands and knees. As she lay in the dirt, panting, she heard something move onto the trail behind her. Terrified, she turned and looked. It had a silver coat and was very large, with pointed ears and a long snout.

And great round eyes the color of October corn.

Miriam stumbled to her feet, keeping her eyes on the monstrous wolf. She had no weapon, but knew if she looked the forest would provide one. Backing away from the creature with its slavering jaws, she searched the ground for something – *anything* – she could use: a branch, a stone, a sharp stick. As she spotted the rock that had felled her and knelt to retrieve it, a further rustling in the underbrush made the gesture futile.

A half dozen shadowy forms emerged from the trees to circle her. At first, Miriam feared it was the rest of the pack.

It wasn't.

These shadows walked on two legs.

It was late but Judith Kingsley could not sleep. She was troubled in her heart about a number of things. Not the least of which was the note she held in her hand. William had left it for her, placing it on her robe beside the bed. She could still feel his kiss on her cheek....

He had planned a trip to the capital for late April, early May. William intended to ask the commandant there for an extended leave and, while he was in New Bern, to complete the preparations for their upcoming nuptials. 'But', the letter said, 'unexpected events' had compelled him to leave early. He cautioned her to keep close to the house, to mind the children – especially Miriam – and ended with the unsettling fact that he had ordered several of his men to remain behind to patrol the perimeter of the estate in his absence. They would check in with her in a day or two when ready to take up their positions. William added as well in a postscript that he would write her as soon as possible with more news.

Judith laid the note in her lap and leaned her chin on her hand. Did these 'unexpected events' have anything to do with Josiah Woodward she wondered? Since informing William of the budding relationship between the young man and Miriam, he had become obsessed. As they had discussed, he had quickly put an end to their daily encounters by transferring Josiah to the stable. And Miriam was set to return to school in the fall. But it didn't end there. Judith knew William had canvassed the servants, bullying them in an attempt to find out all he could about the young man his father had brought home. And when it seemed Josiah Woodward *had* no past, William had stretched the power of his authority as a servant of the King and ordered several of his men to backtrack and find out where Josiah had come from and what he might be hiding. Judith laid the note on the desk and tapped it with her finger. It was possible William only sought to prove the young man's parentage, hoping to eliminate his own father as the sire. But somehow she doubted it. Bastard children, whether white or colored, were nothing new to the aristocracy even though the law frowned upon them. Her own father had several. No, there was something troublesome – and more sinister – about William's interest in the young man.

And the only cause she could think of was his relationship with Miriam.

How William's middle girl reminded her of herself! Headstrong and prideful. Dissatisfied with the status quo. Intelligent. *Too* intelligent for a world where a woman's duty was to hang off of a man's arm and glitter for a day, while enduring endless months of misery and monotony alone.

It was not a life *she* would have chosen, had she any choice.

With a sigh Judith straightened up and reached for the candle that rested near the pile of papers stacked neatly on the desk. She really should get to bed. For some reason, she hesitated to have the day draw to a close – almost as if she sensed something ominous in the one to come. Shaking off such foolish nonsense, Judith rose to her feet and turned.

Just in time to see a shadow pass the door.

"Caroline? Is that you?" she called, lifting the half-spent candle. When there was no reply, she took a step toward the hall. "Martha?"

The shadow returned. A sheepish and mildly chagrinned George Foxwell followed it, stepping into the room and the meager circle of her candle's light. George was haphazardly dressed. His stock collar was askew and – though she could not be certain – Judith thought his boots unmatched.

"George? What brings you to the house?"

"I am sorry if I frightened you, Judith," he said, removing his hat.

"Startled, perhaps. But not frightened. We see you all too infrequently. I hope it has not taken some trouble to bring you to the house...."

He shook his head. "No. No." George's hand trembled slightly as he raised it to his forehead and ran fingers through his tousled hair. "Have you seen Josiah tonight?" he asked without preamble.

Judith shook her head. "No. Should he be here?"

He laughed nervously. "I thought he might. I seem to have misplaced him."

"Should I check on Miriam?" she asked suddenly. Her eyes went to the note that lay open on the desk. 'Stay close to the house,' William had warned. If the girl had run away to some tryst in the woods.... Judith started toward the tapestry bell-pull. "I'll send for a servant," she said.

George moved quickly and caught her hand. "No. I have spoken to Josiah about that. There will be no more midnight rendezvous." He met her dubious stare as he released her. "How long have you known? About the two of them?"

"Since shortly after my arrival." Judith studied him for a moment and then decided to take him at his word. At least for now. She was interested in speaking to William's father and interviews such as this were rare indeed. The older man had grown quite reclusive and seldom left his studio for reasons other than business. Returning to the desk, she picked up the letter and folded it, placing it safely within the embroidered pocket tied at her waist. Then she sat down. Indicating a chair close by, she said softly, "Please, George. *Father*. Join me."

His ice blue eyes went to the drawing room door. He gazed longingly at it as if anxious to escape but did as she asked, taking the seat before the empty hearth that William usually occupied.

"Did Miriam tell you?" he asked.

She shook her head as she folded her hands in her lap. "No. By word and look it was not hard to deduce. I found myself in a...*similar* situation many years ago. I told her so. And I told her it *must* not be." Judith paused and then added with some fire. "I am surprised you allowed this to occur."

"Allowed?" George laughed again as he settled back in the chair. "Where Miriam and Josiah are concerned, there is no such thing as 'allowed'. In the beginning it was simply a childhood friendship. I am not convinced it is *anything* more than that now. Still – "

She shook her head. "It is more. Or very close to being more. Take my word for it."

He was silent a moment. Then he asked, "And William? Does he know?"

"Miriam is his daughter," she answered.

The older man nodded. "Just so."

"And the young man," Judith began, settling her piercing brown eyes on his face, "*is* he your son?"

William's father shifted. If he spoke the truth, it did not sit comfortably with him. "Yes. He is."

"And you have permitted this infatuation with Miriam to grow, even though he would be her uncle? Why not tell her and have it over with? It is irresponsible – and immoral – to allow it to continue."

George pulled at his collar. Though the late night had proven somewhat chill, at least within the house, sweat beaded on his forehead. "They are children," he replied and then fell silent.

Judith rose. She crossed to where he sat and looked down at him. "*No*. They are not. And the young man is not your child either, is he?"

Her soon to be father-in-law looked up at her. He blinked as though confused. For a moment it seemed he could not form the word and then he asked, "What?"

"Josiah Woodward – if that *is* his name – is not your son. Is he? Or William's brother? You are not the kind of a man who would allow Miriam to form a romantic attachment to a blood relative. And there is something about that young man – I do not think he comes from the West Indies. My father had several servants from Bermuda. He does not put me in mind of them." Judith knelt beside his chair and laid her hand on his. "Who is he, George? And why are you protecting him, to the possible detriment of your family?"

George Foxwell seemed to come back to himself. He placed his other hand on top of hers and patted it. "I like you, Judith," he said. "William is fortunate to have found you."

She was not about to be put off subject. "Answer my question, George. Who is he?"

For a moment he was silent, then – sounding incredible weary – he asked her, "Do you believe in miracles, Judith?"

Without a moment's hesitation she answered, "Yes."

He nodded. "That young man is a miracle. I should never have found him. He should *not* have lived." George raised a hand to his head and rubbed his temple. Then he massaged his upper arm with a frown. "There is something for him yet. I know it. Something only we can give him – "

"Are you all right?" Judith asked him suddenly. He had grimaced as if in severe pain and closed his eyes.

"A sudden ache in the head," he answered, his voice weak. "I cannot see clearly." George rose, but wobbled. As Judith caught him and lowered him back to the chair, he added, "I think I had best go to my bed...."

"What? What is it?"

"Dear Lord," he whispered. "I can't feel my arm."

Seconds later he was slumped against her, unconscious.

"George!" The sudden impact of his solid frame almost carried her to the floor. "Martha! Martha! Fetch Doctor Wallington! Quickly!"

The circle was tightening.

Miriam held very still as the furtive figures moved from shadow to light, revealing themselves to be neither wolves nor brigands, or highwaymen as she had feared –

But Indians.

From what little she had overheard of her father's conversations regarding the native population of their colony, she thought them to be warriors. Tall and powerfully built, their faces were tattooed with shapes – animal, flower and star. They were dressed in a combination of colonial and native attire. All wore cloth shirts, most with legging-moccasins, though at least one was barelegged. His painted and oiled skin shone a deep blue as he stepped into the waxing moonlight. For the most part their heads were shaved and mounted with deerskin roaches, the tails of which trailed down their backs and onto their shoulders. Around their throats a few sported silver gorgets of British import, but most wore simple shells. Brightly painted bags hung from their broad shoulders and the belts at their hips held an assortment of knives and striking weapons, as well as pistols. Several had muskets.

They looked as if bent toward war.

Miriam remained seated in the dirt as one of the Indians stepped forward. Over his shirt and leggings, he wore a heavy cloth robe with a braided edge. He was an older man – perhaps her father's age – and seemed to be the leader. Copper rings encircled his arms. One ear had been slit as was their custom and stretched so as to appear gigantic – the thick sliver of skin that hung at the bottom near his collar was also banded with copper. Near his feet a furred form moved, weaving in and out of the shadows. Miriam gasped as a frighteningly familiar pair of yellow-gold eyes fastened on her.

With a snarl the wolf leapt forward.

"Ha-le!" The Indian in the robe barked a command and the animal halted. It whimpered as he scolded it and brought its head close to the ground. Then it backed off. Miriam could see now that it was not a wolf as she had thought, but some sort of a large dog that resembled one – or perhaps a mixture of the two. The savage touched its head affectionately as he moved past it and came to stand before her. Extending a finger, he pointed at her and asked a question. When she did not answer, the Indian grew impatient and asked it again, his tone harsh.

Miriam shuddered. Each unintelligible syllable he uttered fell into the silence of the forested world like the chop of an ax on a block. "I'm sorry," she replied, trembling. "I don't know what you are asking me."

"Yo-ne-ga," the robed Indian remarked to someone behind him.

"V-v," the other man replied.

That one Miriam *had* heard. 'Yo-ne-ga' was Cherokee and it meant 'white' or 'English'. The question was – was that good or bad? Her father had told her that most Cherokee were friends of the British. But, he warned, there were renegades. From the look on the robed man's tattooed face it seemed the word left a sour taste in his mouth.

Stepping back, the leader beckoned the other man forward. The Indian who emerged from his shadow was not so muscle-bound as his compatriots and was, perhaps, half a foot shorter than the one who had spoken to her. The waxing moonlight revealed a clerkish figure – a thin, studious man wearing a tattered frock coat and, of all things, glasses! His hair was not shaved, but was close-cropped, as if he sometimes wore a wig.

"Who are you?" he demanded.

"You speak English?" Miriam replied, mightily relieved.

"Yes. Who are you?" His words were clipped. His tone, brusque.

"My name is Miriam," she answered, hesitating to use her father's surname. William Foxwell had a reputation for cold calculation in war and had made many enemies among the various tribes. These men could very well number among them. "Miriam Colbert," she concluded, claiming her mother's maiden name instead.

The man with the glasses turned to the Indian in the robe and translated what she had said. Then he turned back to her.

"I am called Two Worlds, for I have walked with both the Yo-ne-ga and Tsalagi. You will stay with me until we arrive at the camp." He looked over his glasses, pinning her with his eyes "Now, you will tell me what you are doing here."

Miriam glanced at the men surrounding them. Some faces were curious, but most were openly hostile. Many had weapons in their hands. "I was taking a walk. I became lost," she answered, choosing to employ at least a part of the truth. She looked past the translator to the Indian in the robe. The older man had not stopped staring at her since they had overtaken her. His interest was beginning to make her nervous. "What are *you* doing here?" she asked him, growing bold. "I doubt you are walking about in the wood for your health this time of night."

Two Worlds hesitated, and then translated her question.

At first the man in the robe seemed angered, but then he laughed heartily and struck the translator's back so hard he knocked Two Worlds' glasses down to the tip of his nose. As the clerkish Indian shoved them back into place, the native in the robe grabbed his crotch and thrust forward, speaking words that made the others in the party roar with laughter.

Miriam felt her face go red.

Two Worlds eyed him with displeasure and then turned back to her. He spoke quietly, "If you knew why we are here, it would mean your death." Then he raised his voice and added, "Green Snake admires your courage. He says you would make a handsome wife. Now, stand up. It is time to go."

Miriam shivered and pulled her cloak tightly about her throat as Two Worlds offered her his hand. The wind was out of the north and unseasonably chill. And the promised rain had at last begun to fall. "Please, let me go," she pleaded, squeezing his fingers. "I won't tell anyone I have seen you."

"I am afraid that is impossible. You *have* seen us. You must be silenced – one way or another," Two Worlds replied, menace and regret mingling in his tone. He indicated the circle of warriors surrounding them with a nod. "They await only one word from Green Snake. Just *one* and you would be dead." He pulled his hand from hers as she gained her feet. "You live now, only because you have not screamed or tried to escape."

Miriam wanted to. *Very* much. And in truth she had *not* screamed only because she knew it would be useless. No one would hear her. Everyone at the manor was asleep.

Asleep. And vulnerable.

"If it is your intention to attack the house, there is no need," she said, suddenly fearing for Anna and Judith, and even the silly old busybody Martha. "If it is money you want, or liquor, then take me home. I can get it for you without bloodshed – "

"A-ye-ga-li!" The man in the robe drew a hand across his throat in a curt gesture calling for silence.

Miriam needed no translation. Fear had made her tongue run. She closed her mouth and did as she was told.

Two Worlds spoke briefly to Green Snake. The tone of his words was apologetic and somewhat fawning. After a moment Green Snake nodded and then turned to speak to his men. The translator turned back toward her and studied her. Miriam used the ever-increasing moonlight to do the same with him. Two Worlds was definitely a man of mixed parentage. His face was narrow. The bones of his face gaunt and high. His eyes were light; his nose thin and straight, though it looked as if it had once been broken. She could not see the color of his skin clearly as the moonlight painted everything and everyone a silvery-blue, but she would have guessed it to be a light gold. Lighter even then Copperhead's.

Where *was* Copperhead?

"You are a woman of some means and intelligence," Two Worlds said finally. "You know these lands belong to the People. We have no interest in the white man's liquor or his money. What we want are *no more* white men." Two Worlds touched the flintlock pistol at his waist. "The People grow soft and weak because of the influx of easy goods. No longer can we provide what we need for ourselves. No longer can a warrior live off the land alone" He removed the pistol and pointed it at her. "When one has seen a musket, Miriam Colbert, how can he go back to the arrow and bow?"

Green Snake spoke commandingly from behind the translator, his tone indicating a need for haste. He whistled and called the wolf dog that had fallen asleep on the path and, as the animal rose to follow, the robed native plunged into the rustling trees.

The other warriors did the same, leaving her alone with Two Worlds and his pistol – which was still pointed at her chest.

The rain was coming in waves now. Thunder rumbled in the distance. She had not seen any lightning yet, but the angry night promised it would come. "What is to become of me?" Miriam asked.

"That has much to do with what happens next," Two Worlds answered, waving the flintlock toward the trees and the dark ingress his fellows had taken. "We go to the meeting place. It is there your fate will be decided."

Chapter Eleven

Judith extinguished the candle and then backed away from the bedside table to stare at the man who lay on the feather ticking, his breathing labored, his color gray as the dawning morn. Dr. Wallington had come and gone, as had the night. George Foxwell, it seemed, suffered from a softening of the brain. The condition had resulted in apoplexy and for the moment, her husband's father could not speak. Couldn't even move.

Though she did not know him well, it was painful to see the tall, once healthy and vigorous man reduced to the state of an unweaned babe. Along with a silent stream of slaves, she and Martha were taking turns caring for him. The doctor said there was hope for recovery.

But it was slim.

Drawing a deep breath, Judith turned away and crossed to the window to look out on the new day. She had not slept at all and her vision was blurred as the water-colored world outside. The night's storm had given way to a gentle rain – the kind that brings renewed life – and the sun was fighting valiantly to break through. Before returning to George's room to check on him, she had made her way to Anna's, and then Miriam's. William's middle girl was still missing. Her bed had not been slept in.

She wondered now if Miriam and the young man, Josiah, had chosen to run away together. Perhaps her interference – telling William – had pushed them into it. If so, it was an ill omen for the marriage.

Judith shook herself and moved back into the room. She walked to the end of the bed and stared at the pitiful creature it held for a moment before turning away, tears in her eyes. Just as she reached the door she stopped. There had been a sound. A rustling of fabric, a sigh.

Something….

Returning to her soon to be father-in-law's side, she leaned over the bed and took his hand. "George? Father? Can you hear me?"

For a moment there was nothing. Then his chest rose and fell with a single deeply drawn breath. He blinked several times and a moment later, opened his eyes.

She pressed his hand tightly between her own. "George? Can you hear me?"

A pause, and then a very slight movement of his head. Almost a nod.

Judith smiled as tears spilled down her cheeks. "Thank Providence! Can you speak?"

George shifted ever so slightly. His jaw moved and his mouth opened, but no sound emerged. She kept a pewter cup with water beside the bed. She sat beside him now and lifted his head and placed it against his lips. He was able to drink, though the most of the liquid spilled over his chin and ran down his neck, soaking his collar. She daubed his chin with her handkerchief and then placed the cup back on the stand. Then she took his hand again and waited as he worked his lips. A few strangled sounds emerged.

"Take your time. The doctor says it may takes days," she said softly. Or months, she thought to herself. Or years.

Or maybe never.

George's right hand balled into a fist. She placed her own over it and smiled sadly. He was fighting. There was fire in his eyes. And anger. Anger and frustration at his own helplessness.

"Is there something I can get you?" she asked, releasing him and rising to her feet. "I can have Martha bring some soup – "

He shook his head.

"Wine, perhaps?"

No, again. More emphatically.

The older man began to grow agitated. Dr. Wallington had warned her that a softening of the brain could sometimes alter people in unexpected ways. The meek could become lions; those once gentle, hard and cruel. She studied him for a moment, fearful that this had happened, and then realized George's right hand was opening and closing as if seeking something. She frowned, and then it dawned on her.

If he could not speak – perhaps he could write.

"A pen?" she asked. "And paper?"

The fight seemed to go out of him. He didn't nod, but she knew that was what he had meant.

"Just a moment."

She had to go to her room which was nearby to fetch some ink, a quill, and parchment. She returned with it and placed the paper on the bed beneath George's hand. Then she dipped the quill and held it in his fingers that she formed for the purpose. When he finished, it was a barely legible scrawl and the effort had cost him dearly. George closed his eyes and fell into a deep restless sleep.

Judith took the paper and walked to the window to examine it. It held only one word.

'Copperhead'.

He was free.

Copperhead sat near the center of a bark and branch lodge, stripped of the white world's clothes and conventions, cleansed of its stench and released from its expectations and insanity.

Free.

For the last six months he had been keeping company with his own kind. At Isaac Watkins establishment he had met Two Worlds, also known as Joseph Samuels. They had struck up a conversation and soon learned they had much in common. At first Two Worlds visits had been infrequent and unexpected. But then the slender man with wire-rimmed glasses began to appear regularly and later, brought others with him. One night after completing his work, he left the tavern to find them waiting for him. Two Worlds invited him to come with them, and then led the group to the edge of the town where they entered the woods. Traveling with them Copperhead had felt as clumsy as one of the elephants in the tales of the Arabian Nights George Foxwell read to him when he was young. The men moved through the leafy underbrush like kindred shadows. The group arrived at a clearing deep in the heart of the forest just as the moon tipped the top of the trees. There he had been introduced to Green Snake, the leader of their clan.

And his life began again.

He and Two Worlds were of the same bloodline. Their mothers' mothers had been cousins. Two Worlds knew of Walker, his grandfather. The old man was still alive. And Two Worlds informed him that the tale of his own bravery in defying the chief and setting out to avenge his murdered family was still told. Two of Copperhead's friends had survived that day and carried the tale back to the People. His story was repeated around the fire and served as inspiration to young men who sought to rid their home of the white menace that was overtaking the wood and the water and the green grass in an unholy blight.

Two Worlds words shamed him.

He had not been a hero. He had not even done what he set out to do. And for the last five years he had lived as a white man and loved a woman born of one.

Even though he had never told her so.

Green Snake's band had accepted him as family and then, begun his reeducation. On the long trips to town he spent his nights not at the inn as he told George Foxwell, but stripped bare and running with his brothers in the wood, learning again to hunt, to track.

To kill.

He had not yet killed a man, but he had seen it done. Green Snake had ordered raids on several farms, burning the white men's cabins and barns to the ground, and killing all the stock and settlers within. Copperhead had watched from the sidelines, not yet trusted enough to participate. But that was to change…

Tonight.

He sat now in the healer's lodge, his hands on his knees, palms turned upward in supplication. Outside the light was dawning. The hard male rain of the day before had ended, giving way to a shower that caressed the earth with the gentle power of a woman, seeking to soothe and heal. Another reason he had not been included so far was that Green Snake sensed the conflict within him. He had sent him here the night before to cleanse himself of the taint of the white man's world.

Free.

Or was he?

Copperhead tossed off the skin blanket that covered his legs and slowly rose to his feet. He stretched and reached for the blue hunting frock Two Worlds had given him as a gift. Donning it over the breechcloth and moccasin leggings he wore, he fastened a beaded belt about his waist to hold his weapons, and then finished with a leather bandoleer that held both powder and lead balls. He was never going back. As of this moment, he *was* Tsalagi.

As he approached the door, he heard a commotion erupt outside the lodge. Green Snake's camp was set deep within the untamed wilderness. Farms and houses were few and far between, and settlements even more so. No one could hear them – even if they whooped and shouted with all of their power. And that was what the men he lived with now were doing. He heard shouts of triumph, cries of conquest, and the grunts and groans that spoke of the hunger of men's loins.

With a frown Copperhead shoved aside the blanket that covered the door and stepped into the dawning day. He noted the expressions of Green Snake's men who watched him as he quickly crossed the camp. Some were welcoming. Others wary. And some, openly hostile. It would take time and action to prove himself – to prove that he had not been altered or changed by the many moons he had spent living among their foes.

As Copperhead approached the edge of the clearing he spotted Two Worlds. His friend stood apart from the chaos of greased and painted bodies, and the clamor of the laughter and boastful cheering that arose from them. Two Worlds spoke as if he was of the People, but admitted there were things that bothered him. He did not care for unnecessary killing. And he did not believe in blood vengeance, saying revenge only led to further violence and – when it came to the People – gave the white man an excuse to exterminate them and wipe their memory from the face of the earth.

Two Worlds caught his eye and slowly shook his head. He signaled to him that he should not speak.

Curious, Copperhead halted at his friend's side to observe the frantic show. Green Snake's men had formed a circle. Many of them were stomping and shouting. He could not understand the words. Several ducked in and out of the circle as if tormenting whatever lay trapped within. As he watched one emerged with a pale ribbon in his hand, shouting with triumph. Another snatched it from him and the two began to tussle in the mud while others cheered and jeered and taunted, making wagers on which would lose. By chance the ribbon ended near his feet. Copperhead bent to examine it. It was made of a costly fabric – silk most likely – and was a pale green. Frowning, he moved forward, determined to discover what lay at the center of such insanity.

It was a woman. A *white* woman.

The pitiful creature lay on the ground, trembling. Her hair was a pale golden-yellow and her tattered gown – what was left of it – a soft moss green like the ribbon in his hand. Her fingers clawed at the earth as though she sought to escape into it. Her feet were bare and bloody. As he watched one of the men, a fierce warrior and survivor of many battles named 'Bear', caught the woman's hair in his hand and lifted her head. Drawing his knife, he sliced a good eight inches of it off and thrust the trophy into the air with a cry of triumph.

The woman screamed and sat up, raising her dirt and blood stained hands into the air as if to retrieve it.

Two Worlds gripped his arm and held him back. "Do nothing," he whispered as Copperhead saw her face.

It was Miriam.

"Colonel Foxwell?"

His brooding interrupted, William Foxwell pivoted and glared at his current aide, Lieutenant Jedidiah Nevilles. "What is it?"

"Sir! The intelligence you were expecting. Sir!"

William nodded as the young man handed him a packet of letters, signed and sealed with the insignia of the Royal Army. "Dismissed, Nevilles. Return to patrol."

"Yes, sir!" The lieutenant saluted smartly, turned on his heel, and marched off.

The small contingent of men of which he and Jedidiah Nevilles were a part, were distributed thinly through the nearby trees, searching for signs of a renegade band of Indians. William Foxwell watched his aide march smartly across the packed earth floor and out of the farmhouse they had commandeered, a half-concealed smile on his lips. Nevilles would make a fine officer one day. He knew the value of proper conduct and order.

And how to *fear* his commander.

As he broke the seal, William Foxwell sat at his desk. He had chosen the farm for his headquarters as it sat on the northern edge of the great wood, not ten miles from his own home. Perhaps a half day's steady jog. He had been to the capital but had returned here in secret. Danger and threat were in the air. The Cherokee renegades in the area were intent on malicious mischief – determined to cause as much damage as they could to the white settlers and their property. These young malcontents had nothing in their heads but glory and a desire for gore, and were a waste of the food it took to feed them and the very air they breathed.

William perused the notes one by one, nodding or shaking his head at their content, until he came to the final two. One was from Judith. He set it aside in order to attend to the last one in the packet. It came from one of the men he had sent to Pennsylvania to inquire into Josiah Woodward's background. Pursing his lips, William broke the seal and quickly read its contents, and then tossed it on the desk. As he suspected there was no record in any church or parish of the boy – though that meant little, only that he was not of noble birth. His father claimed the boy had been born in the West Indies anyway. In retracing the old man's steps as best they could, using military records and purchase orders, his men had found out only that George Foxwell had taken a leave of absence and when he returned, the boy had been with him.

The only tidbit, the only morsel of news meaty enough to chew on – horrific as it was – was a statement from a German farmer who said he had provided lodging overnight in his barn at about the same time for a man in a red coat who went by the name of 'George' and a wounded Indian boy. When asked how he knew the boy was 'Indian', the farmer said he had seen the paint and heard the boy muttering in what he believed was the Cherokee tongue.

An *Indian*!

Damn the old man! What was he thinking?

William Foxwell crushed the letter in his hand and flung it across the room. The farmer's wife who was feeding and looking after them while they occupied her house looked up from her chores with a question in her eyes. The letter had fallen near the blazing hearth. He hesitated, but then nodded when she asked him if he wanted to save it. Taking the vile thing in his fingers, William smoothed it out and placed it in his satchel, and then turned the key in the lock, sealing it away from prying eyes. Then he took up Judith's note. He noticed immediately the haste with which it had been addressed. His last name was spelled incorrectly and there were several drops of excess ink on the face. Puzzled, he looked again. It *was* Judith's hand.

Such carelessness was uncharacteristic for her.

Frowning, he broke the seal and opened the letter and began to read.

'William, come home,' Judith's high, noble cursive begged, 'your father may be dying....'

"No!" Two Worlds warned, gripping his arm. "Do nothing."

Copperhead struggled to break free, but his friend held him fast. "But it is *Miriam*! I can't – "

His friend's teeth were clenched. He whispered through them. "Yes, you *can*." Two Worlds nodded toward the edge of the chaotic circle of frenzied warriors. Green Snake was there, watching with satisfaction, a broad grin painted on his darkly tanned face. "I thought that was who she was. She gave another name. Copperhead, my *brother*, you are no longer a part of her world. Let her go."

"I will not let Miriam be abused or harmed – even if I *am* no part of her world! Release me!" Copperhead's knife was free of its leather sheath and rested in his hand. "*Now!*"

Two Worlds forced him to meet his eyes. "Mark me. This action will prove to them where your loyalties lie. Take care which side you choose."

Copperhead cringed as he heard Miriam cry out. "She is a woman!"

"She is *nothing*. Tonight you might be ordered to burn her home to the ground. To kill her sisters and brothers. To put them *all* to the knife."

Another scream from Miriam decided it. Copperhead broke free and with a fearful cry of pent up rage and pain, plunged into the melee. Miriam was on the ground sobbing hysterically. What was left of the bodice of her green gown had been ripped. The laces of the stays beneath had been slashed and the remnants of both fell loosely about her breasts. She struggled to hold them closed. When Copperhead reached her, he planted one foot firmly in the wet earth on either side of her prone form and challenged them all.

"You say, my brothers, that you are *not* the animals the white men claim!" He caught the eye of several of them, the brutish Bear included. "I say you are wrong! If this were a deer you would not torture it so. The kill would be clean. You are cowards! *Cowards*, every one!"

A general chorus of outrage and anger was his reply. He knew he had insulted them, but he had also called the men on their honor. Simply appealing to them for mercy would have done no good. Too many of them had lost family members – friends, lovers – to the white man. Male, female, young or old, whites were the enemy and they were to be conquered, destroyed, defeated, and driven out.

Miriam was the enemy.

As he stood there, breathing hard, every muscle tense and alert, Bear stepped forward and thrust the truncated lock of golden-blonde hair in his face and then turned and held it out to the mob. "I do not wish to kill this woman," he proclaimed, striking his chest. "I claim her!"

Copperhead glanced down. Miriam had been sobbing, but now she had grown quiet. Her pale face was turned sideways so the dawning light struck it, illuminating a countenance both fearful and wretched. Then, as he watched, she passed out.

Looking up he met Bear's hungry stare. "No."

"No?" Bear repeated, coming closer. The powerful warrior's lustful hunger had deepened into one for blood, and Copperhead could see his death in his eyes. "And what will you do, son of the white man's world, to stop me from taking her?"

Bear was twice his size and nearly twice his age. In the world of the People if you were more than thirty years old then you knew how to kill, and kill with ease. And how to survive. The life of the Tsalagi seldom afforded the luxury of becoming an old man.

Copperhead drew several deep breaths and centered himself, driving the image of Miriam's battered and abused form beneath his feet from his mind. He shifted into a striking position and brandished his knife. "If you want her, you will have to go through me to get her."

A slow sneer crept across Bear's dark face, drawing his lips up and baring his teeth. "From the first day Two Worlds brought you to us, I did not trust you. If I thought you were a man, wanting to use this woman for your pleasure, I could respect you enough to fight you for her. But you are weak." Bear pivoted sharply and addressed the hushed mob. "He is *weak*! The white man's world contaminates him! No matter how many days he passes in the healer's lodge, he will *never* be clean." Bear turned back and spat in Copperhead's face. His voice was acid. "I will not fight you...."

"But I will gladly kill you."

The spittle trailed down Copperhead's cheek and onto his shirt, but he ignored it, focusing on the movements of the tall warrior before him. There would be some sign before Bear struck – a twitch of his lips, a sudden tensing of his muscles – something. And that small edge might be all he would have.

Bear stepped away from him and bellowed a name. One of his circle of warriors handed him a rifle with the pan open and primed. With a vicious smile Bear closed the metal lid and, placing his finger on the trigger, spun and pointed the musket at his chest.

"Where is the honor in this?" Two Worlds shouted, approaching the pair. "Bear! Tell me!"

The rifle did not waver as Bear sighted along it. "He is a dog and will die as one."

"Put the rifle...down."

Copperhead's gaze shifted from the primed barrel of death pointed at him to Green Snake, who had spoken – in English. The clan leader had observed the growing tension between them with keen interest, but said nothing until now. Bear stiffened at the command, resisted, and then did as he was told, dropping the point of the musket but not relinquishing the gun. Green Snake approached Bear. With his hand the Tsalagi leader forced the barrel into the wet ground.

Then he turned to him.

Copperhead was breathing hard and feeling light-headed. In preparation for his night in the healer's lodge he had not eaten or taken drink since noon the day before. The rush of adrenaline upon seeing Miriam in danger had carried him through, but now he had to fight just to keep from shaking.

Green Snake stopped before him. He said nothing, but held Copperhead's gaze as if reading what lay inside. Then his eyes went to Miriam. "What is ...the Yo-ne-ga woman ...to you?" he asked.

Green Snake's English was broken and he seldom used it. Copperhead wondered why he did so now.

To make a point?

"She is nothing to me," he lied, answering in kind. "But she does not deserve to be abused. We are *not* animals." His gaze flicked to Bear who was leaning on the rifle, seething.

"She is da-na-da-s-ka-gi," the older man declared, meeting his eyes.

The 'enemy'.

As the warriors in the circle nodded and muttered their agreement, Copperhead considered his words. Green Snake was right. Hard as the root was to chew – if he was to be one of them, Green Snake *had* to be right.

"You must choose," the clan leader said, and then he turned and crossed to Two Worlds and spoke to him in the People's tongue. Copperhead caught Miriam's name, but their words flew faster than arrows on the wing, and he could make no sense of the rest of it.

The translator responded once or twice. Then he nodded and lowered his head.

"Bear," Green Snake called, turning to the warrior.

"Yes?"

"Hear my words. You do nothing. For now."

Bear's jaw grew tense and his hand formed into a fist. Copperhead could see that he was not satisfied. But Green Snake's power was implicit, and after a moment the warrior nodded and with a jerk of his head, called his men to follow him. Moments later they disappeared into the trees surrounding the camp.

Within minutes the rest of the warriors had dispersed, leaving only Miriam, who lay unconscious, Green Snake and Two Worlds. And him.

The clan leader spoke to the translator again. His Tsalagi words came too quickly for him to understand. There was something about 'sundown', and then Green Snake too was gone.

Copperhead waited. When Two Worlds offered no explanation, he asked, "What did he say?"

"Take the woman," his friend answered, nodding toward Miriam. "Place her in the lodge we share. She is yours – for now."

There was something in his friend's voice. "And then?"

Two Worlds shook his head. "You did not head my warning. You have brought this on yourself."

"What? Brought what?"

"Tonight at sundown we go to burn the white man out."

Copperhead frowned. He knew this. Then the meaning of Two World's words dawned on him as surely as the sun would dawn tomorrow on a day of decision and hard choices. "No...."

"Yes. It will be *this* woman's home."

"And what of Miriam?"

Two Worlds walked to her side and knelt, placing his hand on her small still form. "Before that time you must choose whose side you are on. If you go with us, you are *one* of us, and therefore this woman is your enemy." Two Worlds slid his glasses back on his nose and rose to his feet. "And to show we are not, as you so eloquently put it, 'animals', Green Snake will not permit Bear to use her. Instead, as you suggested, the kill is to be clean.

"And you are to do it."

Judith stood outside the house near the ivied wall that guarded the estate, watching the path that ran before it, praying for a sign of William's missing child. His other daughter, Anna, was bedridden with worry and being cared for by her nursemaid. The house servants were on edge. She was feeling very much alone. The only one who might have understood – William's father, George Foxwell – she dare not tell the girl was missing, not in his condition.

Nor could she tell him that the young man, Josiah Woodward, who was for some inexplicable reason so close to his heart, was probably responsible.

The doctor was with George now. He had come again near noon. Dr. Wallington had pulled her aside in the house to tell her that the small responses the older man had made to his tests were 'encouraging.' She wondered now if she should have written to William, asking him to come home, but at the time she had thought his father was dying. Judith sighed and began the short walk back to the house. Oh, well, it mattered little. William was days or even weeks away, and by the time the letter reached him – well – anything could happen.

As she crossed the lawn the sun finally managed to overcome the clouds that lingered from the night before, and with its appearance the breeze grew a little less chill. While pausing to loosen her shawl, Judith happened to glance toward the western end of the house and was startled to see movement there. Most of the servants were occupied in or away from the house today. It was not the time for grounds keeping, unless Miller or one of the other slaves had decided to work on the beds near the manor late in hopes of chasing the brown reminders of winter away. Catching her skirts in her fingers, Judith moved with haste to see who it was. Then she remembered William's postscript. He was going to send soldiers to keep watch over them. Would his men have taken up their posts without informing her?

A sad smile quirked the edges of her lightly painted lips. Knowing William? Most likely.

Holding her skirts above the mud, Judith moved quickly over the uneven ground toward the jutting corner of the manor house where she had seen the fleeting shadow. Just as she reached it, she heard the crunch of a branch broken underfoot. When she turned, no one was there. Puzzled, she hesitated for a moment and was unexpectedly caught in a shower of pine needles that rained down from the large spruce tree shading the western face of the manor. Looking up she saw nothing – no animal or bird – in its branches. Of a sudden a chill overtook her and she became afraid. Was someone there?

Was someone *watching*?

Just as she shifted around the tree's massive trunk, meaning to take a look from the other side, she heard Doctor Wallington call her name. With one final glance at the nest of branches and sprouting buds above her head, she denied her unease and hurried toward the front of the house.

In the dark womb of the tree a lean figure clothed in soft leather and linen crouched. It watched until she disappeared and then silently slid down the trunk and entered the forest behind the house, racing toward the clearing where Green Snake awaited word.

Miriam shuddered and woke in a cold sweat, totally exhausted. It had taken all of her strength to swim up through the nightmare of savage faces that leered and jeered, and painted and tattooed arms and legs that struck and kicked her; to move past the rough touch of their hands on her face, her legs, her breasts – to forget the horror of the stench of grease and wood-smoke, of blood and sweat mingled with animal lust. Her eyes flew open and she gasped and then sat up, expecting to find herself in her bed at the manor, the victim of a horrific night terror.

Instead she found she was lying on a rough pallet of branches and dried grasses suspended a few inches above the floor and covered with several soft animal skins. In the center of a primitive hut a fire burned low. Smoke trailed up from it, passing through a crude hole in the ceiling above like a lost soul seeking Paradise. Miriam shifted and cried out in pain. *Everything* hurt. She looked and found bruises on her arms, her chest, her legs.

It had *not* been a nightmare.

The dam of her denial broke and memories of her horrific journey to the Indian's camp rushed in. She remembered being taken in the woods. Remembered those rough hands shoving, tossing, striking her, and forcing her to run even after she had lost her shoes. Her feet were raw clumps of flesh. She was filthy, bathed in sweat and covered in mud and blood. Her gown was gone and she was left naked, wearing only a torn chemise. Her once beautiful hair had been chopped short and its jagged edges hung tatterdemalion before her eyes, decorated with pine needles, twigs, and cockle-burrs.

Miriam's hands closed into fists and she began to shake. Everything - *everything* her father had ever told her about the savages was true.

She *hated* them!

For a moment she sat very still and then, gathering her courage, glanced about the interior of the lodge, noting its lack of furniture and fineries. She started to slip off the bed, thinking herself alone, but then a shadow shifted within the deeper shadows of the room and she knew someone was there.

A face flashed before her mind's eye – a powerful dark-skinned savage, holding a mass of shining pale-yellow hair.

And Miriam began to weep.

For a moment the living shade did nothing. Then she heard an intake of breath. Whoever it was approached her bed – slowly – coming to within three yards of where she sat before it stopped. The shadowy figure was careful. It remained just without the circle of light thrown by the meager fire so she could not see its face.

"Who are you?" Miriam trembled so hard the rough pallet on which she lay was shaking. "Do you mean to hurt me?"

The in-taken breath was released in a sigh. "Miriam, why did you follow me?"

Her heart had been racing, preparing for the worst. Now it leapt within her. He had come to rescue her! "Copperhead?" His name was a whisper of hope. "Copperhead!"

He hesitated, and then moved forward so the fire illuminated his long, lean figure. She saw him wince as she choked back a cry.

She did not know him.

Copperhead might have been one of the men who had tormented and abused her. All aspects of the civilized man he had become – the man called 'Josiah Woodward' – were gone. His deep bronze hair, while not tied back or shaved in the usual Indian fashion, was greased so it lay flat against his head, and adorned with feathers and beads. His striking face was stained red and black and covered with stars and other mystic signs. Copperhead's chest was bare beneath a deep blue frock coat. He wore buckskin leggings and a breechcloth that was painted and fringed with shells.

At her horrified look he hung his head, ashamed. "Miriam…."

"Does this mean you are one of them? Of those savage *brutes*?"

"Miriam, they are my People – "

Her temper flared as she regarded him and understood the choice he had made. "So *this* is where you have been coming! To join with these evil creatures!" She could hear the hysteria creeping into her voice, but she didn't care. "How *could* you? *How could you!*"

He fell on his knees beside the low bed. A painted hand reached for hers. "Miriam, I would never – "

"Don't touch me!" She shifted back, away from him, away from everything he had become. Curling up into a ball Miriam turned her face to the dry unforgiving wall of the lodge and began to sob. "Stay away from me!"

After a minute she grew quiet. When Copperhead said nothing, she couldn't help it, she *had* to look. She had heard him rise and thought he might have left the lodge, but when she rolled over she found he was still there – standing near the door with his hand on the blanket that covered it.

Choking back tears, Miriam threw the skin that covered her off and planted her feet on the floor. He was *not* going to run away. Copperhead owed her an explanation and she was going to have one! As she moved forward he turned toward her. His handsome face was haunted. He shook his head and then dropped the blanket that covered the door, sealing them in.

As he returned to her side she folded her arms over the torn fabric of her chemise and glared at him.

"Miriam," he began, his voice soft, his words insistent, "you may hate me now – and have every right to. But you *must* trust me."

"Trust you!" she scoffed. "*Why?*"

"The sun is almost down. We must go before it sets."

"Go? Go *where?*"

Copperhead inspected her, starting at her head and finishing with her toes. Though it made her uncomfortable, she held her ground. A moment later he removed his frock coat and held it out. "Put this on. I am taking you home."

She took the coat from him, but made no move to put it on. "But I thought..." she began.

"Thought what?"

Miriam shook her head, confused. "Are you not one of *them* now? These *savage* creatures?"

"They are not savages. They are men."

"Well, most men *are* savages," she snapped. "Look at that one with the robe! He does not intend to let me go. I could see it in his eyes."

"Green Snake?" Copperhead seemed confused. Then she watched it dawn on him – the clan leader had not let Bear have her because Green Snake intended to take her for his own.

As she watched, his fear and apprehension rolled through shame into rage. Copperhead crossed the lodge in several long strides. Picking up a gourd, he poured water from it into a wooden bowl. Wetting his hands, he ran them up and down his arms, over his chest and across his face, obliterating the symbols painted there and the men they tied him to. He tore the feathers and beads from his hair and crushed them underfoot.

When he looked at Miriam there were tears in his eyes.

"I do not know where I belong, but it is not here with these men," he confessed as he approached her. "With the setting of the sun, Green Snake will come. He will ask if I *am* with them and if I say 'no', he will kill us both. If I say, 'yes'..." Copperhead paused. He reached toward her, but stopped just short of touching her short butchered hair. "If I say 'yes', he will hand me a knife and I am to kill *you*."

Copperhead was breathing hard. The fire's light glinted off his taut, muscled chest, the water used to cleanse it making it gleam. His deep brown eyes were fixed on her and in them she saw just a bit of the battle he waged – and a hint of the long and difficult path she would walk if she did not turn away.

"Miriam?"

She caught his hand between her own and pressed it to her lips. "I am sorry," she whispered as the tears flowed freely. "I am *so* sorry...."

He touched her hair and her cheek. Then he pulled away. "There is no time," he warned. "The sun will be down in less than one hour. We *must* escape."

"But won't they expect us to try?" she asked as he helped her to don the frock coat and then offered her a pair of moccasins.

"Sit," he urged her.

Miriam did as she was told. Copperhead paused for a moment with his hand on one bruised and bloodied foot, but then slipped the leather shoe on and tied it about her ankle so it would not fall off. "Yes, they will expect it," he said reaching for her other foot. "Bear, at least. I have a friend who is watching outside. So far, there is no sign of him or anyone else. But that does not mean that they do not await us in the wood."

She touched his face and made him look up at her. "Bear *wants* me. Doesn't he?"

He rose to his feet and pulled her up after him. "But he will not have you. Not until I am dead." Copperhead motioned her toward the back of the lodge. Once there he began to pull at the dried mud and branches. She fell to her knees and helped him. Within minutes there was an opening large enough for them to slip through.

Copperhead told her that he would go first, to make certain the way was clear. As he ducked into the opening, she caught his hand and pulled him back.

"What?" he asked, slightly annoyed.

She caught his face with her other hand and kissed him.

"I love you," she said. It was an admission to her as much as to him. "Whither thou goest, I will follow. Wherever the path may lead."

Copperhead said nothing but nodded, and disappeared into the night.

Chapter Twelve

Judith returned to George's bedside to keep watch over the ailing man. The day was almost gone and the new moon had risen, but it did little to light the night sky. She sat in the chair, nodding, a book balanced precariously on her knee. Though it wasn't terribly late, Anna was already in bed. The girl had cried herself to sleep, convinced that her sister was dead. Judith fought to hold off such feelings, knowing it more likely that Miriam had run away, but there was something in the air – a sense of something dark and dreadful impending – that made the notion almost impossible to dismiss.

A sudden noise roused her. Judith shook herself awake and then looked at William's father. The older man was sleeping peacefully. It hadn't been him.

Rising to her feet she crossed to the door and opened it a crack and listened. There were voices in the lower hall – loud, strident voices. She hesitated, attempting to discern one from the other. Then she recognized one. The promise of it and the protection it offered caused her to fling the door open and run down the stairs like a giddy girl unexpectedly visited by her beau.

William was home!

He caught her in his arms and held her as she sobbed, even not knowing why she did. With more tender care than she had expected, he waited until the tempest had passed before holding her at arm's length and forcing her to meet his worried gaze.

"Judith?"

She sniffed and fought for control. She knew William hated weakness. "Yes?"

"This is more than my father, isn't it?"

She didn't know how to answer that. "No. And yes. William, there was someone outside the house earlier today. I know most likely it was a vagabond, but their presence left me unnerved. And ever since – "

Instead of dismissing her notion as the foolishness of a woman, he shot off a series of questions rapid-fire. "Someone outside the house? Where? What do you mean? It was not one of the servants or slaves? You are certain?"

"By the great spruce. And no, it was not one of the servants. Nor a slave. I had McNeil check. There was no one there." She drew a quick breath. "At least no one I could see."

William snapped his fingers. "Nevilles!"

Lieutenant Jedidiah Nevilles had been waiting near the door. He stepped smartly up. "Sir!"

"Increase the patrol. Canvass the edge of the estate, focusing on the eastern perimeter, and be sharp about it!"

"Sir! Yes, sir!"

"William, what is it?"

He shook his head. Then he took her hand and drew her into the drawing room, away from the remaining soldiers and the servants and house slaves that had appeared to welcome him home. Once within the wainscoted and polished cotton draped room, William closed the doors and leaned heavily on them.

Judith was trembling. "What in Heaven's name is going on?"

"It is my belief that we will soon be under attack," he answered curtly as he moved to the window and gazed surreptitiously at the lawn from behind the cover of the drape. "Whoever you saw was probably a front man, acting as a scout."

"Attack? Who...."

"Savages," William growled. "The intelligence I spoke of in my letter – you received it?"

She nodded.

"There is a band of the red devils in this area – renegade Cherokee." He tossed his tricorn hat on the chair near the hearth and moved to pour himself a whiskey. "While most of the Cherokee know what side their bread is buttered on and work hard to keep in the good graces of His Majesty, these renegades are bent on nothing but destruction and murder most foul. It is their sole purpose to drive the white man from these shores." He lifted the etched glass as if in a toast. "Here's to the devil with them!" And with that he drained the spirits in one gulp.

"But why here? Why attack us? We have done them no harm."

"They hate me," he answered, pouring another shot. "With good reason. That's all you need to know."

Judith knew better than to question him when he was in one of his moods. "What should we do?"

"My men are patrolling the grounds. I have brought as many as I could muster, and more are to follow. Still, the savages will most likely outnumber us. But what we lack in numbers, we shall make up in superior intelligence and firepower!" He drained the next glass and then turned to her. "What servants are able, we will arm. You and the other women need to remove to one of the inner rooms near one of the end stairs."

"Why near the stair?"

He came to stand before her. "In case they try to burn us out." As she began to tremble almost uncontrollably, William took her by both arms. "Judith, I need you to be strong. It is one of the qualities that made me choose you."

"I will put my trust in Providence and you," she assured him, her voice barely above a whisper. "What about your father?"

"Where is he?"

"In a room close to ours. I have been caring for him. Well, Martha and I have been – "

"Leave him there." He released her and turned away. "Most likely the savages won't bother with a half-dead old man anyway."

Judith was shocked. "William! He's your father."

"He's nothing to me," he snarled. "Do you hear me? *Nothing!*"

She squared her shoulders. "I will *not* leave him. One of the servants can help me lift him and remove him to the room where we will be staying."

William whirled and pointed a finger at her. "Don't you dare defy me, woman!"

"It is not Christian to abandon anyone to such a fate, let *alone* your own parent," she countered. "Dear God, William, why do you hate him so?"

He flung the glass across the room. It struck the fireplace mantel with a resounding crash. In a second he was on her and slapped her so hard she stumbled and fell to the floor. Dropping to his knees beside her, William caught her arms and forced her to meet his vitriolic gaze. "You want to know what that old man did? I'll tell you. He betrayed my mother – not with some doxy from the town, not even with a Barbados slave, but with some ignorant slut of a squaw!" He shook her and then pushed her away as he rose. "That boy – Josiah Woodward – he's a filthy Cherokee half-breed!"

Judith drew a deep breath. Her lower lip was bleeding. She wiped it as she righted herself. "He's still your…father's son," she breathed. *And if not by blood, she thought, then by love.*

For a moment she feared William would strike her again. He came close, but then turned and, whiskey bottle in hand, dropped into the chair by the fire. From it he watched the flames and fell into a morose silence. Judith waited until she had calmed and then rose and went to stand opposite him. "How long do we have?" she asked.

"They usually attack when they think the household is sleeping," he said, his voice dead and without feeling. "An hour. Maybe two."

Judith hesitated. Then she said it. "And do you intend to spend that time getting so drunk you are of no use to any of us?"

William gazed up at her, his eyes deep wells of anger and self-inflicted pain, and then something snapped back into place. Most likely his military training. He really looked at her – noting her swollen cheek and split lip – and then at the whiskey decanter in his hand. Rising, he threw it into the fire where it shattered and, for a moment, fed the flames.

William listened to it crackle and spit for a moment, and then turned to meet her accusing stare. Then he nodded. Once. "Thank you," he said.

Startled, Judith found she had nothing to say.

As he moved away, William tossed over his shoulder, "I will send one of my men to help with my father, to remove him to whatever room you choose. Is there anything else you need of me before I rejoin the men?"

Judith shook her head. She remained silent until he reached the door and then, just as he opened it, called softly after him, "Aren't you going to visit your father before you go?"

William stiffened but did not turn or look at her. A moment later he passed through the door and into the hall.

Judith held onto the chair near her for a moment longer and then fell into it and dropped her head into her hands and wept.

They had made it past the perimeter of the renegade Cherokee's camp. Copperhead held her hand tightly and led the way. Miriam gritted her teeth and denied tears, but they streamed down her cheeks anyway. The pain was excruciating. Unaccustomed to the soft-soled moccasins, with the bottoms of her feet broken and blistered, each step was agony. But she was resolute and did not complain. In fact neither of them had said a word since they entered the trees. Unlike her, who had no earthly idea of where they were or which way to go, Copperhead knew the way and led them unerringly forward. She realized now that they had never been that far from the manor. The Cherokee who took her had turned her round and round so she would lose all sense of where she was. Only a few minutes before she had recognized the place where she had fallen and been taken.

Impossible as it seemed, it appeared that their escape had gone unnoticed. Miriam was certain they would have been accosted by now if such were not the case. She started to say something about it to Copperhead, but he put a finger to his lips and shook his head calling for silence, wary as ever.

Gripping his callused hand as a lifeline, Miriam trusted him to lead her blindly through the dark night. The moon was cloaked and the shadows cast by the ancient trees and obstructing underbrush masked the narrow path that cut through their heart. They traveled for another quarter of an hour before Copperhead stopped. Miriam brightened when she recognized the cheerful voice of the slender stream that emptied into the pond near the house. They were close to the boundary of her father's lands! Relief made her giddy. She grinned and released his hand and began to run toward the safety of home.

"Miriam! No!" Copperhead called, running after her. "Miriam!"

The path to civilization lay before her. The path to her father's house and her soft feather bed in the room with the double-door that could be locked and barred to keep all of the unpleasant things of the world outside – just where she wanted them. So keen was she on reaching this earthly Heaven, that Miriam almost missed Copperhead's call. When she heard it, she halted and turned back. His slender, well-muscled form, illuminated by the scanty moonlight, was frighteningly reminiscent of her captors. Copperhead *was* an Indian. If she stayed with him, she would have to surrender it all: Her home. Her father's protection. Her relationship with Judith, and her sister, Anna. Safety and security.

All of it would be gone.

Miriam closed her eyes. She thought she had made her choice back in the lodge when he had rescued her. But now, faced with the *reality* of it, she found it hard.

Opening her eyes, she started toward him. Copperhead, I – "

He was gone.

"Copperhead?" Miriam walked quickly and then began to run back to where she had last seen him. "Copperhead? Where – "

From out of the shadows came a hand. It closed over her mouth, and a pair of powerful arms gripped her tight. Miriam struggled against the brute who held her, smelling not only danger but the familiar scent of grease, smoke, and sweat commingled. But it was of no use. She was smaller than most women –

And Bear was a powerful warrior in his prime.

Slinging her easily over his shoulder, Bear carried her off the path and into a shallow ravine bordered by weeping willows; their budding branches brushing the ground with a soft, sad sigh. At the bottom of the ravine Copperhead lay unconscious, one arm twisted beneath him, and a great bruise growing on his temple where Bear had struck him hard with the club he wore at his belt.

Bear caught him by his hair in passing and lifted him up. "So much for your savior!" the powerful warrior growled as he advanced into the woods, carrying her, and dragging Copperhead's limp form behind.

Copperhead awoke in intense pain. He groaned and lifted his head and looked around, uncertain of where he was and what had happened. He saw Miriam lying on the ground not far away and tried to rise, but found he could not. He was bound, hand and foot, and his body lashed to a tree. Choking as the rope that circled his neck bit into his flesh, he coughed and gasped for air.

A second later a knife was at his throat.

"So you awake, Wudigeas," Bear snarled, crouching in front of him. The Cherokee warrior forced Copperhead to lift his head by pressing the tip of the razor sharp blade into the tender skin beneath his chin. "Did you think I had forgotten the insult you paid me?"

Copperhead couldn't answer. Not without chancing being stuck.

"I knew you would go. *Knew* you would betray us. I told Green Snake so. He said nothing, but knew I would take care of you." Bear ran the knife down his chest, cutting a slow, bloody path. "I will get much pleasure, *dog*, from your death!"

Copperhead bit back a cry, refusing to give it to him. "Death holds no fear for me," he declared, his teeth clenched against the pain.

It was true. In many ways death would be a relief.

Bear grinned wickedly. He turned slowly towards Miriam, savoring Copperhead's horror. "And for her?"

"*No!* Do what you like with me! Leave her alone!"

"I will leave her," Bear said rising, "in the grave. But first," he slowly began to remove his bandoleers and weapons. "First, I will *have* her while you watch."

Copperhead struggled against his bonds. Blood pounded in his temples and stung as rage and guilt surged through his veins. "No! I will *kill* you!"

Bear had taken a step toward Miriam. He turned back. "When I have had my pleasure you will be released. Then, we will see."

He fought with his desire to plead for her life. Begging would do no good – he knew it – it would only multiply the brute's sadistic pleasure. As Bear walked away, he focused his attention on Miriam. She was starting to stir.

Copperhead could not – he *would* not look away no matter what happened and so, with his eyes open he began to pray to his Creator, to the one who first made the People and set them on the Earth, and to the strange god of the white men, Miriam's god – the Jew on a wooden cross whose story George Foxwell had read to him so many times. "Creator," he whispered as Bear bore down on Miriam and she began to scream, "I care little what happens to me. But save her. *Save Miriam!*"

COPPERHEAD

Bear was on her quickly and tore away what was left of her white chemise, revealing her breasts. Tears streamed down Copperhead's face as he saw Miriam's tender flesh crushed in brutal hands. Bear rose above her, howling, spreading her pale legs wide and then suddenly stiffened – but not with pleasure.

With surprise.

Copperhead was breathing so hard the smoke from the musket fired close by his head choked him as it curled into the air. When he was able to wrest his tear-filled eyes away from Miriam who was shrieking and shrieking as she struggled to free herself from Bear's bloody and lifeless corpse, he found a young British soldier in a scarlet coat staring at his own weapon as if surprised that it could kill.

Then he recognized him.

"Lieutenant Nevilles?" he whispered.

The soldier looked down at him. They did not know each other well, just in passing. William Foxwell's current aide had come to the manor while Miriam's father had still been in residence, and they had spoken several times. Nevilles had always had a kind word for him – even if his commander had not.

"Josiah? Josiah Woodward?"

Now the tears did flow, unashamed. "Miriam," he whispered, nodding toward her. "Help Miriam."

"The Colonel's daughter?" Jedidiah Nevilles paled when he saw Miriam on the ground with Bear's lifeless body sprawled on top of her. He ran across the open space and rolled the dead man off. Copperhead watched helpless as at first Miriam fought against the British soldier, still caught in the nightmare of what had almost occurred. Then she recognized Nevilles and calmed.

Flinging her arms about the young man, Miriam began to sob.

Moments later Jedidiah assisted her to her feet and brought her to Copperhead's side. Placing her on the ground beside him, the soldier set to work cutting his bonds. Once loose Copperhead caught Miriam in his arms and, touching her face, spoke her name. Then he pulled her to his chest.

"I could do nothing," he began, ashamed. "Nothing...."

She reached up and touched his lips, hushing him. "Shh, I am safe now."

William Foxwell's lieutenant watched them for a minute, saying nothing. Then he cleared his throat. When they looked up, he told them, "I think you two should know. The Colonel's at the house."

"What?" Miriam had been trembling – Neville's news brought her to the edge of hysteria. "Dear God! *No*! What are we going to do? We have to go! Find a place to hide...."

"You can't. There are patrols everywhere."

Copperhead nodded, understanding, as he sought to soothe her. And even though he knew the answer, he asked the soldier, "What is happening?"

"There's savages bound here." Jedidiah indicated Bear with a nod of his head. "This one's probably part of it. Our spies say they mean to attack the colonel's house. Burn it out. Colonel Foxwell got wind of it a couple of days ago." Lieutenant Nevilles' eyes went to Miriam. "He said he told you to keep close to the house. What are you doing out here, Miss Miriam? Josiah?" When they said nothing, he looked from one to the other. Miriam was leaning into Copperhead's embrace, her face buried against his bloody chest. Copperhead was stroking her hair.

"Oh."

After a moment, Copperhead gently pushed her away. He met her puzzled gaze and said, "We have to get you to the house before the others arrive."

"No! I won't leave you!" she protested.

"You must. Jedidiah, can you get Miriam through the lines?"

The soldier nodded. "What about you?"

Copperhead struggled to his feet, pulling Miriam after him. "I am part of the problem, so I must be part of the solution as well. I know these men. I can take you to them. I know the path they will choose."

Jedidiah stared at him, seeing for the first time the remnants of paint and his native attire. "So it's true then?"

"That I am an Indian? Yes."

Nevilles whistled. "Now if that don't just take the biscuit! *And* old man Foxwell's kid?" When Copperhead didn't answer, the soldier shrugged. "As they say, 'the business of my betters isn't mine'. Wait here. I'll get Jenkins and a few of the others. Someone can escort Miss Miriam home and we can go play the hero!" He cast a look over his shoulder and added darkly, "First, I'll make sure the savage is really dead. Wouldn't want him popping up later."

Miriam trembled in Copperhead's arms as her father's aide moved to Bear's side, and then hid her face when Nevilles plunged his bayonet straight into the dead man's chest.

"He's dead as a nit and gone to the diet of the worms," the Englishman announced with pride. Then with a short salute he disappeared into the trees, leaving them alone.

The night breeze stirred the leaves about them. It held a hint of rain, promising another storm to come. Miriam clung to him as if her very life depended on the touch.

"I am sorry you had to see this," Copperhead said, his voice torn with grief and regret. "It is all my fault."

Her head shook against him. "I could have trusted you – "

"And you would have been wrong. If not for your coming, I would be marching in the company of the men who intend to kill your family and burn your home to the ground."

She grew stiff in his arms. Then she looked up. "Would you have? Really?"

He glanced at Bear and remembered the lawless frenzy of her arrival in the camp. "No," he answered softly, shifting a ragged lock of hair out of her eyes. "My home is not with the People."

"Then where is it?" Miriam asked.

Copperhead grew suddenly solemn. "I have no home. If I die tonight and make right what I have done, then I will *be* home."

She caught his hand and kissed it. "Your home is with me."

"Miriam, we both know that is impossible. I cannot provide for you. After tonight I will not be welcome at the manor – or in the town – and *you* cannot live in the wilderness."

"Let me decide that," she answered just as Lieutenant Nevilles and about a dozen men in scarlet coats broke through the underbrush.

"Corporal Jenkins will take her," Nevilles said as he drew abreast them.

Copperhead nodded. He pulled her pale hands from his deeply tanned flesh, but then he froze, suddenly alert.

"What's wrong, mate?"

He turned in the direction they had come and closed his eyes, listening. Then he looked at Nevilles.

"It is too late. They are here."

"Sound the call!" William Foxwell shouted. "Bring the men in about the house!" He glanced at the upper window behind which he knew his wife-to-be, his youngest daughter, and the serving women of the house were sequestered. He had ordered them to close all the shutters and await word. A lump formed in William's throat as he turned back toward the forest and scanned the tree line. He had only just learned that Miriam was missing. His daughter might be a prisoner by now. Abused. Dead.

Or defiled.

When he asked Judith about Josiah Woodward's involvement, she had conveniently been too busy to answer. After his obscene outburst in the drawing room before, William had chosen not to press her. It could wait. If the boy were not involved, he would find him later. If he was –

He would kill him.

As his men began to stream out of the woods William heard a heathen cry go up close behind them. He recognized it immediately from the last war. One of the enlisted men in the company, a young man barely seventeen named Jeffries, paused and asked him, "Is this it, sir? Is it the savages?"

William Foxwell pressed the lad's shoulder with his hand. "Aye, boy. A chance for glory, and to serve God and King!"

"Sir!"

"Have you seen Lieutenant Nevilles?" he asked Jeffries as he started to move away.

"He was deep in the woods, sir, with the left flank." Jeffries grinned. "Knowing Jedidiah he was probably the one to sound the alarm."

William nodded, dismissing him. In all he had about three dozen men of the company with him. Another two dozen were on their way from New Bern, but there was no way of knowing if they would arrive in time. Hopefully there were no more of the savages than the spies had reported. They placed the red man's number at fifty – men and boys.

In the last war he would have taken out that many before sun-up and then settled in for a light breakfast. But this was his home. His family.

This was *personal*.

"Grove!" he called, addressing a swarthy sergeant who was running past.

"Aye, sir!" the man replied, skidding to a halt.

"I am going inside. Assemble the men and have them form a ring around the exterior of the house. The outbuildings are expendable. The horses have already been removed to a place of safety so these renegades cannot make use of them. Your men's job is to protect the house. Dismissed."

"Sir!"

William Foxwell turned and marched toward the manor. It was his intention to run an inspection tour of the house interior and make certain nothing had been overlooked – that there were not any windows or doors left unlatched or unbarred. The brick structure was large and built in the latest fashion and, unfortunately, appointed with a great many of both. This was not feudal times. The manor was *not* a fortress. When the plan for it had been conceived back in England, the idea of a full-scale attack had not been in his mind. Rather arrogantly he had thought his reputation of ruthlessness on the battlefield would keep them safe.

Showed what a damn fool he was!

As William approached the house he recalled something Judith had said concerning the great spruce leaning perilously close to the eastern end of the house – about seeing someone or something in it earlier in the day. Turning his feet that way, he hastened along the walk. When he arrived he leaned back and examined the branches that appeared to be empty. Then, William looked at the house itself.

The second story window was open.

Copperhead and Jedidiah Nevilles left the shuddering trees and entered the manor's yard near the studio. They searched the small building first, making certain George Foxwell was not within, and then moved with stealth toward the great house itself. The old man had not been there the night before either when Copperhead had made up his mind to leave. He had thought it odd at the time. The fact that Miriam's grandfather had not been himself of late had made it all the easier for Copperhead to take advantage of his trust and to slip in and out unnoticed. Guilt and shame stabbed him at the thought. This was *all* his fault.

If anyone died….

"There! Look!" Jedidiah Nevilles hit him in the arm, drawing his attention.

Copperhead saw them. Painted shadows, light and dark, clothed in leather and wearing beads, shells, and feathers, moving in sinister concert toward the house. Jedidiah raised his musket and took aim, but Copperhead stopped him from shooting.

"No. Not yet," Copperhead said. "You do not want to alert those already inside."

"What? There's savages *in* the house?"

He nodded. "It is the usual way. Make a bold frontal attack while others sneak in from behind, unnoticed. Take what hostages you can to bargain with." Copperhead swallowed hard. "They can always be killed later. The plan is to conquer on two fronts. I need to get inside, Jedidiah. You can warn the others – "

"Pauley can do it. I'm staying with you."

Copperhead looked at him. He nodded. "I understand. You do not trust me."

William Foxwell's aide laughed. "Hell, no! I know what you're like. I've watched you with the old general. You take better care of him than Captain Will. And you're smart. And able. I'd rather have an Indian I *can* trust watching my back than any of these blokes come from Devon and Jersey," he said with a grin. "If you get my drift."

For a moment he didn't know what to say. "Thank you."

"And you really *are* an Indian?"

"Yes."

"Well, pinch me then! Just checking." Jedidiah shifted ahead of him. "Come on, Josiah. Time's a wasting."

He could see them out on the lawn, fierce painted savages with deerskin roaches, bathed in mud and marked all over with evil signs. William Foxwell had sent Sergeant Grove to check the west wing, and then canvassed the east wing of the house himself, first checking on the women and then heading further down the corridor to where he had spotted the open window. He leaned out and looked up and down, and then closed it with a frown. Kneeling, he checked the floor beneath it for signs of bare feet and moccasins. He saw nothing, but when he bent and ran his hand over the Persian rug, William found it was wet. Further on toward the center hall he found traces of mud. The savages were no doubt searching the house, trying to determine where the women and children were. Bloody *animals*! If they didn't kill the women outright, they would take them and turn them into slaves, or torture them for their pleasure. During the Seven Years' War he had had to remove a white woman from a burnt stake. She had been roasted, her skin blown open like a pig left on the spit too long; her eyes and teeth white against the horrific field of charred black flesh. It was a sight he had never forgotten.

Or forgiven.

William followed the damp footprints and they led him, not unexpectedly, to the back stair. There they parted, one heading into the servants' wing of the house and several more descending the steps toward the attached kitchen and the yard beyond. He paused on the landing, listening. Their old house slave, Ben, had volunteered to guard the rear door, and Albert Pennyworth, an Englishman who had been with the family since William had been a boy, was positioned in the hall near the front. He should have heard some indication that at least Ben was there – a sigh or a shift of body weight – but there was nothing below.

Only eerie silence.

William cautiously descended the stair, pistol drawn, expecting at any moment to trip over one of the men's butchered forms. Near the bottom, just before he would have emerged into the kitchen, he froze. A hue and cry had gone up from his men outside and a volley of shots accompanied the savage's defiant screams.

The battle had begun.

Every impulse in Colonel William Foxwell insisted he enter the fray, but years of wartime experience had rendered him immune to that inner voice. Instead he calmly continued on. There was little he could do in the house. The women were secure and he was needed with his men. He moved through the attached kitchen toward the small door that opened onto a short stair and led down into the root cellar.

If he could pry the lock free and manage to use the outside entrance to emerge unnoticed – God and fate be willing! – he would take a few of the savages by surprise.

Copperhead glanced at Jedidiah Nevilles and then removed the padlock that held the root cellar doors closed. As a trusted servant of the house, he had the key. The native who had been stationed there by the Tsalagi to keep watch at the back of the house – a young man called 'Smoke' – lay dead at their feet, felled by a single shot from Neville's gun. Copperhead held the soldier's gaze for a moment and then leapt back as he threw open the doors. Seconds later, certain it was clear, they approached the cellar together. The large earth and stone room beneath the manor was strung with ropes from which nets of onions and sacks of tubers dangled. Wooden crates filled with sand held vegetables and eggs. The room was dry and musty, and dark as a tomb.

Copperhead nodded to his companion and then lowered himself in. He descended a half dozen steps and then turned to assist Nevilles who had caught the strap of his cartridge box on one of the door's rough hinges. As he did something shifted behind him. Instantly alert, Copperhead turned – barely in time to miss having his skull broken by the butt of a British pistol.

"You! By *God*, I knew it!" William Foxwell roared, his voice shaking with rage. "I will beat you within an inch of breathing, boy! And then when you have told me what I want to know, pound you into so many pieces there won't be enough *left* to feed to the dogs!"

Miriam's father drew his short whip. The braided lash struck the hand Copperhead had lifted to shield his face and split his palm in two.

"By all that's holy, Colonel! No! Colonel Foxwell, no!" Jedidiah screamed as he broke free and rushed down the steps. He caught his commanding officer's arm with both hands and held the whip away. "Josiah's on our side!"

But the bloodlust was on William Foxwell. He pivoted faster than Copperhead's eye could follow and brought the handle of the whip up under Jedidiah's chin, knocking the soldier back and upsetting several crates of eggs.

Then he turned back to beating him.

As the tip of the lash came down splitting his cheek and barely missing his eye, Copperhead looked away to find Jedidiah rising. From a crouching position, the soldier flung his broken strap out and caught his colonel's ankles. As William Foxwell took a step forward to strike

Copperhead again, the strap caused him to stumble and fall to his knees. Jedidiah rose and quickly placed himself between them.

"Colonel William! There's no time for this. The savages are on us and they're bearing torches. We need to get the women out and secure the house." Jedidiah Nevilles was breathing hard. "You may not want to believe it, but Josiah here is the one who gave the alarm."

William Foxwell remained on his knees. Sweat streamed down his cheeks. He was breathing hard. He glared at Copperhead for several heartbeats, struggling to master his hatred and rage, and then he said, "All right, but *he* stays here. Lock him in."

Jedidiah didn't budge. "Sir. This man saved your daughter, Miriam's, life. I think you owe him."

Miriam's father blinked as if stunned by a grenade blast. "What?"

"The reason he's dressed as a savage is – " Jedidiah shot Copperhead a quick look and then lied. " – he was scouting for us. Since he looks like one of them, Josiah offered to help."

"When was this?" William Foxwell's tone was more than skeptical.

"Yesterday, sir. Just after the mistress disappeared. A savage had her, sir. Held in the woods. He's dead now." Jedidiah swallowed and lied again. "Josiah was the one that done it."

"Where is my daughter now?"

"Safe."

Copperhead wiped blood from his lips. He couldn't understand why Jedidiah was doing this for him.

William Foxwell was silent for a moment. He rose and dusted himself off and then gave Copperhead an order. "On your feet, Woodward!"

It took two tries but he managed it.

"You can come with us, but by *God*, boy, you stay where I can see you or I will mistake you for one of the enemy and shoot you like a rabid dog!" Miriam's father drew close and lowered his voice. "This doesn't mean anything, you understand that? Once this is over, *nothing* has changed between us."

Copperhead nodded. He resisted the urge to add, "I hate you too."

"Come on, both of you," Jedidiah called. "The women are in the east wing."

"Where is Master George?" Copperhead asked.

"There as well," William Foxwell answered as he turned into the room and headed for the stair that led up to the kitchen. Near the top he paused. Copperhead heard him sniffing. "Dear God!" he declared in horror. "That's smoke! They've set the manor on fire!"

The three men rushed up the stairs and burst into the kitchen, Nevilles and Foxwell with weapons drawn. The old slave, Ben, lay on the floor and the door at the rear was wide open. William Foxwell checked him. He was not dead, but had been partially scalped.

"Lieutenant!" Foxwell snapped, "tend to him! And you," he pointed at Copperhead, "come with me!"

The entry hall was billowing with smoke and savages. An acrid gray cloud filled the hall but, for the moment, the fire seemed to be contained to the lower west wing and dining room. As the two of them battled their way to the bottom of the main stair, William Foxwell ordered him to, "Check the drawing room!" Then he sped off down the corridor in the opposite direction toward the blaze.

Copperhead checked it. He found nothing there but more smoke. Coughing, tears streaming down his face, he stepped over the bodies littering the hall and backtracked, following in William Foxwell's footsteps.

The fire in the dining room had been kindled by several flaming arrows that had become lodged in the costly draperies lining it. The painted pine beams of the ceiling directly above the great cherry table were already charred. As Copperhead paused in the doorway, a strong breeze struck him, lifting his hair from his shoulders and chilling him. Several of the expensive glass panes had been broken by stone or axe. Then wind was feeding the flames. Behind the table, near the western wall, William Foxwell struggled with one of the renegade Tsalagi. The older man was tall and wore a long robe.

It was Green Snake.

Copperhead searched for a weapon. He found one in the brass poker near the cold hearth. With a fierce battle cry he leapt on the table, slid its length, and ended near the pair. Green Snake had just struck William Foxwell in the temple with the butt of his knife, knocking Miriam's father senseless. The clan leader pivoted at his cry. When he recognized him, Green Snake's lips curled in a sneer. Then he shifted the knife into his other hand and prepared to throw.

At that moment a momentous 'crack' sounded above their heads and a shower of flaming embers rained down. Copperhead jumped from the table and rolled across the patterned floor toward the windows just as the gigantic pine beam above the table broke in two and crashed to the parquet floor.

Green Snake was killed instantly. William Foxwell, who had managed to press his tall form into the unlit fireplace, escaped the worst of it, but his right leg was crushed under a portion of the burning wood.

For a moment Copperhead considered leaving him. It was no more than he deserved.

The man was his enemy.

But William Foxwell was also Miriam's father. And Copperhead knew what it was to lose a father.

Picking himself up, Copperhead leapt the remnants of the beam and crossed to William Foxwell's side. He found a portion that was not yet on fire and, using his back, lifted it up and shifted it several inches. Foxwell's leg came free, but the man didn't move. He lay there as if stunned. Copperhead grabbed Miriam's father under the arms and half-lifted, half-drug him out of the now raging inferno and into the hall just as the remainder of the dining room ceiling collapsed.

Falling to the floor, Copperhead coughed and vomited black ash. With his cheek against the boards he watched the fire rage for a moment or two.

And then he knew no more.

Until he heard Jedidiah Nevilles' voice in his ear and felt a hand on his shoulder trying to rouse him.

"Josiah. Josiah! Are you alive?"

With a grudging grunt Copperhead awoke. He found himself on the lawn. He coughed again and then turned and looked at the house. The western half of the manor was still in flames though the fire seemed to be abating. A steady rain had begun to fall and a line of William Foxwell's men, free of their scarlet coats, muskets and hats, were passing leather buckets from one to the other, pitching water on the fire. Providence had saved them, Jedidiah told him. Providence *and* hard work. Copperhead raised his face to the heavens and let the rain cleanse it, washing away the sweat and blood and soot.

And coughed again. Speaking was not easy. "The women?" he asked, his voice little more than a rasp.

"Safe. And before you ask, so is the general." Jedidiah paused, but seemed to think better of what he had been about to say. "They've taken them all to the studio. It isn't big, but it escaped the fire." The soldier rose to his feet. "And it's far away from all of this."

"What happened?" Copperhead asked, struggling to sit up.

Nevilles helped him. "The rest of the company from New Bern arrived. Overwhelmed the savages, they did. The Indians are all dead." He shrugged. "Leastwise, we didn't find any alive."

Copperhead was numb. He didn't know what to feel. For many moons those 'savages' had been his brothers and *this* world – the one of manor houses and British soldiers – the one he meant to turn his back on.

145

"Was there...a thin man...with glasses...in a white man's clothes among them?" he asked.

Jedidiah shook his head. "Not that I seen."

So, perhaps Two Worlds was not among the dead.

"And Miriam?"

"With the women. Jenkins kept her safe and then brought her in after the fighting was over." Lieutenant Nevilles shifted his hat back on his head and looked at the house. He let out a long, low whistle. "It'll take something to put this back together, won't it?" As Copperhead coughed again, the soldier looked at him. "How are you feeling? Can you stand?"

He nodded, 'yes', though he wasn't really certain. Jedidiah helped him to his feet and supported him.

"Why?" Copperhead asked.

"Why what?"

"Why...are you doing this for me? The things...you said to Colonel Foxwell. And you must have pulled me from the house...."

The young soldier was quiet for a moment. "There's some things a man can't say. All I'll tell you is that her name was Oheo. And that's enough said."

Oheo. That was Seneca.

"You're wanted in the studio, Josiah," Jedidiah told him, "if you feel well enough to walk there."

Copperhead drew a breath and suppressed another cough. Breathing was its own kind of 'fire'. "Wanted?" he asked with a frown.

The British soldier laughed and slapped him on the back, bringing on another round of coughing.

"You're a hero, Josiah Woodward. Didn't you know that?"

The walk was longer than it had ever been before. Along the way Copperhead was startled to be cheered by the other soldiers. The cumulative effect of the day, his decision to stay with – and then desert – the People, Miriam's capture and near rape, his beating at Foxwell's hands, the fire and the smoke, taken all together were nearly enough to break him. But he clutched Jedidiah's arm and made it to the stone walk. Ten yards from the door the soldier gently disengaged his hand and stepped away so he stood under his own power.

"Got to keep up appearances," Nevilles said softly as he knocked on the door and backed away.

A very weary and worried Judith Kingsley opened it. She took one look at Copperhead and burst into tears and then hurried forward to crush him in a close embrace. Releasing him she took his hand and led him into the studio where Miriam sat with her sister, Anna. Both were comforting their old nursemaid, Martha. When Miriam saw him, she rose to her feet and joined them. She was tired and obviously still shaken from her ordeal in the woods, but instantly Copperhead knew something else was wrong.

Terribly wrong.

Miriam's deep blue eyes fastened on him even though she spoke to Judith. "Does he know?" she asked.

The older woman shook her head. "I thought I would let you explain, and go with him."

"But what if Papa returns?"

"I will deal with William if he does." Judith kissed Miriam on the forehead and then took her hand. Turning to Copperhead she asked for his as well, and then linked them. "Young man, I was wrong about you. Perhaps in time we can convince Miriam's father that he is wrong as well. You two have my blessing."

As Judith walked away, Copperhead turned to Miriam. The fatigue he felt fled in the face of so many unknowns. "What is it?" he asked her.

She nodded toward the room which he used to care for sick horses.

"It's Grandpapa," she said.

The room had been hastily cleaned out and blankets laid on the floor. Several soldiers with minor burns lay on them, moaning as they struggled to sleep. There was one empty bed. Miriam explained it was her father's. The moment William Foxwell had awakened – in spite of the burns on his face and hands, *and* the fact that his leg had been half-crushed – he had insisted on returning to his men. On a pallet set aside in the corner, near Copperhead's workbench, lay George Foxwell. Miriam gripped his hand and together they approached the old man. Her grandfather was sleeping. Copperhead noted that the left side of his face was drawn down, and the arm on the same side curled up against his body. And that the old man's skin looked like parchment stretched too thin. He knew the look. He had seen it before – in the village as a child.

A man no longer useful, marked for death.

"They call it a softening of the brain," Miriam whispered, tears streaming down her dirty cheeks. "Doctor Wallington says he *may* recover...."

Copperhead remained silent for some time. Then he asked, his voice breaking, "When did this happen? Tonight?"

"No. Yesterday. It's *not* your fault." She squeezed his hand. "None of this is your fault."

He touched her cheek and then gently disengaged his hand. He left her and went to kneel by George Foxwell's side. As he did, the old man opened his eyes and the shadow of a smile formed on the right side of his mouth.

"Cop...per...head..." he breathed. The sound of the old man's voice was dry as the brush of a dead leaf on stone.

He had never known quite what to call him. 'George' had seemed too personal. 'Master Foxwell' too removed. When very young, 'sir', had sufficed. Lately, he had not called him anything. They had not talked.

"Yes, it is I," he replied.

George Foxwell lifted his right hand and beckoned him closer. Copperhead took the hand and, in spite of the pain, pressed it between his own.

"Stay..." the old man said. "Stay...with...me."

A tear escaped Copperhead's eye to trail down his bloodied cheek. The sting of this man's son's attack was still sharp, and the place where William Foxwell's lash had struck him, split to the bone. He had told Miriam there was nowhere he belonged. He had been wrong.

He belonged with this old man.

"Father," Copperhead whispered, bending over to kiss George Foxwell's forehead. "I will stay."

COPPERHEAD

Chapter Thirteen

Copperhead stood with his hands linked behind his back, his head held high. He had been summoned to the area of the manor devastated by the fire, to the very room in which he had saved the life of the man in the dark green frock coat who haltingly paced the scorched tiles before him. William Foxwell's physical dexterity had been compromised – his crushed leg forced him to move about with a cane – but his sense of what was right and proper in the world remained intact.

A sense that Copperhead's very existence challenged.

It had been five days since the blaze. The two of them had not spoken since then. Attending to the aftermath of the Indians' attack, seeking out any who had escaped and burying those who had not in a mass grave far from the house, notifying the kin of the soldiers who had perished and beginning the work of restoring the burnt-out west wing had occupied them all. The work left little time to think, let alone consider the monumental nature of the events, some of which had begun – and others ended that night.

Copperhead waited as patiently as he could, not knowing what to expect from Miriam's father. No matter what, he had made his choice. He intended to stay.

William Foxwell would have to kill him to separate him from the old man in his need.

Foxwell crossed to the place where the beam that had injured him lay. The charred remnants of the giant pine timber were scattered across the table and what remained of the scorched patterned floor. He limped to the window and stood there, staring at the rising sun as if seeking a calm center from which to speak, and then turned back to look at him.

"Who are you?" William Foxwell asked without preamble.

Copperhead did not hesitate. "George Foxwell's son."

The older man swallowed a look of distaste and forced his face to remain neutral. "Really? You have proof of that?"

"Ask your father."

"Don't be impertinent with me, boy! Whether or not you pulled a burning timber off of me matters little. I still have my suspicions that you were in on this raid. That you were one of *them* – and not us." William Foxwell was managing his anger, but it lay just below the surface, seething – seeking a reason to explode. He limped forward until only a few feet remained between them. "You are *not* my brother," he growled. "And you will never claim to be, or I will seek you out and personally see to it that your miserable life is cut short at the end of a rope!"

William Foxwell desired power over him, but he was afraid – and Foxwell's fear gave his enemy strength. Copperhead said nothing, knowing that was all he needed to say.

Miriam's father glared at him. When he did not back down, he pivoted on his heel and returned to the burned and broken cherry table. Leaning his back against the part of it that remained upright, he eased the weight on his bad leg and stifled a sigh of relief, unwilling to show any weakness.

"If you are to remain here, on the property, certain rules of order must be established and observed without fail. My father, in his weakness, insists that he cannot continue in his present state without your presence in his life. That you must remain by his side. If this is to be the case, you and I must see each other daily. Not a prospect I cherish, I must admit."

"We know one another," Copperhead answered softly.

William Foxwell nodded. "Yes, we do. But do we understand one another? *That* is the question. You will be treated as a servant – as any *other* servant of this household. Punished, corrected, and rewarded in the same fashion. And as a servant, the same rules apply. You are not to have contact with my children in any other capacity than *as* a servant. Is that understood, Master Woodward? Especially Miriam."

Copperhead had learned how to play the game. He lowered his eyes and asked humbly. "May I ask a question, sir?"

William Foxwell was taken by surprise. "Well...yes."

"Is the mistress not then to return to school?" It had been her father's intention that Miriam be shipped off to Scotland again once the new term began. Something must have changed.

Foxwell snorted. "I seem to have no influence with Miriam anymore. Judith says she needs her here, to help her." He pushed off the chair and came closer, wincing with the pain in his leg, and pinned him with a hateful stare. "By necessity you will both be in the manor house. You will *not* take advantage of that to speak to Miriam. Is that understood?"

Copperhead kept his eyes averted. "Perfectly, sir."

William Foxwell said nothing. Glancing up, Copperhead saw that Miriam's father regarded him with a mixture of wariness and well-controlled – if not entirely concealed – rage. The older man moved even closer, lowering his voice before continuing. "What game are you playing at, Josiah Woodward? What do you hope to gain by shackling yourself to an old man whose time has come, who is months – if not *days* away from death's door? Is it money? Do you think you will inherit something as a bastard son?" He shook his head slowly. "I can tell you that you will not get one farthing while I live. And *that* is a promise. The minute the old man dies, you will be out on your ear!"

"The minute the old man dies I will leave this place, and you will never see me again." Copperhead looked up and met his adversarial stare. "*That* is the promise I make you."

William Foxwell nodded. "Then we *do* understand one another."

Copperhead went from the interview with Miriam's father to sit by George Foxwell's side. The frail old man had been given one of the lower rooms in the east wing with an outside access, a room that looked onto Miriam's late mother's garden which was blossoming and bursting into life. It was late April. The time when the world looked forward and not back. When the defeat of winter, with its dead brown branches and dry brittle leaves, gave way to the triumph of Spring.

Copperhead knew the man who lay before him would know no such victory. Even though George Foxwell might live many years, the man who had rescued him – the man he had known – was in many ways already dead. But he would honor him so long as the old man drew breath, and stay so long as he needed him. Rising, Copperhead touched George Foxwell's hand and leaned forward to gently kiss him on the forehead before turning to leave.

Tremulous, quaking fingers caught his and held him back. As he looked, the old man's lips parted. He drew a breath and tried to speak, but could not. Still, he managed to gesture toward the pewter cup filled with water that rested on the stand beside the bed. Copperhead retrieved it and then lifted him up, and helped him to drink.

"Stay," George whispered after he did.

He nodded. "Yes. What is it you would like me to do?"

"Just...stay."

Without releasing the old man's hand, Copperhead returned the cup to the stand and then sat on the edge of the bed. Minutes passed and George Foxwell remained silent. Copperhead shifted once or twice, uncomfortable with the moment. It did not surprise him. One thing he had learned by his time among the Tsalagi was that he had changed. The white world *had* corrupted him. He felt the need to 'do'. He was quick to speak, and found unnaturally long silences unsettling. Two Worlds had chided him for forgetting who he was. Green Snake told him he had 'lost himself'. Perhaps they were both right, but what he understood best was that long silences challenged a person to think, to consider their life and the choices they had made.

It was easier not to think.

It was easier to just to sit here in the warm sunshine, holding the old man's hand, waiting for him to die.

"Read...to me," George said at last, the words slurred so he only just caught their meaning.

Copperhead glanced around. Several books were stacked haphazardly on a table by the outer door. He released the old man's hand and crossed to wooden stand. The calfskin volumes contained an assortment of poems, prose, and religious matter. The Book of Common Prayer was on the top. The Bible at the bottom.

He turned to the older man and asked, "Which would you like me to read?"

"The...Bible...."

Copperhead's smile was gentle. Why did that not surprise him? He palmed the dark leather tome and walked back to the old man's side. He started to sit in the chair, but George indicated by patting the bed linens with his good hand that he wished him to return there.

"And which book would you like to hear?" he asked as he complied.

"Ma...Matthew...five forty...three." George's index finger created a lazy circle indicating he should keep reading until he stopped him.

Copperhead ran his hand over the book, enjoying the touch of the soft calfskin, and then opened the Bible to the back, where the gospels were. After flipping a few pages, he located the passage in question and scanned it quickly. It was one he knew and had read often. His deep brown eyes went to the old man.

George's mouth was turned up on the right side in a smile.

"Read...."

Copperhead did as he was instructed, knowing the words were meant for him and not for the old man lying in the bed.

"Ye have heard it was said, thou shalt love thy neighbor and hate thine enemy, but I say unto you, love your enemies and pray for them that persecute you; that ye may be sons of your Father who is in heaven: for he maketh his sun to rise on the evil and the good, and sendeth rain on the just and unjust." He paused, but George wagged his fingers, indicating he should continue. "For if you love them that love you, what reward have ye? Do not even the publicans the same? And if ye salute your brethren only, what do ye more? Do not even the Gentiles the same? Ye therefore shall be perfect, as your heavenly Father is perfect...."

Copperhead fell silent.

George caught his hand and squeezed it. "Listen."

He shook his head. "I cannot do this."

The smile remained. "You...can. You are...strong."

Copperhead pulled away and rose to his feet, flinging the dark tome on the bed. "Is it strength to love a man who hates you, who seeks to destroy you? Who despises the land your feet touch, the very air you breathe? Is it *strength* to forgive, and not to seek revenge?" he demanded angrily.

"It is…the way…to peace."

"No. It is not *my* way. My way is – "

"Death. It…is death." The old man sighed and closed his eyes, wearied by the effort.

Into the silence that descended the sound of a soft footfall fell. He knew it, and so he was not surprised when shortly Miriam appeared at the inner door. Copperhead turned to look at her. It had been several days since they had seen one another – she had been busy with Judith and work in the house, while he had assisted with the burials. Miriam was dressed like a servant, with a pinner apron covering a simple calico dress, and a day cap masking her cropped golden hair. Her face and hands, as well as her apron, were covered in soot. One short gleaming ringlet managed to escape the cap's unflattering prison to cascade down the middle of her forehead and trouble her eyes.

She brushed it aside but only succeeded in smudging her nose. "I didn't know you were here," she said, her voice the soft sigh of longing. "I came to see how Grandpa was doing."

Copperhead picked the leather book up from the bed and crossed to the table to replace it. "He is sleeping."

She must have noticed something – his knuckles white on the book's dark binding, his tightly clenched jaw – for she asked, "Is it my father?"

He glanced at her but said nothing.

Miriam stepped into the room. "You know he will be gone soon. The marriage is only a few weeks away. After that we will not have to worry about – "

"Nothing will change. Do you think he will not leave eyes and ears behind?" he replied.

Miriam frowned, whatever hopes she had, dashed. "Do you care?"

She had said she loved him. He had told her nothing in return. Since the fire, he had begun to wonder if her father was not correct – if his presence in her life *did* bring her nothing but pain and sorrow.

If not for the old man he would have left.

"Yes, I care," Copperhead answered, surprising her. "But not for me. For *you*."

Miriam bristled. "I can take care of myself, thank you *very* much, and make my own choices. If I want to be with you, I will be. And there is nothing my father can do to stop it!"

No. Nothing her father could do.

Only *he* had that power.

"Miriam, I...."

"Miriam? Child...." George Foxwell coughed and lifted his hand, beckoning her to his side. "Miriam...."

Miriam shot him a look that would have killed if it had been an arrow loosed from the bow, and then flew to her grandfather's side. Once there she gripped the old man's hand with her own. "How are you, Grandpapa? Better today?"

As she bent to kiss him, Copperhead took the opportunity to slip out of the room. He walked slowly down the corridor, nodding to the slaves he passed. Moving through the kitchen he left the manor by the back door, and then fled into the shade and sanctuary of the leaves.

If he truly loved Miriam, the best thing he could do for her was to let her go.

Judith watched from her bedroom window as the young man who had saved her soon to be husband's life bolted from the house into the woods. Josiah Woodward was an enigma. A puzzle she had yet to unravel. She had thought the claim that he was William's brother merely a ploy, but now it seemed William believed it, though he told her the boy's mother had not been a native of the West Indies but a savage George had apparently been involved with when a younger man.

If true, it put a new wrinkle on Miriam's attachment to Josiah. As before, Judith did not sense 'sisterly' feelings in the girl, but out and out infatuation. And while it was not unheard of, that still made the boy her half-uncle and blood, and such things were not to be tolerated.

At least in the New World.

Frowning, Judith turned back into the room and crossed to the chair by the fire. William had come in late to speak to her and fallen asleep in it. She had left him there and gone to bed still wearing her clothes. The sunlight pouring in the windows had awakened her and she had risen to find him still there. She took the book he had been reading from his hand and placed it on the table beside him. Then she nodded to Caroline, dismissing her. She had called her lady's maid in to stay the night so no one could question William's visit and paint it as improper. Caroline had been doing some tambour-work. She rose and curtseyed and left the room.

As Judith took the seat opposite him, William stirred and opened his eyes. She wondered if the door closing behind her maid had been enough to wake him. He blinked and shook himself and then sat up, yawning. William had been deeply asleep. His injuries were more severe than he cared to admit, and he had not stopped once since the fire occurred.

"How are you?" she asked gently.

"Tired," he admitted in a moment of unusual candor as he sank back into the chair. "*Very* tired."

Judith remembered the first time she had met him. His wife, Charlotte, had been alive then. She had been living with her father – a barrister in New Bern – at the time. When the Seven Years' War ended there had been a great many celebrations. A fantastic ball had been given in honor of the signing of the Peace Treaty, and she and her father had been invited. William and Charlotte had been in attendance, as well as William's father, George. Both were decorated and celebrated veterans of several of England's conflicts. She and the couple had exchanged pleasantries and, at the time, Judith had thought the high-strung, socially minded Charlotte – who was a bit of a flibbertigibbet – very ill-suited to the brooding but fascinating and extremely handsome Lieutenant William Foxwell.

After Charlotte's death they had begun a correspondence, first occasioned by some work her father had done for him. She acted as her father's secretary. They had found they had a mutual liking, and William had recognized in her a tidy mind and skills of organization that would well suit his and his manor's needs, as well as his girls'.

She didn't know if he loved her, or if he ever would.

She believed she loved him. Though there were times when he frightened her. Especially when he drank.

William rose and stretched again and then leaned on the mantle staring at the remnants of the fire. He remained still as if thinking for a few minutes and then glanced out the window. When he realized a new day had dawned, he turned to her with a chagrinned smile.

"I will make an improper woman of you yet."

"Or a very proper one," she countered with a grin. "In just thirteen days."

He nodded and reached for his pipe that he had left on the mantelpiece the night before. Stirring the coals, he found enough life in them to light it. William took a couple of puffs and then admitted wearily, "I am hesitant to leave, with all that has happened."

Judith drew a deep breath. They were set to travel to the capital to wed, and then to take an extended honeymoon in New York. The spring season would just be starting. There would be theater and balls, and all sorts of entertainments. She was to see her old friends and acquaintances – and to be seen *by* them. She had to admit that she took secret joy in the knowledge that some of the belles who had been so unkind to her would suddenly find 'old maid Judith' on the arm of such a handsome, desirable man. But she understood William's fears. They were her own.

"We do not have to go," she said. "The parish priest could marry us."

William put the pipe back on the mantel. "You are all I believed. An *excellent* woman," he said.

She nodded, holding back the tears.

"I thought perhaps we could still travel to the capital for the ceremony," he went on. "And stay for the week. I am not comfortable being gone several months. My father can no longer look after the horse trade, the workers need instruction, and there are a great many arrangements that need to be made before I return to duty. And then there is Miriam and this...*boy*."

"We can still go?" she asked, incredulous.

He leaned down and kissed her on the cheek. "I know how much it means to you."

The tears fell in earnest now. "That is kind of you. Thank you."

William took her hands and pulled her to her feet and then embraced her. She lay her cheek on his chest. "Every day, in every way, my dear, you prove your worth," he said. "What more could I ask? When I leave I know my children, all that I have will be in good hands – competent hands. And the whole of my affairs will be minded and managed by a woman with a great heart and well-ordered mind."

And that was probably as close to a confession of love as she was ever going to get.

Judith leaned into his strength and remained there, allowing him to stroke her hair. She had never dreamed she would have a husband, a house, and perhaps children of her own. All of this William gave her, even if he could not give her his heart.

Gently, he moved her away and then kissed her again before taking up his pipe and turning toward the door. "I must be about the business of the estate. The architect arrives today. I think we will make a few changes to the west wing, since Providence has seen fit to force us to rebuild." He ran his hand over his stubbled chin and glanced at his soot-covered hands. "I'd best see to myself before meeting him."

"You look quite handsome," Judith said softly.

His grin suited the rake he must have been when a young and callow youth. William bowed deeply and exited with a gallantly spoken, "My lady!"

Judith closed the door behind him and then returned to her window to face the growing day. She needed to change her clothes and prepare as well. She and Miriam were lending a hand, assisting the servants in removing the soot from the floors and walls, a time-consuming and laborious task at best. She had changed before William had come to call the night before and now needed to return to her work clothes. As Judith gazed out the window she saw the young man, Josiah, return from the woods. He walked with determination toward the studio that was his home. William told her the young man had vowed to stay by his father's side so long as George lived.

She wondered if that decision might not bring about, in time, a different kind of firestorm.

Chapter Fourteen

Miriam smiled at her sister, Anna. Judith and their father had left the week before for their wedding journey and the two of them were free – for the most part. Martha and Caroline had been left in charge of them and, between the young and the old maids, the two spinsters had found more than enough work to occupy most of their waking hours. This morning she and Anna had begged and pleaded and finally been allowed to escape to their mother's garden which was in need of a loving hand. Amidst the budding branches and growing green things sprouting in the thick brown earth, they had found a sort of haven. Miller, the gardener, a kindly old negro slave, had brought them the fruits of his winter labor – tiny seedlings nurtured with care, which would produce a myriad of brightly colored blossoms as the summer dawned. They had been hard at work for several hours when Miriam stuck her trowel in the earth and sat on her haunches, deciding it was time to take a rest. As she removed her gloves and wiped her hands on her apron, her eyes fell on the plot of green grass to the east of the garden. She could almost see her older sister, Kate, sitting there, teasing her about the 'secret' in their grandfather's studio. So many things had happened since that day, so many terrible unpredictable things. Kate and their mother's deaths, their grandfather's illness, the fire. She drew a deep breath of the fresh spring air and removed her straw hat, shaking her head to free the sweat from her cropped hair. That was another dark moment. One she tried hard to forget. Sometimes she could still feel the savage, Bear, on top of her, pressing into her, handling her breasts....

Miriam shuddered.

"Is something wrong?" Anna asked.

She shook her head. "No. Just a chill."

Her sister scowled at her as she thrust her own spade into the soil. "Stop treating me like a child."

"What?"

"You treat me like I am still nine years old. I am not. I'm almost a woman now. Some of my friends are engaged to be married."

"I'm sorry, Anna. I don't mean to." Miriam replaced her hat and began to tie the silk ribbons beneath her chin. "Let's get back to work."

"Just because you are the oldest now doesn't mean you can order me around." Anna crossed her arms and huffed. "Sometimes I wish *you* had died and Kate was still here!"

"Anna! Whatever is wrong with you?" Up until this moment Anna had been unusually quiet, but Miriam had just assumed that her sister was lost in the same dreamy state that working with the earth and green things always created in her. She *had* noticed that Anna had changed since the fire. Her sister's soft metal had been passed through the flames and the result had not been a stronger blade, but a brittle one. Anna was prone to tears and fits of temper, and had become unpredictable. "Why would you say such a thing?" she demanded.

"It's true. If it hadn't been for Martha sending us out here, all I would have seen of you today is when you came in to order me to bed. You never spend time with me anymore. You're too *busy*."

"I have a lot to do," she responded, reaching for another seedling. "Judith relies on me, and Grandpapa – "

"He's just going to die. Why do you even bother?"

Miriam turned to her aghast. "You don't know that!"

Anna stood. As she shook her skirts free of dirt she said, "Yes, I do. I heard papa say so."

"Well, 'Papa' doesn't know everything," Miriam countered. "Grandpa George is getting better. He is speaking more and – "

"I know why you go there," Anna said, dropping her voice and drawing closer. "To see *him*."

"Grandpa? Of course, I do…."

"No. *Him*." Anna indicated the tree line that partially hid the studio where Copperhead now lived alone. "Josiah."

Miriam rose as well and followed her sister's gaze. Copperhead was there, working outside the studio, chopping wood. His fine linen shirt hung on a fencepost beside him and his deeply tanned muscles rippled in the mounting sunlight as he worked. She chewed her lip and then turned back. "I'm not certain what you are suggesting, Anna."

"I'm not *suggesting* anything. It's plain as the nose on your face that you are in love with Josiah. Everybody knows it. Including Papa."

"You're imagining things," Miriam said as she bent to gather up the debris from her gardening. She motioned to Miller to come over and take it. As the old man did, executing a short bow, she turned back to her sister and said, her tone brooking no disobedience, "Let's change the subject."

Anna anchored her fists on her hips and did not move. "That's it! Tell me what to do. But you can't tell me what to *see*. And I have seen you, you know. I've seen you sneaking out to be with him." She dropped her voice again. "Did you know the servants say Josiah is part savage? And that he's Grandpapa's bastard."

"I don't have to listen to this," Miriam said, pushing past her and heading for the house.

"Mama would have been ashamed of you."

Miriam pivoted sharply. She walked back to her sister's side. "You take that back."

"Why? It's the truth!" Anna glanced around and then asked with an insinuating whisper, "Have you *been* with him? I bet you have. Papa thinks so. I heard him tell Judith."

"And just how many keyholes do you sit with your ear next to, you little snitch!" Miriam had done a good job holding out so far, but now she lost her temper. "If I wasn't a lady, I'd…. Well, I'd make mice feet of you!"

"Why don't you try?" Anna shouted, shoving her. "Brawling goes with being nothing but a piece of laced mutton!"

A second later the two of them were rolling on the ground in the middle of their dead mother's garden, flattening the seedlings they had just labored so hard to plant. Miriam caught her sister's strawberry blonde ringlets and yanked hard. Anna screamed and kicked her in the stomach so she fell back, unable to breathe.

Then she jumped on top of her.

Miriam could hear the elderly negro servant howling and calling for help. He must have thought they had lost their minds.

They had, but she didn't care. She was *so* angry!

"You little witch!" she screamed, catching hold of her sister's apron and ripping it and the fine expensive gown beneath. "Get off of me!"

"I hate you!" Anna shouted back while grinding dirt into her face. "I *hate* you!"

All of a sudden Anna stiffened and her mouth formed a round 'o' of surprise. A pair of deeply tanned hands circled at her waist and she was lifted up. Miriam looked up to find Copperhead holding Anna, his arms wrapped tightly around her sister's middle. He had thrown his soaked linen shirt on and run across the lawn to separate them.

"Anna! Miriam!" he shouted. "What do you think you are doing?"

Her sister struggled against him, kicking and screaming. "Let me go! Let me *go!* I'll tell on you – on *both* of you if you don't!"

Copperhead held her close. "Tell what you like. I will not let go of you until you calm down."

His deep brown eyes sought Miriam's as he effortlessly contained her sister. In their familiar stare she read a mixture of surprise and a quiet sort of amusement. Miriam suddenly felt quite ridiculous and every bit the child she had earlier accused her younger sister of being. What must she look like? Her hair was hanging in her eyes, her gown was torn, and she was covered in dirt and grass-stains.

"Young ladies!" a strident voice called from close by. "Mary and Joseph! What is wrong with the two of you?"

COPPERHEAD

Miriam winced. She turned to find Martha standing just without the wall of the garden. The old woman was wringing her hands. Miller, who stood at her side, was doing the same.

"Get up, Miriam!" Martha ordered and then wagged a bony finger at Copperhead. "And you, young man, release the colonel's daughter this instant!"

Copperhead opened his arms. Anna was still fighting to break free and so, when he did, she fell forward striking her elbows and knees on the ground.

And then Anna began to wail.

Martha was having none of that. "Stop it, child! Stand up, both of you! I am ashamed of you. You two are a *disgrace* to the name of Foxwell! Miriam, help your sister up."

Miriam did as she was ordered. She took hold of Anna's arm and helped her to stand. Once her sister was on her feet, Anna defiantly jerked her arm free and then, at Martha's disapproving look, lowered her head and stared at the ground. Miriam glanced at Copperhead who had retreated to the edge of the garden and then turned to face the storm of her old nursemaid's righteous wrath.

"I *am* sorry, Martha. I don't know what got into us...."

"Lucifer and all of his demonic hosts by the look of it!" the old woman replied, throwing her arms in the air. "Jesus might as well come and take me now. Imagine an old woman like me having to deal with two young *minxes* such as you! I'll surely end the Spring wrapped in a winding sheet and sealed in my grave! Now, both of you, march straight into the house and go to your prayer closets, and repent yourselves of this unseemly behavior." Martha pinned them both with her watery eyes and shook her head sadly. "What *would* your lady mother think? And you," the indignant old woman pointed at Copperhead again, "what are you smiling at? Off with you, boy. Off with you! And the next time you come near the house make certain you are decent! I never...."

Martha kept muttering as she turned around, lifted her skirts, and marched toward the house expecting the two of them to follow obediently in her wake. Miriam stole a glance at Copperhead before she did. He gave her a sympathetic smile and then, lacing his shirt, turned back toward the studio.

She watched him a moment and then sighed. "Come on, Anna. Let's not drag our heels or Martha will surely confiscate our shoes and we'll be stuck in the house forever. We're in trouble enough." She turned toward her sister. "Anna?"

Her sister hadn't moved. She was watching Copperhead walk away.

"Anna?"

"I hear you!" Anna snapped as she turned and headed for the house. As her sister drew abreast her, she muttered under her breath, "I still don't see what Josiah sees in *you*!"

Miriam stared after her. Then she turned and looked at Copperhead who – with his shirt on – had resumed chopping wood.

Could it be?

Was Anna *jealous?*

Later in the day a knock on the studio door brought his head up. Copperhead was sitting on the low cot he had used since George Foxwell had brought him to the estate, practicing his reading, but his mind was far away. The book he held was not the Bible the old man always wanted him to read, but a collection of poems by a man named Dante. Even though the words were hard and not formed in the fashion he was used to, he liked the visions Dante's writings evoked. Images of autumn, of a soul feeling like a 'dried sheath, bound up at length for harvesting' intrigued him, transporting him away from the world in which he found himself – a world that was troublesome and confusing at best.

Laying the book down he crossed to the door, but hesitated before opening it. If it was Miriam, he was not certain what he would do. Forming an excuse in his head, he lifted the latch, stepped back, and opened it.

Only to find Jedidiah Nevilles standing on the stoop, a wide grin splitting his freckled face. "Hey, there, Josiah!" he said. "I have some time free. I thought maybe you'd like to do something, or maybe just talk. If your work's done for the day."

Jedidiah was out of uniform, wearing only a pair of buff breeches and a pale linen shirt with a brown woolen vest thrown over it, and a leather pouch with a strap. His sandy hair shone in the late afternoon sun, gleaming like spun gold. The pale-skinned, blue-eyed son of an English merchant who had vowed to use his modest income to make certain his children had a better life, had an easy-going nature that made everyone like him.

Copperhead certainly did.

He smiled and retreated, clearing the way into the studio. "Come in, Jedidiah. I am finished as well, other than cleaning up in the annex. One of the horses was well enough today to return to the field."

"Glad to hear it." Jedidiah crossed the threshold and then stood with his hands anchored on his hips, looking around. Copperhead had managed to put the studio back together once the refugees from the fire had returned either to their own homes, or to the manor. Jedidiah whistled low. "Not too many that has this kind of space to himself. I bet you like it." He stepped into the main room and went to stare at one of George Foxwell's paintings. "Me. I'd be lonely. I grew up in a large family – ten brothers and sisters – and went straight into the army where I have dozens more." He laughed as he turned back. "Too much space and *way* too much quiet for me."

"I like it quiet," Copperhead said as he moved across the room and took a seat on the cot.

"I bet you do." Jedidiah took a seat in a chair close by. He fell silent for a moment. Then he shifted as if nervous and uncertain of what to say.

Copperhead hid his smile. "Do you have a question?" he asked.

"Yes. Well, *tons* of them really. If you don't mind."

"You saved Miriam's life – and mine. Ask me anything you want."

Jedidiah shook his head. "You don't owe me anything. You would've done the same for me."

"No. I would not have. Not then." It was painful to admit, but true. "The men who attacked the house…. Well, for a short time, I *was* one of them."

Jedidiah sat back in his chair. "No."

He smiled sadly. It seemed his confession had done the one thing he had not thought possible – silenced Jedidiah Nevilles.

After a moment, the young man stirred. "What do you remember? About who you were before – before you came here?"

"Why?"

"Just tell me."

Copperhead rose and walked to the window where he could look out at the lawn. The sun was almost down. "I remember my grandfather's lodge. It was made of branches and mud. The floor was dirt, but we were warm in the winter and cool in the summer, and always had more than enough. And I remember feeling as if I belonged. Not to just my grandfather, but to the whole village."

"Why did you leave then? What happened?"

"My family had been slaughtered. I was angry." His fingers balled into fists. "My father and one brother were murdered by soldiers as I watched. Then the soldiers went to my village and killed my mother and many others. When I close my eyes, I can still see the bodies, and smell the fried flesh." He looked at his friend. "I sought revenge in battle, but what I found instead was death – the death of my friends, and almost my own. If not for George Foxwell, I *would* have died."

"Then you aren't…." Jedidiah hesitated. "You aren't the old man's son?"

Copperhead was tired of lying. "No. I am not. He found me wounded, almost dead, and brought me here."

"So I bet 'Josiah' isn't your real name either, is it?"

"No. It is Wudigeas."

Jedidiah's brow wrinkled and he thought about it for a few seconds. "That's Cherokee, isn't it?"

"You know the language?"

Jedidiah laughed. "Cock and pie, no! I recognize the sound of it though. We've had some dealings with the Cherokee while I've been in Colonel Foxwell's regiment. A few of them have even been spies for the colonel. So what does it mean?"

"Copperhead," he said simply.

"Like the snake? How'd you come by that?"

"One called a 'Beloved Woman' gave it to me, an elder of the village."

"You remember that then?"

He nodded. Memory was odd that way. He couldn't recall his father's voice, the touch of his mother's hand.... But he could remember the rituals. "When about a week old Cherokee children are taken and immersed in the river and a name is given to them, based on how they look or act. I was born with much hair, or so I was told, and it was not black or brown, but copper as it is now."

"It's a good name for you," Jedidiah grinned. "Copperheads are swift and deadly, but only when forced in a corner. I think that fits you." He held out his hand, "Well, Copperhead, since I know your name now, I should 'formally' introduce myself, Jedidiah Beldhem Nevilles. But you can call me Jed, all my relations do."

Copperhead took his hand and shook it. "Hello, Jed," he said with a grin.

Jed fell silent for a moment. When he released his hand, he admitted, "I didn't come here by accident, actually. This is the first time I've had free – since the colonel is gone – and I have something important to show you. I just wanted to make certain the risk was worth it." The young man met his puzzled stare. "From what you've said today, I think it is."

"Risk?"

"After the fire I was sent to gather up the colonel's things. I found his satchel in the drawing room. It was undone and when I picked it up, several letters fell to the floor. I sort of took a look at them...." Jed reached into the leather pouch he carried and pulled out a letter partially covered in soot.

Copperhead frowned as he crossed the room to accept the letter and then examined it. The address was written in a large bold hand. It was from one of Foxwell's junior officers. On the back there was a map.

"What is this?" he asked.

Jed shook his head. "You better read it. And sit down when you do."

Copperhead frowned at him and began to read William Foxwell's personal mail. It was in a hasty hand and was hard for him to decipher. Script was still difficult for him. He recognized his name – Josiah Woodward – and several references to records that the officer had been told to seek out. Finally he held it out to his friend and admitted defeat. "The printed word I can read," he said, slightly embarrassed. "This is too hard."

"Oh. I hadn't thought of that. Sorry." Jed took the letter back. "This man, Ensign Thomas Ward, was sent by the colonel to find out who you are – or were. He backtracked and checked all the parish records in the area where General Foxwell was stationed during the last war. Thomas couldn't find any reference to a child born to him. Of course, I know why that is now. But what *you* need to know, is that Colonel William knows it as well."

Copperhead shrugged. "Records can be lost. And many are never written to begin with. It proves nothing. And the map?"

"That's the important part." Jed rose to his feet and pointed to an 'x' near the top of the drawing with some letters beside it. "There was a German farmer, name of Schaffner, who told Ensign Ward that he remembered a British officer who had come to his cabin with a young Indian boy who had been shot. This is the map to the farmer's house – and I would imagine, to your home and the people you left behind."

Copperhead's hands began to shake.

"I told you to sit down," Jed said quietly.

He did.

"I thought we could copy it, and then I could slip the letter back in the satchel. Or say I found it on the floor, or buried in the midst of the debris of the entryway. I doubt the colonel remembers whether it was in or *out* of his satchel."

He didn't know whether to be excited or terrified. "Thank you," Copperhead said, meaning it. "But Jed...."

"Yes?"

"Why? I asked you that before. Why help me? Why put yourself at risk? I don't understand."

The usually ebullient young man returned to the chair and sat, hanging his hands between his knees. Jed pursed his lips and then began quietly, "You remember I told you I had ten brothers and sisters?"

Copperhead nodded.

"Michael, the second to oldest – he's about ten years older than me. He came over here during the last war, fought with Prideaux and Johnson at Niagara. While he was serving he fell in love...with a native woman. Her brother had fought with the French and was killed at the fort. She was Seneca, I think. Oheo, that was her name. Meant 'beautiful'"

"Was?"

"She was raped and murdered. In front of her children," Jeb said, his voice breaking. "For the fact that she had the courage to love a white man."

Copperhead closed his eyes to shut out the images of the past, and of a future he was coming more and more to fear. A future involving Miriam. "And the children?" he asked quietly.

"Michael has them. He lives in one of the frontier settlements now near the border with Canada. There was no way he could take them back to England. I visited him before I made my way down here to my assignment." Jed rose to his feet. He came to his side and placed a hand on his shoulder. "So, you see, Wudigeas, I understand. And I find Colonel Foxwell's blind prejudice unacceptable. A man is a man, no matter the color of his skin."

Copperhead placed his hand over his friend's. "You are a good man, Jed. Would that every man felt the way you do. But that is a dream, I fear."

The young soldier held his other hand out, asking for the letter. "Now let's get this copied and back in the colonel's satchel before someone figures out what we're about."

Miriam had been reading to her grandfather from the Book of Common Prayer. He had fallen asleep and she had continued on her own. It was early evening and the sun was nearly gone, only a few pale strands of light lingered in the west casting the shadows of the tall trees across the lawn in pale purple stripes. She rose to light a taper from the fire, intending to carry it across the room to where the brass candlestick waited on the bedside table, but a sound made her stop and turn toward the door. Just as she did, a shadow crossed the threshold. When no one entered, she blew the taper out and stepped into the passageway. Looking right and then left, she saw Copperhead's long lean form silhouetted in the dying light that crept in through the open window.

"Please," she called, moving toward him, "please wait."

He remained still a moment and then stepped into the shadows.

Miriam rushed after him, slightly angered. Her father was away. This was their chance to meet, to talk – not to run from one another. As she rounded a corner, she almost ran into him. His strong hands caught her shoulders, stopping her, and then he released her and stepped back.

"I thought you had left," she said.

"I should have. Nothing but ill can come of this."

"Why? Why can we not at least be friends?"

His dark eyes met hers. "You know the answer to that."

"I don't care what my father thinks! I am old enough to make my own choices." Miriam fought to keep her voice level and low enough that no one would hear and discover them. "I love you."

"You think you do," he replied.

"What is *that* supposed to mean? You sound just like Papa! Do you think I am a child who does not know her own mind, or one so infatuated with danger that she would seek an illicit romance? I am no child, and I know what I am doing." She stepped close to him and touched his arm. "I know what, and *who* I want."

"You want Josiah Woodward," Copperhead responded quietly. "Not Wudigeas. You want me in white man's clothes, living a lie, pretending to be something I am not."

Miriam protested, "I don't want you to lie...."

He reached out and touched the front of her silk gown. "Are you willing to trade this for doeskin? And your fine linen shoes for moccasins? Will you carry your little ones with a strap tied to your head and beat the corn for crows, and wear your fingers to the bone grinding grain into meal on a stone?" Copperhead took hold of her hands and turned them over, showing her palms. "There are no calluses here, Miriam. And there never should be."

"But I don't – "

Copperhead reached out. He sighed as he brushed the ends of her butchered blonde hair with his fingers. "This, is my fault," he said. "Bear and the men who burnt your home, they are of *my* world. I will not make you a part of it. I will not take you to my people." He pulled his hand away. "And I cannot stay here forever."

"No," she whispered, catching his hand and pressing it to her lips, "we can make it work."

Copperhead pulled away. "No, we *cannot*. I will not hurt you anymore."

She sniffed as tears flooded her eyes and spilled down her cheeks. "Then you do care? At least a little?"

"Miriam...."

He took her in his arms and held her while she cried. For the longest time they remained, just as they were – he, with his hand on her hair, she with her arms about his waist. Outside the sun set and the evening's shadows overtook the corridor, casting them into total darkness.

"You must go," he said at last. "You will be missed."

"No…. I want to stay here, with you forever."

Copperhead kissed her hair and then pushed her away. "This place is not real. It is a dream. When the sun rises, it will vanish."

"Will you?" she asked quietly, her voice robbed of strength.

He frowned. "Will I what?"

"Vanish, with the rising of the sun," she said. "Are you leaving?"

Copperhead remained silent for several heartbeats. When he spoke, his voice broke with pain. "I promised your grandfather I would stay, and so long as he lives, I will do just that. But we cannot meet again. This cannot continue."

"Why? What is different? What did my father tell you?" she asked, growing angry. "Did he threaten you?"

"This has nothing to do with your father. I do not fear him. What I *do* fear is hurting you. I will never be accepted in your world, Miriam, you know this. And I will not make you a part of mine."

Each word was like a nail driven into her heart. "You have no right to make that decision for me," she countered weakly. "No right at all."

He smiled sadly. "It does not matter. I have made it. It is over." And with those words Copperhead turned and disappeared into the shadows that had overtaken the corridor.

Miriam stood, stunned. She leaned one hand on the wall to steady herself and then began to cry in earnest. Great sobs wracked her slight form until she couldn't breathe. Then, when she heard her sister calling her for supper, she ran headlong down the corridor and out into the yard, not stopping until she entered the maze and fell to the quickening grass as one dead.

Chapter Fifteen

The annex was dark and a safe sanctuary away from the desires that tortured him, from the dreams he dare not dream, and from the pain he had seen in Miriam's eyes – pain *he* had inflicted.

Copperhead slowly, steadily pulled a brush across the fine black coat of George Foxwell's mare, Molly. The horse was his now that the old man could no longer ride. She neighed and struck the floor with her foot. Tossing her shining ebon mane Molly pushed her head up under his hand, seeking his touch. Copperhead laid the brush down and wrapped one arm around her neck and stroked her, speaking soft words of comfort and assurance. Molly mourned for her fallen master.

Even as Copperhead mourned.

A sudden noise startled him and he looked toward the door. It was past midnight and he did not expect company. Patting Molly's nose, he released her and walked toward the opening that led from the studio's annex into the common room. Peering into the interior he saw nothing. With a frown Copperhead moved into the room and stood searching the shadows. Finally, satisfied that no one was there, he turned back to the task at hand.

It was then he heard a woman speak.

He pivoted, but still could not make out a shape. "Miriam? You shouldn't have come – "

A slender form – taller, broader than Miriam – dressed in a fine cambric chemise with a short bed-jacket of leaf green over it, stepped into the square of light cast by the studio window. "It's not Miriam. It's Anna."

"Anna?" he asked, surprised. Then, noting her nearly undressed state, he added quickly, "You shouldn't be here. Not alone."

She shrugged. "I know. I just…. Well, I couldn't sleep. I *had* to come. I wanted to apologize."

Copperhead picked up a linen cloth from the table beside him and wiped his hands. He had been working with Molly and they were covered with dust and dirt.

Besides, it gave him something to do.

"Apologize? For what?" he asked.

"My behavior earlier. Out on the lawn."

"Oh." Copperhead tossed the cloth down and headed for the hearth. "There is nothing to apologize for. At least not to *me*."

Anna made a little strangled noise low in her throat. "I suppose you mean I should apologize to Miriam."

He glanced at her as he reached for the poker to rouse the dying embers. "Yes."

"I will. Tomorrow. I promise."

Copperhead put a fresh log on the fire and replaced the poker before turning back to face her. Anna was just standing there, staring at him.

"Is there something more?" he asked.

Anna had her head lowered. She looked up at him demurely. A coy smile lifted the corner of one of her rouged lips as the crackling firelight caught in her blue eyes and sparked like flint. "Yes," she answered. "You can tell me if you accept my apology."

Copperhead did not have much experience with women. He remembered his mother, his grandmother and sisters. But since entering the white world there had seemed to be neither the time – nor the desire – to interact with females. Isaac Watkin's had laughed and cuffed his head one day when he asked about a spirited mother and daughter who frequented the store attached to the tavern. The pair was always sure to find something they needed for him to do – fetch an unlikely item from a high shelf, carry their supplies, or load and maybe *reload* their wagon. When the mother asked him to make a delivery to their residence Isaac had warned him to watch out – and then told him with a grin to 'enjoy himself'. Copperhead declined the invitation. He knew the pair would have happily taught him all he needed – or wanted to know. But there was always something else of more import to think about – George Foxwell's expectations of him, Two Worlds and the challenge of his friendship, William Foxwell and others like him and their irrational hatred....

Miriam.

Copperhead studied Miriam's little sister. Anna's eyes held the same invitation as the two at the tavern. Her fingers played with the edge of her chemise, undoing the laces, shifting the white fabric so it revealed the tops of her breasts.

"Anna..." he began.

As she closed the distance between them, Anna's smile turned into a well-practiced pout. "Well? *Do* you accept my apology? I don't think I could stand for you to be angry with me."

Behind him the log crackled, sending sparks into the air. He turned to tend it, but before he could Anna's hand was on his arm, holding him back. Copperhead frowned as he caught her hand in his own and squeezed her fingers.

Hard.

"Anna, this is not only foolish, it is dangerous. And not only for me. For *you*. You know how your father feels about me – "

"That hasn't stopped you from meeting with Miriam, has it?" she snapped, her expression passing quickly from pout to petulance. "Is she so much prettier than I am? Miriam's such a *tiny* little thing. I can assure you," she pulled his hand toward her exposed breasts, "I have more to offer. *Much* more."

"Anna! No!" Copperhead backed away. "No...."

For a moment she looked as though she might cry, and then Anna's anguish hardened into hate. "Who do you think you are? You think you can turn me down? My father *owns* you! All I have to do is rip my chemise and tell him that you tried to ravish me. Who do you think he will believe? *You*?" Her laugh was bitter. "They will take you and beat you, and you'll be sorry!"

"Why are you doing this? I have tried to be your friend – "

"I don't want to be your *friend*!" she countered. Anna's voice dropped to a throaty whisper as her hand ran down his chest. "I want *you*. And if I don't get you, I will make your life – and Miriam's – hell." She batted her eyelashes and smiled a sickly sweet smile. "And that's a *promise*."

Copperhead caught her hand. Anna Foxwell was beautiful, like her sister, but it was a beauty bent by sorrow and marred by insecurity and conceit. Anna would have what Anna *would* have and if not, then someone would pay. As she struggled to break free, he gripped her wrist tightly and pulled her close.

"I am sorry that life has not given you what you desire, Anna. I am sorry that your mother and sister died, that your house burned, that your grandfather is unwell. I am *sorry* that the world is not fair."

"What? What *are* you talking about?"

He caught her other arm and held her so she was forced to look into his eyes. "I am sorry that I do not love you, Anna."

Like an enraged animal Anna's lips curled back to reveal perfect pearl white teeth. "Let me go!" she snarled. "Let me go or you will regret it!"

He held her tighter. "No. *You* will listen to me. You are better than this. You are *worth* more than this."

Tears appeared in her eyes. "No.... Let me go...."

"Anna, listen to me! Even if I did love you, it would not work. Your father will never accept me. He *hates* me. That is why I have told Miriam that I must go."

Anna struggled for a second more and then she froze. "Go?" she asked, her voice small and frightened as a child's.

He nodded as he released her. "Yes."

"When?"

"Soon. I stay only so long as your grandfather lives."

Anna sniffed. She struck a tear from her cheek with her fingers and then pushed the loose blond curls back from her face. "Does Miriam know?"

"Yes. I will not see her again. I told her so earlier tonight."

For several heartbeats neither of them said anything. Then Anna reached up and caught her chemise and pulled its two sides together. Without looking up, she said softly, "You must think me a whore."

He shook his head. "No. I have known loss – loss *so* great I did not think I could survive. What I had to do to continue, I did. This is nothing more. We do what we have to."

Anna's lip trembled. "I don't want you to go."

"It is for the best," he answered. "For everyone."

She glanced up – just for a moment – but in that moment Copperhead saw something that frightened him. A need. A sense of determination.

But to what end?

Anna started for the door but stopped halfway there. Framed by the argent light that fell through the skylight she looked back at him. "Men," she snorted, "you always think you know what is best. But you don't. How can breaking my sister's heart be 'best'? Or breaking mine?" She took a few more steps and laid her hand on the latch that opened the door. "I'll show you what's *best*...."

And with that, she was gone.

Copperhead followed Anna out the door and watched as she dashed across the greening lawn to the manor house.

The wind had changed.

It was time for him to go.

Something woke her, but she didn't know what. A sense of movement. Voices.

Someone crying.

Miriam raised her head and shook herself, aware for the first time that she was still outside. She shifted her aching body and sat up, and then leaned against the stone bench behind her and looked up at the moon. It must be well past midnight. She couldn't believe no one had come looking for her. But then Judith was gone and ancient Martha, who was probably wrapped in her shawl and seated diligently in her chair by the staircase keeping a careful watch, would be fast asleep by now.

Miriam placed a steadying hand on the bench and rose to her feet. She frowned trying to remember what had driven her here. And then the waking terror of her parting from Copperhead struck her, and a wave of pain and loss and immeasurably deep sorrow greater than any she had ever known – even when her mother and sister died – swept over her pulling her down, threatening to drown her. She gasped for air. Suddenly weak in the knees, Miriam dropped onto the stone bench and lowered her head into her hands.

What was she going to do?

If Copperhead had been dead, or even if he had gone away, she might have been able to go on. *Might*. But to have him here, to see him daily, to know that he was near and not be able to be a part of him, that was a torture worthy of the worst fiend of Hell.

She couldn't bear it.

Lifting her head Miriam tossed her short curls back and straightened her dress, seeking to control something – even the smallest most unimportant thing in her life. Then she rose to her feet and walked to the edge of the maze. From the living framework of its doorway she gazed at the manor house, thinking of Grandpa George lying in his bed and of all he had been to her, of the things he had taught her that were now a part of the fiber of her being. Of Judith and her kindness, and the older woman's words of wisdom. Of her warning.

And of her father, William, and the life he intended her to live.

'Will 'love' keep clothes on your back, or food in your children's bellies?' he once asked her. 'Will 'love' till the fields and bring in the harvest?'

Before her lay two paths – one to the manor, the other to the studio where she knew Copperhead would be. She could choose either. She could choose to remain William Foxwell's daughter and to grow up as her father demanded, to become sensible and staid, and marry someone like Charles Matthew Spencer who could give her all that this world had to offer of safety and security. Or she could choose to be true to herself and to put her fate in the hands of the man she loved, even if it meant giving up every thing she had ever known.

Miriam hesitated, staring at the dark woods beyond the studio, remembering the faces, the fevered frenzy, the ferocious nature of the natives who had taken and accosted her. A shudder ran the length of her slight frame. What if Copperhead chose to go back to his people? Would she, could she go with him? He had spoken to her often of the hardships – the backbreaking labor, the seasons with no food that forced you to move from place to place, of not knowing where next you would call home. There *were* Indians who lived in houses, who farmed, who tried to fit in, but Miriam knew in her heart that in the end such efforts would come to naught because there would always be men like her father who would hate them just for the color of their skin.

Who would *never* let them fit in.

COPPERHEAD

Miriam looked at her hands – they were white and perfect, protected from the sun and any serious work. A hard day's labor in the garden might mean a callus, but there would always be Martha or one of the servants or slaves to make it better, to remind her that it was not her place, to tell her that she should let them take care of it. Let them take care of *her*.

She wanted to take care of someone.

She wanted to take care of Copperhead.

Lifting her skirts Miriam turned away from the manor and headed for the studio. There was a light within it so she knew he was awake. She would tell Copperhead that she was certain, that she knew what she wanted. And she wouldn't take 'no' for an answer. She was his. She would go away with him. Marry him. *Become* an Indian if she must. But she would not let him go, not tonight.

Not ever.

Judith Kingsley pulled a soiled glove from her hand and flung it on the settee next to the other one. She removed her hat and shoved an unruly lock of brown hair out of her eyes and then turned just in time to see William stride into the drawing room of the manor. He was in the worst temper she had ever seen. They had made it no more than twenty-five miles from the estate when a courier had overtaken them from Charles Town with a letter for Colonel William Foxwell.

A letter carrying a royal seal.

William read it, crushed the parchment in his hand, and then ordered their carriage back to the manor. He had not told her much, only that the marriage would not be postponed but that it would have to be performed here, by the local priest, and that the honeymoon would have to wait.

Judith was tired and disappointed, but accepted her marching orders like a good soldier. There was no use in arguing or complaining. She was no love-struck child who was prone to a fit of temper when thwarted in her plans. She would be William's wife and she would care for his children and his home while he was away, and welcome him back when his duty was done.

William on the other hand was behaving like a spoiled child. He had a supply of liquor with them in a spirits box and had opened one of the decanters and begun drinking the moment their fortunes turned. And was drinking still. When they stopped at the parish priest's home to see if he would marry them the next day, the elderly man had regarded her with knowing and sympathetic eyes.

The best thing Judith could do was get William to bed right away and let him sleep it off – away from her and anyone else he might lash out at in his drunken state.

"Damned inconvenient! Bloody *damned* nuisance!" William roared as he entered the room, glass in hand. "Where is Pennyworth? And Martha! Is there not a servant in the house?"

"It's past two in the morning, William. Everyone is abed."

"Well, let's wake them up, then. Shall we?" He took hold of one of the drawing room doors and slammed it with a vengeance. Opening it again William stepped into the hall and bellowed, "Wake up, you slackers! The master's home!"

"William! Get control of yourself!" Judith declared while carefully maintaining a safe distance from him. "I don't understand what has put you in this mood. I am disappointed, yes, about not getting to take our trip, but we are still to be married. Providence does not always deal us the hand we desire."

He stopped and stared at her. With a crooked sneer William lifted his glass. "Or *deserve*!" he toasted and downed the remaining whiskey.

Growing bold, she asked him, "What was in that letter? Will you tell me?"

William crossed to the bar and refilled his glass and then, with bottle in hand, moved to the fireplace and threw his long frame into the chair before it. "I am being recalled to England," he said as he took another drink. "I am to report as soon as possible to the Fisher's estate in Catawba Town for new orders. The King's advocate is there."

"England?" She hadn't considered that possibility. "Why?"

He shook his head. "This country is a powder-keg. The Indians, the French, the colonials themselves – men like this rabble Samuel Adams spreading sedition. People protesting their proper taxes, and this recent messy business in Boston. Some sort of rebellion may be on the horizon." He finished the remainder of the whiskey in his glass and poured another. "The King wishes me to return to England to train new recruits."

Judith sat heavily in the chair opposite him. "How long will you be gone?"

He shook his head. "Months. Years."

She had begun to shake. "Years?"

He nodded. Then he fixed her with his ice blue eyes which were keen and clear as a hawk's in spite of the amount of liquor he had consumed. "Still want to marry me?"

It had not been her intention to be a military 'widow' before she was a newlywed bride. And this meant that the entire responsibility of the estate – the servants, the slaves, the family business, Miriam and Anna, William's ailing father – would all be on *her* shoulders.

Judith drew a deep breath. "It is not what I would have wished."

William snorted. "Life seldom is." He downed the drink he held and moved to pour another.

"Don't you think you have had enough?" Judith dared to ask quietly.

For a moment she watched the drunken rage within him war with his reason. He stiffened and made as if to rise. Then reason won and William sank wearily back into his seat. He placed the whiskey bottle on the chair-side table and, leaning his chin on his hand, regarded her with an affectionate smile.

"I told you that you are good for me," he said.

Judith crossed to the hearth and knelt before him and began to remove his boots. She paused when she sensed movement outside the door. William's drunken ranting had no doubt roused one of the servants. Judith glanced toward the opening expecting to see Martha, or perhaps Pennyworth. Instead it was a pale and visibly shaken Anna Foxwell who hesitated just outside the painted pine doorway. Judith rose and moved quickly to her side.

"Anna? What is it?" She glanced at the girl's feet and hair. Even though Anna was dressed for bed, it was obvious she had been outside. Her bare feet were dirty and her hair, tousled and tangled from the wind. Behind her, Judith heard William stir within the confines of the chair. Anna couldn't see her father from this angle. She wondered if the girl had heard him, or if his presence remained unknown to her. "Well?" Judith asked when Anna failed to answer.

"What are you doing here?" the girl asked. "Is my father here?"

"Yes."

"I thought you were to be away for several weeks."

"There's been a change of plans," Judith replied.

"But the wedding? Are you married?"

She shook her head. "Not yet. Now, you answer me – where have *you* been?"

Anna met her gaze with a defiant stare. "If it's any of your business – which it's not – I went to see Josiah. I told him that I loved him."

Judith could hear it. The hammer being cocked. And the moment of tense silence before William Foxwell exploded in blind rage.

"By God, you did *what!*" William rose from his chair rigid with righteous indignation. He advanced like a storm without warning, his outrage striking the girl with the force of a hurricane. "I won't have my child acting like some Drury Lane vestal! Where's my whip! I'll take it to your backside first and then skin him alive!"

"William!" Judith shifted and placed her body between him and his daughter. Anna was white as her chemise and trembling from head to toe. "What she did was *very* wrong. But you can't – "

"I can *damn* well strike her down where she stands if I like! And you as well! There is no court in this land that would rule against me if I did. A man has a right to protect – and punish his own," he growled. William's complexion was scarlet as his coat. *"Now, get out of my way!"*

"William, take a moment to collect yourself. You don't want to do anything you will regret later." Judith's eyes were trained on his upraised hand, waiting for the blow to come. *"Think* about what you are doing."

He was seething. Barely able to stand in one place. Barely in control.

But for the moment he *was* in control.

"Did he touch you?" William demanded of his daughter. "Well? *Speak!"*

Judith glanced over her shoulder. Anna's head was down. She saw the girl shiver. Heard her sniff. And watched as emotions ranging from rage to regret tightened her jaw and sent tears trailing down her cheeks.

Anna said nothing – and everything.

She nodded.

Judith drew a deep breath before turning back. She faced William and waited for the lightning and thunder of his hateful fury to sound throughout the room. Instead, he grew calm.

Terrifyingly calm.

An acid smile quirked the edge of William Foxwell's upper lip and he laughed.

"Ha! *I have him!"*

Chapter Sixteen

Miriam didn't knock at the studio door. It was already open. She could see Copperhead sitting within. He didn't stir as she entered, didn't look up. She passed through the patches of pale moonlight that striped the floor and sat by him on the cot. For a moment he did nothing. Then he took her hand and gripped it in his own.

For some time they sat just so. At last his lips parted and he said three words – words that in themselves meant little, but by their implication spoke volumes.

"Anna was here."

"Anna?" Miriam frowned. "In the middle of the night? What did she want?"

Copperhead's expression was more than enough of an answer.

"Dear God!" she exclaimed. Then, her voice hushed by the horror of it, asked quietly, "Did anyone see her come here? Do you know?"

He shrugged. "I have no idea. I am still here – and alive – so I assume no one is aware that she came."

"Martha is probably asleep. Thank the Lord my father and Judith are away! What could have gotten into her? I suspected Anna was infatuated with you. But this?" Miriam rose and began to pace, anxious to mend this, to *fix* it in some way. "I'll go find her. I am sure I can swear her to secrecy. I certainly know enough things to keep her quiet. I – "

Copperhead rose and came to her side. He took one of her hands in his own, while pressing the fingers of the other to her lips. "Miriam. It's over. I have to go. *Now*."

Tears flooded her eyes. She wanted to argue with him, but he was right. They both knew from experience what was deemed 'just' punishment for a man of color who dared to touch a white woman.

Still, she couldn't let him go.

"Copperhead.... No. I can't lose you."

He reached out and touched the soft blond curls that framed her face, brushing them back from her eyes. "You already have."

"*No*. I will go with you. I was coming here tonight to tell you that." She held his hand tightly, refusing to yield when he tried to pull away. "I have made up my mind. I don't care where you go – I want to go there to!"

"Miriam, no."

"If you don't let me, I will follow you," she replied, growing heated. "I won't be left behind! This life – endless days spent in useless pursuits, jockeying for position and power, wedding and bedding to secure one's place in the world – it is not my life anymore. I *cannot* be what my father wants. Through you, I have seen there is something more."

"I cannot ask you to go where I am going," he answered.

"But don't you see? You don't *have* to ask. I have already agreed." Miriam squeezed his hand. "Copperhead, please? Don't turn me away."

They were standing in a patch of moonlight. It turned his hair the color of weathered bronze. He wouldn't look at her at first but when he did his eyes, deep brown as freshly turned earth, were troubled; haunted by thoughts of all that lay ahead, by knowledge of the nearly insurmountable chasm that separated them, and by what *she* would have to endure to bridge it. Copperhead drew a deep, shuddering breath and then released it. Raising his hand, he touched her cheek.

And nodded.

Joy and sorrow commingled moved through her – a profound joy tempered both by the reality of her choice and by the knowledge that she was about to bid farewell to everything and everyone she had ever known. Miriam moved into his embrace and laid her head on his chest.

"I'd like to let Grandfather know," she said quietly.

Copperhead held her close. He placed his chin on her hair. "You should take time to gather a few things as well. Anna seemed embarrassed. If she tells her story, I doubt it will be before the sun rises. We should have a few hours. I will meet you on the lawn outside his room in half an hour."

"No." Miriam pulled back and met his gaze. Something, some inborn sense, told her they should not be parted. "I'll wait. We'll go together."

"Miriam...."

"Please. Don't make me go."

Copperhead wiped a spent tear from her cheek with his thumb. "It will be all right. Go. Gather your things." He paused a moment and then added with a rueful smile, "I did not get to say goodbye to my people. I do not want you to have that regret."

She bit her lip as she turned from him and gazed at the house. Copperhead spoke again from the voice of experience. And he was right. Even if she could not say goodbye to her father, or to Judith, she *could* bid farewell to the life she had known and gather a few mementos for the journey – her mother's pearl and gold chatelaine, the watch her grandfather had given her, Grandma Maggie's cross. In answer to his worried look, she nodded. As she released his hand she pleaded, "Don't be long," and then turned toward the door.

"Miriam."

Pivoting to face him, she asked, "Yes?"

"I have wanted to do this for so long...."

Copperhead took her again in his arms. But this time his embrace was potent – powered by the muscles of hard manual labor and fueled by a desire denied for years. He crushed her to his body, and then bent down and kissed her with the passion and fire of a love both sense and sanity forbade.

When he released her she was breathless.

"Now go," he said. "Thirty minutes. I will be there."

Miriam nodded.

It would be a half hour that would change their lives.

Judith Kingsley paced anxiously from one side of the entry hall to the other, wringing her hands against the skirts of her pale blue silk gown. She was exhausted but there was no way she could sleep. William had been *truly* frightening as he calmly walked from the house and mounted one of the horses to make the journey to nearby Fisher Hall. He was going to get the King's advocate. Justice would be swift and severe.

The young man, Josiah Woodward, would hang this day.

William's explosive anger would have been easier to accept. If he had flown off in a rage and beat the boy, or even killed him.... Well, after what had happened, she might have been able to understand – and to forgive. But this cold calculation, making certain everything was in order, that there would *be* no questions, was tantamount to plotting an assassination.

She had to ask herself – just who *was* William Foxwell? And was he a man she could marry?

Judith drew her shawl tightly about her shoulders as she sat heavily on the lowest step of the hall stair. Today was to have marked the beginning of her new life – marriage to a man she loved, becoming a part of a family, knowing she was secure and safe and would be taken care of. Now all of it had come crashing down around her. William was to go away. She would be left alone with his daughters, and if Josiah Woodward *were* hung both of them would be in despair. And what would Miriam do once she had found out that it was her sister's words that condemned him?

It was more – *much* more – than she had bargained for.

Judith rose and for a moment, did not know where to go. Then she thought of the gentle old man who lay at the rear of the house, confined to his rooms – of the only voice of reason she might find in this crisis. But could she? Did she dare disturb an invalid, dare burden him with this? Was it not rather cruel and selfish to do so? Especially when George Foxwell could not respond as would be his wish.

No, she determined, it was *too* unkind.

Still, it would not hurt to go and sit with William's father. Just to see him, to hold his hand and find some comfort in his presence.

Judith began the journey to George Foxwell's rooms, but stopped at the foot of the stair and glanced up. First she must make certain Anna was all right. The foolish girl had run off in tears when her father dismissed her and confined her to her room. The memory brought a scowl to Judith's face. William had struck Anna so hard that it had left his handprint in crimson on her cheek.

Who *was* William Foxwell?

She was not certain she wanted to know anymore.

Judith lifted her pale blue skirts and placed her foot on the bottom step.

First Anna.

And then she would see to her *own* soul.

Miriam entered the house by the back door and crept to the foot of the main stair. She stopped when she realized someone was ascending them. A quick glance showed it to be a woman. With a frown she realized Martha must have awakened and be looking for her. She would have to move quickly and be careful. If Martha caught her she might be delayed, or worse, confined to the house.

And she had no time.

Quietly following the other woman up the stair, Miriam waited until the skirted shadow entered her sister's room. Thinking of what Anna had done – no matter how innocently – of how she had altered forever the course of their lives and put Copperhead's very *life* in danger, made Miriam burn with indignation. Anna should have known that he would want no part of her. Known that the two of them were in love....

Even though they had never admitted it to themselves.

Until now.

Leaving the corridor Miriam passed into her own room and began to silently gather a few things. She located her cloak and short coat, and a bonnet, and tossed them on the bed for easy retrieval. Then she opened the armoire and rummaged through it until she found a cloth bag into which she tossed her comb and brush as well as a half-dozen other personal items. After that she hastily scoured the room, searching for other things she did not want to leave behind. In a silver box she found her mother's chatelaine and, beside it, her grandmother Margaret's miniature portrait with the gold and ruby cross draped over it. Taking a moment to place the cross about her neck, she fastened the catch and then swept up the remainder of her jewelry and the portrait and placed them in the bag. Finishing with the ABC book her grandmother had painted, rescued from the studio years before, Miriam crossed to the door and stood beside it, listening. Hearing nothing, she stepped into the corridor and pulled the door too behind her and then turned around –

Only to find herself face to face with Judith Kingsley.

Judith was very pale; her skin grey as the iridescent sheen of the pallid blue gown she wore. The older woman was disheveled, her shawl had slipped off her shoulders and trailed on the floor. Her brown hair was unkempt.

It was obvious she had been crying.

Judith drew a deep breath and then let the sigh out in words. "I *thought* I heard something. Miriam. Child." Then Judith's eyes lit on the satchel and noted Miriam's cloak and bonnet. Her hand went to her throat as she asked, "Where are you going?"

Miriam was sure her own pallor matched the other woman's. If Judith was here, then where – "Is my father here?" she asked, breathless.

Judith drew a step closer. "No. But William will return soon." She inclined her head toward the cloth bag. "Are you leaving?"

Miriam's knuckles grew white on its bone handle. "Yes."

"With Josiah?"

She nodded, her jaw set. "You *won't* stop me."

Judith had been holding herself very tightly, her slender form rigid. Now it softened, melting with her words. "For the love of God in Heaven, Miriam, I would not try."

"What? What do you mean?"

Judith reached out and took her hand. "I was wrong when I told you before that you must forget love. Go, child! *Be* happy. Even if it is only for a few years. Do not make the mistake of settling for less."

Judith's words dismissed any lingering fears Miriam had. In the older woman's face she saw the reflection of where she would end if she hesitated. "Are you married then?" she asked.

"No." Judith answered as she released her. "A courier found us on the road. Your father has been recalled to duty in England. We are to be married here, later today, by the parish priest."

Miriam sensed her doubt. "And will you? Marry him?"

Tears flooded the older woman's eyes. She looked away. "I don't know. The events of this night may decide it." Suddenly Judith turned back. "Where is your young man?"

She hesitated, but then answered honestly. "Saddling Molly. I am to meet him at grandfather's room. I wanted…. I *need* to say goodbye."

"How long does it take to get to the Fisher's estate?" Judith asked.

The question seemed nonsensical. "The Fishers? Perhaps an hour's ride," Miriam answered "Why?"

Judith turned and put her foot on the top step. "That is where your father has gone. The King's man is there. William brings him back so he may pronounce a sentence of *death* on Josiah."

For a second she could not breathe. "Death? For what?" Miriam descended and took her arm. "What did Anna tell Father?"

Judith placed a hand over hers. "My dear.... That Josiah invited her to his rooms and there accosted her."

Miriam went rigid. She stepped back onto the landing. "The little *trull*! How dare she? When I get my hands on her, I will – "

Judith caught her hand and held her back. "Miriam, I *must* know. Are you certain there is nothing to the charge? Do you know that you can believe Josiah? Over your flesh and blood?"

She met the other woman's troubled gaze. "Yes," she answered, "I know."

Judith studied her face for a moment and then nodded. "All right. But whether or not Anna's charges are true, it matters little. You *know* whom the authorities will believe. And Anna is so terrified of your father that, even if she thought better of the lie, she will not retract it. We must get you and Josiah away from here." Judith gripped her hand and started to descend the stair.

"Come, we will go together to your grandfather's room."

Copperhead had saddled Molly, walked her to the back of the house, and tied her to one of the trees that skirted it. He had taken a moment to gather a few things – his great coat, the kit he had already prepared, a lantern, knife, and the Scottish flintlock George Foxwell had given him. Tucked away as well within his coat was the copy of the map Jedidiah Nevilles had taken from William Foxwell's bag. He prayed it would not come to it, but if he had to use the flintlock to defend Miriam, he would.

He would do *whatever* it took to protect her.

Moving with stealth Copperhead approached the manor, confident in his ability to avoid the servants and guards who patrolled it. He had been a part of the estate for so long he knew its heartbeat as well as his own. The servants were old and would be asleep, and the soldiers who remained behind, keeping watch over Colonel Foxwell's property, were far away to the south at this hour.

At the window of George Foxwell's room he paused to peer in. The old man was alone and appeared to be sleeping. A single candle in a pewter holder sat on a table next to the bed, guttering – a good indication that the servant who was assigned to check on him had already come and gone.

It should be safe to go in.

Putting his hand to the latch he opened the door and entered the room. The air was stale, musty, as though it had not been aired out for days. Copperhead crossed to the old man's bed and sat in the chair beside it. George's skin was grey and transparent. His breathing shallow. His hair, which had once shone like silver, was dull as pewter and needed cutting.

What would life be like for George Foxwell once they were gone? Anna was too frightened to care and his son, William, would as soon see him dead. Judith Kingsley was the only one who was kind to the old man.

If Miriam's grandfather could have traveled, Copperhead would have taken him with them.

But he could not.

As he sat there, thinking, George Foxwell stirred and opened his eyes. The pale blue orbs looked up at him with remarkable clarity.

"Copperhead...my boy," he said, his voice clear as a bell tolling on a rain-flecked plain.

"Father," he answered and gripped the old man's hand.

George Foxwell wet his lips and patted the bed with his hand. "Come. Sit. Beside...me."

Doing as he asked Copperhead perched on the edge of the bed. For a moment he said nothing. When the words finally came, he found there was no need for them.

"Father. Miriam and I are – "

"You are...going," the old man said

Copperhead nodded. "How do you...?"

"Knew it would come...to this. William...." George Foxwell drew a deep breath and coughed. "Never accept you. Promised you could stay, but I knew...."

"I do *not* want to leave you," Copperhead told him.

Miriam's grandfather smiled a crooked smile as only one side of his mouth answered the call. "Know that too. Be...all right."

"Father, I...." Copperhead tensed and pivoted toward the door. There was a noise. Footsteps.

Two pair.

Rising quickly he palmed the knife he had tucked into his belt and ducked behind the door. He waited, tense, expectant. Then he heard Miriam's voice.

But who was with her?

Through the crack in the door Copperhead watched Miriam enter. He shifted and followed her with his eyes as she rushed to her grandfather's side. When the second figure moved toward the sickbed to join her, Copperhead recognized the slender form and rich brown hair piled high.

It was Judith Kingsley.

Judith who should have been in New Bern with William Foxwell.

"Miriam," Copperhead declared as he stepped from the shadows. "Miriam. What is this?"

Judith jumped and then pivoted to look at him. "Josiah. I have no intention of stopping you. You needn't fear me," she assured him quickly.

"And what of William?" he asked as he stepped into the room.

She drew a sharp breath. "That is another matter. You must go. *Now.* William left nearly an hour ago for Catabaw Town and the Fishers'. Josiah, you have perhaps an hour to get away. If you are fortunate."

"He knows then?"

"That you are running away? No." She glanced at Miriam.

From her grandfather's side, the woman he loved answered, "Anna lied. She said *you* seduced *her.* Father has gone to get the King's man who is staying there."

Copperhead shut his eyes and steadied himself. It was all happening just as he feared. And worse. If Miriam went with him she would become, not a recalcitrant child sought by an angry parent, but a fugitive. And he would be branded as a criminal and hunted until the day either *he* or William Foxwell died.

"I should go alone," he said quietly.

Miriam shot to her feet. "No!"

Judith reached out and placed her hand on his arm. "I agree."

"I will not have Miriam live in fear, looking over her shoulder every minute. I will not stand by to see her punished or thrown in a prison because of me. You know William can say anything he wants, make up any lie, and it is *he* who will be believed!"

"William will do nothing to harm his daughter. He *loves* her," Judith spoke the word with distaste, as if its meaning was tarnished by the association. "William loves her in the only way he knows how. Miriam is his possession. He will hunt you, yes, but if you are found, he will not harm her." She glanced at Miriam and then returned to meet his anguished gaze. "If you leave her here, alone, Josiah, *you* will be the one harming her. Now, go! *Both* of you."

Miriam had risen and crossed to his side. She took his hand. "Copperhead, please. Listen to her...."

Judith frowned. "Copperhead? Is that your name?"

He nodded. "Yes. It is not Josiah Woodward. It never has been. I am Wudigeas. I am Cherokee."

The older woman paled. "Then William was right? You *are* George's son by an Indian woman?"

"No. I am a full-blooded Cherokee. George Foxwell found me when I was dying. He brought me here. He *saved* me." Copperhead looked at the older man. Miriam's grandfather was watching their exchange with fascination from his sickbed. "I am not his son. Nor William's brother."

Judith turned a wondering gaze on Miriam. "Are you prepared for this?" she asked

Miriam took his hand. He felt her lean into his strength.

"Yes," she answered. "*Wherever* the path may lead. I am ready."

Judith stared at the two of them for a moment, and then she went to sit in the chair beside George Foxwell. She looked at him and the old man nodded once, as if giving them his blessing. Judith gripped his hand and turned back toward them. "Do you believe in miracles?' George asked me once. He said there was something for you yet, Josiah... Copperhead. Something yet to come. Is this it?"

Miriam picked her satchel up from the floor and handed it to him. Then she went to the older woman and kissed her on the cheek. "Take care of grandpa for me, will you, Judith? You are all he has now." As Judith nodded she crossed to his side and leaned over and kissed him on the forehead. "I will come back, Grandpapa," Miriam said softly. "You wait for me, do you hear? You are not allowed to die."

She was crying. Copperhead went to her and put his arm about her shoulders. George Foxwell met his troubled gaze with a weak smile.

"God protect you both," he said.

He and Miriam would have been well away before morning if not for the fact that Molly threw a shoe.

They made it to the far end of the estate before it happened, near the stable that had been their meeting place. Copperhead kept supplies there, prepared for just such an eventuality – though he had thought at the time he stowed them that he would be fleeing the Foxwell estate alone. He led Molly into one of the stalls of the abandoned building and set about cleaning her foot and replacing the shoe. As he worked Miriam paced back and forth just inside the door, breathless, nervous, terrified that her father would appear and descend on them before they could make good their escape. Outside the ramshackle building the sun was dawning, trailing rose-red fingers across a blue sky that left in their wake pale purple ribbons of light. It had begun to rain. A lavender mist rose from the wet grass to fill the shallow bowl the stable lay within.

Miriam turned to him and asked, "How much longer?"

"A few minutes," he replied, keeping his tone deliberately calm.

"Can't you hurry?" Her voice was strained. Almost angry. "Each minute brings my father closer."

"If I hurry it will only happen again," he answered. "Beyond the estate there are few houses and even fewer supplies. Keep watch. Listen. I will finish as soon as I can."

Miriam stared at him for a moment and then nodded before turning back to the door. He watched her walk to it and place her hand on the jamb and look out on the ripening day before he turned back to the task at hand. Freedom lay there – not three hundred yards away – through the surrounding wall, down the road and out of the estate, and then over the river to the south where their destiny lay.

"There," he said releasing Molly's foot and patting her on the rump. "Give me a moment to check the straps and we can go." When he had finished, Copperhead patted the animal's neck, reassuring her that he knew she had not meant to harm them. Then he turned to look at Miriam.

She was gone.

Puzzled, he left the horse and stepped outside. The mist that rose with the morning hung like a gossamer curtain, obscuring the woods and the rolling hills beyond. Copperhead called Miriam's name and waited. When she didn't show he took several steps forward, but stopped as the mist parted to reveal an officer dressed in a scarlet coat – and a half dozen more soldiers following behind. One of them held Miriam in his arms. As she struggled, crying out for him to 'run!', the officer advanced until he was no more than six feet away.

It was William Foxwell.

Chapter Seventeen

Miriam's father unhitched a mule skinner's whip from the belt of his scarlet coat and advanced toward him, backing Copperhead over the threshold and into the stable. As he did, he struck the looped and braided lash against his palm so it snapped with menace.

"So, here we are at last, boy!" he snarled. "I knew one day that I would have you – that *one* day you would overstep your bounds. *Good God*! As if seducing and wrecking the life of *one* of my daughters wasn't enough!" William Foxwell flicked the lash free and let the tail drag through the debris of the stable floor. "I warned my father that you were a viper in the nest, only waiting for the right moment to strike. What a blind *fool* the old man is! If he knew you like *I* do – "

Copperhead was cornered, pressed up against the rough boards that formed Molly's stall. The horse stomped as she sensed the threat to him, and whinnied with fear. "You don't know me at all," he countered. "You don't want to!"

Miriam's father took another step. "But do you know *me*, boy? *That* is the question – do *you* know *me*?"

"I know what you are capable of." Copperhead's answer was defiant. "I know your kind – heartless, inhuman. Arrogant and cruel." In his mind's eye he saw a shadowy figure – dressed in the same scarlet coat – standing over his father's body, driving a bayonet through his still-beating heart. Copperhead swallowed over the bile that rose in his throat. "*Merciless.*"

William Foxwell snorted. "You dare to call *me* 'arrogant'? I have never met a more arrogant bastard than you – and *your* kind. Oh yes, I know. I know you are a 'breed' born of the filthy loins of some grunting squaw!" Miriam's father strode across the remainder of the straw-covered stable floor, quickly closing the gap between them. The quirk of his cruel lips, the glint in his steely eyes, showed how much he was enjoying himself. His triumphant sneer was caustic. "I have seen that look in other black eyes. In the faces of savages as they died at the end of my bayonet. You think yourself superior. *Better* than us. Better than *me*."

In many ways William Foxwell was a coward. He would not have had the courage to take him on alone. But here, with the stable surrounded by his men and Miriam held hostage against any reprisal or escape, he had become judge, jury and executioner.

It was over.

Copperhead drew a breath and sealed his fate.

"I *am* better than you."

William Foxwell's rage painted his face scarlet as his coat. He rammed the handle of the whip under Copperhead's chin and forced his head up. "I will *relish* your death, boy."

"On what charge? For what crime do I die?" he countered.

"I don't need a charge," his tormentor growled. "If I wanted, you would die merely because I said it is so. However, as I want there to be no question as to the *legitimacy* of this execution of justice...." William Foxwell's ice blue eyes flicked to Molly where she stamped and snorted in the stall, and then back to him. "To spare my daughter the shame, I will not bring up her indiscretion. You will be branded a horse thief. That's *more* than enough to hang you."

Copperhead could have protested. Molly was a gift. But then Miriam's father knew George Foxwell could not testify to that fact – even if there *was* a trial.

Which he knew there would not be.

"Well? Are you just going to meekly accept your fate? Where's your spine, *breed*?" William Foxwell paused. He lowered the whip and took a step back. "What *is* your name, boy? Certainly not 'Josiah'."

Copperhead shook his head and held his peace.

Miriam's father frowned. Then his jaw went rigid with anger. He raised a quaking hand and lashed out, taking him by throat. "Oh, that's right. You won't *honor* me with it. Well, I'll find out what it is one day, breed, and then I will wipe it from mankind's memory. I will dance on your grave, boy. You have made a fool of me for long enough!"

There was a noise. Someone clearing their throat. Then a pallid face appeared at the stable door.

It was Jedidiah Nevilles.

William Foxwell's aide stepped in and saluted smartly. He kept his eyes trained on his commanding officer. "Sir! The King's man, John Leighton, is at the manor," he announced.

Miriam's father answered without looking at him. "Have Jenkins show Mr. Leighton to the drawing room. Give him a cup of tea and make him comfortable. I'll be a few minutes yet."

"Sir!" Jedidiah saluted again. Then he hesitated and his gaze shifted to Copperhead. As he met his friend's stare, Jedidiah shook his head in dismay.

William Foxwell sensed his aide's uncertainty. He pivoted and shouted, "Get on your way, man! Once Jenkins has been dispatched, take charge of my daughter and send Sergeant Grove and Ensign Ward in here. *Now*, soldier!"

Jedidiah saluted smartly a third time and stepped out the door. Seconds later two men, Grove and Ward he presumed, stepped in. One was a brawny, powerfully built man, swarthy complected, with the gait of a sailor. The other was whip-thin and mean, and obviously his lackey. Both regarded him with hatred and disgust.

"You will be my witnesses," William Foxwell told the pair as he stepped back and leaned against the stall. "We are going to do this properly. The criminal will be interrogated. And *when* he resists...."

Miriam's father signaled the soldiers and Ward and Grove moved in for the kill.

Miriam fought furiously to escape Jedidiah Neville's grasp. Her father's aide held her tightly, refusing to let her run into the stable.

She knew her father. She *knew* what was coming.

"Let me go! Dear God, let me go! Jedidiah, he'll kill him!"

"Miss Miriam, think! What good can you do?" Jedidiah's young face was a study in misery. He glanced back over his shoulder at the open stable door. "What can any of us do? The King's advocate came here with a warrant. It's all proper and legal. Copperhead's been accused of a crime and there's nothing we can do to interfere!"

The use of Copperhead's Indian name startled her into submission. Miriam met the young soldier' stare. "You know then? About Josiah being an – "

He nodded. "I know. I know who – and *what* he is. I have since the fire."

"He said you two had become friends. But I didn't realize...."

Jedidiah shrugged. "I sort of figured it out. My brother was married to an Indian woman."

"*Was?*" she prompted.

He winced and the nodded. "White men killed her. Just like they're going to kill Copperhead."

"*No!*" Miriam began to struggle again. "Let me go! I'll *beg* my father to – "

"You think that's going to help him?" Jedidiah snapped. "Go on then! *Show* your father how much you love him! Give the Colonel a reason to shove the bayonet in another inch!" He gripped her arms and shook her hard. "Nothing you can say is going to help. *Nothing!* Admitting you love Copperhead is just pounding another nail in his coffin!"

Above their heads the sky broke into morning. Dawn's pale fingers advanced to part the clouds and a brilliant white light poured through the opening, dispelling the mist and revealing the dozen or so silent soldiers who ringed the stable.

Into that moment of silence and light came a dark, terrifying sound.

Copperhead screamed.

"Oh, God! No!" Miriam's fingers clawed at the braid on Jedidiah's sleeves. "For the love of *God*, let me go!"

Jedidiah refused. "No."

A second scream – longer, louder than the first – stabbed her. Tears filled her eyes, spilling over to pour down her cheeks. If Copperhead had cried out, the pain had to be unendurable. Otherwise, he would never have given her father the satisfaction.

"You say you're his friend! How can you listen to that!" Miriam sobbed. "Jedidiah, *please*!"

"It's no use, I tell you! *Anything* we do will only make things worse – " Jedidiah's sentence ended in an abrupt frown. As he released her and stepped back, he spoke to someone behind her. "Begging your pardon, Ma'am. But what are *you* doing here?"

Miriam pivoted to find a pale but determined Judith Kingsley standing behind her. The older woman's eyes were on the stable. Her hands were clenched in fists and she was breathing hard.

"Putting an end to this," Judith declared.

The stable was a wash of grays and browns – swirling, eddying, spiraling, pulling him down.

Down.

Down

Copperhead jerked awake. He couldn't think, could barely breathe. Pain pounded through his bound wrists and shot down his extended arms. Blood from the lash striped his bare chest and soaked his breeches as it trailed down his legs and dripped from his bare feet to form a crimson puddle on the stable floor.

The two soldiers who had beaten him laughed, boasting loudly. William Foxwell had watched as the pair asked him questions to which there were no answers and then, when he remained silent, tortured him by displacing several of his fingers. That was the first time he had shamed himself by crying out. The next came when, after Ensign Ward had stripped him and tied his hands together, Sergeant Grove tossed a thick rope over one of the stable beams and together the two of them hauled him above the straw-covered floor and left him dangling by his wrists.

Then, he had been flogged.

Swimming up through a sea of pain and nausea Copperhead forced his eyes open, determined to meet his death with honor. In the brief time he had been unconscious William Foxwell had crossed the stable to stand below him. He waited now, gazing up at him. When Foxwell saw he was awake, he made a sharp cutting motion.

A moment later Copperhead crashed to the straw-covered floor.

William Foxwell crouched beside him. "Get up!" he ordered. "Get up, *savage*!"

Copperhead bit his lip so as not to moan. The taste of iron on his tongue galvanized him and he struggled to rise, but fatigue and blood loss unmanned him. In the end he succeeded only in lifting his head to look at his enemy.

Miriam's father rose and signaled one of the two soldiers. "Grove! Get this animal on his feet. Then, you are both dismissed."

Sergeant Grove kicked him savagely in the side before gripping him and hauling him up. His fingers dug into Copperhead's flesh, grinding dirt and filthy straw into the wounds the lash had opened. When Grove released him it was all he could do not to collapse and fall back to the floor.

But he managed it.

Closing his eyes, Copperhead sought his center as his grandfather Walker had taught him. Then he opened them and defiantly met William Foxwell's exultant stare.

"Well? What have you to say?" Miriam's father moved in. He raised his hand and clenched his fingers a scant inch from his face. "Let me hear you beg for your life, boy. I hold it in *my* hand."

"You hold *nothing*. You may...kill me," Copperhead declared, his voice ragged with pain, "but you will...*never* break me."

William Foxwell's face grew livid. "By *God*! I will do *more* than break you!"

And then Miriam's father began to pound him with his fists.

Copperhead had no idea how long the withering blows rained upon him, nor how much time passed. He only knew that, as the light dimmed and sound and sight were swallowed up in numbing pain, a woman's voice intruded.

A note of compassion in the midst of a deafening storm of hate.

Judith still felt the sting of Miriam's anger. She pitied Jedidiah Nevilles. The young man had a hellion on his hands. But it would not have done to have Miriam in the stable – not at all. The girl would have been a distraction. And what she found there, devastating.

Judith wasn't certain the boy, Josiah, was not *already* dead.

"William! William! By all that is holy, *stop*!" She couldn't believe what she saw. Josiah Woodward lay on the stable floor, half-naked, his body a mass of welts and blood. William stood over him, looking down. He was breathing hard and his knotted fists were raw and covered with the young man's blood.

"*My God*! What have you done?" she breathed.

William blinked. He looked at her and seemed to notice her presence for the first time. "Judith. You shouldn't be here. This is Crown business. Your place is in the house." He stepped away from the boy's prone form and pointed toward the door. "Go there at once!"

Judith shook her head and refused to be cowed. "Crown business?" she shot back. "This? This is the *business* of brutes! Have you murdered him?"

William wiped his hands on his scarlet coat. "Murder, Madame? Hardly! Try justice dispensed."

"Justice?" she countered, crossing to where he stood. "Try *vengeance*. I see no court. I see no judge. I see no justice!" Judith met her fiancé's eyes and did not know him. "Only an executioner."

William met her fierce gaze and said nothing for a moment. When he did speak, she sensed his anger shifting toward *her*. "This is none of your business, woman! Nor is it your place to tell me what to do."

"It is my place as the woman who…loves you…to stop you from destroying yourself!" Judith drew a steadying breath. She glanced at Josiah where he lay silent and unmoving on the stable floor. "If you kill this young man, you *will* be a murderer. He has done nothing wrong."

"He tried to *rape* Anna – "

"William! You know as well as I do that that is a lie." He denied it, but she could tell by his reaction he suspected it at least. "I spoke to Anna. *She* went to him, and this young man refused to touch her! Her hurt her by that refusal and she wanted to hurt him back. So she lied." Judith measured William's reaction as she spoke. So far sobriety had no place in it. He was enraged. Shaking violently. His complexion a livid red. "Face it!" she continued. "You can't *bear* the fact that a child of yours could be attracted to a savage. That she could love someone you don't even consider a man."

William's knuckles began to bleed afresh as they curled into fists. "You go *too* far, Judith!" he warned.

"No. It is *you* who have gone too far. *You* who are the savage!" Judith paused as tears flooded her eyes and stained her cheeks. She shook her head. "And to think I meant to marry you!"

As she turned away William struck out and caught her by the arm. "Judith…"

She pivoted to face him. Her words were measured, but burned with intensity. "If you *touch* me I shall go to your superiors and tell them the truth. I may not sit high in society, but I am not without connections. There are many in power who know me – and my father – who know I do *not* lie."

William continued to hold her for a moment and then released her. When he did, his eyes lingered on the handprint left on her pale flesh. A handprint drawn in Josiah Woodward's blood.

"*This* is what liquor brings a man to!" she told him. "Why, William? *Why*?"

William met her accusing stare but said nothing. Then he shook his head and looked down.

Judith gathered her skirts in her hands and turned toward the door. "I will send Pennyworth for Doctor Wallington – "

"No. No!" When she looked at him, William finished, "I will have my regimental physician attend to him. There is no need for this to go any further than those of us who have been involved tonight. I regret… I regret losing control."

What he regretted was doing so in plain sight. "What do you intend to do?" Judith asked. "I will not allow you to dump him in some ditch somewhere…."

"I won't let him die, if that's what you fear." William's voice was stronger. Sober. "But neither will I have this redskin *bed* my daughter. I will not allow a child of mine to bear breed children."

Judith hesitated. Could she condemn him for that? What father *would* if he had a chance to prevent it?

"William. I don't know…."

"Judith," he approached her and, after seeking permission with his eyes, reached for her hand with his own which was bathed in the boy's blood. She shook her head and stepped back. William nodded, understanding, and withdrew it. "I will see to it that he is well tended, and then send him away. Miriam *will* forget. She will be forced to move on, to grow up. This is a gift that we – as her parents – can and *must* give her."

"William…. I don't know."

"I promise you, I will not drink again." He stood straight and looked her in the eye. "Judith, I do not want to lose you. Stay. Please. Will you stay?"

Her gaze went to the young man who lay silent at his feet. It was against her best judgment. Even though she knew he *would* try, she was almost certain William could not change. And yet, could she desert him in his need? Could she desert Anna – and Miriam, who even now she could hear crying out in pain?

Once the young man was gone William's daughters would need her more than ever. And then there was George. Who would look after him? William was certain to send Miriam away again as soon as possible, back to school in Scotland, somewhere – *anywhere* to heal and to forget.

Judith met his hopeful gaze and nodded once.

Then she turned and walked out the door.

Miriam bolted from Jedidiah's arms and ran toward Judith as the older woman wearily crossed the ground before the stable. Judith was alone. Her father was still within – with Copperhead.

The soldiers her father had called into the stable had emerged a few minutes before, their uniforms spattered with blood. The pair stood sentry now on either side of the open door. Jedidiah had obeyed Judith's command as if it had come from his colonel. He had held her back, refusing to yield.

Even when she swore she would hate him for the rest of her life.

As Judith drew near Miriam noted the bloodstain on her arm. The older woman looked as if every inch of strength had been wrung from her by the interview. Miriam rushed to her side and took one of her hands and pressed it between her own. "Oh God," she panted. "Dear God…all the blood. Judith, is he…?"

Judith squeezed her hand. "You must come with me, Miriam."

"No. Copperhead…." She started toward the stable only to have the older woman pull her back. "Judith?"

"He's been severely beaten." Judith's jaw tightened as if she were trying to convince herself of the veracity of her own words. "I have your father's promise that he will send for the regimental physician. Copperhead will be looked after – "

"His word!" Miriam jerked free. "The word of a *murderer*!"

"Copperhead is not dead. He *will* live," she said it with confidence, if not conviction. "But he will not be allowed to stay. You must *never* see him again if you value his life."

"No. No!" Miriam tried to push past her. "Copperhead!"

Judith caught her arm and held her back forcefully. "Miriam, use your head! Copperhead is a *savage*! There is no court in this country that will listen to his claim. *One word* from your father and he is dead." Judith's brown eyes were stricken with grief. "Have you ever seen a man's death by hanging?"

Miriam grew very still. She nodded.

"This way he will live. It is the only thing – the only *gift* you can give him now. You *must* let him go."

"No...."

"Yes." Judith released her. "Return to the house. Go to your grandfather. Find what comfort you can in his presence."

Miriam looked past her to the stable door. Her father's tall frame filled it. Anger and a profound grief fought for control within her – anger at her father, at Judith, at herself, and grief for the loss of not only Copperhead, but *of* her father, of Anna....

Of everything she had ever known.

"Where will he send him?" she asked, her tone wretched.

Judith touched her hair.

"That, child, you must never know."

William Foxwell finished washing his hands. He ran them, still cold with the water, over his neck and face and then accepted a towel from his aide. Nodding to Nevilles, he watched as the young man took the bloody basin and left the kitchen of the manor house to toss it into the tall grasses outside the door. Jedidiah avoided his eyes while doing so. It was evident he did not approve. Still, the young man was enough of a soldier that he kept his mouth shut and did his duty. So there was no need for dismissal.

Besides Nevilles knew too much. It was better to keep him close at hand.

"Will there be anything else, sir?" his aide asked as he returned and replaced the basin on the stand.

William shook his head. "No." Then he rethought it. "Yes, actually, there is. Is the King's man – what was his name?"

"Leighton, sir. John Leighton."

"Right. Is he still here?"

"Yes, sir."

William patted the back of his neck with the cloth and then tossed it in the empty basin. "See if Mr. Leighton would do me the honor of granting me a brief audience in the drawing room."

"Sir!" Nevilles saluted again and then disappeared.

William followed him slowly. An idea had been forming in his head since his interview with Judith – a way to deal with the problem that was 'Josiah Woodward'. In fact, he had his father to thank for the plausibility of the scheme. A sly smile lifted the corner of William's upper lip.

He would have to remember to pay a visit to the old man and let him know just how helpful he had been.

Sucking on one of his sore knuckles, William entered the main hall and made his way through the darkened corridor to the drawing room. As he passed the central stair he spied Judith on the landing. She was headed for Miriam's room. Even here, far below, he could hear the girl weeping inconsolably.

William spit out blood and wrapped a fresh linen handkerchief around the knuckles that would not stop bleeding. She would get over it. This whole affair had to do with the loss of her mother and sister. Insecurity and inadequacy had forced Miriam to seek out danger. To strike out and rebel. Her feelings were mere infatuation. After all, the boy was a savage.

What else *could* they be?

As William entered the drawing room he was surprised to find John Leighton already occupying it. The King's Advocate sat in one of the chairs by the fire. When he entered Leighton made as if to stand. William shook his head and indicated he should remain seated. He asked Leighton if he would like a drink and poured him one when he indicated 'yes'. William's hand lingered on the decanter. He debated pouring one for himself. Then he replaced the stopper and left his own glass dry.

This was a night for sobriety. Tomorrow he would rethink what he had promised Judith.

"Master Foxwell," John Leighton said as he accepted the glass.

"William. Please."

"William, then. So I understand from young Nevilles that your 'problem' is solved? And you will have no further need of my services?"

William took the seat opposite him. He pursed his lips. "Solved? No. Not solved. The young man is still a problem. And I still need a warrant for his arrest."

Leighton took a sip and nodded. "Excellent," he said, "and the charge?"

"Thievery, plain and simple. He took my father's horse."

The King's man took another sip of his drink and regarded him coolly over the rim of the thick glass. "A serious charge indeed. Why not simply string him up?"

William adopted a look of chagrin. "There is a complication, Mr. Leighton."

"John. *Please.*"

"John. You see the boy – well, I hate to admit this – but he is my father's bastard by some red skin trollop. As such, I cannot hand him over to the authorities. It would not be…proper."

"Ah. A difficult situation." John placed the empty glass on the table by the chair and then leaned back. "But what is it you think *I* can do for you?"

William studied the fire for a moment. Then he remarked – almost casually, "I understand that – in England – it is quite common for the illegitimate offspring of noblemen such as you and I to…well…take long 'holidays' in the depths of some dank feudal castle or keep. Locked away until they are…forgotten."

John nodded, understanding. "And you would like me to arrange such a 'holiday' for this young man? Joseph, was it?"

"Josiah. Josiah Woodward."

John Leighton rose to his feet. "You understand, do you not, that such 'holidays' do not come cheap. The upkeep. The need for the boy to be…attended at all hours…."

William leaned on the arm of the chair and placed one bruised knuckle under his chin.

"Are you a family man, Mr. Leighton?"

John paused, surprised by the question. "Yes, I have two sons."

"Then you know. The boy – Josiah – is my half-brother. You are to give him what he deserves.

"No matter the cost."

Chapter Eighteen

Copperhead awoke in misery in a damp odious place without light. He shifted and instantly regretted it as blinding pain shot through his bound wrists and elbows, terminating at his dislocated shoulder in a gasp and oblivion as he passed out again. But it was only a moment's respite. All too soon he awoke to a new awareness of his plight. Coarse ropes cut into his bruised and broken flesh, steel shackles gripped his bare ankles, and a gag had been placed between his teeth to make certain he would not cry out.

Only his eyes were free, and with them he explored the abysmal hole he found himself in. The floor was dank and malodorous, reeking of fish and brine. In the ceiling above his head a line of light traced the outline of a door. Dangling from it were ropes, some loaded with sandbags at the end, others with coarsely woven tow-cloth sacks. On one of the sacks was a fat rat. It stared at him, its peckish eyes gleaming as it considered which would make the better meal – the foodstuffs that lay within the sack –

Or him.

Copperhead turned to look behind. As he did the wooden floor beneath him unexpectedly rolled and the room lurched. The sudden movement dislodged the rat and set the tow sacks and sandbags overhead to swinging. And his stomach to churning. He swallowed hard as bile rose in his throat. In spite of the chill rising from the damp floor, a wave of heat rolled over him and he vomited tasting blood on his tongue.

Copperhead laid, his face against the fouled boards, panting and shaking uncontrollably, listening to the sounds of what he now recognized was his prison cell. It was hard to sort out what he heard. There were a great many voices, some agitated, others excited. Above them all one man's rose in command, shouting orders. Beyond the voices there was another sound – a constant, consistent roar like a storm wind walking through the forest.

As he lay there trembling with cold and fear, the floor beneath him lurched again and the world of which he was now a part pitched sharply to the left. Copperhead cried out as he rolled over his damaged fingers and came to an abrupt halt against a large wooden crate. As he lay there, gasping, there was a tremendous 'crack' from the beams overhead. In answer the planks beneath his trussed form groaned like a woman giving birth.

In the ceiling above the outline of light unexpectedly expanded to form a blinding square. A door opened revealing a wooden ladder, and a shaft of pure white light penetrated the false night of his cell. Clean, fresh air flooded the rank chamber. As Copperhead drew a breath, savoring its sweetness, a pair of highly polished black boots landed on the plank floor near his head. The man who wore them straightened his scarlet coat, using his fingers to dust off the single silver epaulet on his right shoulder.

William Foxwell looked down at him. His smug voice echoed the cruel pleasure written on his face. "So how do you find the 'accommodations,' breed? Are they to your liking?"

Copperhead said nothing.

Miriam's father waited a moment and then squatted by his side. He sniffed and added with a look of disgust, "You've soiled yourself, savage. But then again, what *can* one expect from a piece of filth – but *more* filth?"

As Foxwell continued to taunt him, Copperhead realized someone else had joined them. A pair of leather shoes appeared. Brown. Elegant. Hand-tooled with fine silver buckles. He shifted so he could see the man who wore them. The stranger was dark, with hawkish eyes, and what white men called a 'Roman' nose.

He didn't know him.

"As you can see, there is no need to worry," the man said, addressing Miriam's father. "We are well underway. This young man is not going anywhere. As soon as I can speak to the captain, I will have him transferred to one of the cabins and – "

"Whatever *for?*" Foxwell shot to his feet. His tone was adamant. "The hold is more than good enough for the likes of him!"

The other man paused, his dark eyes flicking from Foxwell to Copperhead and back again. When he spoke, his voice was laced with something new – a hint of threat perhaps?

"I thought you wanted him alive at the end of the journey, William. Or have you changed your mind? Do you mean to *murder* the boy after all with contagion as your weapon?"

Miriam's father strode to the bottom of the ladder. Placing one hand on a rung, he turned his face upward, so the sunlight struck it. William Foxwell's aspect was hard as the steel of the blade that hung from his belt, and just as cold.

"I don't want this vermin to see the light of day until you reach England," he ordered. "Once I leave you to join my ship, I expect you to keep him in solitary, here, below. I have paid you enough to make certain it is so." He placed one black boot on the ladder. "I will not have some soft-hearted idiot taking a liking to him and aiding his escape. Is that *understood*, Mr. Leighton?

England!

Suddenly, sickeningly, Copperhead realized where he was. He understood now why the floor lurched as it did, and what had caused the dank boards beneath him to groan. He was on a ship! He had never been on a ship before, but as a boy had watched from the safety of the trees as the massive wooden vessels glided into the bay, the great white sheets that propelled them billowing like clouds heralding a storm. Omens of evil, his father had called them.

Harbingers of change and doom.

Mr. Leighton remained at Copperhead's side. The man's demeanor was calm, but the toe of his shoe beat an impatient staccato on the floor as he endured William Foxwell's tirade.

"I can appreciate the 'situation' you find yourself in, Colonel Foxwell," he began, "but I did not enter into this contract to become your bastard brother's executioner. I will keep the young man contained – and see him delivered to prison – but that is all. I am no murderer – nor any man's pawn!"

"I don't want the boy…dead, John," Foxwell responded, though his tone indicated otherwise. "It is just that…. Well, if he happened to die during the journey over, no one would think there had been any *intent* to harm him. Dozens of men die on ships everyday."

"Your father, General Foxwell, is well known and liked. If this *is* his son – " Leighton moved to the bottom of the ladder. "As you said before, Colonel, this should be done 'properly'."

"Yes. Yes! *Damn* you!" Miriam's father made a dismissive gesture with his free hand before placing it on the ladder next to the other one. Then he began to ascend. "From this moment on I don't care what you do with Josiah Woodward. I just want him to cease to exist! Can you at *least* see to that?"

John Leighton remained still, his face tilted upward, gazing at the sky above. When he spoke at last, Copperhead was not certain to whom his words were addressed.

"You have my word, I will see to it the boy is taken care of."

With John Leighton's departure Copperhead's consciousness waned, and he fell into a black place. When he awoke he no longer lay on the ship's floor, swimming in foul water and filth, but was in a bed. Above it, to his right, was a small round window punched into the vessel's wall. It framed a crescent moon set against a backdrop of indigo blue. He shifted to look out it, but found he lacked the strength. As he reached out to steady himself, he realized his hands were no longer bound. His mangled fingers had been set with a splint and expertly bandaged.

Copperhead stared at both a moment, disbelieving, and then lifted his shirt to check his chest. The telling trails of William Foxwell's lash had been concealed by linen bandages. He nosed a sweet salve. Someone must have applied it to soothe his pain.

Copperhead closed his eyes and lay back as an all-too familiar wave of sweat-soaked nausea rolled up and over him. Its origin, he guessed, lay not with the beating he had taken, but with the pitch and roll of the ship he was captive on. Long ago when he had been a boy, some of the men of his village had boarded one of these great ships to accompany a party of white men up river as scouts. When they returned months later the men had spoken of how it had unmanned them, telling tales of laying in their own vomit for most of the journey. 'Sea-sickness' it was called.

Copperhead's stomach was the definition of it.

Opening his eyes again he sat up on the straw ticking. Pressing a hand against the thick-bubbled glass of the window, he gazed out. The moon was gone from view. She was bedded down with the stars in a bank of black clouds. Still, a few shone, scintillating above the vast unending water.

"I see you're awake."

John Leighton spoke, surprising him. Copperhead pivoted toward him and instantly regretted it as a fresh wave of nausea forced him back against the sheets.

"The effect will lessen in time as you grow used to the movement of the ship," Leighton said. He moved to Copperhead's side as the door closed behind him and reached out to adjust the blanket covering him. "You should take some water, Josiah. There is a jug on the table. I'll have my boy bring you some bread. I wouldn't try anything else just yet. Though some ginger tea might serve you well." John Leighton paused at his look. "What? What is it?"

"Why are you being kind to me?" Copperhead asked, his tone laced with suspicion.

The man with the hawkish face shrugged. "I have a son about your age."

"A *white* son."

Leighton stared at him for a moment before turning away to fill a horn cup with water. As he turned back, he nodded. "Yes. Two. John and Geoffrey. They are in England. I hope to see them before I return to the Colonies." He held the cup out. "Here. Take this. You've had precious little in the last week."

Copperhead met the man's kindness with a stubborn shake of his head. "And what is it you save me for, John Leighton? Imprisonment? Death? I will not drink. *Or* eat."

"Then you will die," Leighton replied as he put the cup on the table beside him. "You may anyhow, if mortification sets in any of those wounds."

"I want to die," he insisted, turning his face away.

"Now *there's* a noble sentiment," John Leighton snorted. "One I am sure would please William Foxwell – if *not* his daughter."

"Miriam?" Copperhead looked at him. "You know her?"

"Yes. She mourns your loss."

"How would you know?"

"I imagine the entire colony knows by now. She did not stop weeping for the two days I was at the manor house. As we were leaving to come to the ship, Judith called the doctor in." Leighton offered him the cup again but when he still refused, set it down and headed for the door. Once there he paused with his hand on the latch. "Even a bleeding did not quiet her."

Copperhead was broken. Weak and deprived of strength. His body ached, and the stripes from William Foxwell's lash pounded with growing fire in spite of the salve, sounding a warning of sickness to come. Suddenly, shamefully, he was unable to deny his tears.

Humiliated, he turned his face to the wall. "It is better for Miriam if I die."

"I doubt she would agree with that." John Leighton lifted the latch, adding quietly, "You know from what William Foxwell told me, I didn't take you to be a coward."

"I am no coward!" Copperhead countered, turning back.

"Then prove it! Choose to live!" Leighton strode back to his side. "Don't lie there wallowing in grief, already dead by despair. Find the anger that fueled you before. *Find it*, Josiah, and hang on to it throughout whatever life throws at you! Throughout this voyage. Through prison. Through decades in *Hell*!" The man was actually trembling. "Live! If *only* to pay William Foxwell back."

"Who *are* you?" Copperhead asked.

John Leighton opened the door and stepped into the corridor beyond. From the darkness that masked it he answered.

"What you need. A friend."

He had been right. Death *would* have been better. For him.

Every time Copperhead's stomach rebelled, each time he vomited the smallest morsel of food and choked on water, as he burned and turned in the midst of fever and filth, and struggled against the infection that fought like a madman to claim him – when he gripped the soiled sheets his skeletal frame lay on with a ferocity that tore the fabric – he remembered John Leighton's words and refused to give in. Refused to surrender.

Refused to die.

In the midst of his delirium Copperhead returned to the forested world of his childhood and walked once again with his Indian brothers. He ran naked through the tall grasses, garmented only by the sun. At first his dreams were comforting, reminding him of who he had been, but as the fever raged and consumed him, they grew dark.

And terrible.

He saw his mother walking. Black bone garbed in ash. In her skeletal arms she bore the charred remains of her youngest child. At her burnt breast the babe sucked blood. Close behind this horror came his father's corpse, his skin putrid, his heart pierced by a British bayonet. That of his elder brother followed, accompanied by the men, the women, and the children of his village. All moaning. All weeping.

All pointing bony fingers at him, crying out; damning him for their murders.

Miriam was there as well. Her beautiful face a brilliant bit of hope set against a black backdrop of destruction and endless death. As her sun ascended the others – his mother, father, brother – faded to nothing. Soon there was only Miriam calling out to him, urging him to live. Her presence brought an unanticipated peace to his tormented soul. He reached out for her and his bruised fingers brushed hers. But then a shadow named Bear rose between them and Copperhead watched as she was stripped naked, brutally abused, and raped. He saw Bear toss her used and bloodied body away like trash.

And he heard William Foxwell laughing.

Laughing as his hand struck him. Bellowing as his whip drew blood. Once. Twice. A dozen – no, a hundred times. Beating him down. Tearing his skin from his bones and hope from his soul. As the lash struck, William Foxwell's venom filled his ears. Jeering. Scoffing. Calling him 'coward'. Naming him a savage and a 'breed'. Proclaiming he could not win. Shouting that he should curl up and die.

And he was right.

He *should* die.

Then, just as he was about to give up, to claim oblivion and peace, there was a flash of light on the horizon – an argent light like summer lightning. It called to him powerfully. Unable to resist, he moved toward it and watched as the light coalesced, becoming a solid form. A giant form with a silver face and fur –

And a pair of wise gold eyes.

The silver fox stared at him, infusing him with strength, renewing and reminding him of the promise it had made his grandfather, Walker, so many years before. When he was close enough it stood up like a man. Planting its paws on his shoulder, it whispered in his ear.

There is something for you. Something more.
Something to live for.

Copperhead awoke, panting. He lay still for a moment, and then struggled to sit up.

John Leighton was right. He *must* live

If only to seek revenge.

They despaired of her life. Miriam knew it. Before he left, she had overheard Dr. Wallington warn her father that she was of the 'nervous excitable type' and that, like her dear departed mother and sister, she was not long for this world.

Dr. Wallington was right.

Miriam didn't *want* to live.

Living meant facing what her father and Anna had done. Living meant returning to Scotland and school. Living meant marrying someone like Charles Matthew Spencer and bearing a brood of children she would grow to despise. It meant day after day, month after month, year after year drawing breath after breath without caring.

Without Copperhead.

Before her father had left the manor to board the ship that would bear him back to England and his duty, he told her that Copperhead was dead. She didn't know whether to believe him or not. Judith insisted he had been alive the last time she had seen him. It didn't matter. If her father hadn't killed Copperhead outright, he was as good as dead – exiled, sent away somewhere to be imprisoned, sold….

Miriam shuddered and pulled the coverlet over her head.

She had barely eaten anything for a week. Judith had worked some broth between her lips and forced her to take water, but she had had nothing of any substance since the interview with her father. At first she had refused to speak to him, even going so far as to lock her door. When he grew angry and broke it down, dear old Martha stood between them. Her father struck the ancient matron so hard he caused her lip to bleed. Gently pulling the old woman out of the way, she had faced her father's wrath and taken her punishment. She was confined to her room. Forbidden to leave the manor.

Exiled to school.

The date for her return to Edinburgh had been set for the first of May. The fifteenth of that month had come and gone, and found her lying in her sick bed. Dr. Wallington had been called in and had left less than an hour before shaking his head. Miriam could still hear his whispered words.

'If the child is *determined* to die....'

She was.

Miriam shifted and pulled the coverlet tight, wrapping it about her shoulders. If she could just sink into sickness, suffocate in the shadows, *drown* in the darkness, she wouldn't have to face any of it. She wouldn't have to face her father's explosive anger or Judith's quiet sadness. Anna's pathetic apologies. Martha's endless weeping.

Or life without Copperhead.

The sound of her bedroom door opening caused her fingers to clutch the thick woven fabric. Someone was coming! Someone who expected her to rise up out of the pit of despair and choose to live. But they were too late. Mortification had already set in. Her heart was dead.

There was nothing to revive.

"Miriam...."

The voice was old. Feeble. But firm.

And familiar.

Miriam's quaking fingers lowered the coverlet. Her eyes peeped over it, seeking the door. Judith was there, and in front of her, an odd looking chair on castors.

And Grandpa George in the chair.

Beyond them two of her father's soldiers waited. Judith thanked them and then, dismissing them, pushed her grandfather into the room and closed the door. Then the dark-haired woman wheeled him to the side of her bed. Judith looked exhausted. There was a gray streak in her brown hair that had not been there before, and sadness cradled her deep-set eyes. Judith opened her mouth to speak, glanced at Grandpa George, and then drew close. Leaning down, the older woman took her hand and squeezed it.

Then Judith left the room without speaking a word.

Miriam remained where she was – hidden, safe – for a moment, and then shifted and sat up with her back to the pillows. She hesitantly met her grandfather's gaze but said nothing. Grandpa George was seated in a curious chair with wide padded wings at the top near his head and rests below for his arms. Near the top at the back there was a shank. Probably for moving the chair.

She had never seen anything like it.

"A gift," her grandfather said, the right side of his mouth quirking with irony. "From...my son."

Miriam scowled.

"Don't...hate him," Grandpapa George said.

"I do!" she almost shouted.

He couldn't quite shake his head, but he tried. The words that came from his lips were breathed more than spoken. "Then...William wins."

"Grandpa! He has killed Copperhead!" Miriam rose up in her bed, trembling. "He told me so!"

"No." Her grandfather's voice was firm. "Will come back...some day." He lifted his hand, which quaked as much as her own, and held it out. "Strong. Be...strong."

She leaned forward and took it, even as tears began to fall freely, wetting her cheeks. "How can I? Without him?"

"*For*...him." Grandpa George struggled for a moment. His lips opened again, but this time no sound issued from them. He closed his eyes and seemed to summon strength from somewhere deep within himself.

A strength that shamed her.

"Would not...want you to die. Copperhead..." Her grandfather's voice broke. A tear trailed down his grizzled cheek. "...want you to live. Miri.... I want...*need* you to live."

She realized at that moment that she had thought only of herself. Not of Copperhead.

And not of him.

Miriam shifted the coverlet and slipped off the bed. Too weak to stand, she knelt by his chair and clung to its arm. Reaching for his hand, she whispered, "Grandpapa, I am *so* sorry...."

He shook his head. "You...love him."

She choked. A sob escaped her. "Yes...."

"Child." Her grandfather's palsied fingers gripped hers with amazing strength. His voice rung clear as it had in his youth. "You must have faith."

Miriam looked up. Her grandfather George's blue eyes were clear as the summer sky and bold as a young man's. She squeezed his fingers in reply. Then she nodded and laid her head in his lap.

Two hours later Judith found them just so.

A week later Miriam set sail for Scotland.

Chapter Nineteen

Nearly half of the forty-odd day voyage had passed. During that time Copperhead saw little of the sea or sky save what showed through the portal window above his bed. His legs, once strong and sinewy, had gone spindly and were little more than bone, barely filling the brown breeches that covered them. His muscled arms, strong from long hours of labor, were now weak – so weak it seemed at times they could not bear the weight of the linen shirt he wore. When he spoke, his voice lacked strength; his words no more than a whisper born of lips unused to speech.

He was in a cabin attached to John Leighton's, one usually reserved for a cabin boy or man's man. He had found out that – after the first day when his fever worsened and it seemed he would die – the mysterious Mr. Leighton had called the ship's physician in to look after him, and dedicated the boy who personally attended him to his service. The boy was known as 'Kip', though his real name was Todd Merrett. But no one called him that. Kip sat beside him now, in a bow-back chair, his tousled blond head nodding over a book on ship's protocol.

When he stirred and shifted his body, Kip awoke with a start and hopped to his feet. "Can I get you anything, Master Josiah?" he asked as he dropped the book onto the seat.

Copperhead shook his head feebly.

"Are you sure? There's broth here. Dr. Standley left it for you. He said I was to *make* you drink it." Kip scrunched up his nose as he lifted the double-handled cup and sniffed the liquid that filled it. "God be thanked it's you and not me. It smells a fright!"

Copperhead couldn't help but agree. The soup's noxious odor permeated the sick room and turned his stomach.

" 'Bones for bones', the Vicar said. Bones for bones," Kip explained in his uncultured English accent. "Marrow soup, that's what it is. Though I can't say what rotten animal old Standley managed to pull from some hidden chink to pound it out of!" The boy's wide blue eyes narrowed and his high tenor voice dropped to a whisper as he leaned in closer. "It's French, the Vicar says. Don't know that I'd trust anything concocted by the Frogs!"

Kip was only eleven. Younger than he had been when George Foxwell rescued him and yet, in much the same way, already a man. Several years before Kip's parents had died in one of London's plagues, and he had gone to work for John Leighton in order to send money home to pay for food and clothing for his four younger siblings. Copperhead smiled as the boy continued to rant about the French. He knew all about Kip. About his likes and dislikes. About the ebon headed girl next door who had slapped him when he tried to kiss her. About his mother's lovely singing voice and his father's habit of drinking too much. Copperhead knew it all because – during the long weeks of his sickness as he attended him, Kip had *never* stopped talking.

Before he could reply Copperhead heard the key turn in the cabin door. He glanced toward it. It opened and Dr. Vicke Standley, the ship's attending physician, entered the room, his usual gold-rimmed glasses posed halfway down his long nose, a hand-tied notebook in his hand. Kip explained earlier how the crew had affectionately dubbed the older man 'the Vicar' as, due to no fault of his own, the sailors he attended most often ended in a watery grave. Behind the doctor's tall but stooped form, Copperhead felt as much as saw two shadows lurking. They belonged to the soldiers William Foxwell had placed outside his door to make certain he would not escape.

Foxwell need have little fear. It was unlikely he could stand, let alone run.

"And how are you today, Master Josiah?" Dr. Standley asked as he arrived at the side of his sickbed. The older man pushed his glasses down to the end of his nose and looked over them at the still full cup of soup. He made a clucking noise with his tongue and then turned on Kip, raising one grizzled eyebrow.

Kip thrust his hands into the air. "I tried! God's little bodikins, I promise I did! Josiah ain't got the stomach for it." The boy shrugged and then added under his breath. "Not that I can fault him in that...."

Dr. Standley failed to hide his smile. "It will wait."

Vicke Standley was a tall man, with thick blond hair going gray. He was whip-thin and his skin, once tanned dark as saddle-leather from years of service in the Royal Navy, was dry and wrinkled like that of a man twice his age. Dr. Standley looked as if he was hard as forged iron. Instead he was a gentle man in both manner and speech, who frequently proclaimed that he had seen far too much of death and dying and men's inhumanity to his fellow man to ever pass judgment on anyone but himself. Kip had told Copperhead that there were rumors of some scandal – of something the doctor had done of which King George had not approved – and that was why Vicke Standley had left private practice and gone to sailing on ships.

Dr. Standley sat on the edge of his bunk and took one of Copperhead's hands in his own. The older man closed his eyes as he took hold of his wrist and listened to the pulse of the blood running through his veins. "Good. Good. Steady. Not so rapid or thready as it has been." The doctor opened his eyes and shifted back. With academic scrutiny he studied him for a moment and then asked, "Do you think you can walk?"

Copperhead's confusion must have been apparent for Dr. Standley laughed.

"Where's he gonna walk?" Kip demanded, exasperated for him. "Josiah ain't allowed out of this room! Colonel Foxwell's orders."

Dr. Standley rose to his feet. He pushed his glasses back into position and pinned the boy with his gray eyes. "I usually don't feel the need to explain myself to cabin boys, however – as perplexing a patient is not good for his health – I will acquiesce this time." With a slight smile the doctor added, "We were boarded two days ago. A rather unsavory bunch. You remember them, don't you, Kip?"

The boy nodded. He crossed his arms and pronounced judgment. "A bunch of nobs!"

Vicke Standley pursed his thin lips and nodded. "Kip, in his rather expressive way, is trying to tell you that the men who boarded us had something of a high opinion of themselves."

"Ain't one of them ever walked a deck before," Kip declared, truly disgusted. "I saw one of them Army blokes turn green!"

"*Army* blokes?" Copperhead asked, confused.

"British regulars," Standley replied. "Came in a fast-flying frigate to escort Colonel Foxwell off the *Renard*." At Copperhead's sudden change in expression, the doctor nodded. "That's right, boy. He's gone."

"I thought the ship...." Copperhead swallowed over his hope. "Are we not headed for England? As William Foxwell was?"

"Yes. But we have several stops to make first. The King was anxious for Colonel Foxwell to arrive and begin training the other boorish oafs produced by state sanctioned inbreeding to take his place in the Colonies." Standley's smile broadened as he moved to a chair opposite the bunk that was flanked by a small writing desk. He watched him for a moment and then said, "Go ahead. Ask your questions."

Copperhead shifted uncomfortably. Lying for so long had left him with sores on his back and legs. Shifting eased the pain in them. But more than that, he was uncomfortable with Dr. Standley *and* the man who had sent the physician to take care of him – the mysterious John Leighton.

"Why have you bothered to save me? When we reach England I am to be shut away in a prison. To be forgotten. To *die*." Copperhead exhaled as he leaned back into the pillow's cool embrace. "Why save me *now* only so I can die later? What am I to you? Or to Mr. Leighton?"

Dr. Standley stared at him long and hard as if weighing his thoughts – and how many of them he should give voice to. At last he said, "Where there's life, there's hope, Josiah. Your crime was a serious one from what I have heard. Horse thievery, was it not?"

Copperhead shook his head. "I stole nothing! The horse was a gift."

Dr. Standley nodded as if that was what he had suspected. "Then it was the other crime. The *more* heinous one."

"What? What other crime?" he demanded.

"Being born on the wrong side of the blanket." Vicke Standley glanced at Kip. He lowered his voice, but continued in spite of the boy's presence and attention. "I understand that you are Colonel William Foxwell's half-brother. Is that right?"

For a moment Copperhead said nothing. Then he countered with a question. "Is *that* why you have cared for me? Because of William Foxwell?"

"It is my sworn duty to care for all who are ill or injured," the doctor answered, showing the first spark of irritation. "It wouldn't matter to me if you had slit old King George's throat!" Vicke Standley rose to his feet and placed his notebook on the desk. "As for John Leighton, you will have to ask him what his motives are." Dr. Standley shoved his gold-rimmed glasses up to the bridge of his nose again and then motioned to Kip who had been standing idly by trying to look disinterested.

"Sir!" the boy snapped.

"Get over here, Kip, and earn your wage. Lend Josiah your shoulder."

Copperhead looked from one to the other. "What for?"

Dr. Standley drew the linen blanket back. After a cursory examination of him, he nodded and then headed for the door. Once there he turned back, the shadow of a smile lighting his weather-beaten face. "I convinced the captain that you would never mend in this dark hole. And that – if not mended – you would most likely die before you could reach England. I intimated that Colonel Foxwell would be *very* upset with him if that happened. John backed me up and added a guinea or two of persuasion." Standley put his hand to the latch. "Though we will not be permitted to go unattended – in other words the villains who have been set to watch you must go with us – I *am* permitted to take you for a walk on the deck.

"In the sun."

The world outside the *Renard's* dark interior was one he no longer knew. The sun's pure white light was a brutal stranger. Its rays, withering. For a time he clung to the shadows, almost as if he desired them, and then slowly, uncertainly, Copperhead let young Kip lead him into the light.

He couldn't walk without aid. Kip gripped his arm tightly and held him up as they moved along the deck, passing first one and then dozens of sailors hard at work. Some smiled or nodded. Most stopped to wipe the sweat from their brows and stare at him with curiosity and even surprise, as if he were a man known dead unexpectedly risen from the grave.

Which he was.

Dr. Standley walked beside them, carefully noting his progress, shaking his head and muttering as was his custom while jotting notes in the book he carried. The *Renard* ran silently over the vast green ocean. Most of its company was at ease. A bearded seaman played a jaunty tune on his piccolo while another danced, hopping from one foot to the other. Another, high in the ship's rigging, called out to the Vicar as they passed, asking the physician to say a prayer for him. Dr. Standley raised a hand and made the sign of the cross in the air and then went back to writing. As they reached the aft end of the ship, the older man placed a hand on Kip's shoulder and pointed them in the direction of a stack of crates resting near the rail. The area about the crates was deserted and their even surfaces offered a welcome port at which to land.

"Time to take a break," Dr. Standley said softly. "Sit down, Josiah. Rest a while."

Copperhead eased onto the crate with a scowl, grunting as its unforgiving wood surface bruised his bones. The progress of his illness had left him frail. Earlier in the cabin he had asked Kip for a mirror. The boy had refused. Looking at his arms and legs now he understood why – the brilliant light flooding the deck revealed how thin he had become. His skin color had faded until it was nearly the same as William Foxwell's.

An irony that was not lost on him.

Dr. Standley closed his book and looked hard at him over the rim of his glasses. "I want you to sit here for a while, Josiah. Soak up the sun. It will do you good." He turned and glanced back the way they had come. Foxwell's men were there – lurking in the shadows cast by one of the ship's broad masts. "And you two," Standley called, addressing them, "you let Josiah be. He's to sit here in the sun, in peace, for an hour or two. Captain's orders."

Copperhead had never seen his wardens clearly. Like wolves on the prowl they hugged the shadows of the corridor outside his sickroom, never seen but ever a threat. Now one stepped forward. The man was of medium height; thickset and powerfully built like a blacksmith or pugilist, with a swarthy complexion. As he moved, the sunlight struck him, revealing his face.

And Copperhead began to shake.

It was Sergeant Grove. One of the two men who had flogged and beaten him, almost to death.

"So long as he don't try to jump overboard and swim back to them heathens he calls kin," Grove growled as he jabbed a finger at him. "You hear me, *breed*?"

"Miscreant!" Dr. Standley muttered under his breath as his hand returned to Kip's shoulder. When the boy looked up, he said quietly, "Kip, stay with Josiah. Don't leave his side for a minute." Then the doctor added, loudly, "Sit down, boy, and wait with my young charge here while I fetch Captain Long. I think it is about time he made young Master Woodward's formal acquaintance."

As the doctor moved away, Copperhead's eyes returned to Sergeant Grove. Foxwell's lackey had slunk back into the shadows where his cohort waited. He would have laid odds that the other man was Ensign Ward.

Kip waited until Dr. Standley disappeared behind main mast and then climbed up on the crate to sit at his side. Copperhead heard Grove and Ward arguing, their voices raised in some sort of dispute. He breathed a sigh of relief as they went below. Still, he knew this was only the beginning. They would return again to inhabit the shadows, to watch and wait for an opportunity to finish the shameful work they had begun in William Foxwell's stable.

Copperhead leaned back and lifted his face into the sun. After nearly a month in the ship's belly, the fiery globe had at first seemed an enemy. Now, it was a welcome friend. As he closed his eyes, embracing its healing rays, he fell silent. All about him the business of the *Renard* continued. Seamen came and went, performing their various duties. Junior officers, unsure of themselves and so, overly confident, barked orders. The sailors obeyed them, muttering their displeasure under their breath as they did. Beyond and above all of this was the voice of the sea breeze breathing out, breathing in, out, in – snapping the ship's standard and filling her sails. And below everything ran the deep satisfied sigh of the emerald waves as the great ship parted them, pushing on toward its destiny. For the moment, Copperhead was content.

Unfortunately young Kip was not.

The boy could not keep still. Kip shifted two or three times and then began to wriggle like a worm on a line. He pursed his lips and echoed the tune a sailor had whistled earlier in passing, but failed to complete it. He drummed his fingers and started a new one. After ten minutes or so, he jumped to his feet. Through half-lidded eyes Copperhead watched him cross to the railing where he stared out at the horizon. Several minutes later he felt the boy's fingers pick at the sleeve of his linen shirt. Hiding his smile, Copperhead opened his eyes and met Kip's earnest gaze.

"What is it, Kip?"

A deep frown scrunched up his freckled nose. "It ain't polite to ask, sir..." he began.

Copperhead thought he knew what was coming. "Call me, Josiah," he answered. "And ask anyway."

Kip nodded toward the mast where Grove and Ward had been. "Foxwell's men, they call you a 'breed'. Are you *really*? The Vicar said you're the colonel's brother.... Does that mean your Mum, well, that your Mum's a savage? Like the ones I seen in London wearing feathers and beads, and painted from top to toe?"

It took a moment for Kip's words to sink in. "London?" he asked, surprised. "You have seen Indians in London?"

"Aye. The promoters, they snatch them, bring them across the water, and put them in shows. They make them fight each other and then bet on which one will win." Kip shook his head. "My old man, before he died, said it was a downright disgrace. Snatching men and women from across the ocean and breeding them just so they could die on a stage for some rich man's pleasure."

Copperhead was stunned. "They *do* that?"

Kip nodded. "Caught you by surprise? Don't know why. Think about it." He nodded toward the shadows Ward and Gove had occupied. "Think about the two of *them*. There's plenty of damned souls like theirs, given over to working evil. Aye, they do that, Josiah. *And worse.*"

Copperhead rose and walked shakily to the railing. He leaned on it and turned his gaunt face toward the ship's prow, looking forward toward the hostile and foreign land for which he was bound. Was that Foxwell's plan? Did he intend to sell him once they reached land?

Was there a cage already waiting?

"Josiah!"

In Kip's voice was a warning. Copperhead pivoted to find that William Foxwell's jackals had returned. Sergeant Grove was leaning against the mast, striking his open palm with a cudgel.

If he lived that long.

Miriam leaned on the fore-rail of the ship that bore her silently and surely away from the new world toward the old. She would disembark in

England, and from its capital city board a coach that would take her to Scotland. Her father's sister was to meet her in London. She had met her aunt Amelia Foxwell Chetwood only once before. Amelia's soldier husband had died in one of the wars and the young widow had come to Foxwell Manor to stay with them, intent on finding another. Failing in that, her Aunt Amelia had packed her bags and returned to 'civilization' as she put it – meaning England – but not before scolding her brother, William, in front of his daughters and informing him that his girls – she and Kate and Anna – would turn out to be little better than 'savages' if he insisted on raising them in the Colonies.

Miriam was not looking forward to their second meeting.

With a sigh she pushed off the rail and went to sit in one of the chairs the ship's captain had ordered a deck hand to bring out for them. There were two and the other was occupied by Martha. The old woman had been exiled as well, sent to keep watch over her until she was safely delivered into Aunt Amelia's hands. Martha came from Enfield, a borough just north of London. She was to spend a month or so visiting her relations there and then to return across the sea before winter set in.

While Miriam went on to Edinburgh and school.

Charles Matthew Spencer had written to her. The letter was in her valise. He had not forgotten her. He had, in fact, kept the promise he had made her all those years ago when he left the Colonies shortly after her mother and Kate had died in order to return to his father's ancestral estate. Charles had pledged his undying love and vowed that he would wait for her

He waited still.

Miriam straightened her crimson silk skirts and reached over to take Martha's hand. Since the dear old thing had risked her father's wrath to stand up for her, they had grown closer. And here, on this ship, in the middle of the ocean, Martha was the *only* thing that tied her to home. To Foxwell manor. To dear sweet Grandpa George. To Judith. Even to rotten, spoiled little Anna.

And to Copperhead.

A chill took her. Miriam caught her shawl with her free hand and drew it close about her throat. One chapter of her life was over. Another beginning. She wondered what it would hold.

And she wondered if she would ever see Copperhead again.

Martha stirred and looked at her. The old woman squeezed her fingers and smiled. Miriam returned the gesture and then turned her eyes once again to the far distant shore.

Only time would tell.

Chapter Twenty

Christopher MacKay yawned, only remembering at the last minute to cover his mouth. He raised one raven-black eyebrow in apology and shrugged as his father scowled. Captain William Long of the *Renard*, who sat across the card table from them, exchanged an amused glance with his father's business acquaintance John Leighton and then returned his gaze to his cards. Leighton had joined them in the captain's cabin for a friendly game of Piquet.

"Are we 'old men' boring you, Kit?" his father asked.

"Boring? Why, of course not, sir. It is just that I had a rather late night last night, and it *is* almost morning...."

"And what, pray tell, might you have found on my ship, young Master MacKay, to keep you thus occupied so late?" William Long remarked as he picked up the deck of cards and began to shuffle. "Don't tell me you've secreted a woman aboard? Bad form, don't you know? Not to mention bad *luck*...."

"He didn't fail for trying," Kit's father exclaimed, slapping the table with his palm. "I caught the young scallywag in an clutch with a buxom doxy on the wharf just before we departed!"

"Father!"

The older man picked up his cards and then eyed his son over the pair of gilded frames perched precariously on the tip of his aquiline nose. "What? She wasn't a doxy?"

Kit stifled a sigh as he rose to his feet. "Might I be excused?"

Lord MacKay examined his dozen cards and tossed two on the table. As he drew replacements from his talon he said firmly, "Sit down, son."

Kit frowned but did as he was told. As he took his seat he caught sight of John Leighton's knowing smile. Kit had spent time at the Leighton's manor house and knew the man's sons, Johnny and Geoffrey, well. In fact he and Geoff had shared rooms at Oxford.

As he added the new cards to his hand, Lord MacKay's eyes returned to his son. "I would hazard a guess, then, that it was your 'other' passion that deprived you of this *much* needed sleep?"

Captain Long's hazel eyes flashed with unexpected interest as they returned to Kit. "Other?" he asked. "So your tastes run to *masculine* charms as well?"

"Oh no, Charles. No!" his father laughed. "No, Kit is most definitely a lady's man. My son's other passion – his *true* mistress, you might say – is his muse."

Kit shifted uncomfortably, feeling a bit like one of his Oxford don's prize specimens on display.

"A man with a muse," John Leighton said, tossing down two cards. "Music or dancing, may I ask?"

Captain Long leaned back in his chair and stared at him hard. "By God! I have it!" he exclaimed, slapping his thigh. "The boy's a writer!"

"One could only be so blessed by Providence above," Lord MacKay moaned as he picked up his glass and downed its contents in one gulp. As the liquor's fire coursed from double chin to gouty toe, he shuddered. Then he placed the cup on the table, punctuating his remark with a resounding clang. "The boy wants to be an *actor*. God save us!"

"Father, there is nothing wrong with being in the theatre," Kit protested as his eyes sought John Leighton again, hoping for a sympathetic nod. Geoff's father's attention had wandered. The dark-haired man with the hawkish face was sipping his wine and looking toward the door as if he longed to escape.

A sentiment Kit understood only *too* well.

"While it may not be the most respected of trades," he continued, "you have to admit many find amusement there – "

"*Trade*? *Acting*? For a scion of the noble classes? Good *God*, boy! Actors are little better than painted and powdered thieves dressed in borrowed clothes. They are vagabonds! *Wastrels*!"

"Hear! Hear!" Captain Long seconded.

"What of William Shakespeare?" Kit countered quickly.

"The man did write excellent poems," John Leighton offered.

"But did he stick to poems as he *should* have? No! He threw his talent away writing bawdy comedies and indulging in overly melodramatic tragedies. No, Kit," his father said with a shake of his head, "invoking Shakespeare will not save you."

Kit opened his mouth to reply, then clamped it shut. It would do no good. He and his father had taken this path more times than he could count. Lord MacKay would never approve of his choice.

Which was why he had made plans.

Kit's gaze skipped from one man to the other. His father was occupied with his cards. Captain Long was drinking and John Leighton – well, Leighton, was still staring at the door.

Kit cleared his throat. "May I go *now*, sir?"

His father nodded absentmindedly. As Kit rose to his feet and moved away from the table, the older man muttered, "You would think a game of Piquet would appeal to a young man bound and determined to live a life of immoral *excess* among prostitutes and procurers...."

Kit swallowed the sigh that longed to escape his throat and bid his father and the other two men a 'good night'. Then he fled the stuffy stateroom, bounded up the stair, and ran past the mizzenmast to the rear of the ship seeking the open vista of the sea. Once on the quarterdeck he caught a fist-thick rope that dangled from the belfry with his hand and leapt up onto the railing. For some time he stood there, watching the moon's argent light rise and fall with the undulating waves. Night had come as they sat in the captain's quarters and passed into the morning of the next day. He and his father were returning via the American Colonies from a journey to the West Indies where their family had holdings. Lord Mackay was intent on giving him an education in the real world equal to the one he was receiving at Oxford. His father meant to groom him to take his place. They were not really 'peerage' as the older man was apt to claim but were minor nobility, descended from a bastard son of one of the English kings. Their ancestral lands and holdings in Scotland were vast. One day Kit would be wealthy and powerful beyond his wildest dreams.

It was a day he dreamed would never come.

Hopping down from the rail, Kit started the long walk back to his cabin that was below deck in the fore part of the ship. Three weeks would find him in London, and another two, back at school. While he loved studying and adored literature and art, he felt stifled by the day-to-day drudgery of achieving a higher education. Too many of the dons spent their time dissecting the works of the men who were their masters – in both wit *and* intelligence – as if their ideas and philosophies were insects that could be pinned to a board. Art, poetry and novels were evanescent things. Ineffable. Indescribable. They were meant to be lived and breathed, not understood.

Meant to become a part of one's soul.

Kit yawned as he walked down the gangway of the main deck. The night before he had spent sitting up memorizing a long passage of Shakespeare's *Henry III* for the coming tour. His father didn't know – no one did. He had been accepted into David Stanbury's acting troupe. One week after the new session began at Oxford, the actors were to set sail for Canada. And he was to go with them. Stanbury had not promised him an acting part, but he didn't care. Checking wardrobe, taking tickets, prompting other actors – *anything* was better than spending another year being pressed into his father's mold. A curious restiveness had gripped him in the last month – ever since they had left the West Indies. The conditions there, the way the men, women *and* children who worked for his father were beaten and abused – not to mention the fact that they spent their lives in squalor, laboring to make *him* comfortable – had deeply disturbed him. He had seen their haunted, hurting faces – black and red – watching him as he rode by in comfort. Envying him. *Condemning* him.

If they only knew. If fate had dealt him a *slightly* different hand, he could have been one of them.

Kit nodded a distracted 'hello' to a seaman who passed him by and then stopped and did a double-take. The thickset man wore a crimson coat with buff breeches and shining black boots, and had the look of a pirate. He wasn't a sailor, though. By his dress, he identified him as one of the soldiers who had boarded the ship at the Carolina coast with Colonel Foxwell. Kit and his father had dined with the colonel on several occasions in Captain Long's stateroom. He had found the man not only a boor, but a brute as well. When one of the cabin boys accidentally slipped during service and spilled a bit of wine on the tablecloth, William Foxwell had boxed his ears so hard the boy cried.

Kit frowned as he watched the soldier hurry up the gangway. There was something about the way the man moved that suggested he was up to no good. The soldier hugged the shadows of the deck and furtively glanced from side to side, as if checking to see if he was being followed.

Kit decided to oblige him and do just that.

The soldier continued to the fore of the ship and then took the gangway off the forecastle and headed below deck. Kit counted to ten and then followed. As he passed down the ladder an unexpected blast of hot air struck him, causing his eyes to water and his exposed skin to prickle with warning. He took a deep breath, closed his eyes, and defied it, even though for a moment it felt as if he descended into Hell. Once on the lower deck, he followed the blur of the soldier's scarlet coat past the ship's oven and copper furnace into a cooler, darkened corridor that led to an open chamber beyond.

Kit hesitated, allowing his quarry time to move ahead. As he did, a light leapt into existence at the far end of the corridor and a brusque voice hailed the soldier. Seconds later a figure appeared carrying a lantern and dragging something heavy behind. The light revealed the man's red coat that was the same as that of the soldier he followed. As the light raced across the wooden floorboards, threatening to expose him, Kit ducked into the first opening he could find – which turned out to be the Captain's Cook Room. Fortunately it was unoccupied.

From this place of relative safety he listened to the soldiers' words.

"The watch is about to end," one said. "Everyone's abed. It's time we toss him."

"It's gotta look like an accident, Grove," the other countered with a quaking voice.

"Don't piss yourself, Ward," the first man laughed. "It will. It *will*. There's a loose bit of railing. He's always standing there at the fore of the ship, looking off toward the horizon. Won't seem suspicious at all if the rail breaks and he tumbles in."

Kit rested his head against the Cook Room wall. Apparently his curiosity had landed him in the middle of a murder plot! He wondered whom the poor bastard was the soldiers were discussing. There were other passengers on the *Renard*. Some like him were wealthy and well known. Others, middle class merchants and such. And then there were those who had come aboard bound and in chains. Prisoners, no doubt. It might be one of them or – even more likely – a sailor. Some poor Jack who had cheated the pair at cards or some other such nonsense and was about to get his just – or *unjust* deserts. The whole affair really was none of his business.

Still, there *had* been that mention of 'tossing' the man. It wouldn't do to just walk away and then learn of the poor blighter's having drowned at the morning watch.

Kit straightened up and turned toward the entry of the Cook's Room, determined to call them out. He halted at a strange muffled sound. One of the soldiers cursed and answered it with a slap. Then there was a thud –

And a groan.

Dear God! Their intended victim was *here*!

Careful not to reveal his position, Kit peered around the doorjamb. The soldiers had their backs to him and, sure enough, the lantern's light revealed a crumpled shape between them on the floor.

"Get him up, Ward!" Grove ordered. "Now! By the time we get him to the deck, the lads will be changing from mid to morning watch. We don't want nobody seeing us."

Kit watched as Ward knelt and then rose slowly to his feet. Their victim, drugged or semi-conscious, dangled limp in his arms. As Grove lent a hand and the pair started to move, he shrunk back into the shadows and waited. Supporting the man between them, the soldiers moved quickly past the entrance to the Cook's Room and headed for the stair. All Kit could see of the poor bastard they carried was a flash of a youthful face with tanned skin, a brownish-red head, and the collar of a linen shirt that was stained with blood.

Following at a discreet distance behind the trio Kit mounted the stair, furiously thinking what to do. If he confronted the men alone, the ruffians would probably kill him and pitch his body overboard as well. He needed a witness and yet, if he took the time to find one, their victim would be drowned before he managed to return.

As Kit topped the stair and stepped onto the main deck, he made up his mind. He would have to chance it and call them out. Hugging the shadows cast by the risen moon, he dashed down the deck and pivoted sharply around the main mast, so he would appear to come at them from the opposite end of the ship. He walked boldly and whistled a lively tune. When the soldiers spotted him they froze like footpads caught with their hands on a lady's purse.

It was all he could do to keep from laughing.

"Gentlemen! Good evening!" Kit called merrily as his gaze went to the still form that dangled between them, perilously close to the rail. "I say, might your companion be in his cups? He doesn't look at all well."

"Aye," Ensign Ward answered, instantly suspicious. "He's pissed-up. He don't want the captain to see him this way. We was...escorting him to his bunk."

"Oh, I see." Kit paused and deliberately took a long hard look at the man's face. "Say, don't I know you? Ward, isn't it? And Grove?"

"*Sergeant* Grove," the older of the two growled in reply as he stepped forward and squinted to see him better, wrinkling the jagged three inch scar that ran from beneath his eye to the tip of his curled lip. "And you? You're Lord MacKay's son, ain't you?"

Kit nodded. "Yes."

"Well, your *lordship*," Grove suggested, his tone mocking, "you must have more important things to think about than this here boosey sailor. We'll take care of him."

"I'm sure you will," Kit answered, his voice weighted with sarcasm. "In fact, I heard you making plans to do *just* that a few moments ago. Below deck near the Captain's Cook Room."

Ward blanched. Sergeant Grove snorted in reply, and then jabbed his less than willing accomplice in the ribs with his elbow to silence him. With a nod in Kit's general direction, the villain leaned over and muttered something in his cohort's ear that made the already pallid man go white as a winding sheet. Kit took a step back, certain he was a goner. Then, as Grove advanced on him with murderous intent, Providence intervened. The sailor set to keep the morning watch miraculously appeared, walking the gangway toward them.

"*Now* you've gone and done it, your lordship!" Sergeant Grove snarled, raising his voice so the approaching seaman would hear. "Our friend's a goner. Or he *will* be once the captain sees he's had more than his ration of ale."

"Captain Long is an old acquaintance of my father. I have some influence with him," Kit remarked quietly. "Leave it to me. I will see that nothing happens to him."

Ward and Grove exchanged nervous looks even as Kit nodded to the passing sailor who had hesitated and was watching them. "That ain't necessary, your lordship," Grove insisted.

"Oh, but I think it *is*." Kit held out his hand, indicating Grove should surrender their intended victim to him.

Sergeant Grove hesitated. He glanced at the sailor and then back at him as if considering whether or not he could take them both. In the end the rogue turned to Ensign Ward and barked, "Leave him! There'll be another day."

Ward glanced at the sailor who was shaking his head as if he had seen it all before. Then at Kit. And then at the semi-conscious man dangling between them. Without warning, he let the man go.

The poor bastard groaned as he hit the boards.

Shooting a venomous look over his shoulder, Sergeant Grove gripped Ward's elbow and hustled him away. Kit watched until the pair disappeared and then he knelt by their intended victim's side. As he rolled the man over, he saw that his first impression had been right – his skin was a little darker than the norm and his hair, an unusual bronze color. There was also a nasty black bruise on his temple. It was evident from that, as well as the blood on his face and collar, that he had been viciously used. It was also evident that he was *not* a sailor.

Touching the man's arm Kit assured him softly, "You're safe now, my friend. Those men cannot harm you. Can you speak?"

The stranger stirred. His dark brown eyes opened but with little focus. "Yes...."

"Can you tell me your name?"

A nod. And then, "Josiah."

Kit smiled reassuringly. "Well, Josiah, you certainly have made a *dangerous* pair of enemies." He slipped his arm around the other man's shoulders and helped him to rise. Supporting him, Kit led him up the gangway.

"Who.... Who are *you*?" Josiah asked.

Kit tightened his grip and helped him to place his foot on the first rung of the ladder that led to the lower deck.

"A friend."

Copperhead opened his eyes to find he was lying on a soft pallet in a strange room. He waited a moment and then shifted. Swinging his feet over the edge of the bunk, he placed them on the floor and then sat there, waiting for the strength to come that would allow him to rise. As he hesitated the door to the cabin opened and a well-dressed man in his twenties, with hair as raven-black as the fine suit he wore, entered. The stranger halted when he saw he was awake. Smiling, he crossed to his side and placed a horn cup filled with liquid on the table by the bunk.

"How are you feeling, Josiah?" he asked.

Copperhead frowned. He winced as he touched the bruise on his forehead. "Where am I?"

"In my cabin. Forgive my presumption. I didn't feel it was safe to leave you alone." The man sat in a chair by the table. "Not with *those* two still out there."

He shuddered with the memory. "Ensign Ward. And Sergeant Grove."

"Yes. It appears they intended to...." The man shifted uncomfortably. "Well, I over heard them making plans – "

"To kill me."

He nodded. "That *was* my assumption."

"And you stopped them?" Copperhead met his unknown savior's stare. His eyes were as black as the cloth of his well-tailored suit. "Why? Why put your own life in danger?"

The man shrugged, and then added with a grin. "Call it a character flaw. My father certainly does."

Copperhead laughed. "Thank you."

"I'd say, 'It was nothing', but that would be insulting." The man rose and held out his hand. "The name is MacKay. Kit Mackay. And you are Josiah…?"

Kit's skin was lightly tanned. The hand he extended, callus free and obviously unused to any kind of hard labor. He wore a close-fitting suit of ebony sprigged velvet embellished with bits of pearl set in nests of finely worked embroidery. The silver buckles on his shoes, as well as the diamond stickpin at his throat, marked him as a child of the privileged classes. Landed. Wealthy.

Like William Foxwell.

Taking his hand Copperhead shook it. "Woodward," he answered. "Josiah Woodward."

Kit didn't release his hand. "Woodward?" he scowled. "Doesn't ring a bell. But I feel I know you somehow. Are you certain we haven't met?"

He nodded. "I would remember."

"Perhaps I've seen you on deck then…." Kit snapped his fingers. "That's it! With Dr. Vicke. Are you his patient?"

Copperhead pulled his hand free. "In a way," he answered as he linked it with the other one in his lap and turned to look out the portal at the growing dawn.

A silence fell between them. It lasted perhaps a full minute. Kit MacKay, like most white men, was uncomfortable with it. He took hold of the horn cup and twirled it in his fingers. He changed positions in the chair. Finally, he palmed the cup and held it out to him. Copperhead sniffed the warm golden liquid within, recognized it for what it was – rum – and then downed it anyway. As the buttery toddy slid down his throat and eased his pain, his host rose to his feet and crossed to the opposite side of the elegant private cabin. Stopping near a small rosewood desk butted up against the wall, he flipped through the first few pages of a journal that lay there as if considering whether or not to take up his pen. Instead he closed it and turned to look at him.

"Why did those men want to kill you, Josiah?" Kit asked bluntly.

Copperhead was tired – *too* tired to invent a clever lie. Over the last few days as they drew nearer and nearer to their destination, Ensign Ward and Sergeant Grove had become his second shadow. The pair followed him every time he went on deck, taunting him with their presence, silently informing him that the days – the very *hours* he had to live were numbered. The afternoon before they had haunted the corridor outside of the cabin where he stayed, waiting until Dr. Standley left, and then confronted him as he and Kip headed for the stair. In so many words Sergeant Grove had made their intentions all *too* clear. Kip was not safe. The boy's life would be in danger if he accompanied him that day. Copperhead feigned weakness and insisted Kip take him back to the cabin. Then, as the boy went about his other duties, he returned to the ladder and climbed to the deck alone and went to confront William Foxwell's bullies.

At the top Ensign Ward grabbed him and Sergeant Grove struck him with a cudgel, and then he had known nothing more until he awoke below decks to the sound of the two soldiers planning his death.

Then his unexpected savior, Kit MacKay, had appeared.

"Josiah?" Kit was watching him closely. "Tell me. Why?"

Copperhead placed the horn cup on the table. "They had their orders."

"*Orders*? From whom?"

He rose shakily to his feet and started for the door. "Thank you for saving me, Kit MacKay. I *am* grateful, but I should go now."

"But you can't go!" Kit caught his shoulder. "That pair will only try again. I'll take you to Captain Long. He should be made aware of what has happened – "

"He is most likely *already* aware!" he snapped as he pulled free.

"What? Josiah, stay," Kit pleaded. "*Talk* to me."

Copperhead sighed. He very much wanted to 'talk' to him. But what he *knew* he had to do was escape. Kit MacKay was intelligent. Perceptive. *Persuasive*. It wouldn't be long before he was telling him his life story, and that was something he did *not* want to do.

"Josiah?"

"I doubt very much such an act could be perpetrated on board a ship without the captain's knowledge," he answered quietly. "Or permission."

"You're not just a deck hand, are you? Who *are* you, Josiah? Tell me. You can trust me." Kit paused. His tone was sincere. "I think you *need* a friend."

Copperhead shook his head.

"Please! I want to help you."

"No. You *don't*." He knew he should hold his tongue. His grandfather Walker would have told him that in naming his persecutor, he gave him more power. But he lacked the strength to lie. "Colonel William Foxwell is not a man you would wish to make your enemy."

The light of understanding dawned in Kit MacKay's black eyes. "You're the poor bastard they've held in chains below! Aren't you? *You're* William Foxwell's heathen half-brother!"

"You know of me?" Copperhead asked, amazed.

"Don't look so surprised. Not everyone knows. It's just...." Kit frowned slightly. "Well, let's just say I took a special interest in your story."

"And you heard it where?"

Kit laughed. "From the *Renard's* captain. My father and William Long are old friends. And the man *can't* hold his liquor when playing cards." His smile faded. "So you're a breed. Who's the savage – your father or mother?"

Copperhead didn't answer. He pushed past him and headed toward the door.

"Josiah, wait. I meant no offense. Don't go!"

His hand was on the latch. He glanced back over his shoulder. "What is it to you?"

"You and I, I think, have much in common," Kit said softly.

Copperhead shook his head. "I doubt it."

The man in black took a step toward him. "Look at me, Josiah. *Really*, look at me."

He sighed as he turned back. "What do you expect me to see?"

Kit met his gaze and held it for several heartbeats. Then he flinched and looked away. "Just a friend," he said as he returned to the table by the bunk and fingered the empty horn cup. "Someone who would like to get to know you better."

Copperhead lifted the latch and opened the door. "For your own good you must stay away from me, Kit MacKay. On this you must trust me. I am *not* someone you would want to know."

After Josiah exited the cabin Kit remained beside the table, staring at the empty cup. Then he returned to the rosewood desk and shifted his journal out of the way. Gripping one of the decorative knobs on an inset panel he gave it a sharp twist. A secret compartment popped open. From its depths he pulled a narrow velvet case. With great care he untied the ribbon that bound it and removed a second case. As he opened that one, a heavy chain with a locket of chaised gold at its end fell into his hand. Dropping both cases on the desk, he crossed to the bunk Josiah had occupied and sat on it.

Kit drew a deep breath as, his fingers trembling just a bit, he used them to pry open the tiny gilded window onto another, happier time.

A woman stared back at him. An Indian beauty whose wide brown eyes crackled with pride. The bone frame of her face was broad, her nose straight, and her full lips quirking with hidden mirth. The thick hair he remembered so well was waist-length even plaited, and black as a lightless night. Kit reached out and touched the tiny painted portrait and then snapped the gold locket shut and rose to his feet. Walking to the desk he opened a drawer and drew out a mirror. Holding it up, he looked at his own face and saw the same deep brown eyes, the same nose and wide cheeks – even if his skin was only half as dark and he had his white father's mouth.

"What do I expect you to see, Josiah Woodward – heathen, *breed* – when you look at me?" Kit whispered.

"Yourself."

Chapter Twenty-One
England

The *Renard's* arrival in England was delayed by the appearance of a fast flying frigate off the port side bearing news to the mysterious and seldom seen John Leighton that a ship of his private line had run aground near Caldy Island, Wales. Leighton's ship, the *Diligence* lay foundered south of their present position on a rugged bit of coast not far from the Wurm's Head – a promontory shaped like a giant sea serpent that marked the most westerly tip of Gower. Her cargo was intact. John Leighton listened closely as the man who boarded them gave him the details, and then took him in hand and went to find Captain Long. Locating the *Renard's* master near the wheel, Leighton explained what had happened, and then offered Long and his crew half of the profits if the captain would, with all haste, detour to Wales to rescue it.

Copperhead had been taking one of his mandated constitutionals with Kip when the frigate arrived. As usual Sergeant Grove and his cohort Ensign Ward dogged their heels. On William Foxwell's behalf the pair vigorously protested the delay, but Captain Long – sensing a quick and easy profit – paid them little heed. The captain of the *Renard* nodded his head and promised he would note their protest in the ship's log and then, to the raucous cheers of his men, shook John Leighton's hand and sealed the deal.

The detour would cost them two weeks.

For the ship's crew the delay came as a mixed blessing. While they looked forward to the extra money it would put in their pockets, the journey south would take them farther from their homes. Most were from the London area and had not seen their families in well over two years. As Copperhead moved among them, he overheard their comments and whispered prayers – some thanked the white man's God for this opportunity, while others sought their Creator's protection against the jagged rocks and turbulent seas ahead. For him the unexpected detour had come as a welcome reprieve. The *Renard* was now headed away from England and from the imprisonment that awaited him there.

As the Captain and John Leighton shook hands, Dr. Standley sought him out and asked if he could 'borrow' Kip for an hour or two. Over Kip's protests, he had agreed. Grove and Ward were not done with him yet and he was concerned they would use the boy's affection for him as a weapon.

Copperhead shifted and glanced in the direction Dr. Standley had gone. More than two hours had passed. There was no sign of Kip and he was growing concerned. The sun had set in the west and a steady breeze arisen. In it was the chill of the winter to be. Pulling the coarse fabric of his woolen jacket close about his throat, Copperhead shivered.

"Josiah?"

He knew the voice, though it had been more than a month since he had heard it last. Copperhead turned to find the mysterious John Leighton standing directly behind him. Surprise, and then anger registered in Leighton's hawkish brown eyes as they lighted on the tell-tale bruises left by the beating he had taken at the hands of the men in William Foxwell's employ.

"Mr. Leighton," Copperhead nodded a greeting. "You have been quite the stranger of late."

Leighton leaned on the railing and turned his face toward the distant horizon. "I must apologize. I *have* kept up with your progress. Vicke has kept me well informed. I, like you, do not take well to the seas," he added with chagrin. "I have been indisposed for the greater part of the journey."

He studied the man. John Leighton was attired in a deep blue woolen suit. His stock collar was crisp and framed a clean-shaven chin. The man's color *was* a bit pale, but he seemed robust – and the picture of health. "I see," Copperhead replied and then added, "your absence has not admitted me an opportunity to thank you."

He appeared surprised. "For what?"

"Kip. And Dr. Standley. For a cabin of my own."

John Leighton dismissed his supposed generosity with a wave of his hand. "A more comfortable prison. I wish I could do more."

"Why? *Why* do you care?"

The older man's lean frame stiffened. Pushing off the rail, he turned to face him. Both his look and his words were hard. "I don't owe you anything, Josiah. Least of all an explanation for my actions. Press me, and I will leave you to fend off Foxwell's dogs alone."

Copperhead followed Leighton's sideways glance. Ward and Grove were close at hand as usual. Ward was leaning against the mast, a basket of apples in his arms. He had bought the fruit off the cook of the frigate before it departed. Grove was peeling a ripe red one. When the surly sergeant noticed his scrutiny, he sneered and brandished the paring knife with deliberate threat.

Copperhead's hands tightened into fists.

He was tired of games.

He met Leighton's stare with a challenge. "Why *don't* you then?"

The hawkish man's dark brows arched and he laughed. "I see Dr. Standley's forced constitutionals have helped you to regain at least *some* fire. That's good. You will need it if you are to survive where you are going."

"You could keep me from prison if you wanted. Couldn't you?" Copperhead demanded.

"No. I signed a deal with William Foxwell. The man is a loathsome pig, but a contract *is* a contract. I have my business – and reputation to consider."

"But you *could* allow me to escape."

Leighton held his gaze. After a moment he replied, "I could. But I won't."

"And you won't tell me why."

The other man's upper lip quirked as if he were slightly amused. "Let us just say, Josiah, that I believe a man must fight his own battles. That is what makes him a man." John Leighton inclined his head as he turned to leave. "Good e'en, Master Woodward. I will see you again before we disembark in London."

Copperhead watched him go with a frown, staring after him until he disappeared down the ship's ladder. Who was John Leighton? And just what *was* the man's connection with Miriam's father? He seemed to loath and yet, at the same time, be bound to William Foxwell. Was Leighton's kindness genuine, or merely a ruse? Did he give him hope only to dash it? There was no way of knowing. All he could do was continue to accept the man's help...

And hope there was not too great a price to pay in the end.

"So you got a reprieve, eh? You know it ain't gonna save you in the end." A thickset frame blocked his view. "You listening to me, *breed*?"

Sergeant Grove had left Ward behind and come to taunt him. "Leave me alone," Copperhead answered, shoving past.

Grove caught his arm and held it. "Leave him alone, he says. What'cha think, Ward?" he called over his shoulder. "Should we leave the *breed* be? Maybe we could turn our backs? Then he can jump ship the minute she cozies up to the coast."

"Let me go!" Copperhead insisted, resisting.

Like a viper Grove struck out, pressing the razor sharp point of the paring knife into his shirt. "What'cha gonna do, *breed*?," he snarled. "Go crying to your high and mighty friend to save you? Look around. His lordship Master Kit Mac-Kay ain't here this time to save your tanned arse." The blade passed through the linen and bit into the skin stretched taut over his ribs. "What's say I stick you like a pig right now and toss your carcass over the railing to feed the fish?" The soldier's sneer showed several missing teeth. "I could always say I slipped. *Oops!*"

As Copperhead felt blood trickle down his chest, a thin sheet of sweat broke out on his skin. There was little he could do. Before he could move, the blade would penetrate his heart.

Even as the thought crossed his mind that this was where he would die, Sergeant Grove snorted and pulled back. With a bellowing laugh he returned the soiled blade to the apple and cutting a thick slice popped it into his mouth –

Blood and all.

"Nah. Not here. Too many witnesses." Tossing the remainder of the apple over the side, Grove finished with wicked pleasure, "Still, I'd advise you to watch your back, mate. One of these days, you'll find this knife *in* it."

Sergeant Grove returned to Ward's side and together they moved off.

Copperhead stared after them for some time and then returned to the railing and leaned there, looking out toward the horizon just as John Leighton had done, and awaited Kip's return.

Aunt Amelia was everything Miriam remembered.

And more.

Miriam stifled a sigh and leaned her chin on her hand as her cousin Dorothea finished a wretched rendition of a Bach fugue to thunderous applause. When Miriam had arrived in London the week before she had found everything arranged – or rather, *re*arranged. Instead of sending her on immediately to school and Scotland as previously agreed, she was to remain with her Aunt Amelia's family for nearly a month in order to be introduced to London Society first. In about three weeks her father would join them, and then he would personally escort her to school. The Head Mistress knew all about it and had lent her enthusiastic approval to the plan, stating that life experience was as integral a part of a young woman's education as Latin or French – and at least *twice* as useful as Mathematics.

Tonight Aunt Amelia was hosting a party. Her daughters Dorothea and Matilda were providing the entertainment. A pack of rapacious suitors circled the pair, their keen eyes fixed on the young heiress' ample bosoms and the jewels set there in fine silver and gold filigree to serve as an advertisement for their even more sizeable dowries. Miriam sighed and shifted and glanced at the pair where they sat side by side on the upholstered bench that fronted the French ormolu and gilt harpsichord. It was a good thing that Dorothea and Matilda were blessed with wealth. Even though they were dressed to the nines in costly fabrics worked with embroidery and punctuated with pearls, to put it kindly, they were as homely as a pair of sows.

No, that was unkind to the sows.

Miriam stifled a giggle as she lifted her eyes to her late uncle Albert's portrait where the tall raw-boned man kept watch over his daughters from the grave and his prominent position on the papered wall above the harpsichord. Less than a half a century before the Chetwoods had been impoverished blacksmiths. Albert's father had made a killing in the copper mines of Cornwall and had used his newfound wealth to buy his son's way into the upper ranks of London society. Albert Chetwood had a ruddy face with a tolerably large mouth, small piggish eyes, and a distinctive and *very* noticeable nose. Dorothea and Matilda would inherit their father's vast estate and personal fortune.

It was unfortunate they had also inherited his looks.

Miriam leaned back in her seat and fanned, masking her amusement. Dorothea had risen, leaving the bench to her sister. Matilda was the eldest and, thereby, the first to inherit. The pack circling the harpsichord drew even closer. A few of the bachelors burst into applause even before her bejeweled fingers could brush the keys. Matilda was triumphant. She smirked, nudging the beauty spot on her upper lip into the shadow cast by her protruding nose, and then put a plump hand to her forehead and declared she was simply *too* fatigued to go on. As the bachelors begged and cajoled, Dorothea fumed. Miriam watched her Aunt Amelia rise from her chair, ready to play her part in the unfolding drama.

This was it.

Her chance to escape.

Miriam rose and, catching her cream silk skirts in her fingers, slipped into the shadows cast by the light of two of the Chetwood's quartet of Meissen candelabrum. Making her way to the back of the room, she headed for the double doors that led to the terrace. Albert Chetwood's London home was spacious and well furnished. The ballroom – as every other room – was stocked with an excess of the costliest of porcelain figures, sterling tea sets, and the finest mahogany furniture money could buy. In order to prove himself worthy, the son of the North London blacksmith had built his house in the fashionable West End, close by the formal squares of Westminster. Within its white stone walls, Chetwood House was a palace. Without, it became a fortress. The chains, padlocks and iron railings that protected the estate proclaimed the truth Albert Chetwood had worked hard to deny. One her Aunt Amelia still fought so hard to conceal.

The truth that the lowborn Chetwoods did *not* belong.

As she opened the doors and stepped onto the terrace with its potted trees and lush hanging baskets ripe with late summer flowers, Miriam breathed a sigh of relief. She crossed quickly to the stone balustrade and leaned on it, gazing out over the ordered gardens below. The sight of the well-manicured gardens made her wonder how her mother's small plot of earth fared back home. The last of the summer roses would be dying. There were things that needed to be tended too. Proper care must be taken in order to insure the fragile flowers survived the fast approaching winter. In spite of the warm night Miriam shuddered and pulled her silk shawl closer about her exposed shoulders. Judith had written to her. She had found the letter waiting when she disembarked. Anna would not be there to watch over their mother's treasures. Her younger sister was to be sent away to school in New York. There would be no one left at Foxwell Manor but the servants, and Judith and her grandfather. Judith had written that Grandpa George was well, though little improved.

She missed him so.

Miriam closed her eyes and let the night breeze wash over her, praying its welcome touch would cleanse her spirit and lift the melancholy mood that had settled on her unexpectedly. Instead it caught her pale blond curls in its wake and deposited them on her shoulders. She shook her head and realized her hair had come free of the ribbon that kept it contained in its stylish tail. Lifting a hand, she reached back to search for it.

And was startled to encounter other fingers doing the same.

Miriam drew a sharp breath and pivoted. A man stood close behind her, cloaked in shadow. "I believe this belongs to you," he said offering her the ribbon. His voice was rich and laced with a sort of affectionate amusement.

She accepted it with a nod. "Yes. The wind.... It must have come undone."

"Your hair is lovely down. Well, it is lovely no matter what. I mean...." The man paused and then added with a shake of his head. "I mean, *you* are lovely no matter what."

"You are rather bold, sir, for a stranger," she said as she started to push past him.

He caught her elbow from behind. "Miriam. I am *no* stranger."

"Miriam? How do you – " She stopped, stunned. In turning, the light had revealed his face. "Charles?"

Releasing her, he executed a well-rehearsed bow. "Charles Matthew Spencer. At your service, Miss Foxwell."

Miriam shook her head. "I wouldn't have known you."

"From the reaction my presence evoked the last time we met, dear lady, I believe that would be a *good* thing."

"Charles. No."

"The truth, now. You thought I was a bore," Charles prompted with a smile.

"No!" Miriam paused. She pursed her lips and gnawed the lower one, and then admitted with a sigh, "Well, yes. I guess I did."

"And you were right."

Charles turned away from her and walked to the stone balustrade. The moonlight struck his manly form as he stared off into the night. He had matured since she had seen him last. Charles' attire was handsome, well cut of a costly forest green velvet, but sober and not in the least ostentatious as it had been when he visited Foxwell Manor. When he spoke, his speech was unaffected. Gone was the toff, the snob, the blustering boor she had despised. In his place she found an earnest and admirable young man.

"I was a fool," Charles continued, turning back toward her. "When you rejected my suit, it made me take a look at myself. A *good* look. I had to learn to see myself through your eyes."

"What does it matter what I thought – or think?" she asked.

Charles crossed to her side and, without permission, took her hand. Pressing it between his own, he said softly, "Because, my dear Miss Foxwell, I love you. I have *always* loved you. And if my suit was to have any chance, I had to become someone *you* could love in return."

Miriam glanced back at the glittering ballroom with its false daylight and fickle denizens. "Did Aunt Amelia put you up to this?" she demanded.

"No. *No.* Your aunt's interest lies in those two harpies roosted at the harpsichord. I was invited to attend tonight in order to make love to Matilda Chetwood." Charles' look was sour until it settled on her face. "I had no idea you were in attendance – or even in London – until I saw you just now, fleeing like a fox before the hounds."

Miriam nodded, accepting him at his word, and then indicated her hand. As he released it, she said, "I should go back inside."

Charles took a step back. "May I call on you at least? With your Aunt's permission, of course?"

Miriam hesitated. She looked at him. Charles *was* handsome. And now that he had put away the fool, a clear intelligent light shone from his wide hazel eyes. He had a head of dark blond curls that fell – contrary to custom – to brush the collar of his velvet coat, and a wide mouth that seemed gentle – even kind.

She looked at Charles, but thought of Copperhead.

Miriam choked back a sob and lowered her head, unable to meet his steady gaze.

Charles said nothing. He simply waited.

After a moment she composed herself. Glancing up she nodded once, and then turned and fled, abandoning the terrace and the dreams of her youth to embrace the cold harsh reality of a life lived without the one she loved.

It was as if someone had driven a stake through her heart.

The *Renard* arrived in the waters near Caldy's Island during the night while most of the ship's compliment was still sleeping. Kit MacKay should have been one of them. Instead he had spent a restive night, haunted by the ghosts of a childhood abandoned – not at his own choosing, but at the behest of another. Upon hearing the sounds of the sailors moving about, he had risen and gone above deck. There he had watched the sun rise and marveled at its beauty. Beyond the rocky precipice known as the Wurm's Head, which was cast in ebon silhouette against it, an aurora borealis of vibrant, almost violent colors was displayed. Purple and crimson clouds lay upon a bed of golden sky, skirted by a horizon of pallid blue.

As a young boy Kit had known such beauty – beauty his adult mind lacked the words to describe. At the time he had roamed the forested land of Keetowah – the land its English conquerors now called 'South Carolina'. He had lived among his mother's people and though he had known hardship – seasons of want, sickness, even starvation – what he remembered most was the sense of *belonging*, of knowing at each and every moment who and what he was. Among his mother's people, called Cherokee by those who were not a part of them, there was no such thing as a bastard. A child born to a Cherokee mother *was* Cherokee. Such a child was wanted. Loved.

Accepted.

The world his Scottish father's wooden ship had borne him to was *not* so kind. From the moment he set foot on English soil – the lost child of a dead mother, barely seven summers old – he had known he did not belong. And even more, he had known there was something he had lost. Something of great importance. It had taken him a dozen years of wine and women and wasted living to remember what it was.

Himself.

Kit shuddered and gripped the rope that hung from the ship's belfry tightly with his quaking fingers. The abandoned hulk of the *Diligence* lay to the lee of the ship, foundering in shallow water, a jagged hole ripped in her wooden hide. From this wound Captain Long's men poured carrying crates and kegs, bearing boxes, carting the remainder of the *Diligence's* rescued cargo to shore. Though the crates contained sugar and other costly spices, and the kegs were full of rum and the finest tobacco leaf, they had been left until the last. Compared to the other cargo the Diligence carried, buried deep within its belly, they were as *nothing*.

Kit was not meant to see. No one was. But see he did, and *what* he saw sickened him.

His flesh crawled as the door cut into the upper deck slammed shut behind William Long's lean upright form with a horrible finality. The captain hadn't seen him watching from the shadows, but the copper-skinned men and women he drove before him, bound and in chains, had –

And thought him one of their persecutors.

Only once before in his young life had Kit known such outrage as he felt now, and that was when his father had taken him on an inspection tour of their 'property' in the West Indies – property that included, to use Lord MacKay's favorite term, the *animals* he owned that walked on two feet.

Unable to bear the shame and guilt any longer, Kit turned away and ran the length of the deck. He slid down the wooden ladder that led to the ship's darkened interior and headed for the familiar sanctuary of his cabin. On his way a man crossed his path. It took him a second, but he recognized the figure as John Leighton. Back at Oxford Leighton's son, Geoff, had hinted that the family 'interests' ran beyond tobacco, sugar and rum. Now he knew what Geoff had meant.

The Leightons dealt in human flesh.

John Leighton was preoccupied. As he passed, they brushed shoulders. The older man halted to straighten his coat and only then, seemed to note his presence.

"Master MacKay," he greeted him. "Forgive me. I didn't see you."

"Too busy thinking of the *profit* that awaits you in London?" Kit asked, seething.

John Leighton's demeanor was strangely calm. "The shipment is not mine," he said quietly. "It belongs to my business partner, Oliver Gerard."

"So that excuses everything?" Kit snapped. "You had to know what cargo the *Diligence* hauled."

"Yes, I knew. That does not mean I approve." Leighton turned to leave. "Now, if you will excuse me, I am needed below."

Kit reached out and boldly caught the other man's arm. "How *can* you, sir, in good conscience – " Leighton's gaze shifted to his hand and only then did Kit realize how hard he gripped him. Releasing him, he inclined his head. "Forgive me, Mr. Leighton, it is just – "

"Never apologize for a display of heartfelt passion, Master MacKay," the other man remarked enigmatically as he straightened his sleeve. "But do not waste it on hopeless causes either. There is *nothing* you can do for the poor creatures locked in the ship's hold. Their fate is sealed. You would do better to expend such energy in helping one who could benefit from it. One who might avoid such a fate, had he such a *passionate* benefactor."

"What?" Kit scowled. "Whom are you talking about?"

"London is a labyrinth. A vast metropolis of some eight or nine hundred thousand souls. If a man could once be set loose in it...." John Leighton's dark brown eyes were haunted. The light in them unexpectedly suggesting some personal gain to be found in the act. "Well, not even William Foxwell and his *dogs* could sniff him out."

"You're speaking of Josiah?" Kit asked.

Leighton shrugged. "Am I?"

As the other man moved away, Kit challenged him. "How can you know I would help him? Why should *I* care?"

John Leighton halted. "Do you remember me?" he asked as he returned to his side.

The light of the lantern hung from the corridors' rafters illuminated the older man's face. Pale skinned but dark haired, with eyes like a predatory bird's. Kit knew it well. "Of course I do," he said.

Leighton shook his head. "No. *Before.* When you were a boy."

"That's impossible," Kit breathed, suddenly unsure. "You cannot have known me then. I spent my childhood in – "

"The Colonies. I know." His voice was soft. Almost wistful. "I remember."

"How? When were you – "

"Oh, I was there. Your father traveled with our company. James was a merchant even then. I was adjutant to a general. We lived for a time among the savages." Leighton shook his head. "*Savages.* That's what we called the red man. They were no more 'savage' than we. I don't recall your mother's name, but I do recall that she was lovely."

Kit stiffened. "You knew my mother?"

He nodded. "Don't be alarmed. Your secret is safe with me – as is Josiah Woodward's."

"*Why?* What have you to gain by your silence?"

"Gain?" the other man snorted. "Perhaps a bit of self-respect. A turn of the key in Saint Peter's gate? Who knows? If I do enough good deeds in the time I have left, I may yet earn entrance to Heaven."

"Are you then already consigned to Hell?" Kit asked him boldly.

"Oh, yes." John Leighton's aspect darkened. "But this is not about me. It is about Josiah Woodward. I have done all I can for him. I can do no more openly. The rest is up to you."

"Me?"

"The boy is to be held in an ancient stronghold north of the city called Spurrell Pode, among the impoverished people of North London. It will be easy to bribe the guards." Leighton's smile was sly. "Use some of that money of your father's to *free* one of your own, rather than to enslave them."

At first Kit missed what he hinted at. Then he bristled. "Do you mean to suggest that *my* father is somehow involved in this pandering of human flesh?"

"Your father's hands are not bloodied by the fate of those upon the *Diligence*. I cannot speak for those in the West Indies. Then again, John MacKay is just a man doing what he must to survive. And isn't that what we all do, Master MacKay? What we *need* to survive?" John Leighton held his gaze for several heartbeats, and then turned his back and descended the stair to the lower deck.

Kit stood for some moments, stunned. Then – his jaw tight and his hands clenched in fists of determination – he left the corridor and headed for his cabin.

Chapter Twenty-Two

"Oh! Miriam. I didn't see you there! You frightened me half out of my wits!"

Miriam smiled weakly. Her cousin, Dorothea Chetwood, had come around the corner into a small alcove reserved for cooks and maids and discovered her there. Dorothea glanced at the leftover mutton with oysters and hours old asparagus ices laying in bowls near her slippered feet and wrinkled her prominent nose.

"Whatever are you doing here?" she asked.

Miriam scowled. She didn't know what she was doing *here*, unless it was hoping to melt away like the ices. Her Aunt Amelia's party refused to die. Though a few of the guests had had the good sense to excuse themselves and go home, the majority remained behind dancing, drinking, and dangling over the costly furniture, so inebriated she doubted they knew who they were. She had sought refuge behind a thick set of damask draperies used to screen the frantic movements of the staff from the Chetwood's socially acceptable guests.

"I just.... Well, I needed to get away," Miriam replied. "What are *you* doing here?"

"Mama sent me to scold the chef," Dorothea said as her piggish eyes flicked to a servant who was hurrying past bearing a tray of Muscadine Ices. "You know, I saw you with Charles earlier. Is that who you are trying to get away from?" Wanton expectation curled the ends of Dorothea's thin lips. "Was he forward?"

"No." Miriam shook her head. "No! Charles is a perfect gentleman."

Dorothea looked disappointed. "Mama wants him for Matilda. You know that, don't you?"

Miriam nodded. "He told me."

"She'll be very cross if she finds out you were speaking with him. And alone."

"It isn't my wish to upset Aunt Amelia. Charles and I have met before, in the Colonies. He just wanted to…catch up."

"Don't you mean *pick up* where you left off?"

"No." Miriam reluctantly decided to abandon the dark sanctuary of the drapes. Gathering her skirts in her hands, she pushed past her cousin. "I have no interest in Charles, you may assure Matilda of that. I have no interest in *anyone*. I don't intend to marry."

Dorothea caught her arm and held her back. "You're a queer one, aren't you, cousin Miriam? Mama said there's something in the country air in the Colonies that makes you Yanks daft."

Miriam gritted her teeth. She pulled free and then pivoted on her heel to face her cousin. "Mama says. *Mama* says! Do you have a thought in your head you can call your own?"

Her cousin looked as if she had been struck. "You don't have to be unkind," she pouted.

"I'm not. I'm being truthful! Do you have to agree with *everything* your mother says?"

"Well, yes...."

"Don't you ever, for just a moment, want to break free and be who *you* are? Think what *you* think? Dorothea, there is more to life than finding the right money to marry and then bedding the man!" As unexpected tears welled in her eyes Miriam turned away. "Excuse me. I have to go...."

"Miriam?"

She halted but did not look back. "What?"

Dorothea hesitated. "I don't really care if Charles courts you. Mama picked him for Matilda and it suits me fine if, just *once*, the cow doesn't get what she wants. But I don't think you *want* him to court you. Do you?"

Miriam shuddered. Tears streamed down her cheeks and streaked the fine brocade fabric of her dress.

"Is there someone else?" her cousin asked suddenly. "Someone back in the Colonies? You can tell me. Really. I'm good at keeping secrets."

She wanted to tell her. Dear Lord, she *needed* to tell someone. She needed a friend, here, in this alien world. But it was too soon. For all she knew Dorothea was playing her for a fool and would fly to her *Mama* with every word as soon as her back was turned.

Drawing a deep breath, Miriam turned to face her. "There was someone once," she said. "But he's dead."

Dorothea's fan flew to her face in a well-rehearsed gesture. "Oh, how terrible! Who was he?"

"I don't want to talk about it."

"Oh, but you should. Pain only lessens if it is shared."

"Did your Mama tell you that as well?" Miriam snapped.

Dorothea looked genuinely hurt. "No." She hesitated and then added quietly, "Experience."

It was Miriam's turn to be stunned. "I didn't.... I'm sorry." She held her hand out and indicated that her cousin should take it. "Don't you think it's time we returned to the party? Your Mama will be looking for both of us."

Copperhead opened his eyes. A noise – something he couldn't identify – had awakened him. He sat up in his bunk and glanced at the floor. Kip was there, on his pallet, sound asleep. Outside the porthole the dawning sun turned the ocean waves to liquid gold. The *Renard* was three days out from Caldy, and two away from London.

Two days of freedom remained.

He lay in his bunk for some time but found sleep elusive. Suddenly thirsty, he swung his bare feet over the side and, avoiding Kip, padded across the floor toward the water jug. Then it came again. The sound that had awakened him.

A gentle insistent scratching on the cabin door.

Copperhead glanced at Kip. He was still asleep. Then he crossed to the door, lifted the latch, and opened it. The passage beyond was dark. Someone had extinguished the lantern that hung close by the ladder to the upper deck, though a bit of light spilled down from the above. He frowned as he poked his head into the corridor.

And was gripped from behind. Copperhead struggled against the hand clamped over his mouth, certain it was Grove or Ward. How could he so stupidly have fallen into their trap? Then a soft voice spoke close by his ear.

"Calm down! It's me. Kit. Josiah, you have to trust me. We have to leave – *now*. They're coming!"

As he was released, Copperhead asked, "Who?"

"No time." Kit nodded toward the ladder. Within the shadows that masked it, darker shadows stirred. Someone was descending. "We have to go. Now!"

He glanced at the open cabin door. "I can't leave Kip."

"Kip is not in danger. *You* are. They mean to take you tonight." Kit gripped the door and pulled it to. "I promise I will get word to Gerard. He'll take care of the boy. Now, come on!"

Copperhead hesitated only a moment and then turned and followed Kit McKay as he dashed down the lightless corridor headed for the ladder at the opposite end of the deck. "Why are you doing this?" he asked as they ran.

Kit glanced back at him. A broad grin split his deeply tanned face. "I've asked myself the same question. We'll see if I can think of an answer by the time we reach our destination!"

As they drew abreast the ladder that led to the poop deck, Kit made an unexpected shift and bypassed it. He led them instead past the Ward Room, and then took the ladder to the lower gallery. When they reached the Bread Room, he halted. Catching Copperhead's arm, Kit drew him into a pool of shadows cast by one of the ship's big guns. He pressed a finger to his lips and then leaned his head against the wall and closed his eyes.

And they waited.

Several minutes later Kit stirred. He stepped forward and looked down the corridor. "It seems we have thrown them off," he sighed with relief.

"Sergeant Grove?"

"And Ward. I was abroad early today. I happened on the two of them making a deal with a seaman named Chambers. Something about removing cargo from the ship before the change of the morning watch." Kit's white teeth flashed again, though his smile was grim. "I presumed that 'cargo' was you."

"But why? When we are so close to land and I am bound for prison...."

Kit faced him. "You have friends here, Josiah. Friends other than me. I do not believe Dr. Standley – or even Captain Long – would stand idly by and let those two toughs take you in hand. The world of the *Renard* is small. It is common knowledge what they did to you."

"So they mean to kidnap me."

Kit nodded. "We must hide you until we reach port. Somewhere they will not find you. Some place they would never suspect."

Copperhead sensed something in his tone. "What are you thinking?"

Kit reached into his waistcoat and produced a key. One ebon eyebrow arched and he grinned as he wagged it before his face. "Captain Long has a great capacity for ale – but mine is greater!"

"You took it?" As Kit nodded again, he asked, "What does it open?"

His companion sobered instantly.

"The gates of Hell."

Copperhead surrendered his shirt and shivered with the cold damp of the hold as he watched his friend disappear behind one of the *Renard's* great guns. Kit had awakened him from sleep wearing nothing but a linen shirt and breeches. Now, in order for his friend's plan to work, the shirt had to go. Kit had explained it to him as they took stair after stair, step after step descending farther into the bowels of the ship. He had reluctantly agreed, not knowing what else to do. Still, he was uneasy.

There were so many things that could go wrong.

The sound of footsteps approaching brought him back to the present. Copperhead looked up to find that Kit had returned. His friend held up hands blackened with grease and powder residue. With an artist's eye Lord McKay's son studied him and then, with a wicked grin, began to smear the foul smelling stuff on his face, chest and legs.

"Unfasten your hair," Kit said. And when he had done so, added, "You look properly filthy now, even if you *haven't* the proper stench." His eyes flicked to a nearby door that led into the lower deck. "Are you ready?"

When he failed to answer, Kit clapped a hand on his shoulder in encouragement and then turned toward the door and inserted the key. Even before it opened Copperhead became aware of the scent of sickness and death permeating the dark chamber that lay below the waterline. Kit choked and reached for a handkerchief to place over his mouth. As their eyes met, he halted and returned it to his pocket. Then, drawing a deep breath, he led the way into what passed on the *Renard* as purgatory.

Briny water, seeping through the boards, pooled on a floor made slick with urine and human waste. The stench of vomit and sweat-soaked bodies choked the air. Copperhead knew the place. It was where he had first been incarcerated upon arriving on the English ship. Someone had cleared it, removing the ropes and wooden crates, but its purpose was the same – within its four fetid walls a dozen or more copper-skinned men were held captive. Shackles cast of iron encircled their wrists and ankles, linked by chains that bound them to the floor.

"Are you ready?" Kit had asked.

No. He was not.

Though it pained him to admit it, nearly ten years passed in the white man's world had altered him. He had grown used to the comfort of a bed with a feather ticking. Become accustomed to linen shirts and the feel of fine fabric against his skin. He craved a room warmed by a roaring fire. A stack of books beside his bed. Creature comforts. The men who hugged the far wall of the chamber, half-naked, foul and filthy, muttering words now foreign to his ear, *were* savages.

And he was one of them no longer.

"It is only for a few days," Kit said softly, sensing his unease. "Until we reach London. I will come for you before we make landfall and get you off the ship – somehow."

Copperhead turned to look at him. "You have still not told me why you do this," he said.

Kit's face was a study in determination. "No, I haven't."

"Will you tell me now?"

His friend's voice trembled as he answered. "It is for my mother as much as for you. And for myself," he admitted with chagrin. Kit lifted a chain that hung around his neck. A gold locket dangled at its end. He pulled the necklace over his head and held it out to him. "Here. See for yourself."

Copperhead took it and opened the locket. From its depths a handsome woman gazed at him – a woman with raven black hair and deeply tanned skin, whose black eyes shone with intelligence and humor.

A woman native as he.

"Your mother?" Copperhead asked, astonished.

Kit accepted the locket back. He nodded even as he snapped it closed and replaced the chain around his neck. "So you see, Josiah, we are *brothers* in a way." Kit bent to pick up a pair of shackles. "I need to get back before someone becomes suspicious. Put these on. I will seal them with an iron nail. They will not be locked. You can get out of them if you need to."

Copperhead nodded and held out his arms.

Still, even with Kit's assurances, the sound of the iron cuffs closing about his wrists resounded within him as a knell of doom.

"I'll come back as often as I am able," Kit promised as he knelt and fastened a second set about his ankles. "But I dare not arouse suspicion. Remember, to the seamen who will come to bring food, you look just the others. No one should recognize you."

Copperhead stared at the cuffs. "They will be hunting me. Grove and Ward," he said quietly.

"Yes, but I do not believe they will think to look here. You should be safe." Kit touched his shoulder again. "Be *strong*, my friend. Until later, then!"

Copperhead watched him go and did not move until after he heard the key turn in the lock, sealing his fate. Then he pivoted to find two dozen black eyes fixed on him. Several of the men were scowling. One strained at the chains that bound him to the floor as if he would tear him apart.

Raising his shackled hands in what he hoped was a gesture of peace, Copperhead backed away until he encountered the wall of the ship. Then he slid to the floor and, sitting in the fetid water, fell into a wary watch.

Miriam closed the draperies in her room, shutting out the night and the perpetual light of London's west end streetlamps, and crossed to her bed. The curtains had been drawn and a brass bed warmer placed inside. A servant had entered silently and laid out her nightclothes, and then vanished before she could tell them 'thank you'. She drew the curtains aside, climbed the small wooden stair, and then sat on the edge of the high bed and let her feet dangle like she was a little girl.

She missed her mother tonight. And Kate. And even ornery Anna.

But most of all she missed Copperhead.

As Miriam sniffed and wiped her nose on her expensive embroidered silk sleeve, she fell back on the bed and stared up at the wooden slats of the tester that held its canopied top in place. She could still feel Copperhead's arms about her. And when she closed her eyes, remember the touch of his lips. In spite of what her father had told her, she didn't believe he was dead. Judith had confirmed as much. Still, her father's hatred had most likely confined him to a life of slavery in some distant country, or condemned him to some other living Hell. Wrapping her arms about her small frame, Miriam shivered and curled up in a tight ball on the bed. She would never see him again.

How could she survive?

As she lay there, softly crying, there was a disturbance in the hall. Someone shouted and one of the chambermaids squealed. Puzzled, Miriam rose to her feet just as the door to her bedchamber burst open and a tall man in a great coat with dark tousled hair and cheeks reddened from his journey stepped boldly inside.

He stared at her a moment and then held out his arms. A broad smile lit his handsome face. "Miri! Good Lord! Look at you! You've grown into a woman!"

"James? James!" Miriam flew into her brother's arms. She hadn't seen him in years, not since that horrible time after their mother and sister had died. He was in his last year at Oxford now, studying criminal law and, according to his most recent letter, had decided to remain in England for good.

James hugged her and then held her at arm's length. "You've been crying," he remarked, his disapproving tone reminding her of their father.

She sniffed. "Yes. I want to go home."

"Whatever for? What is there in the Colonies to induce you to return?"

"I miss Grandpa George...."

"Crazy George will be dead soon, Miri." When she scowled at him for being so callous, he softened his tone – but not what he said. "You know it is the truth. Grandfather is old and unwell. You have to think of yourself. Of what is best for *you*."

James had matured. She sensed in him a certainty he had not had when under their father's thumb. Ignoring his words, she asked him, "What are you doing here? Did Aunt Amelia send for you?"

"Good *God*, no! I'd have run the opposite direction." James laughed as he tossed his hat and coat on the bed and then dropped into the wing chair before the fire. "That old shrew has tried to marry me off three times now! How the woman can know so many unpleasant cows I have no idea..."

"James!" Miriam laughed.

"There, that's better," he said with a smile as he patted the chair indicating she should join him.

She crossed to him but remained standing. "What brought you here then?" she asked.

James looked up at her. "You."

"But how did you.... Did father write you and tell you that I was here?"

He shook his head.

"Then how?"

One word. "Charles."

Miriam frowned. She had forgotten that they were friends. It was James, after all, who had brought Charles to Foxwell Manor all those years ago. "Oh," was all she said.

James leaned forward. "Do you like him, Miri? Just a little?"

She thought about it and then shrugged. "He's kind enough, but....."

"But what? 'Kind enough' but too *pale* for your tastes?" James words were hard. "You're not still panting for that dead *savage* are you?"

Her jaw tightened. "Don't be cruel," she said.

"I'm not." James rose to his feet and leaned on the mantle. "You are no longer a child, Miriam, with the luxury of a child's dreams. Soon, you *too* will be old. Consider Charles' interest carefully. You could do much worse."

"So I am to settle? Just to avoid something worse?" she snapped.

"You are a woman, Miriam. Like it or not, you wield little or no power in this world. And what power you do have, must come from the man you choose, the children you bear him, and the station you find yourself in. Charles is wealthy. He could have anyone he chooses, but he wants you. Charles *loves* you. That is more than most can hope to obtain in a match."

"But I don't love him," she said softly.

James crossed to her. He placed his hand on her cheek and kissed the top of her hair. "Love is a luxury, little Miri. One you cannot afford."

As her brother straightened up, there was a knock at the door and a light voice with an Irish lilt called out, "Would it be all right, Miss, if I banked the fire for the night?"

"Come in, Peg." Miriam blinked back tears. "James, I'm tired. Can we talk about this another day?"

He nodded, and kissed her again. Taking her hand he said, "Think about what I've told you. Promise me you will."

Miriam lowered her head and nodded as Peg entered the room.

"Oh! Master James!" the Irish maid exclaimed. "I thought you'd gone, sir."

James spun, a devilish smile on his face. "Would I leave without telling you goodbye, my girl? Have I ever?"

As Peg giggled and bustled past, James gave the serving girl a swat on the behind, his hand lingering on her rump for just a moment with obvious familiarity. Peg playfully batted his hand away and then favored him with an adoring look that would have been the envy of any of the gods.

Coming close to the girl's ear, he added in a stage whisper, "See you in the larder later, my girl." At Miriam's' startled look he laughed and winked, "Well, I'm ravenous after my long ride! For food *and* company." Striding across the room, James grasped the doorknob. Then he turned back to look at her. "Oh. I forgot to mention that there is a fête at the Leighton's London house at the end of next week. Charles asked me to test the waters for him. Will you go?"

"A fête?" she squeaked.

"A masked ball." James winked and lowered his voice. "Plenty of opportunity for mistaken identities and stolen kisses. Well? What should I tell him?"

"Tell him he can ask for himself," she answered quickly. "And tell him, I don't bite."

James snorted. "Well, that will be a disappointment!"

Miriam picked up a book on her nightstand and threw it at him.

"Goodnight, Miri! Peg!" he laughed as he ducked out the door. "I'll be waiting in the larder with the butter warmed."

Miriam crossed to her bed and sat on it with a 'whoosh', sinking into the fat feather ticking. As she closed her eyes, Peg came to her side and asked, "Is there anything else I can get for you, Miss?"

Yes, she thought. A thousand things. Passage back to the Colonies. A moment in her mother's garden. A walk with her grandfather.

Copperhead's arms.

"No, Peg," Miriam answered woodenly, "I wouldn't want you to keep James waiting."

Kit turned the key in the lock, consigning Josiah to the darkness. He prayed the natives would accept him as one of their own and not look on him as a spy and suspect him of some treason. Running a hand across the back of his neck he massaged it, seeking to ease some of the tension there. He was still deep in the belly of the ship and had quite a journey ahead of him. With one last glance at the door, he pocketed the key and moved past the row of guns, heading for the ladder that would lead him to the next deck up. Outside the portals the sun shone, its brilliant light white as the high capped waves. The day had dawned and his father would soon be abroad, looking for him. As he continued to walk, he considered what story he would concoct to explain his absence. As there were no women on the ship, a game of cards, perhaps? Or gambling on the cocks? Kit laughed as he placed a hand to the ladder rung. There was little chance of that! Most of the birds taken on board at their last port had already been sacrificed to the pot and Captain Long's peckish appetite.

At the top of the ladder he paused to look around. They had thrown Grove and Ward off the scent, but William Foxwell's dogs were most likely still on the prowl. If they found him here, this deep in the ship, there would be questions – uncomfortable questions he would not want to answer. When it seemed he was alone, Kit emerged. He had gone no more than six feet when a harsh voice spoke.

"Well, well, what do we have here? If it ain't your high and mighty Lordship McKay." Sergeant Grove left the shadows of the after-stair he occupied. As he approached, he rubbed the fingers of one hand against the other. The glint of something coppery revealed the metal knucks that decorated them. "Your father'd be right proud. Lookin' out for the welfare of a poor bastard heathen. Charity. That's the heart of the nobility, ain't it, Ward?"

"You're right there, Grove," Ensign Ward answered as he joined them. "What's got your interest down in the hole, your Lordship? Beside them heathens?"

"I was visiting with Dr. Standley," Kit stammered. "He and I – "

Before he could finish the sentence, Ensign Ward gripped his arms and pinned them behind his back. Grove drew close. The smell of rum and the threat of its reckless power were heavy on him. As the sergeant took hold of Kit's stock collar, he raised the brass knuckles he wore and grinned, showing several broken teeth.

"Bright idea, your Lordship. If a little *premature*...."

COPPERHEAD

Chapter Twenty-Three

Copperhead groaned as he shifted his head and pain exploded through it. Something had struck him. Hard. He couldn't remember what. All he could remember was the door to the cell he occupied on the *Renard* opening onto a lightless corridor, and the thought that Kit must have forgotten to tell him something.

Then nothing.

As he waited for the throbbing to subside, he slowly became aware of the world he occupied. The filthy scent of urine and salt water was gone, though his body still rocked from side to side as if he was on the ship. Beneath his feet the floor was soft and padded. Dry. And from close by came the sound of horses' hooves striking hardened earth.

What was going on?

Steeling himself, he opened his eyes to find Sergeant Grove sitting opposite him, leering like a cathedral grotesque.

As Grove snorted Copperhead became aware of the ropes binding his hands and feet. Glancing about he found he was in a closed chariot – the type of coach hired for speed, and only by those who had enough gold to waste on such a luxury. On its back wall was a heraldic device – a double-griffin worked in gold bearing a shield with the letter 'L'. Its windows were curtained and its doors, undoubtedly locked. Moving forward on the seat, he sought to peer through a small rent in the thick velvet drapes. As he did Grove took hold of the ropes that bound him and shoved him back. The villain grinned as he threw the curtains wide, revealing the dawning world beyond. Then he settled in again, pushing his brown coat aside and fingering the handle of his flintlock pistol.

"Now, don't you go getting' any ideas. You hear?" Grove snarled. "Just sit there nice and quiet, and you'll make it all the way to your new *accommodations*."

"Where am I?" he asked.

"I just told you. On the way to your new home."

"But how…. How did I come to be here?"

Grove drew the pistol from behind his belt and rested it on his knee. "You don't remember nothing?"

Copperhead frowned. His memories were vague at best. The door of the hold opening. Someone moving toward him. One of the natives shouting, and then a blow to the back of the head. Hands gripping him, lifting him. A rancid smell, and then sinking into a deep black sleep that robbed him of everything – even who he was.

And then, being here.

His eyes returned to the man sitting opposite him. Sergeant Grove was obviously enjoying his predicament. Copperhead wanted nothing more than to wipe the smirk off of the villain's scarred face – permanently. But first he needed answers.

He had not been *alone* in the hold.

"I remember a cowardly attack in the dark," he growled.

Grove's upper lip twitched with irritation. "Watch it."

"What have you done with Kit?"

"Kit. Kit? Oh, you mean his high and mighty lordship?" Sergeant Grove ran his finger along the fine filigree embellishing the Scottish pistol. "He got what he deserved."

Copperhead shot up in his seat. "If you've harmed him. I'll – "

"You'll *what*?" Grove barked. He cocked the weapon's trigger and pointed it at his head. "Go ahead, breed. *Give* me a reason."

He considered it. What lay ahead of him was anathema to his soul. Which would be the less grievous sentence, he wondered.

Prison? Or death?

But then he thought of John Leighton's words, of Kit's actions on his behalf, and of William Foxwell's debt, and he knew suicide was the path only a coward would walk.

Sinking back, Copperhead deliberately turned his face to the window. Grove gave another snort and then placed the pistol on the seat beside him in what was obviously an open invitation. Copperhead ignored it and focused instead on the world rushing past the open window – on an alien landscape of vast estates and rolling hills which the rising light was just coaxing from the deep purples of night. London, it seemed, was not his final destination. There was no sign here of a mighty metropolis peopled by tens of thousands. Grove must be taking him somewhere in the surrounding countryside.

"Spurrell Pode," the soldier announced suddenly, breaking into his reverie.

Copperhead looked at him but said nothing.

"That's the answer to your question, breed. It's where you're going. Outside the bailey, past Surrey. *Nice* accommodations. You'll even have your own room, courtesy of Colonel William Foxwell, with your fire lit in the morning and tea at four, I'm sure." A sly smirk twisted Grove's thin upper lip. "The Colonel hopes you'll be happy there for a *very* long time."

"Spurrell Pode is the name of the prison?"

"Nah. It ain't a prison. It's a *boarding house* for Lord's second sons. Old man Sneath'll take care of you, just like he's taken care of all the other bastards sent there." Grove sneered with triumph. "He'll bury you so deep that filthy red skin of yours will be white as your betters' in no time."

Copperhead's eyes flicked to the pistol lying beside the sergeant.

"Why don't you try it?" Grove's voice was soft as the rattle of a snake poised to strike. "I'd like a chance to blast a hole through that copper hide of yours."

"Why don't you? I thought Foxwell wanted me dead. Not alive and buried."

"The Colonel? He told us 'dead or alive'." Grove patted the pocket of his great coat and grinned as coins jingled in its depths. "But there's others willing to pay more to keep you alive."

That surprised him. "Who?"

"Like I'd tell you," Grove snarled. He picked the pistol up and placed it on his knee again. "Now shut up or I'll gag you."

Copperhead continued to stare at the villain for several heartbeats and then did as he was told. He was puzzled by this new revelation. *Who* was his protector? His eyes flicked to the 'L' detailed on the coach's velvet lining. Could it be John Leighton? But why? What was the life of one copper-skinned son of the colonial aristocracy to him – *him*, who traded in copper skin?

They rumbled on in silence for what must have been a half an hour before a male voice shouted something from above. It took Copperhead a moment to recognize the driver's voice as Ensign Ward's.

Sergeant Grove eyed him and then leaned forward to call out the window. "What is it?"

Ward's reply was muffled. Copperhead could only catch one word. Three? Or maybe *tree*?

"Go 'round it!" the sergeant yelled, confirming his suspicion.

Ward's answer came this time in the form of frightened horses neighing and a sudden lurch of the coach that threw Sergeant Grove against the door and Copperhead to the floor. Even as he had a thought to make a break for it, Grove pivoted with his pistol in hand.

"Don't!" he warned.

Copperhead raised his bound hands in surrender and shifted back against the seat.

Seconds later the coach door opened and Ensign Ward stuck his head in. "There's a tree across the road the size of London Bridge. We'll have to move it or find another way."

"You bring an axe?" Grove grumbled.

Ward nodded. "You want me to hack through it?"

Grove turned slowly. He aimed the pistol at Copperhead.

"Not you. *Him*."

Miriam took her brother James' hand and stepped out of the carriage. She pulled the hood of her emerald cloak fast about her face. They had left the hustle and bustle and the thousand lights and fires of London behind to travel into the North Country. Here, far above the bustling city, she felt the icy hand of the approaching winter.

As James greeted the estate's head of staff and made arrangements for the disposal of their things, Miriam stood staring up at the imposing edifice that was John Leighton's country home. After entering the great stone gates crested with a pair of gilded griffins they had traveled perhaps a mile – maybe more – by coach, passing a homely chapel and moderate size zoo occupied by exotic animals and birds, before arriving at the manor that was impressive – if a bit run down. The Leighton family was old, though not *so* old as many who panted after the peerage. Still, there *was* wealth and tradition here that strolled back centuries.

Miriam stifled a sigh and smiled sweetly as her brother took up her valise and then offered her his arm. Aunt Amelia's maid, Peg, who had come with them, curtsied as she accepted a second case and then did a nice little bump with her rear as James ordered her to proceed them into the house. Mrs. Leighton was dead and so one of John Leighton's sisters, who acted as mistress of the house, greeted them at the door to bid them welcome. Miriam disliked her instantly. Bridget Leighton was tight waisted and tight lipped, with a chignon of white-blond hair whipped into submission and held captive by a golden net. Bridget barked an order to one of the hall's male servants and then turned them over to his care.

Miriam's brother leaned over and whispered in her ear. "The locals call her 'frigid Bridget'. It's said she hasn't had a man in years."

Miriam scowled and elbowed him in the stomach. As James huffed, pretending to be hurt, she moved ahead of him, following the manservant to their rooms. At the door she brushed off her brother's request to come in, politely accepted his kiss on her cheek, shooed Peg out the door, and then threw her valise and herself on the bed and let the tears flow.

What *was* she doing here?

It had been almost a week since James had broached the idea of attending the masque at Leighton Hall. At the time the thought had seemed promising as it offered a temporary escape from Aunt Amelia and her never ending schemes. But now, the central object of those schemes – the rich and handsome Charles Matthew Spencer – was due to arrive any minute, and that meant she would have to see him and talk to him, and she knew *what* Charles was going to want to talk about. While all she wanted....

Well, *all* she wanted was what she could not have.

Stifling tears that were childish and pointless, Miriam rose to her feet and opened her valise and began to unpack. She paused as her hand encountered a thin velvet pouch. Opening it, she allowed her mother's silver and pearl chatelaine to drop into her hand. With a sad smile, she followed its elegant lines with a finger. Then she quickly replaced it and tied the ribbons that sealed the pouch.

Then she reached for what lay beneath.

When she knew she was leaving the colonies she had sought it among his things. Her fingers quickly found the rumpled vellum pages. She steadied herself, and then drew out the tattered ABC book her Grandmother Margaret had painted for her, oh, *so* many years before. The book was a powerful talisman – a link to all that had been. To everything she had dared to hope – but dared to hope no more.

To Copperhead.

Miriam began to tremble. The book fell from her fingers and fluttered to the hardwood floor. She followed it, landing in a heap of white linen petticoats and fine leaf-green damask beside the tester bed.

Sinking her head into her hands, she began to cry.

A few minutes later a light knock on the door brought her head up. She struck away as many tears as she could with her sleeve as she rose and called out, "Give me a moment." But before the moment was given, the door to her room opened and a pale ringletted head peeked in. For a moment Miriam thought it was Bridget Leighton, but then she realized the form revealed by the light of the lamp it carried was petite.

About *her* size in fact.

"Excuse me," the woman's lyrical voice apologized. "James told me you were here. I came to see if you need anything." The woman, wrapped in a blue silk saque gown that shimmered silver when she moved, stepped in. "Bridget can be a little stern, and not the most welcoming of hostesses – Oh! You've been crying."

Miriam turned her face into the shadows. "I'm fine. Really. I need nothing."

An awkward silence fell between them. Several heartbeats later the woman turned to leave. But then she hesitated. Crossing the room instead, she dipped to the floor and rose with something in her hand. "Here. You must have dropped this."

Miriam didn't look. She *knew* what it was. "Put it on the bed. Please."

"The hand is lovely. Did you do it?"

"My grandmother. She's dead now," she replied woodenly.

"Oh. Well, I'll be going then. I will see you when we break fast in the morning." The stranger walked toward the door, but then changed her mind and came instead to her side. The light of the lamp revealed her face. She was, perhaps, eighteen. Her hair was not white as she had thought, but a rich golden-blond, drawn back in a fashionable pony's tail.

Miriam didn't know her, but just as instinctively as she knew she did not like Bridget Leighton, she knew she *would* like this woman.

"Rosalyn Castell," she said, holding out her hand.

Miriam wiped the tears from her own and took it. "Miriam Foxwell."

Rosalyn smiled. "Are you staying until the ball?"

She nodded.

"Good. Then we shall have time to get to know one another."

Miriam sniffed and smiled. "I think that I would like that."

Copperhead curled his fingers around the axe's wooden handle and lifted it high above his head. Then he brought it down, sending a shower of splinters into the air. He jerked the axe from the tree's flesh and repeated the action five more times before leaning it against the trunk. Raising a hand to his brow, he wiped away the sweat. As he glanced at the sun where it hung halfway to the horizon, he placed a hand in the crook of his back and frowned at the ache in it and in his arms. It had been months since he had done any such labor. And in those months he had been near death more than once. He was but the shadow of the man he had been. And there was only one name on which to hang the blame.

William Foxwell.

"Stop your slacking," Grove growled from the shade of a nearby tree. "Keep at it!"

Copperhead closed his eyes, fighting the desire to take up the axe and split the villain's head open with it. "No," he said.

For a moment, Grove said nothing. "What do you mean, 'no'?" he demanded.

Copperhead opened his eyes as he tipped the axe over and let it fall to the ground. "I mean 'no'. I assume, even with your limited education, that you know what the word means."

Grove stormed across the short space between them and quick as lightning had him by the shirt collar. "Listen, here, redskin!" he thundered. "You will do as *I* tell you. Now, *pick up that axe!*"

There was no smell of rum today. Without liquor to back the bully, Grove was dangerous but weak. Impotent.

"No."

Grove's pistol came out from behind his waistband. Seconds later it was pressed beneath his chin. "Nothin' would give me more pleasure than seein' your red brains decoratin' this highway," he declared.

"You won't kill me and we *both* know it. You admitted as much in the coach." Copperhead's words were low, meant only for the sergeant's ears. "You have no power over me."

Grove shook with rage. "I can still deliver you to hell!" he bellowed.

Copperhead laughed. "When someone slits your throat in a back alley and you die, Grove, drowning in your own blood, remember this.... I'll *be there* waiting for you."

Sergeant Grove's knuckles were white where they gripped his collar. His face a livid red. The soldier breathed in and out, once...twice...fighting for control, and then suddenly released him. Then without warning he backhanded him so hard it split his lip and sent him reeling to the ground.

"Bind him!" Grove barked. "Bind the *breed* and gag him so tight he'll drop for lack of air. And toss him in the coach!"

Ensign Ward hustled to Grove's side. "You want I should tie the redskin up?" he asked, puzzled.

"What'd I say?" Grove snapped.

Ward glanced at Copperhead and then at the tree which was only half cut through. "Then who's gonna finish clearing the road?"

Sergeant Grove said nothing. He just glared.

Ward swallowed hard and turned to Copperhead who still lay in the dust of the road. He shook his head when the ensign offered him a hand up and rose of his own accord. When they arrived at the coach Ward gripped his arms and bound them tightly behind his back. He didn't care. Copperhead tossed his sweat soaked hair back and laughed. It had been a small skirmish and a *minor* victory.

But it was *his*.

An hour or so later as he lay on the coach seat bound and gagged, tasting blood, Copperhead heard the approach of hoof-beats. Struggling into a seated position, he leaned against the chariot's door and looked out the window. It was candle-lighting time. Dusk had settled on the land. At first, he could see nothing. Then he noticed a cloud of dust and heard a voice calling for more speed. Whoever it was, they were moving *fast* –

Toward a rendezvous with a fallen tree.

Copperhead shifted so he could look forward. Ensign Ward was there, struggling to drag what remained of the tree off the roadway. Sergeant Grove had turned in the direction of the approaching figure. A cruel smile lit his face.

Whoever it was, they were not going to make it.

The rider was close now. The sound of his horse's hooves thundered through Copperhead's aching head. He heard a shout of alarm and then both horse and man became airborne.

The sound of the tree's jagged wooden fingers scratching horseflesh.

A cry of 'Damnation!'

An exclamation of disbelief and then a curse.

And then the sound of horse's hooves striking earth and quickly fading into the distance.

Whoever he was, he made it!

Copperhead leaned back in the coach and closed his eyes. He didn't know why, but the stranger's sudden appearance and miraculous escape struck him as an omen.

He did not think he would be in prison very long.

Miriam sat in the Leighton's drawing room, warming herself by the fire. She had chosen a book from their vast library, but it lay unread in her lap. Across the room Rosalyn Castell sat at the family's harpsichord playing a simple tune by the protégée Wolfgang Amadeus Mozart, her child size fingers flying fast as a chariot's wheels. Miriam had learned that, like her, Rosalyn was here for the ball. She was a friend of John Leighton's son, Geoffrey, who was due home soon from school. Miriam was not certain, but it seemed from their conversations that Geoff had aspirations of something more than *friendship* where Rosalyn was concerned, and that Rosalyn did not share his hopes. There was someone else. A woman could tell. And even though Rosalyn had not said so, Miriam had a feeling she was hoping this man – whoever he was – would be in attendance at the ball.

Rosalyn hit a sour note and frowned, her pert nose wrinkling like a pampered pup's. She leaned forward, tracing the notation with her finger, and then tried it again. No improvement. With a sigh, Rosalyn caught the hand-written sheets in her fingers and rose to her feet. In a rustle of rust-red satin, she shifted off the bench and approached Miriam, music in hand.

"The carrier was careless and it has gotten wet. I can't read these notes. Can you?"

Miriam took it, but no sooner had her fingers closed on the vellum than the door to the drawing room burst open and a wild looking man in an ebon cloak and tricorn hat, with mud on his jack-boots strode in. He took a moment to remove the cloak and hat and toss them on the settee. Then he turned toward them.

He was a handsome man. With shining black hair that spiraled in unruly curls across his forehead. He was clothed in a costly suit of deep blue velvet, though the garments had seen much wear and looked as if he had slept in them. His waistcoat was cut of cloth of gold and embroidered with delicate flowers, crimson and sapphire. An angular face, with prominent bones, served as the seat for a pair of intense black eyes. As Miriam rose to her feet, he opened his arms and grinned.

Magnificently.

Her companion gasped. "Kit!" Rosalyn cried.

And flew into his arms.

Chapter Twenty-four

Copperhead soon had reason to regret his moment of triumph.

Stripped to his breeches, suspended by aching wrists from a wooden beam over a stone floor rank with the blood of others unfortunate enough to have merited Ruskin Sneath's attention, flogged to the bone and bitten by flies, he was *welcomed* by its master to Spurrell Pode Prison.

Sneath was a whip-thin man with a narrow face and a bone ridge of a nose that bore a pair of tarnished silver spectacles perched so low they pinched his already nasal voice. He was dressed from turkey flap neck to pointed toe in black, against which his paste gray skin shone like ghost-flesh. As an underling wielded the whip, the jailer wielded the words of the same Bible George Foxwell had cherished, declaring it God's judgment that the wicked should be punished

Sergeant Grove was there as well. William Foxwell's underling leant a willing hand as his jailers stripped him and, when those in Sneath's employ bound his wrists and hauled him up, Grove punched his stomach until he blacked out. Now the villain took a knife and cut him loose, and bellowed with callous mirth as he struck the chilling stones with a thud. Someone lifted his head and spit in his face and he knew no more.

Until he awoke to the sound of a heavy door banging shut with terrifying finality.

Copperhead stirred. He worked his way into a seated position, and then used the back of a filthy hand to wipe the blood from his lip. The cell he had been placed in was lightless and smelled of fouled straw and death. He had just risen and begun to prowl the limits of this new 'world' when he heard a click, and a square of light unexpectedly appeared on the floor. Ruskin's Sneath's unwelcome visage soon appeared within the framework of a small window that opened in the door.

"Master Woodward, are you awake?" Sneath's voice was fingernails on slate. "You *will* answer me."

Copperhead said nothing.

"You will find, Master Woodward, that no quarter is given here. Compliance is rewarded and *rebellion* quashed. Do you understand this, Master Woodward?"

When he remained silent, the light was suddenly eclipsed – not by the shutting of the window, but by the application of Sneath's black Bible to the opening.

"Hear the word of the Lord God, Jehovah!" Sneath declared. " 'But if ye will not hearken unto me, and will not do as I command, and if ye shall despise my statutes, or if your soul abhor my judgments, I also will do *this* unto you'." The leather tome was lowered and Sneath's languid gray eyes appeared within the window frame. "'*I* will appoint over you terror, and cause sorrow of heart,'" he intoned, the words becoming his own. "*I will set my face against you, and then I will punish you seven times more for your sins. I will break the pride of your power, and your strength shall be spent in vain!*'" The jailer paused to catch his breath. "Understand this, Master Woodward, I *am* God here. You will obey or you *will* be chastised. For your indiscretion *this* day, you shall have no food and precious little water for a week, nor will you speak to any living man. At the end of that time I will come and see if you have repented yourself of your sins.

"May God have mercy on your soul."

Miriam felt somewhat embarrassed in the lovers' presence and sought to excuse herself, counterfeiting that she needed something from her room, but before she could slip from the chamber she heard Rosalyn exclaim and turned back to see what was the matter. Kit shook his head as if he wished her to remain silent, but there was no going back. Rosalyn's face reflected a horror Miriam had known –

That of a woman terrified for her man.

"Kit! Dear God, what happened? What villain did this to you?" Rosalyn demanded.

"Rosalyn, hush!" he ordered.

"Excuse me, sir," Miriam said, feeling *quite* unwanted. "I was just reading by the fire. I didn't mean to...." Her words trailed off as she saw what Rosalyn had. The side of Kit's face was a road map of bruises running from his left temple, where the skin had been split and hastily stitched, to his upper lip which was swollen nearly twice its size.

Once he realized he could not escape her scrutiny, Kit's well-bred manners took over and he extended his hand. "I don't believe I have had the privilege. Miss?"

"Foxwell," she replied. "Miriam Foxwell."

"Of the Marlborough Foxwells?" he inquired politely – as if he had just dropped by for tea instead of looking like an escapee from one of the clubs in the lower east end.

She shook her head. "Of the *Carolina* Foxwells."

"Carolina? Oh, the Colonies? You are from America?"

As she nodded, Rosalyn came to her side and took her hand. "Kit," she began. "You are being deliberately difficult. You cannot hide that you have been in a fight. What is this? Who *did* this to you?"

One ebon eyebrow arched and he favored them both with the most charming sheepish grin. "If I tell you, you will grow angry."

"Kit, no!" Rosalyn's sudden shift in tone seemed to prove him right. "You have not – tell me you have *not* been boxing again!"

Kit shrugged. The smile remained fixed on his handsome face. "Anything you ask, my dear. I have *not* been practicing the manly art of pugilism."

Kit was tall – well over six feet. Rosalyn was a good foot shorter than him. Still, she went toe to toe with him, and emphasized her point by driving one of her talented fingers into his chest. "I have *told* you before what I think of pugilists. They are no better than beasts! You had best watch yourself, Kit MacKay, or I may give Geoffrey Leighton a nod and it is *you* who will be out on your ear!"

"Rosalyn...."

The petite blonde's jaw was set in stone. Rosalyn caught her rust-red skirts in her fingers and straightened her back, and with an 'hmmph!' stormed out the door leaving the two of them alone.

Miriam felt every second of the awkward minute long silence that fell between them. She thought of a thousand different ways to excuse herself, but every one of them seemed lame. She started to speak, stopped at least twice, and then fell to looking at her hands.

Kit drew a deep breath. When he spoke, his words were hushed and heartfelt, and they brought Miriam's head up. "Miss Foxwell, I regret you were placed in the middle of that. Please accept my apologies."

Miriam nodded, puzzled. "Pray think nothing of it. I took no offense, sir."

"Kit. Please."

"Kit." Miriam hesitated and then added, "Pardon me if I am too bold. You really should have that attended to." She indicated the stitched wound. "It looks fresh and fevered."

"It is nothing," he answered curtly, and then moved past her to take a seat before the fire. As he sat a sudden fatigue seemed to overcome him. He leaned his head back against the embroidered fabric and sighed.

"Sir.... Kit, can I get you something?" Miriam asked. "A brandy perhaps?"

He started to shake his head, but then nodded. When she delivered the glass, he took a sip and said softly, "Thank you for your kindness to a stranger."

"You seem fatigued, and look as if you have ridden hard."

"All night and into the day without stopping," he answered. "I needed to see Rosalyn before...." Kit paused and looked toward the door. "That did *not* go well."

"You lied to her. She knew it," she said.

His ebon eyes flew to her face. "What? How would you know that?"

Miriam laughed. "Men. You know everything and nothing at the same time. Would you like me to call Rosalyn back?"

He took another sip. "She will not come."

"If the matter is dire, she will. You said you *needed* to see her – "

"I cannot stay." Kit downed the remainder of the brandy and rose from the chair. "I have an errand I must perform. A *friend* I must rescue. I meant to tell Rosalyn." His eyes met hers. "Forgive my boldness. I think… If I see her again, I may not be *able* to go. Will you deliver a message for me?"

His smile was disarming. As were the silken tones that accompanied it. "If I were Rosalyn, I might be tempted to kill the messenger," she answered with a wry grin. "Especially if it was another woman."

He laughed. A genuine heartfelt sound. "Miss Foxwell, I pray you and Rosalyn will become fast friends. What a world of good you would do her in this household!" As Kit continued, he sobered. "Rosalyn knows where my heart lies. There is no doubting it. Will you take the message?"

She was reluctant, but she nodded.

Kit crossed quickly to the mahogany secretary that graced the east wall of the drawing room and hastily scribbled a note. He did not take time to seal it, but gave it to her in trust. "Will you deliver it tonight?"

"The moment you depart. But please, *do* have that cut looked to," she said, gently urging. "You will do your friend no good if you fall from your horse and lie languishing in a fever in some ditch along the way."

He placed the note in her hand and then closed her fingers over it, pressing them with his own. "Providence has placed you in my path, Miss Foxwell. May it reward your kindness with the fulfillment of the desires of your heart."

Tears entered her eyes and she lowered her head.

"Mistress! Forgive me. I did not mean…."

She pressed his fingers in return. "God speed, Kit" was all she said, and then Miriam fled into the hall and up the stairs.

Copperhead explored the narrow confines of his cell at Spurrell Pode and found there was a window in it. It was set high in the western wall and had been boarded over at some time. By anchoring his fingers and toes in the chinks where mortar was missing from the stones, he managed to raise his exhausted body high enough to grasp the cold iron bars over which the board was fixed. As he tried to push it away, his strength failed and he fell to the straw-covered floor, knocking the wind out of his lungs and losing consciousness for a few seconds. Placing his back against the wall, he sat for some time unmoving, feeling every strike of the Ruskin Sneath's lash. He was weak and growing weaker. He hadn't eaten since before Kit had roused him from sleep and taken him to the hold of the *Renard*. He had no way of knowing how many days had passed in-between since he had been drugged when Grove and Ward secreted him away from the ship. Seven days without food might not kill him, but it *would* probably break him.

And William Foxwell would win.

Copperhead leaned his head against the stone wall and breathed slowly, gathering strength. Then he rose, trembling, to his feet. With his arms shaking and blood running down his back, he placed his fingers in the chinks of the mortar and slowly began to draw his body up the wall again.

Rosalyn Castell stood with her lover's note dangling from her fingers, gazing out the open window of the room she occupied in John Leighton's house. Miriam waited to see if she had anything to say. When the other woman remained silent, she turned to leave.

"Please stay," Rosalyn said suddenly.

Miriam turned back. "If you are certain you want me to."

"Yes." Rosalyn faced her. "I am sorry if I was rude. It is just…this…." She indicated the note. "I am afraid Kit is involved in something dangerous."

"Dangerous?" Miriam crossed to her side. "Another fight?"

Rosalyn's fingers closed on the note even as she retreated to the edge of her bed. "That was a *feint*. There was no fight. It was an easier explanation than the truth."

"Which is?"

The other woman was bursting to tell her, but shook her head. "I cannot say. More than Kit's life would be in danger if I did. And – "

"You do not know me," Miriam finished for her. "You have no reason to trust me."

"But I *do*!" Rosalyn held her hand out, beckoning. "Dear Miriam. Sit by me?"

Miriam allowed herself to be drawn to the silk coverlet. They sat for a moment in silence and then she said, "He seems a fine young man."

"Kit?" Rosalyn beamed. "He is! Handsome, and with the voice of the gods. You should hear him sing. Perhaps he will the night of the ball." The smile faded. "*If* he returns…."

"He shall." Miriam patted her hand. "He shall."

After a short pause Rosalyn asked, "Are you in love, Miriam?"

The question took her completely by surprise. "Love? Me?" She laughed it off. "No. Of course not."

"What of Charles Spencer? Your brother said – "

"James knows nothing!" she snapped.

Her unexpected anger startled Rosalyn who quickly apologized. "Forgive me. I didn't think...."

"No. No, you must forgive *me*." Miriam's eyes clouded with tears. "Charles means nothing to me."

"Then there is someone else?"

Miriam's sadness drove her from the confinement of the bed to the freedom of the open window. "There isn't," she sighed, relenting, "but there was."

"I'm sorry," Rosalyn said, joining her. "Is he dead?"

The tears were flowing uncontrollably now. She sobbed and reached out to steady herself with a hand to the window frame. "I don't know. My father did not approve. He drove him away. He may be dead. Or worse, sold into slavery in some distant land."

"*Sold?*" The horror in Rosalyn's voice was evident.

Miriam looked at her. "He was a servant in my father's house. We did nothing, but were accused of all. My father...beat him until he was almost dead. He told me he *was* dead."

"But you do not believe him," Rosalyn said as she took her hand.

Miriam shook her head. "I would know."

They stood, hand in hand, as the icy wind of winter whipped the pale blond hair on both their heads, chilling them. Rosalyn shifted and opened her arms, offering her understanding and strength, and then joined Miriam in her tears.

Kit McKay walked into the back room of a tavern of ill repute situated somewhere between the Leighton's country home, which occupied a 400 acre plot of land near the north-eastern extreme of the fashionable West End, and the sprawling urban blight that was North London. He laid a coin on the serving tray of an attractive but wasted serving girl who was passing by, relieved her of an ale, and then slipped behind an oak table in the far corner. Kit scowled at the watered down drink and then sat the mug down on the table's heavily marred surface.

Tapping his fingers against its pewter side, he waited.

A quarter of an hour later the girl came to the table and asked if he would like another. He showed her a half-crown and told her to tell the tavern-keep that he wanted *real* ale this time and was willing to pay for it. Her eyes round as the coin, the girl made a stab at a curtsy, said, 'yes, milord,' and fairly flew across the floor to the bar where a rough and disreputable looking man was keeping custom.

Kit snorted and dumped the remainder of the watered ale on the floor where it could do nothing but improve the finish. Then he leaned forward, steepled his fingers under his chin, and considered his options.

The man he was here to meet was a seaman from the *Renard*. He was, in fact, the one he had seen William Foxwell's toughs – Ward and Grove – bargaining with the night Josiah was taken. Before leaving the ship Kit had sought the sailor out and threatened to expose him, *unless* the man found out where the scoundrels were taking their victim. They had made arrangements to meet here. Kit shifted back in his chair and looked around the tavern. It was peopled by the flotsam and jetsam of England. Sun-baked soldiers and drunken sailors, lying brigands and ever-watchful thieves, scallywags looking to work a scam, and the women who followed them – the lagan of life who did not float but sunk and died. Lost women, just like the serving girl who approached – *this* time with a fine silver tankard brim full of a rich golden ale. Kit relieved her of it, took a sip, and nodded his head.

"Thank you. Miss?"

The girl shoved an unruly lock of copper hair out of her eyes and snorted. "Miss? I ain't no 'Miss'. Call me Milli."

"Milli. That's a lovely name. From Millicent, I imagine?"

She shrugged. "Wouldn't know. Me folks been dead since afore I can remember." Milli drew closer and leaned her hip on the arm of his chair. 'What's it to you? You interested?'

Kit looked at her. Milli was more bones than skin, and what skin she *did* have was sallow and gray from lack of light and compassion. Her copper hair was an obvious fake and when she smiled – which she did infrequently – she showed several missing teeth. "I *am* interested, but not in what you think. I am waiting for a man." He caught her hand and pressed a half sovereign into it. "This is for you if you make certain he makes it to my table unmolested."

"It's always the handsome ones," she said with a sigh as she dropped the gold coin into her cleavage. "What's he look like?"

"A seaman. Small in stature. Brown hair grizzled with gray at the temples. No beard. He wears two golden rings in his right ear." As Kit spoke the tavern door opened and the object of his vigil walked in. When the man headed directly for the bar, he said, "There he is now. Bring him here. And Milli...."

She turned back. "Aye?"

"Bring another silver mug and a bottle of your best rum."

A half hour later the sailor, whose name was Chambers, had downed most of the bottle. Kit waited until he was certain the man's self control was *well* compromised and then asked him, "Do you have the information I need?"

"What's in it for me?" the seaman growled as he lifted the bottle to pour another.

Kit placed his hand on the rim of the cup and waited until the sailor met his eyes. "Escape from the hangman's noose. And though you don't deserve it," he slid his other hand forward and lifted it, revealing two gold crowns beneath, "this. Now tell me what I want to know."

"It warn't easy to find out, milord."

"I'm sure it wasn't," Kit agreed.

"I had to put myself in danger."

"A pity."

The man's eyes darted from his face to the coins. "They'll kill me if they find out."

"So will the Crown when I reveal what you did. If it was I, I think I'd rather be *shot* than hanged. Now do you have what I need?"

Chambers filled his cup and downed the last of the rum. He wiped his lip with his hand and belched. "They've taken that poor jack to old man Sneath's."

"Sneath? Who is that?"

"The master of Spurrell Pode, milord. It's an old castle north of here. Stone from top to toe, it is. Sits on a wooded hill near the river. Hundreds of years ago someone lived there, now it's a 'school' for the sons of rich men that have that which they *don't* want – and need to bury it. Deep."

In other words a prison for bastard children of the nobility. Sons who have no proper place in the order of things. "How do I get there?" Kit asked, his hand firmly clamped over the money. "Tell me and it's yours."

Chambers scowled. "I could draw you a map."

With his other hand, Kit reached into his pocket and drew out a small memorandum book. He shoved it across the table to Chambers. Then he called, "Milli!" When the girl came running, he asked her for a quill. She brought one, along with a well brimful with cheap brown ink, and then remained to watch as the sailor sketched a map to Josiah's prison. Kit snatched it from the table the minute the man finished. "Bring him another bottle of ale," he told her as Chambers claimed the coins on the scarred tabletop. Then Kit slipped not one, but two gold sovereigns into her hand.

"What is this, milord?" she asked, astonished.

"Leave this place," he told her

"But, where would I go, milord?" she asked him as he headed for the door.

Kit glanced back at the grim faces that lined the darkened interior of the tavern – condemned inhabitants of a living hell, every one.

"Anywhere but here."

It took five successive tries but he did it. Copperhead scaled the cell wall and, working with his bare fingers until they were bone and blood, managed to loosen the board that covered the window and push it away. He hung from his fingertips for a moment, gathering strength, and then pulled his weary body up far enough that he could look out.

What he found was overwhelming.

He had supposed he was underground, and that by reaching the window he might find a hope of escape. Instead he found he was caged – not in the bowels of some ancient fortress – but high within a tower, overlooking a stream that meandered far below. From this vantage point he could see the city of London spread out like a great cancer on the land.

How could he hope to escape?

Shifting to ease the pressure on his fingers, Copperhead surveyed the area beneath the window. It was vast. Unending. Even if he *did* manage to lower himself down the wall, where would he go? His skin color would mark him for what he was. It was unlikely he would find any locals sympathetic to his cause. He had no money. He knew nothing of the city or the lands beyond. And, if he was honest, he had grown so weak it was likely he would die of hunger or exposure long before he made it anywhere.

There was no way out.

Exhausted and utterly discouraged, Copperhead released his grip on the stone lintel and slid back to the fetid floor of his prison. For some time he lay there unmoving. Then he did something he had not done for a very long time.

He cried.

Chapter Twenty-Five

Kit had one more stop to make before putting his plan to rescue Josiah into action. He struck the top of the chariot ceiling with the butt of his pistol and called for the driver to halt. Slipping out of the coach he flung the man a coin and ordered him to wait, and then opened the door and entered the ground floor of a slightly more respectable tavern than the one he had left some ten miles back. Halting just inside the door, he searched for a certain feminine face.

Finding it Kit stifled a shudder. Isabella Mary Margaret Catherine Pursglove was holding court in the tavern's back corner, one hip placed with calculation on the edge of an oaken table – the better for the men who surrounded her to notice her finely padded rump. Isabella was the leading lady in David Stanbury's troupe of actors. Kit's audition had been working a scene from Shakespeare's Scottish play with her. Isabella was five feet of Irish perfection topped with lustrous mane of hair the color of a highly polished copper coin. Her well-proportioned figure had been poured into an emerald saque gown.

When she saw him, Isabella boomed in a stage voice. "Why, if it isn't my mournful Lord! Come and give us a kiss on the cheek, love."

Every head in the tavern turned his way.

His face as red as her hair, Kit hurried to her side. "Miss Pursglove, if you could be a *little* more discreet…."

"Worried someone will find out what you are about, are you then? Running off with the heathens?" Isabella laughed as she slid off the tabletop and came to stand before him. She was at least a head shorter, but every inch his match.

And she knew *he* knew it.

"Miss Pursglove – "

Isabella ran her fingers up his thigh and pressed into him. "Make that 'Issie', lover," she breathed softly as she pulled his head down and kissed him on the lips.

The men of her court burst into laughter and applause – which would have been fine, except Kit recognized two of them as infrequent business associates of his father.

Catching Isabella by the waist, Kit danced her into the shadows of the hall. With a grin he leaned down and gave her a longer, more succulent kiss on his own terms. Then he suggested in her ear, "Can we go somewhere a little more…private?"

"Thought you'd never ask, love."

Isabella gripped his collar and pulled him toward the stair that led to the private rooms. At its foot, Kit stopped her. She turned back puzzled. One finely trimmed mouse-skin eyebrow arched as she realized what he *didn't* want. Locking her hands on her padded hips, she cursed, "May Hell roast you then! You strike the flint but spit on the spark. What is it you're about if it's not a tumble?"

"Isabella, I...er...have an appointment to keep, or I would most *certainly* be unable to resist your inestimable and unmatched charms," Kit began.

She wagged a finger, indicating such flattery just *might* eventually buy him back into her rather questionable graces. "Aye. So what is it you want, Master Kit Montagne?"

Montagne was his stage name. "Are you still on to perform at the Leightons the end of this week?"

Isabella frowned. "What's it to you?" Then with a wry crinkle of her painted red lips, she added in her best Irish brogue, "Is Stanbury letting you take the place of Petruchio's *ah-ss*?"

Kit drew a deep breath and counted to ten. There was no time to rise to her bate. Chambers had explained that Josiah was in a holding cell for the moment. Once he was condemned to Spurrell Pode's hellish dungeon, there would be little hope of liberating him. He needed to get there. *Now.*

"Isabella. A life depends on it."

"Does it now?" she smirked. "And 'tis she blond and doe-eyed, or has the trollop hair the color of ebony?"

Kit's gaze flicked from the powdered and pampered tease at the foot of the stair to the tavern's common room. One of the men he had noticed earlier was heading their way.

"Yes or no, Issie!" he demanded.

She followed his gaze and then eyed him suspiciously. "We'll be there," she said at last, "'tis our last performance in London. Then we're off. You still coming along?"

"Look for me on the pier." Kit started to turn to go, but Isabella caught his hand and held him back. "Yes?" he asked.

She leaned in close, nipped his ear, and then breathed in it. "May the cat eat ye, and may the cat be eaten by the Devil if you *ever* do that to me again!"

And to emphasize her point, she kneed him in the groin.

Then, with a bump of her bum roll, Isabella ascended the stair, leaving her court behind and retiring to the royal chambers.

Kit squeaked out a 'goodbye' and fled through the tavern door.

Copperhead sat, knees to chin, his arms coiled tightly about his bare lower legs, one bleeding shoulder braced against the cell wall; his near black eyes fixed on a wooden bowl of fresh water placed by his feet. For four days he had refused to drink and for three of them, he had been beaten for it. This day the jailer had looked at him, and then left without a word after placing this new temptation at his feet. Ruskin Sneath took great pleasure in his captives' pain but he did not *want* them to die. If they did, the master of Spurrell Pode would lose the fees their absent fathers paid. After seeing the vast labyrinth of the world that lay outside his window – and of how he was imprisoned high above it with no hope of escape – Copperhead made up his mind to die. Even though the thirst drove him near to madness, even though his tongue was so thick he could not swallow and his head pounded like a war drum, he would *not* drink. He had listened to the holy men of his village when he was a boy. A man could live for months without food, but a man could last no more than a week without water.

It would soon be over.

Since the jailer had left, he had grown cold. His hands and feet numb. The beat of his heart slowed and he grew tired – so tired he knew he would never rise again. The world he occupied became a nightmare dream of waking. His only reality, the one he saw when he closed his eyes. He watched as his mother, cradling his suckling brother, rose to her feet to greet his father. Bear Paw had just returned from the hunt, a fat buck over his shoulder. His sister and elder brother ran to join them, with cries of joy. Copperhead's father crossed to him and touched his head, and then told him to step outside. *There is something for you there*, he said.

Something waiting.

In this reality he was strong. Copperhead rose with ease, moving with the vigor of a child of thirteen summers. His mother smiled at him as he passed, and nodded as if she knew the surprise. He stepped outside – only to be confronted by the silver fox of his grandfather's vision. The animal stared at him with wisdom eyes and then lunged, snapping its sallow teeth near his face.

Copperhead moaned. He opened his eyes to find he was still in the English cell. He ran his tongue across his parched lips, but it did no good. Weakening, his eyes went to the bowl of water on the cell floor again, but he did not find it.

Instead he found the silver fox.

The pale gray animal lay close by, its massive head resting on its forepaws. It watched, as if waiting for him to speak. When he did not, the fox shifted and rose to its feet revealing the bowl behind it. It bent its head to the water and drank, long and deep. Copperhead's whole body shuddered with desire. Its silver beard dripping, the animal raised its head and fixed him with its yellow gold eyes.

Then it spoke.

Drink.

Copperhead barely had the strength, but he shook his head.

Drink and live.

"No..." he groaned.

The fox's spotted lips, raw red and pink, curled in a snarl. It crouched, ready to pounce.

Then you die a coward!

Copperhead jerked awake. His foot hit the bowl and spilled a good half of the liquid in it. He leaned back against the cold stone wall, panting hard. His eyes searched for the fox, but it was nowhere to be found. Shifting his gaze to the up-turned bowl, he watched the straw beneath it come alive with insects that vied for the wasted water. Dropping to his hands and knees, painfully crawling, Copperhead obeyed the fox and joined the fray. He chased the insects away and then, trembling so hard he could barely control it, raised the bowl to his lips and drank.

For a second it sickened him, and then blessed relief washed through his dehydrated form. He closed his eyes, relishing the sensation. A little later, feeling a bit stronger, he worked himself into a seated position and continued to sip the tepid liquid. As he did, a light crept into the room. Copperhead looked up at the square cut into the cell door. It was open. And through it he could hear voices.

"Surely you are not suggesting, sir, that I can be bribed! What I do here is a sacred duty!" The man's whine identified him as Ruskin Sneath.

"Nae such a thought entered mah mind," a voice, thick with a Scottish brogue replied. "Ah ken you are a God fearing mon, Sneath. And as such, ye will desire to aid me in mah cause."

"This young man's family have given me custody over him. They have *entrusted* me – "

"With a portion o' their wealth." The brogue paused. "Whot are they paying ye per annum?"

"That is none of your concern, sir!"

The brogue bellowed. "Then *why* in the guid Lord's name, hae ye brought me here?"

Copperhead placed the bowl on the floor and rose shakily to his feet. He waited for a wave of nausea to pass and then, using the wall as a prop, headed for the door.

"He will be missed. What shall I say when they return?" Sneath asked just as he arrived.

"Bury a body in the courtyard below, and place a marker on it and the question is answered. I'm sure you hae a sufficiency."

"Not of his...*particular* color," Sneath said after a pause.

"Toss quicklime on it, then there will *be* no color. Noo, open the door, mon, and let me see him."

Copperhead fell back. He slid to the floor on the far side of the room as a key was inserted in the lock. The door creaked open and the two men stepped in. Ruskin Sneath crossed quickly to him. He stared hard at him and then took hold of his hair and forced his head up so the light from the lantern he carried illuminated his face. Copperhead blinked, blinded.

"Aye, he'll do," the stranger said.

"You'll want him made complacent, I presume?" Sneath asked.

The stranger hesitated and then nodded.

"But take care! Dinnae ye damage the merchandise."

Miriam occupied a stone bench on the rear terrace of John Leighton's ancestral home. Dawn was just breaking in the sky, turning the stone balustrade and the courtyard below a pale pink. Nearly a week had passed since she left London, and Miriam found the gloomy atmosphere of the fading country estate produced in her a melancholy air. After speaking with Rosalyn the night before a sense of loss had seized her. Even though she had proclaimed to the other woman the certainty of her conviction that Copperhead lived, she did not really believe it.

Such hope was the lifeblood of a childhood fancy age must force her to abandon soon.

Miriam closed the book she held and rose to her feet, drawing a thin shawl close about the shoulders of her apricot gown. The morning was chill and she was being foolish, but she didn't care – nature had always been her refuge. The sight of God's handiwork freed her from the constraints of the world His creation had made.

Leaning on the terrace's balustrade she watched the sun rise in splendor, changing from pink to a fiery red-gold, and then to fading into a pale purple sky. It was late September, the time of harvest back in the colonies.

The time for reaping what one had sown.

"Miriam?" a voice called from close behind her.

She drew a slow breath and closed her eyes. She knew who it was. He had arrived the night before. She had seen him from her window.

"May I join you?" Charles Matthew Spencer asked.

Winter was next. And then, if she would let it come, spring – and new life.

Miriam turned to face him. "I own no monopoly on the Leighton's terrace, Charles. You may do as you please."

As he approached her, the early morning light caught in his hair, gilding the tousled yellow brown curls. Charles was dressed simply but elegantly, in a deep russet suit with a stock collar and matching solitaire. No ornament graced his lapel. The appearance given was that of a sober young man on a mission.

Of conquest.

Charles stood easily at her side and met her wary gaze. Without preamble, he asked, "Who is he?"

"He?" she replied, startled. "What do you mean?"

"This man you love so deeply that you cannot let him go."

Miriam shook her head. "There is no one."

Charles frowned. "Please. Respect me enough to be truthful. I have done so with you."

"Forgive me. It is just…." She dipped her head. "I can't speak of it."

"Is he dead then?" he asked.

Miriam shuddered. Admitting it was the sound of her own death knell. "Yes."

Charles reached out and took her hand. He remained silent until she looked up. "I can wait," he said. "I can wait until you forget."

Her jaw tightened. Tears stained her shawl. "I won't."

He touched her cheek. "I can live with that as well."

"Charles, no!" Miriam broke away. "It would not be fair to ask you to do so."

"You don't have to ask. I am a *willing* volunteer." He smiled gently. "I love you, Miriam. Let me prove to you that I am a man *you* can love as well."

She stood on the edge of a precipice with her back to an insurmountable wall. No matter what choice she made, she would fall. Miriam's slight form trembled and she began to shake uncontrollably. Tears fell freely and a great sob wracked her.

Charles took her in his arms. He kissed her gently on the forehead, and then held her until the tempest had passed.

For the second time in a week Copperhead awoke to the jarring motion of a fast flying coach. He felt doubly sick. Groaning, he shifted and only the fact that he had not eaten in days kept him from vomiting.

Strong hands caught his shoulders and steadied him. The voice that spoke was male. "Take it slow. Hang that villain! Sneath used opium." A hand touched his face. "Your skin is cold. Combined with your other injuries, that is *not* a good thing." The stranger pulled a blanket about his shoulders, wrapping him in warmth. "It may take some time for this to pass and, *damn* it to Hell! We have precious little time."

Copperhead tried to focus on the speaker, though his apparent savior was little more than a blur. It appeared that the man sitting opposite him – caring for him – was the *brogue* who had bought his release. Though the brogue itself was gone.

He licked his cracked lips and croaked, "Who are you?"

The man released him and sat back. He removed his tricorn hat and turned the collar of his greatcoat down.

Kit MacKay smiled with relief.

"Someone who is very glad to see you."

John Leighton looked up from his papers to watch the couple on the terrace. He had arrived home in the middle of the night and after a few hours sleep risen to go to his study, hoping to catch up on affairs before the household of giddy young guests his son Geoff had invited descended the following night. John leaned back in his chair and rested his chin on his hand. He had been surprised to find William Foxwell's young daughter, Miriam, at the house. He had not known she was in England. John's sister, Bridget, informed him she would not be for long. Apparently Miriam was bound for Scotland and school – and from the looks of it – a new life in the arms of Charles Matthew Spencer.

Apparently her infatuation with Josiah Woodward had not been so deep, or so immutable as her father feared. William would pay handsomely to have the boy kept at Spurrell Pode. From the intelligence he had received it seemed the MacKay boy had not been able to prevent Josiah's incarceration.

A pity.

John Leighton remained still for several heartbeats and then, with a glance to make certain the door to his study was shut, leaned over and opened a low drawer in his mahogany desk. Removing its contents he pressed a concealed lever, and then lifted out the hidden bottom to reveal the treasure secreted there – a double frame of gilded wood, containing the miniature images of a young man and a woman nearly twice his age. He stared at it, noting with irony the resemblance of the boy to the other two – Woodward and MacKay. He had the same deeply tanned skin, the same India ink hair, the wide-set eyes and angular jaw. The woman looked like MacKay's mother. As well she should. The two were of the same tribal clan.

Her name was simply 'Water'. *A'ma.* And the boy? Well, his name was John.

After his father.

John Leighton touched the boy's painted face with his fingers and smiled a smile laced with sorrow. He had done everything he could, but he hadn't been able to save them. He had thought – no hoped – that perhaps he *could* save Josiah Woodward.

But it seemed Providence had no intention of smiling on John Leighton.

At a sound in the corridor John replaced the portraits and the thin board that concealed them. He closed the drawer just as his youngest son, Geoffrey, burst into the room. Geoff was still in the black suit he wore at law school, and appeared studious and respectable. The problem was, appearances lied. Geoff studied the law only to learn how to break it without being caught. His youngest son's tastes were dark. Geoff's ambitions, dangerous. And his pursuit of both as unrelenting as his desire for Rosalyn Castell.

John rose and opened his arms to his son. "I see you have decided to mark tomorrow's festivities with all the grave respect they deserve," he remarked, indicating Geoff's sober garments.

"Miss Castell must see that I am a serious man, sir. And deserving of her," Geoff replied, accepting the embrace and then pulling away.

"Kit was here," John said, turning away in order to mask the *genuine* emotion teasing the edge of his lip into a smile.

"So I have been informed. The villain! Making love to Rosalyn behind my back! I will challenge him to duel and have it over with!"

John Leighton glanced at his son over his shoulder. "And here I thought it was *Kit* who wanted a life in the theater. Such dramatics! Have *you* decided to take to the boards?"

"You mock me, sir!" his son all but shouted.

"I mock the passion of youth," John replied as he dropped wearily into his chair. "But don't listen to me." He glanced at the terrace again. The young lovers were gone.

"I am feeling old today."

Chapter Twenty-Six

Miriam declined at first when Rosalyn suggested it, but it *was* the perfect joke. She was going to the masque, and going as Rosalyn's twin. They had ordered identical costumes from the seamstress – sprigged velvet gowns of forest green inset on the stomacher with a paisley brocade and open to an underskirt of cloth of gold. Their hair was arranged identically, piled high on their heads in a nest of curls dotted with paste jewels, and both would wear feathered butterfly masks.

They would be indistinguishable.

Rosalyn was merry with the idea of teasing Geoffrey Leighton, who panted after her like a dog in its season. Miriam had no desire to tease Charles, but hoped the masquerade might afford her an opportunity to escape his attentions – if only for a little while. Charles was a dear and gallant man. The problem was, no matter what her answer to his proposal – yes or no – she was going to hurt him in the end.

Miriam sighed, which made Rosalyn turn on her heel. "No. I *absolutely* forbid sorrow tonight!" she declared. "We shall put men entirely out of our minds and enjoy our sisterhood – all the while driving them a little mad!" Rosalyn's grin was wicked, like a little girl caught with her finger in the cream. "Now, we must practice our voices. Only *they* can give us away."

"Perhaps it is best if we simply do not speak," Miriam suggested hopefully.

"Perfect! Silent *and* mysterious. That *will* drive them crazy."

Miriam caught the full green and gold skirts in her fingers and went to study herself in the mirror. What looked back at her was a woman grown both weary and wise. The girl who had lived in the Colonies, who longed for love and freedom was dead.

And buried with Copperhead.

"Our life was fairly simple in the Carolinas. I think we only had one ball, though there were many fine suppers. Mother *so* loved to entertain guests," she said as Rosalyn joined her. Then she fell silent.

"I am so sorry." Rosalyn took her hand. "You must miss her."

Miriam glanced at her friend, and then turned back to the stranger in the mirror. "It's not that. I was just thinking of how much mother would approve of Charles. And of how I have become *exactly* what she wanted me to be."

Copperhead stood before the full-length mirror in Kit's room trying not to sway. He reached up with trembling fingers to adjust the collar of the black coat his friend had helped him don. The suit hung on him. The time he had spent in the hold of the Renard and in Spurrell Pode had changed him. He had lost the musculature of his youth. He was slender now. Transparent. Part of life surrounding him and yet apart from it.

Kit, who stood by his side, was concerned.

"It will do, though we may have to pad it a bit." Kit snapped his fingers. "No, wait! A cloak. Along with the hat and mask, no one will be able to tell you are not I. Let me get it."

Kit had returned to John Leighton's house through the front door as a guest, and then snuck him in through the back. This was his plan: the two of them would dress identically and then exchange places. Then, with Copperhead pretending to *be* Kit, he would leave in his friend's stead, traveling with the actors to the ship *Anna Lee* moored on the nearby river, and from there to Canada and freedom. Only a handful of the actors knew Kit Montagne well enough to notice the difference – at least at first.

Kit returned with the cloak and tossed it about his shoulders, and then set the tri-corn hat at a jaunty angle on his head. Then he stood back, placed a hand to his chin and inspected him. "You'll have to stand straighter. You're a good inch or two shorter than me anyhow," he said.

Copperhead did as he was told. "Is this better?" he sighed.

Kit looked chagrinned as he crossed to him and placed a hand on his shoulder. "I know this is hard, Josiah. You have barely had time to shake off the effects of the opiate, let alone nerve yourself to face one of Geoff Leighton's parties. If not for Rosalyn, I wouldn't go within twenty miles of one."

"Why not?"

"They are tedious affairs marked by the archaic mating rituals of certain male birds of high plumage." Kit scowled as he adjusted the hat. "I dislike intensely the feeling of being a *dish* placed on a board to whet some society dame's appetite."

"This woman you mentioned. Rosalyn. Will she not be there?"

Kit nodded. "She will. And she will help us, *if* she is still speaking to me. It will aid in your escape if Kit and Rosalyn can be seen taking a turn on the dance floor, even *as* they are escaping to the actor's coach. Still, I gave Rosalyn the slip the other night. She has every right to be angry. I sent a note through – " Kit stopped. He listened for a moment and then his finger went to his lips. "Shh! Someone is coming."

Kit rushed him behind the moss-green drapes that cloaked the room's high window and then moved to the mirror and began to primp. Copperhead peered from behind the heavy fabric and watched as the door opened and a young man entered unannounced. He was dressed in a rich blue suit of fine silk covered with silver filigree, and carried a mask that was a fantastic lion's head, complete with silver mane.

"The festivities are starting, MacKay," he announced, his tone brusque. "Aren't you ready yet?"

Kit glanced at him as he straightened his cravat. "What no *bauble* on your arm, Geoff?" he asked.

"Rosalyn has granted me the first dance," Geoffrey Leighton trumped.

"Has she? Well, to the victor the spoils," Kit tossed off as he headed for the bed where his mask lay. It was a raven's head with iridescent feathers and a black-jeweled beak. "Hadn't you best go lay claim to your spoils?" he inquired as he placed it over his face.

Geoffrey Leighton glared at him, and then turned on his heel and exited the room.

"Charming chap," Kit sighed as he returned to the bed and drew an identical mask from beneath the pillows. "Do you remember how to find your way to the court outside the ballroom, Josiah?" he asked as he held it out to him.

Abandoning the draperies he nodded. "Yes. But do you really think this will – " Copperhead stopped cold.

They were not alone.

No sooner had Geoff Leighton left the room, than a diminutive blonde woman entered. If Copperhead had not known better he would have thought it was Miriam. As the strange woman entered the room and fell into Kit's arms, planting passionate kisses on his lips, a clap of thunder sounded through him leaving him weak.

It wasn't Miriam. Would never *be* Miriam.

The woman he loved was lost to him forever.

"Rosalyn, this is Josiah," Kit said as wrapped his arm about her corseted waist and walked her to his side. "We will make the switch when the dancing begins anew after the performance is ended. When Rosalyn and I dance into the courtyard, you and I will exchange places. I will return to the festivities while you two follow the actors. Then you will go with them in my place. No one will be the wiser."

Rosalyn's eyes grew wide. Anger crackled in their cobalt depths. "You were going to leave? Tonight?" she exclaimed, pulling out of his embrace.

"I had intended to. For a time," Kit admitted. "To get away from my father. *Never* from you. I meant to tell you tonight."

Rosalyn's jaw was tight. "We'll discuss this later. Josiah, I am pleased to meet you," she said, extending her hand, "and even more pleased to help you escape such a horrible fate."

Copperhead nodded as he took her hand and bent over it.

She smiled. "Such courtly manners. Where did you learn them?"

"As a servant to a rich master who now wishes me dead," he replied coldly.

Rosalyn froze, at a loss for words.

"That was a *bit* uncalled for, old man," Kit chided him.

"No. It's all right," Rosalyn said as he released her hand. "I understand you mean to return to the Carolinas. Whatever for?"

Copperhead slipped the raven mask in place, concealing the fire in his eyes.

"I have some unfinished business there."

Oh, how *proud* her mother would have been.

Miriam stood on the threshold of the Leighton's grand ballroom, one gloved hand on Charles Matthew Spencer's arm. Charles was attired in a fine taupe suit, his mask that of a stag fashioned of genuine deerskin with gilded antlers. She drew a deep breath and held her head high as he led her forward. She was here. There was nothing she could do.

She might as well enjoy it.

At their entrance every head turned. The fine English belles and their mamas began to chatter. Charles was the 'catch' of the day and he was hers. Every fashionable, socially well-placed woman in the room both hated and envied her.

How little they knew. She would have abdicated her position in a heartbeat.

The small orchestra John Leighton had hired for the occasion turned their instruments to a Scottish country tune. Charles smiled and indicated the patterned parquet floor where others were beginning to gather. Miriam nodded, accepting his invitation. It just wouldn't be proper to refuse him on the first dance.

Later she would feign fatigue and escape.

Out of the corner of her eye she noticed Rosalyn entering with Geoffrey Leighton in tow. The belles and their mamas were nonplussed. Who was who? Was *this* Rosalyn Castell? And if she was with Geoffrey Leighton, then *who* was Charles Matthew Spencer making love to?

The evening's entertainment was assured.

Charles placed a hand on her waist and then offered her his other. As she took it, she felt both strength and confidence flowing from him. He wanted to be her protector. To care for her. To keep her safe.

To cage the lark and assure her that the loss of her song was well worth the price.

Miriam nodded to Charles as the music swelled and placed her foot where propriety demanded.

The order of the evening was this – dancing, dinner, the performance, and then more dancing before retiring. Copperhead had hours to kill. He found a comfortable spot near a clump of trees pruned to resemble a coach and a pair of horses and settled in to wait. The light of an ostentatious trio of chandeliers bearing dozens of candles fell through the window glass, staining the frosty ground. Copperhead pulled the collar of his jet-black coat close and adjusted the troublesome mask. Winter was on the wing. The air had an icy chill and he could see his breath. The lateness of the season was the main impetus for Kit's hurried flight. Another week or two and the journey David Stanbury's troupe planned across the Atlantic would prove too dangerous to contemplate. As it was, there was barely time to make Canada before the winter gales began to blow.

Copperhead drew on a pair of black calfskin gloves as he rose to his feet. Gazing through the windows, he spied Rosalyn Castell dancing in the arms of a man in a light brown suit who wore the mask of a stag. He frowned as they passed one of the doors that opened onto the courtyard. He had managed through his ordeal on the *Renard*, and then at Spurrell Pode, to put Miriam from his mind. But Kit's love – so like his own – was a painful reminder of all he had lost. Miriam was better off without him, he reminded himself for the thousandth time. It was *right* she think him dead. In fact, the woman in the emerald gown whirling about the Leighton's ballroom could be her. *Should* be her.

This was where Miriam belonged.

Returning to the shadows, Copperhead propped his back on the stone footer of the topiary chariot and closed his eyes. Minutes later he fell into a restive sleep.

He awoke sometime later to the sound of voices approaching. Weary beyond imagining, Copperhead roused himself and peered around one of the topiary's wheels. It wasn't Kit and Rosalyn, but another young couple – one obviously seeking some privacy.

And headed straight for his hiding place.

Crawling on his hands and knees he moved away, toward the back of the ornamental sculpture. The pair was walking slowly, aware of none but the other, which allowed him time to escape. He passed into the house through a side door but then hesitated, unsure of his bearings. Close by he heard voices, and the clatter of dishes being washed. Knowing he must remain close by the courtyard, he made a choice and then moved with haste through a shadow-lined passageway. At the end of the passage, Kit had explained, there were three doors that opened into the ballroom. Hopefully he could avoid them and escape being seen by any of the Leighton's guests.

Turning a corner quickly, Copperhead nearly knocked Rosalyn down. As he backed away and apologized, she stared at him as if puzzled, and then shifted past. He was just about to ask her where Kit was when the man in the pale brown suit and deer's head mask appeared at the end of the passage and headed to the left. Rosalyn glanced over her shoulder, saw him, and then grabbed Copperhead's hand and, without a word, drew him down the passage and onto the dance floor.

The performance had just ended. The orchestra was striking up a minuet – which was fortunate as both his experience and *talent* at dancing were limited.

Rosalyn was nervous. She missed steps and stumbled once, almost losing her balance. She continued to glance over her shoulder and, when the man in the light brown suit reappeared, steered their dance so it led them away from the courtyard toward the back of the chamber where a double door led back into the Leighton's home. As he followed her, barely managing to avoid stepping on her toes, he wondered who the mystery man was, and what threat he posed.

Rosalyn halted as they danced behind a bank of draperies, and then she squeezed his fingers hard. Rising up on tiptoe, she planted a kiss on his cheek.

"Thanks for rescuing me," she whispered, and then fled into the hall.

Copperhead stared after her, perplexed. Something had obviously gone wrong with Kit's scheme. He turned back into the ballroom and searched the crowd for his friend. The partygoers were dispersing, some leaving, others taking up the dance. A long thin man in a pea-green suit was speaking to John Leighton. That must be David Stanbury. A pouch changed hands. Careful to hug the shadows cast by the flickering chandeliers, Copperhead moved into the crowd in search of Lord MacKay's son – and found him. Kit was standing off to one side of the stage.

With Rosalyn on his arm.

Copperhead halted and turned back toward the double door through which the masked woman had fled.

Who was it he had danced with then?

Even as the question formed in his mind, he was forced to action. Kit had begun to dance with Rosalyn and was steering her toward the courtyard, which was the agreed upon signal. The actors, more than satisfied with their compensation, were breaking down the stage and

COPPERHEAD

packing their wares in preparation for departing.

The moment of his release had come.

Pulling his collar up to aid in concealing his face, Copperhead crossed the room and entered the corridor, quietly passing through it and into the courtyard.

Almost immediately upon leaving Rosalyn, Kit returned to the dance floor in search of Miriam. Her presence was not a necessity but, as he told Josiah, it would help allay suspicions if he and 'Rosalyn' were seen to be in attendance at the ball. Even now the true Rosalyn was walking Josiah to the coach. Still dressed in the raven mask, hat and cloak, Josiah would board the coach and do his best to remain unseen until Stanbury's troupe was aboard the *Anna Lee* and the ship had put out to sea. Once the switch was discovered, there would be little anyone could do. It wouldn't matter to Stanbury anyway. A stagehand was a stagehand. Josiah would grow stronger and be well able to carry out any of the duties afforded him – and maybe even have a little fun playing a bit part in one of the Bard's plays.

He deserved a little fun.

Kit circled the room, seeking his elusive prey. He found Charles Spencer standing at the side surrounded by a bevy of beauties, but Miriam was not among them. Just as he was about to approach the man and ask him what he knew, Kit noticed John Leighton beckoning him. He nodded and began to make his way through drunken remnants of the party to the door. Next to Geoff's father was a tall man in uniform. As he drew close the man removed his cockaded hat and ran a hand through his salt and pepper hair, the nervous gesture saying more about his mission than the crimson coat he wore – whoever he was, he was ill at ease.

"Kit," John Leighton said as he drew abreast them. "Miriam Foxwell, have you seen her?"

"Not since before the performance. Why?"

His host indicated the martial man. "Kit MacKay, I'd like you to meet Colonel William Foxwell. Miriam's father."

Kit swallowed his surprise. Josiah had told him something of the man – none of it to his liking. And to think they had missed each other by mere minutes!

"A pleasure to meet you, sir," he managed. "May I ask what brings you here?"

Colonel Foxwell eyed him. Whatever judgment he made remained his own. "I have come to fetch my daughter."

"Ah. To take her to school?" Miriam had mentioned the intended plan to Rosalyn.

"No. I am afraid I have distressing news. Her grandfather is dying."

It hadn't taken very long for Copperhead to be found out.

He had taken off his mask and donned a hat that he kept low, and pretended to sleep as the troupe jostled toward London. He had managed as well to avoid the boisterous celebration as the actors boarded the ship and they set sail. But when a redheaded woman named Isabella came looking for Kerr Montagne with a bottle of wine in her hand and a fire in her bright blue eyes, there was no hope of continuing the charade. Isabella knew instantly that he was not Kit MacKay. She threatened to reveal him to David Stanbury, and to have him cast off the ship. As there was nothing else to do, Copperhead told her his story.

At the end of an hour he and Isabella were sitting side by side on a crate lashed to the deck. The actress' face was wet with tears, and the wine bottle was empty.

Now, as he stood alone on the foredeck of the ship *Anna Lee* as it pulled away from the English coast, gazing at the buxom ebon-haired masthead that graced her prow, a slight smile touched his full lips. Beyond his name, Copperhead remembered precious little of his native tongue. Still, one word remained crisp and clear as the vision of the forested world he had inhabited as a boy. A word his grandfather Walker had often used.

An-i-li. Fox.

Anna Lee. The name of the ship that bore him home.

His grandfather Walker's spirit and the spirit of the silver fox were with him. Even here, so far from home. The fox would not let him die – then or now – for as the silvery animal had told his grandfather all those years ago, there was something he still had to do.

And now he knew what it was.

No matter where this voyage ended, no matter how much he had to endure, he would return to Foxwell Manor.

And William Foxwell would die.

Chapter Twenty-Seven
Foxwell Manor, late January

Miriam roused herself and walked to the window. She stood there for a moment, thinking, and then took her hands and drew back the draperies. It was late afternoon. The winter sun was weak. Its light offered no warmth as it spilled through the opening into the sickroom where she kept vigil. Outside the world went on, but here – in her father's house – time was suspended. It seemed years ago that she had opened the door to her chamber in John Leighton's English home to find, not a frustrated Charles Matthew Spencer but her father, William, standing in the passageway. According to a letter he had received from Judith her grandfather had taken a turn for the worst. The doctor said there was no way of knowing how long he had, but a quick end was inevitable. Grandpa George was asking for *her*. Her father pronounced the journey 'futile'. The 'old man', he said as they walked to the coach he had hired to take them to the wharf where a fast ship awaited them, was most likely already 'food for the worms'. Still, her father had admitted with chagrin as he helped her board, he *had* promised Judith he would fetch her.

That had been three months ago.

Leaning on the sill, Miriam studied the sky. The portents were not good. As she watched, the sun gave one last dying gasp and then slid behind a mountain of ominous gray clouds and it began to rain. The wind was out of the north – uncommonly bitter, and strong enough to strip the needles from the spruce trees. Already there was a thin sheen of ice on the pebbled drive that ran in front of the manor and the branches of the bare trees glinted like sugared fruit.

A storm was on the way.

At a sound, Miriam pivoted and walked to her grandfather's side. When she first arrived home she had come in to find him sitting up and reading from his Bible, in apparent defiance of Doctor Wallington's dire prediction. Now he could no longer sit, and the period when he was lucid diminished daily. She skirted the painted screen that protected his weakened eyes from the light and took a seat by his side.

"Grandpa, it is Miriam," she said softly. "What is it you want?"

She had thanked God many times that her father did not know the name, for her grandfather's answer was the same every time.

"Copperhead,' he breathed. "Where…is Copperhead?"

She took his hand in hers. "I wish I knew, Grandpa," she replied, as *she* did every time. "I wish you could tell *me*."

Grandpa George fell silent. She held his hand and turned to look out the window at the approaching storm. Then she felt a squeeze and turned back in surprise toward him.

"Grandpa?"

He was trying to smile. It failed to materialize on the damaged side of his face, but his ice blue eyes sparkled like the glazed earth outside. "He's...alive," he said, his voice dry fingers on parchment. "Copperhead's...alive."

Miriam stifled a sob. She turned away so he could not see her tears. "No, Grandpa. No."

"*Yes*." The word and his grip were firm. "He...is...*here*."

"Grandpa, it isn't possible." She didn't want to hurt him. Between them, they had never uttered the word 'dead'. But it was true. Copperhead was long dead and buried in some unmarked grave; his bones bleached white as the freezing rain falling outside the window now. Miriam disengaged her hand and rose to leave. "You mustn't excite yourself. I'll go now and fetch your supper."

"Why...won't you...believe me?" Grandpa George gasped, growing fatigued with the effort. "Miri.... Why...."

He hadn't called her Miri for years. Tears wet her cheeks as she returned to the bedside and leaned over to kiss his forehead. "I have grown old, Grandpa. I am not Miri anymore," she said as she straightened up. "I have put away childish things – like hope. Now try to get some rest. I will return with food soon."

Miriam pressed his hand within hers and then walked to the door. As she entered the corridor tiny missiles of ice began to clatter against the many-paned window at the end of the hall. Miriam pulled her shawl tightly about her shoulders and shivered. Then she descended the stair.

An hour later as the cook was dishing up the soup, preparing a plate for Miriam to take to her grandfather's room, the window at the end of the second floor passage opened and a slender agile figure wearing charcoal breeches and a storm gray coat slipped from the spruce tree outside into the house. Pausing near the window, it occupied the shadows as it gained its bearings and then moved down the hall. In one hand it held a hunting knife. Behind the belt that circled its heavy woolen vest was a flintlock pistol. The sound its black jack-boots made as it moved along the corridor was deliberately muffled by rags drawn tightly about their soles. The figure's face was dark, both in appearance and mean. Lampblack had been smeared across the angled plains to mask its features and the color of its deeply tanned skin.

At the top of the stair the figure paused to listen to the lifeblood of the house as it pulsed below. A woman was playing the harpsichord and singing. Her voice was rich and mellow as a violin's, with a just a touch of the timbre of age. The sound of servants' feet flying fast indicated food was about to be served. Candles were being lit. Wine bottles uncorked. Someone called out and the music ceased. Then into the hushed silence came a new sound.

The voice of his enemy calling his wife to supper.

Copperhead dared to descend two steps so he could peer through the railing. At the foot of the stair Colonel William Foxwell's fat hounds lay, sleeping and dreaming of foxhunts they would never run. He had followed Miriam's father home, keeping a discreet distance, able – but not wanting – to overtake him on the road.

He wanted to take the villain here, in his home, where he felt safe.

A sudden noise from below – a jingle and chink, as of china meeting spoon – made him retreat up the steps. Glancing left and right, he seized on a door near the end of the corridor that was standing partially open and passed inside. From what little observation he had time to make, the manor had suffered in the years he had been away. The renovation to repair the house after the fire had never been completed. And he had seen fewer than a dozen servants on the grounds, though William Foxwell's company of Redcoats was in evidence. Judith Kingsbury, now Judith Foxwell, was here as well. He had seen her greet the villain on his arrival. But George Foxwell must be long dead by now. And Miriam....

Miriam was in England.

Copperhead stopped just inside the door. He removed his hat, shook the sleet from his long coppery hair, and then replaced it. The *Anna Lee* was halfway to Canada before he found out. Isabella Pursglove had been quite taken with Charles Matthew Spencer and had asked a servant about him before they departed the Leighton's estate – him *and* the woman on his arm. Her name was Miriam, she was informed, Miriam Foxwell. Daughter of the war hero, Colonel William Foxwell.

She and Charles Spencer were to be married.

Leaning his head back, Copperhead closed his eyes. He had held her. Danced with her. And had not known it. It only went to prove that what they had was dead.

Dead as her father would *soon* be.

At a sound Copperhead started and opened his eyes. He drew his pistol as something shifted and sighed within the moonlit interior of the room. Cautiously, he crept forward and peered around the end of a silk screen painted with elaborate vistas of foreign lands. Behind it was a bed. And on that bed, an old man.

He should have known. Even though they had moved the sick room, something had drawn him here. Something....

Fate.

At first he didn't recognize him. George Foxwell had grown ancient and perilously thin in the time he had been away. His gray hair was pure white now and thin as the skin that covered his protruding bones. Copperhead locked his pistol behind his belt and then moved to the foot of the bed and stared at him. Death had not claimed the old man who had saved him, but its watch was set.

It would not be long.

As he debated whether or not to make his presence known, the old man's lashes fluttered and his eyes opened. Copperhead held very still. George Foxwell could not know him. He would make an excuse and leave the room. Then he would find some place to hide until the manor had fallen asleep –

And take his revenge.

"My...son...." The old man's voice was a brush of the grave.

"Sir, I think you are mistaken," Copperhead began, pitching his voice low. "I am but a stranger who has lost his way – "

"I am...certain...of that." George's lip curled upward in an awkward smile. "Come... here. Sit."

He shook his head. "I must go. I cannot stay."

"Been...years. Please.... Come."

Copperhead drew a deep breath. It was dangerous. The sleet outside was striking a sharp staccato on the windowpanes. The storm was intensifying. If he should be discovered, it would render flight nearly impossible.

"Copperhead, please. I...haven't long."

He hesitated only a moment longer and then went to sit beside him. Placing his hat on the table nearby, he leaned forward so the moonlight struck his blackened face. The old man's eyes welled with tears as he looked at him. George lifted a palsied hand to touch him. Copperhead caught his fingers and pressed them between his own.

"Father," he said, his voice breaking.

For a dozen heartbeats they remained as they were. Then he lowered the old man's hand to the bed. Copperhead met the unspoken question in his eyes and could not lie.

"I am here to kill your son."

George nodded. "I know." Squeezing his fingers, he asked him, "Do you remember? Matthew five...forty three...."

"Do not quote the Bible to me, old man," Copperhead snarled, loosing his hand and rising. "Those words mean *nothing* to me! I have been *beaten* with them, had my bones *broken* upon them." He palmed his knife and raised it before his face. "You cannot love your enemy – you can only *kill* him!"

The sound of the door opening startled him. Copperhead glanced at George Foxwell and then retreated into the shadows cast by the folding screen. He heard the sound of rustling cloth and the door closing, and watched as the silhouette of a woman carrying a large tray rounded the corner of the screen.

"I hope you are hungry, Grandpapa," Miriam said. "Cook made your favorite soup."

The rising moonlight streaming in through the icy window struck her petite form as she moved into the room. She was dressed simply, with an apron over a pale blue skirt and long bodice; her honey gold hair bound tightly back in a tail and fastened with a ribbon. Her mother's silver and pearl chatelaine was firmly fastened at her waist. For the months since her return she had been her grandfather's caretaker. When he died – which must be soon – she was to return to England. She had made up her mind to accept Charles Matthew Spencer's proposal of marriage.

With Grandpa George gone, there would be nothing for her here.

Miriam turned to place the tray on the table by the bed, but halted as an unexpected item occupied its usually empty surface. Bracing the tray with one hand, she touched it and frowned.

It was a man's hat – and it was wet.

"Grandpa, what?"

It was then she saw him, standing in the shadows at the head of the bed. A stranger with his face blacked, holding a knife in his hand.

"Don't scream," he ordered, his voice rough and threatening.

She shook her head.

"Back up. Let me pass."

Doing as she was told, Miriam left the tray on the table and moved toward the window. The man abandoned the shadows and quickly darted past the screen. As he did, her grandfather grew agitated. He struggled and lifted his body as she had not seen him do in months and called out in a quaking voice, "No! Copperhead...."

The man was at the door. His hand was on the latch. He paused at the name and then opened it and fled into the hall.

Miriam glanced at her grandfather who was gasping. She started for him, but he waved her to the door.

"Go! Child.... Go after him!"

For once in her life Miriam did what she was told. She flew to the door and out into the corridor. For a moment she could not find him, then she did – he was at the window, one foot on the ledge, reaching for the icy branches of the spruce tree.

"Wait!" she cried, running toward him. "Don't go!"

The man hesitated. He turned toward her. The silver moonlight streaming in the window struck his blackened face.

It was he.

"Copperhead?" Miriam's voice was small. Robbed of strength by surprise. She reached out toward him and then, overwhelmed, crumpled to the ground.

When she awoke it was in his arms.

Miriam blinked. She lifted a hand to touch his dirt and soot stained face. Copperhead had aged since she had last seen him – more than the years accounted for. He was too thin and, like sinew, seemed to have hardened with the stretching. There were scars on his flesh, indicating life's harsh handling of him went far beyond this place. But it was his eyes that frightened her. Only once before had she seen them like they were now – that night when he had saved her in the maze, when the savage had overtaken the boy she knew and the lust of killing come upon him.

He caught her hand and held it. Started to speak. Then shook his head as he released it. She nodded, understanding. Then said, with the voice *of* that child. "I thought you were dead."

"I am, to you," he said. "You must forget that you have seen me."

"How can I do *that*?" Miriam caught him in a desperate embrace. "You're here. I am holding you. We're *both* here. What is more important than that?"

"Miriam, it is useless!" he growled as he pushed her away. Copperhead stood and looked down at her. "There is nothing. Nothing left, but *vengeance* and the grave."

"Vengeance?" Miriam rose to her feet. "Here? In this house? What do you mean?"

He gave her no answer. With a glance down the stair, he headed once again for the open window.

Her gaze followed his. Below, in the dining room, the family was preparing for supper. Her father would call her to prayer soon. "My father? You've come here to kill him," she said, stunned.

Copperhead adjusted his hat and pulled his collar up so it masked his face. "You were not to know."

"Well, I do now. Do you *still* mean to kill him?"

He would not look at her. "I do not know."

"What benefit will his death serve? It cannot give you back the years you have lost. It cannot erase the scars you bear – in the flesh or on your soul."

"He is an evil man, Miriam – "

"Yes." Her words were hard. "And so are you if you mean to *murder* him." Miriam paused. "You are better than that."

He shook his head. His laugh was bitter. "No. No, I'm not."

She stared at him and then walked to his side. Even though he tried to pull away, she caught his hand in hers. Gazing up at him, she pulled it to her lips and kissed it. A slight smile lifted the ends of her rose-petal lips. "Take me with you," she said softly. "We can leave together."

"No. Miriam, no! There is no place for *us*. Not with your people."

"Then what about yours?"

It was his turn to look stunned. "No. Go back to England, Miriam. Marry Charles Spencer. Live the life you were born to live."

"I was born to be with *you*. I have known it since first we met. You cannot stop me." Her fingers crushed his. "I told you before. Whither you go, I will follow. Whether you want me to or not."

Copperhead drew a deep breath as he placed his hand on top of hers. "I cannot dissuade you?"

She shook her head.

"It means leaving everything you have ever known," he warned. "Leaving, for the most part, what *I* have known. My people are but a memory. There may be no more welcome among the Cherokee then we find here at Foxwell Manor."

"If I am with you nothing else matters. Copperhead, please…."

He gazed into her eyes for a moment and then released her hand. Raising his own, he framed her face with them for a moment and then encircled her waist and crushed her small form to his. Then he leaned down and kissed her with all the passion of a love thought lost, found again.

She forgot to breathe. And into the silence of that lost breath, sound bled.

"Damn that girl, where is she? *Miriam!*"

Miriam gasped as her father's voice preceded him up the stairs. She shoved Copperhead away. "Go! Go quickly!"

His pistol was in his hand. "Get behind me."

"No!" She caught his free hand and tugged on it. "Grandpa's room! You can hide there." When he failed to move, she pleaded with him. "Please! Copperhead. The beginning of our life together *cannot* be written in blood…."

He hesitated and then nodded, and then the two of them bolted down the passageway and entered her grandfather's room. Sleet still struck the windowpanes, but otherwise the room was silent. As Copperhead ducked into the shadows cast by the screen, she took her usual place at her grandfather's side and reached for his hand. It had grown cold, though the echo of his beating heart beneath her fingers told her he lived still.

"Miriam!" The door to the room was flung open and her father entered. "Are you here, girl?"

She rose to her feet and went to greet him. "Father. Keep your voice low. Grandpa should not be upset."

William Foxwell strode into the room. He glanced about as though suspicious and then asked her, "Why did you not answer when I called?"

"I didn't hear you. The sleet falls with a heavy hand, and I was busy with Grandpa."

He scowled. "Leave it. Supper is on the table."

"Sir," she said quietly, "I am not hungry. I beg to be excused."

"You eat too little," he replied. "You are nothing but skin and bones. Come."

"I prefer not to leave Grandpa."

For the first time he looked at his father. Miriam tensed as his gaze brushed the shadows cast by the screen. But he saw nothing. "Is he dying?" he asked.

She nodded.

"About time," he growled.

Miriam's fingers clenched into fists. Controlling the anger that raged through her she said, her voice shaking, "You wouldn't want him to die alone. Would you? Father?"

William Foxwell remained absolutely still for several hammering beats of her heart. Then he nodded – and exited the room without another word.

She followed him to the door and closed it. Then she returned to the bed to find Copperhead had taken her place at Grandpa George's side. He held the older man's hand in his. There were tears in his eyes.

"Is he...?" she asked.

He shook his head. "Not yet. But soon."

As she crossed to the other side of the bed, her grandfather's mouth opened. Instead of a death gasp, she was startled to hear him say, "You...must...go."

"Grandpa!" Miriam fell to her knees beside him. She took his other hand. "I cannot leave you."

"You...must." George Foxwell drew a hard breath and turned his face toward Copperhead. "Love ...her."

He nodded. "I will."

"Not if you...have hate...in your heart." With unanticipated strength, her grandfather drew their hands together. "Must...forgive"

Copperhead looked at her. "I don't know if I can."

"Together then," she said, placing her other hand on his. "Grandpa, will you give us your blessing?"

"...have it...child. The good Lord...bless you and...keep you."

"Miriam, we must go," Copperhead urged.

As she looked up at him, George Foxwell spoke again. "Something...for you. In the top drawer..." He indicated the clothes press nearby.

Copperhead frowned but did as he was told. He crossed to the press and opened the drawer and drew out –

George Foxwell's red coat.

Returning to the bed, he held it out, puzzled.

"Remember," the old man said, his voice fading. "What you fear may be a blessing in disguise...."

Then his hand fell limp.

Miriam sobbed. Tears flowed down her cheeks. Even as Copperhead rose, she refused to let go. Then she felt his strong arms encircle her. Taking her hand in his, he drew her to her feet. Casting the scarlet coat first about her shoulders, he then caught a blanket from the bed and wrapped her in it. Seconds later he swept her off her feet and carried her into the corridor and down the back stairs, and out into the howling, storm-tossed night.

In the entrance hall below William Foxwell listened to a report from one of his company. A horse had been found tethered nearby with no rider in sight, as well as a trail of shattered ice-coated branches that led from there to the house. One of the men, a young ensign named Caldwell fresh from England, had spied a man close by the old spruce that was married to the second floor. Lieutenant Jedidiah Nevilles had been with him on patrol. Nevilles had tried to dissuade Caldwell from reporting, telling him the man wasn't a stranger, but had worked at the manor once upon a time.

William Foxwell ordered Nevilles found. Then he roused his dogs with a shout and called for his musket.

The damned redskin had returned.

Chapter Twenty-eight

Copperhead cast a worried glance at Miriam. There had been no time to go to her room to gather her things. She had nothing but her grandfather's coat and the woolen blanket he had dressed her in to protect her against the stinging sleet and the frigid night. Shivering from the cold and wincing as the icy pellets struck his flesh, Copperhead led her through the night toward the place where he had left his horse tethered. He needed to get her to warmth and safety. She needed winter clothes. Warm shoes. A cloak. Once he had her on the horse, he would take her to the nearest town. His time with the actors had not left him a rich man, but with little to spend it on, even his meager wages had added up to enough to equip them with the items they needed – as well as buy them shelter and food for a month or so.

Then....

Then, he didn't know.

Copperhead caught Miriam as she stumbled, and shifted his grip from her arm to her waist. "It is not much farther. Can you make it?"

She nodded, though it was a lie. Miriam had grown whisper-thin. He could feel her backbone even through the multiple layers of cloth and stays. She admitted grief had caused her to eat little since her return from England. The lack of food, coupled with their flight and the frightful night, worked together to break her. She was exhausted and near collapse.

"Let me carry you again," he offered.

"No. You may have need of your strength later," she whispered in reply, clinging to him.

Every movement was a gamble. The path, treacherous. If George Foxwell's God blessed their flight, he chose a strange way to show it. Even as Copperhead spied the broken branch that marked the tree where he had left his mount, a sudden wind rose – howling like the angry dead – and nearly blew them off their feet.

Placing Miriam behind an outcropping of rock, he shouted near her ear. "Wait here where there is some shelter! I'll fetch the horse."

Miriam grasped his hand. "No. Don't leave me!"

"The animal may be frightened. He does not know you." Copperhead glanced toward the great emerald-green fir tree where he had left the horse tethered. He had purchased the animal in a nearby village and, despite the seller's claims, it had proven skittish. He was afraid it might strike out with its hooves and hurt her. "It is best if I go alone."

She held his hand for a moment and then released him. With a nod and a 'God speed', she sent him on his way.

Copperhead turned his face into the bitter air and pulled his collar up against the continued assault of the frozen rain. The only good thing about the weather was that it should impede any pursuit. At this point there were precious few patches of dry earth left, but there *were* a few – protected by tree and leaf. The horse should be able to find some footing there. If those in the house did not discover their flight for hours, the storm's work would be complete.

The ice might buy them not only a day or two – but also their freedom.

He halted when he reached the spot where he had left the horse and turned in a tight circle. The animal was nowhere to be seen. Kneeling, he scoured the icy earth for clues, finding few not obliterated by the storm-tossed night. Copperhead rose and went to look at the tree itself. Had the horse broken free, there should be a frayed end of the rope still attached to it. Striking tears from his cheeks, he blinked in the wind and reached out. Yes, the rope was there.

It had been cut.

At that moment he heard a high-pitched cry. Pivoting, Copperhead discerned the glow of an approaching lantern and knew they had been found out.

Seconds later, his daughter in tow and a company of Redcoats at his back, William Foxwell broke through the trees.

Miriam struggled to break free. It had surprised her to find Jedidiah Nevilles among the company pursuing them, and shocked her when the freckle-faced lieutenant – according to her father's wishes – ordered her gagged and bound. Nevilles stood now, his face hard as the frozen earth beneath their feet, holding her tightly in his grip.

Between the roaring wind and the stinging sleet, which had forced her to hide her face, she hadn't seen them coming. Suddenly hounds had been milling at her feet and she had looked up to find her father, his face scarlet as his coat with rage. When she screamed, he struck her so hard he knocked her to the ground. After she had been bound and gagged, he had caught her chin in his fingers and forced her to meet his hateful stare.

'This time, I will do the job myself,' he promised, his raised voice no more than a whisper above the gale. "*This ends tonight!*"

Now, she watched – horrified – as her father raised his musket and took aim for Copperhead's heart.

He stood beneath the fir tree, a coil of rope grasped loosely in his hand. Copperhead did not flinch or attempt to run away, but raised his head and stepped directly into her father's sights as if daring him to shoot. Sleet still fell, coating the land about them, though a portion of it turned to light snow. The night grew suddenly still. Above their heads a crescent moon broke through the clouds, etching the world in silver.

"William Foxwell," he called. "Will you meet me as a man?"

Her father snorted. "I will put you down as the animal that you are."

"Are you afraid, then?" her love countered. "That this *animal* might best you?"

"Good try. I know your game." He took a step forward. "You are slippery as a snake, *breed*. One too many times have I unwittingly aided your escape. No more."

Miriam watched the upper edge of Copperhead's lip curl with a knowing smile.

Many years before, after a young Indian boy had pointed his finger at the painting of a colorful snake her Grandma Margaret had included in her ABC book and told her his name, her Grandpapa had explained –

A Copperhead only strikes when he is threatened.

Miriam heard the hammer of her father's musket cock and saw his finger slide toward the trigger. "We'll see how well you laugh with a hole blown through your belly, breed," he growled.

Copperhead spat on the ground and spoke one word. *One* word only.

"*Coward*."

"Give him a pistol, Colonel," Jedidiah Nevilles called, startling her. "Show the *breed* how superior you are."

Miriam glanced up at Jedidiah. His words were double-edged. On the face they supported his colonel, but hoped dawned in her as she recognized them for what they were – Copperhead's only hope. Colonel Foxwell's honor could not be preserved by shooting a man who had challenged him, not without first offering him satisfaction.

Miriam watched as her father pivoted and glared at Jedidiah, and then turned to the others of his company. He had to hear them. Just as she could. Muttering. Questioning.

What is this? his men asked. *Was* the Colonel afraid?

"*If* you were a gentleman," he remarked, turning back to Copperhead. "I *might* give you such satisfaction. But you are not even a man."

Her love nodded. He stepped into the rising moonlight. "I may not be a man. But I *am* your brother."

The wind rose, whipping Copperhead's burnished hair about his face and tossing Miriam's golden curls into her eyes. It gripped her father's heavy greatcoat and snapped the scarlet fabric against his dun colored breeches. The dead trees clattered, their ice-covered branches striking one another. And the frozen leaves, like vellum sheets freed of their binding, fell to the ground. Jedidiah Nevilles' fingers tightened on her arms in expectation.

William Foxwell lifted a hand and snapped his fingers.

"Give the bastard a gun."

Copperhead stood back to back with Miriam's father, a pistol gripped tightly in his hand. There had been no mention of seconds – this was not a duel. William Foxwell's only concern was that he preserve his honor before his men. Miriam had been passed off to a private and, out of spite, Jedidiah Nevilles chosen to perform the task of counting out the remaining moments of his life. Copperhead nodded his gratitude to his friend. He knew what Jed had tried to do. It mattered little. He was not skilled with firearms – they held little interest for him other than defending himself and his own – and Miriam's father was a trained marksman. In issuing the challenge Copperhead did not expect to escape death. Even if his shot was true – and Foxwell's was not – they were surrounded by the colonel's men who would be duty bound to carry out their leader's orders.

He simply did not want to die like an animal in front of Miriam.

For a *brief* moment he had thought it possible. Their escape. A life together. But now he knew it was just a dream. Miriam would grieve for him. Bury him. And then return to England and marry Charles Matthew Spencer as she was meant to.

When he was a boy and George Foxwell had taken him, dying, from the field of battle and borne him toward his son's home, he had asked the white man 'why?'. 'God alone knows', the old man had replied.

Even now, facing death at the hand of the father of the woman he loved – only the Creator knew why.

"Ready?" Jedidiah cried.

Copperhead nodded as William Foxwell said, "Yes."

"On a count of ten, then. One. Two. Three...."

He faced Miriam. The horror written on her perfect face pained him. Either way she would lose – him, or her father. And most likely both.

"Four. Five. Six...."

Sweat trickled down Copperhead's collar in spite of the icy night as he readied to turn. It would be better for her if he *was* the one to die.

But he didn't want to die.

"Seven. Eight. Nine....Ten!"

As Jedidiah finished shouting out the final count, Copperhead pivoted, raised the pistol, and took aim. As the weapon discharged, its heavy recoil caused him to stumble back onto an icy patch. His feet shot out from under him – providentially – for as he fell he felt the wind of

William Foxwell's ball pass by his cheek. The crack as it splintered the hide of the tree behind him echoed through the night. Copperhead struck the ground with an 'oomph' and immediately rolled over and struggled to his feet.

Across the icy field Miriam's father lay on the ground, the breast of his white linen shirt growing crimson where the ball had entered his shoulder. With the exception of Jedidiah, the men of his company were gathering around him. The soldiers exchanged words and worried looks, trying to decide what to do.

William Foxwell, of course, let his opinion be known. "Nevilles! I order you to kill him!" he screamed even as he loss of blood made his voice grow weak. "Kill…the bastard… now!"

One of Foxwell's men crossed to Jedidiah and handed him his weapon. Being a party to the duel, he had surrendered it earlier. Jed stood staring at it for moment, and then lifted his head and marched to Copperhead's side. Miriam was there as well. When her father had fallen the ensign had panicked and released her, and she run to his arms.

Now they stood together, facing his approaching fate.

Jedidiah Nevilles stopped a few feet away. He glanced at his commander who had fallen unconscious, and then turned back to Copperhead. "If I don't shoot you, they'll hang me," he said.

Copperhead felt Miriam's fingers dig into his arm. "I know."

"He won't ever let you be," Jed's words were quiet. Pitched only for their ears. "You know that, don't you?"

He nodded. "Still, we have to try."

Jed hesitated. Then he nodded. Raising his musket, he pointed it at him and waved him toward the foundation of shadows that lay beneath the nearby trees. "Walk with me. Once we're out of sight, I'll fire off a shot. Tell them I got you, but you managed to crawl away."

"And Miriam?"

Jedidiah shrugged. "I'll say she took fright and ran off. With the Colonel out of commission, it will take some time to organize a pursuit. I'm the senior officer here. I can delay them. Your horse is tied about a quarter of a mile back. No one's watching." He waved his musket. "Now turn around and put your hands up."

Copperhead did what he was told. As they began to walk, he glanced back at William Foxwell. The colonel's men were huddled around his supine form, paying little heed to what they did. As they entered the shadows Jedidiah called out in a loud voice.

"Ensign Caldwell!"

"Sir!" The young soldier snapped to attention.

"Keep watch." Jedidiah shoved Copperhead with the barrel of his gun. "This won't take long."

Minutes later as the shot was fired, Miriam covered her head and slipped away unnoticed into the night.

The following morning dawned cold and golden. Copperhead and Miriam lay together in a sheltered niche cut into the side of a rock-face, surrounded by bushes and trees laid low with ice. As the sun's light struck the frozen world it was transformed, creating for a moment, heaven on earth. Miriam murmured and turned in the circle of his arms to gaze up at him. Her honey colored hair had fallen loose. She was dressed now in the extra suit of clothes he carried, and wearing his greatcoat over her grandfather's scarlet coat for warmth. Gone was the well-ordered and predictable restraint of her father's world, which was a good thing –

Since her father's world was gone as well.

"Where shall we go?" she asked him. There was no fear in her voice, only the promise of a brave new world.

"To my people, I suppose," he answered.

"Do you know how to find them?"

He nodded. The map that Jedidiah Nevilles had drawn for him years before was emblazoned in his memory. "It is a long journey. Full of peril."

Miriam snuggled up against him. She took his hand in her own. "So long as it is with you, I care not."

"I do not know what we will face when we find them."

She laid her hand alongside his cheek and kissed him. Then she rested her head on his chest.

"That's all right. God alone knows."

OTHER TITLES AVAILABLE
BY MARLA FAIR

My French Rebel: A Revolutionary Tale

Goodnight Robinson
A Tale of Love Across Time

Coming 2009
the sequel to My French Rebel
The Flowering Thorn

All titles available at
www.marlafair.com &
www.a-writersgroup.com